COLONEL DAVID HALE, RET

THE REAL WAR

AMY PURDY | **JAMES PURDY**

COPYRIGHT

TABLE OF CONTENTS

ACKNOWLEDGEMENT

Although this book is a work of fiction, the historical characters are real. President Harry Truman was the 33rd President of the United States of America. Other historical figures are General John "Mac" Magruder; Helen Magruder; Colonel William Quinn; Captain Joseph Rochefort.

The writers have made a sincere effort to accurately depict the personality of these noteworthy individuals.

Literary license has been taken with their parts in this book, but the characters themselves are part of American history. Without these brave Americans, this story could not be told.

We appreciate these American heroes for their contribution to making America and the world safer during a time of great turmoil.

CHAPTER 1

January 1947

The sun shone brightly through the three stately windows flanked by dramatic floor-to-ceiling blue-green drapes at 1600 Pennsylvania Avenue. The Oval Office was designed to intimidate, and the room certainly fulfilled its calling, the intruder thought randomly. Although the room did smell faintly of furniture polish and the president's favorite after shave, bringing a curious hominess to the space. Its current peaceful state certainly belied the trouble this room had seen over the years.

The Theodore Roosevelt desk, newly restored after the 1929 Christmas Eve West Wing fire, spoke of the history and power wielded here over the past two centuries. While the artwork spoke of the President's Missouri home and of the man himself. Multiple frames featuring military aircraft aloft in the clouds flanked the doors and spoke of his personal military service. A majestic ship with its billowing sails propelling it forward through rough seas was indicative of his determination and fortitude. And portraits of past presidents were set in place both to inspire and encourage the man currently occupying the Oval Office.

"The new rug is just wonderful," the intruder's wife whispered interrupting his thoughts. "The new presidential seal makes it so regal. It's so very dramatic and really adds something to the room."

"Yes, I'm certain that's exactly what the President had in mind when he ordered it, dear," he replied quietly only half listening.

"You can tease me all you want, but I know I'm right," she returned in muted tones. "I actually tiptoed as I walked across it. Now that's saying something."

The intruder smiled and breathed out a sigh as the magnitude of the task before him settled squarely on his broad fifty-nine-year-old shoulders. Regardless of how charming the new rug was he knew the next fifteen minutes could determine the fate of not only a nation but the world. He pushed every idle thought from his mind as he mentally prepared himself for the most crucial mission of his life as his wife settled herself serenely on the sofa. *I must convince them,* he told himself as he slid a little farther behind the open door and stilled his breathing as he heard the man approaching just outside.

"Good morning Mr. President," his secretary, Rose Conway, greeted with crisp efficiency. "South Carolina Senator Maybank had an emergency and had to reschedule to next week," she continued as the morning's most urgent considerations were handed to him. "You have fifteen minutes before your first appointment. Colonel Quinn is already in the building."

"My, my," the President replied distractedly as he filtered through the morning mail, "What will I do with all of that free time?"

Rose smiled politely as she watched her boss clad in his typical double-breasted suit with peaked lapels hang his trench coat and Stetson fedora on the coat rack and then disappear into the Oval Office.

"Good morning, Mr. President," the intruder said softly as he quietly closed the door.

President Truman swung around, obviously startled. "What the…" He stopped short when he recognized the man standing behind him. "General Magruder? Helen? Is that really you?"

The intruder smiled warmly as he nodded the affirmative and extended his hand. Truman shook his hand heartily. "By God, it's good to see you both. My apologies for being so curt, but Rose didn't tell me you were here," he said as he crossed the room and bent to give Helen a kiss on the cheek.

"It's good to see you too, sir," Mac responded as he took a seat in one of the two upholstered chairs facing the President's desk. "Don't be too hard on Rose, she didn't know we were here."

"Didn't know you were here? Well then, how did you get in? Maybe we need to increase our security," Truman said with a chuckle as he sat down.

"That probably wouldn't be a bad idea," Magruder responded quietly, with his smile fading a bit. He forced the broad grin back on his face as he said brightly, "We watched your State of the Union address last night. The first one ever televised. Very impressive."

"I'm not sure this television thing will last, but I was told it would be something history might remember, so I agreed," Truman said modestly. With the pleasantries out of the way, the President's jovial attitude quickly faded as he cleared his throat and asked, "If you saw the broadcast last night, then I would assume that you've not been held captive. Where have the two of you been Mac, and why no contact? Do you know how many tax dollars have been spent trying to find you and Helen? I have people who are convinced that the Russians have been holding you hostage trying to get a direct line into our intelligence services!"

"I'm sorry for any distress we may have caused, Mr. President. Helen and I both appreciate every effort you've made on our behalf, sir. I know this has been a trying time for you and others wondering where we have been…"

"Apologies aside General Magruder," Truman cut in, "I need to know where you've been and why you've made no contact for the past six months. Have you and your family been under threat?"

Magruder took a deep breath and let it out slowly. "Can this wait until Colonel Quinn arrives?"

"Yes, Mr. President," Helen chimed in. "I'm quite certain that Colonel Quinn will be very interested in what we have to say as well."

"How…" the President started when there was a light knock on the office door. Mac quickly moved from his chair to open the door, careful to stand just out of sight.

Colonel Quinn entered and saw Truman sitting behind his desk. The Chief of Operations of the Central Intelligence Group (CIG) strode confidently toward the President, then stopped a respectful distance away and waited for the President to acknowledge him. "Good morning, Mr. President," Quinn began, only to come to an abrupt stop as he saw the concerned expression on Truman's face. He followed Truman's gaze and slowly turned around to see Helen on the sofa and Mac quietly locking the Oval Office door.

"Hello," Helen said cheerfully while giving a little finger wave. "It's nice to see you again Colonel."

"Hello Bill," Mac greeted the man that had stepped into his position when he went missing months before. "It's been a while," he said cordially as he stepped forward and extended his hand. Quinn stood slack-jawed and seemingly rooted to the floor. So, Mac allowed his hand to return to his side.

When the Colonel regained his power of speech he exclaimed, "Good God, man, we've been looking for you and Helen for, what, six months? Where the hell have you two been?"

"Well…that's rather complicated," Mac said carefully as he walked over to the chair he had previously occupied. "Break it down for us," the President said tersely with his patience wearing thin. "We're reasonably smart guys; we'll try to keep up."

"Okay," Mac said, as much to himself as to the two other men in the room. "We should just face this head-on."

"I think that would be prudent," Truman responded. "What's going on, Mac?"

Mac gestured to Quinn to take the other chair by the President's desk then he sat down as well. "We were…in training, of sorts."

"You and Helen were in training?" Quinn asked, with disbelief in his tone.

"I know you both have a myriad of questions, but there just isn't time to answer all of them right now," Mac hedged. "There are other, much more important things to discuss. We need to move on."

"Oh, for goodness sake. You might just as well be out with it, dear," Helen said primly from the sofa. "After all that's what we're here for."

Mac shot a let-me-do-it-my-way glance at Helen then tried to continue. President Truman held up his hand as he looked at Mac intently for a moment. "No," he said firmly. "No sir. When one of my top intelligence officers and his wife just disappear without a word, then show up in my office unannounced six months later, I need more than it's complicated. I need to know that you haven't been compromised. So, General, you should take your wife's advice and just tell me where in the hell you have been. Pardon my crude expression, Helen."

"No offense taken, Mr. President," Helen said with a dismissive wave of her hand.

A tense silence enveloped the room until resignation registered on Magruder's face, and he reluctantly spoke. "As I said, we have been in training. We were recruited suddenly without the opportunity to notify anyone and have been unable to make contact until we returned yesterday."

"Recruited?" the President asked with raised eyebrows. "Recruited by whom?"

Magruder took a deep breath, then looked at the President directly when he answered. "An alien race we call the Greys. They took us involuntarily to warn us of an impending threat to earth. We then stayed voluntarily for training once we were convinced that the threat might be real."

Truman and Quinn waited quietly for the punchline they were certain was coming. Then turned their eyes toward Helen who smiled sweetly and nodded in confirmation.

"Aliens," Quinn stated in utter disbelief. "So, you disappear for six months and the best excuse you can come up with is aliens abducted you? Good Lord, Mac."

"Do you think I don't know how this sounds?" Mac said forcefully, as he stood to his feet and began pacing. "It took the Greys several weeks just to convince us that what was happening was actually real. And we knew this would be just as hard for you to believe. Why do you think we didn't come to you yesterday right before your State of the Union address? This messes with your mind, I know, but I need you to believe me… both of you."

"I want you both examined," the President said with concern. "Just to make sure you haven't been brainwashed in some way."

"No! No, what we're discussing cannot leave this room," Mac insisted as he continued pacing.

"My personal physician can be called in. He's very discreet. This needs to be done before this goes any further, Mac," Truman said with finality.

"Well gentlemen, it seems you have some things to discuss," Helen interjected as she stood to her feet and shook a wrinkle from her skirt. "I think I'd best leave so you can get to it. Colonel lovely to see you again. Mr. President it's been an honor…and, oh, I absolutely love the new rug. It's so impressive."

The two men stood politely as she walked over and gave Mac a peck on the cheek. "I'll go prepare for that other thing, dear. Until next time, gentlemen."

Then she was gone…just gone.

"What the hell…" was uttered in unison by the President and Colonel Quinn as they stood stunned by the lady's sudden and unusual departure.

"So sorry," Helen apologized as she reappeared by the sofa. "I forgot my purse."

And in a blink, there were again only three people in the room.

CHAPTER 2

"Well, as the lady said, I guess I should just get to it," Mac said resolutely as Truman and Quinn sank slowly back into their seats. He took two steps to his right, then sighed heavily and pointed to the center of the room. "Your whole world is about to change forever, gentlemen," he said with a hint of deep regret.

"General, wait. What just happened? Where is Helen?" President Truman asked once he could finally speak.

The President's train of thought was interrupted when suddenly three figures manifested in the center of the Oval Office. Both Truman and Quinn gasped out loud as they jumped from their seats in response. Quinn's abandoned chair toppled to one side as its previous occupant forgot protocol and took refuge behind the stately desk with the President. They shook their heads and pinched their eyes shut as if to clear their vision, completely unsure of what they were witnessing.

"Holy God almighty!" Quinn gasped, unconsciously summoning a higher power to steady his reeling mind. Two of the "guests" were seated on the floor, with the third standing next to them. All of them appeared to be in some kind of deep sleep. It was apparent to everyone in the office that the two seated beings would be extraordinarily tall if standing upright, easily eight and ten feet respectively, with torsos more than twice the size of a man's, and elongated legs that splayed across the room. The more massive beast was horribly grotesque and had enormous hands and feet with specific recognizable bodily features. The second creature was almost human looking but still incredibly ugly with a contemptible face. The third being was what appeared to be a very handsome young man about five-feet-six-inches tall with pale skin and beautiful white, flowing hair.

"There is no reason to fear," Mac announced quickly as he recognized the unmitigated expressions of shock on his captive audience's faces. "Each of these beings is in a state of stasis right now. They can neither see nor hear you. The two tall ones are called Anakim. They are hateful and dangerous beings with incredible physical strength. The one that looks like a young man is from a race called the Shalanaya. While the two Anakim are large and imposing, it is the Shalanaya that pose the greater threat at the moment. I'll explain later, but you need to recognize your enemy and know what we're up against."

"Jesus, Mary, and Joseph," Truman uttered incredulously.

"I know. This is a shock to the senses. Believe me, when Helen and I saw this, we had the same reaction as you two. It just doesn't seem real, but I can tell you without hesitation that these beings are very real, and they pose a very real threat. They are not only a threat to the United States but to the entire planet. If we don't move quickly and purposefully, we will lose our world to these alien invaders. The entire planet will be enslaved. Those are the stakes gentlemen."

Truman spoke up tensely. "Aliens? Like in Buck Rogers, aliens? Outer space… not from earth, aliens?"

"Yes, sir."

"But that's not possible. It can't be possible. That's just what you see in shows at the motion picture theatres."

"As I said, sir, we had the very same reaction. However, these beings are very real. This is not from a Hollywood movie."

"And they pose a threat to us?" Quinn asked, still trying to overcome the shock of what he was seeing.

"Oh yes, a very real threat. Oh c'mon, do you really think I would be standing here telling you this outrageous story if I didn't believe it with everything in me? Truth be told, they have been a threat for decades, but we had no idea they were even here."

"Trust me, I would have noticed one of those things if I saw it," Quinn stated emphatically, pointing to the sitting creatures.

"But would you have noticed him?" Mac asked, pointing to the handsome young man. "According to the Greys, the Anakim and certain Shalanaya have been collaborating to take over earth for a long time now. Shalanaya conspirators have infiltrated many nations and governments in their quest."

"So, all of this information has come from those you call the Greys? And how exactly do we know they can be trusted?" the President asked with concern.

"We don't," Mac stated flatly. "That's why I'm here. If the threat is real you had to know, but we must search this out. If what the Greys told us is true, then we don't have much time before it happens again."

"Before what happens again?" Quinn asked hesitantly.

"War."

Truman and Quinn looked at one another, then at the aliens, before finally turning their eyes back to Mac. It was clear they were having an enormous problem processing what they had seen and heard thus far. And Mac couldn't blame them; after all, he had gone through the exact same process six months earlier, along with his wife.

"Let me get rid of these creatures so I can fill you in. I can't hold them in stasis much longer, anyway. Helen is back at home helping with this part of the mission, as it takes more than one person to keep these beings in a vegetative state. We'll send them back to the Greys for safekeeping."

The aliens then disappeared as quickly as they came, with only the stench of them remaining in the room to remind the men that someone – something had actually been in their presence. Mac stumbled on the way back to his chair but managed to catch himself by leaning against the President's desk. They noticed his hands trembling a bit as he rested there a moment and said, "I hope you don't mind, Mr. President, but that exercise took quite a lot out of me. It doesn't seem to faze the Greys, but my human frailties make tasks that they do easily more difficult."

"The Greys," Truman began, "The other aliens."

"Yes, Mr. President. Let me try to answer a few of your questions before I have to leave."

"Leave? You just got here!"

"Yes, sir, but I have a few things that need attending after a six-month absence. Not to mention following up on some rather cryptic leads they gave us."

"I thought the Greys were an ally," Quinn interjected quickly. "You said…"

"Slow down, Bill. I'll get there. I promise. Just take a breath."

Truman and Quinn, with minds reeling, remained silent as Mac took several deep breaths in an attempt to regain control. As they waited for Mac's explanation, Quinn stood his chair upright once again and the three of them sat down.

"We are hoping to gain more control and strength as we use our new skills," Mac told them as he rubbed his tingling fingers. "We have had intensive training and some internal physiological changes to allow us to do what you just saw. Why we were chosen by the Greys is a mystery to both of us, but it is what it is." Color began to return to his face as he continued. "You were correct, Mr. President, we don't know any more about the Greys than any of the others and because of that we must verify the information they shared."

"War," Truman stated with dread, "you said a war would happen again if what they said was true. What did you mean by that?"

"What better way to take over an entire planet than to decimate the natives through war? According to the Greys, Shalanaya spies incited both world wars here," Magruder answered solemnly. "Only the United States intervened both times before the devastation was extensive enough for their plans. To put it bluntly, sir, they're gunning for us now."

Truman removed his glasses and silently rubbed his eyes with his free hand. After returning the spectacles to their place, he responded quietly, "I hardly have the words to explain what's going through my head right now. I don't know if I'm having a hallucination or if I have a madman in my office. Either way, there is no way in hell I can simply accept what these aliens…these so-called Greys said without some kind of additional proof. Even seeing it with my own two eyes - this is just too far-fetched to be believed, Mac."

"I couldn't agree more, Mr. President," Mac said as he stood to leave.

"General," the President said, waiting for Mac to turn and look at him. "The last thing we need is another war."

Mac locked eyes with the Commander-in-Chief before responding. "Understood, sir," and with that Magruder disappeared from the room, leaving Truman and Quinn staring at the empty space he had just inhabited. Quinn stood up and took two steps toward the center of the room, then sniffed the air. The repugnant odor of the Anakim was still hanging in the Oval Office.

Quinn finally mumbled, "Son of a…"

"I'm so screwed," Truman exhaled as he slumped back in his chair.

CHAPTER 3

Magruder stood for a moment with his eyes closed while the buzzing in his head subsided. It was a dangerous habit; he knew. One could never be absolutely certain who might be waiting on the other end when you entered, but here he could indulge himself. He opened his eyes slowly and smiled as his head cleared, and the peace of being home settled over him.

He allowed a moment of nostalgia as he recalled how Helen, his wife of twenty-nine years, had purchased this little gem while he was on assignment fifteen years ago. She had waylaid him upon his return after the particularly contentious briefing at the White House with the then Commander-in-Chief and drove him to see the two-story Colonial-style home.

"It's already done," she had told him without apology. "We need a place where we can breathe, Mac, and it's only ten miles from D.C. The apartment was, well, you know, it was beautiful but just stifling. Relaxing there was hard. But this place," she sighed contently, "well it's warm and comfortable, and it has *actual* trees!"

Her excitement had sold him before he ever set eyes on the place. After all, the apartment had been purchased solely out of convenience; he had no particular attachment to it. She had always been home for him, and if this is where Helen wanted to be, this is where he wanted to be.

His body reverberated slightly, and there was a residual amount of nausea in the pit of his stomach from his very recent experience in the Oval Office. *Nobody said this would be a cakewalk,* he reminded himself. Besides, it was far better than some of the missions he had endured in his thirty-plus years of military service.

He wanted to get his bearings before announcing himself, so he stood a few seconds longer, gazing out the large living room window at the mass of snow-covered trees on his property as he took stock of his person. Although a seasoned veteran, physically transporting himself and others inter-dimensionally to different locations was more than a little out of his wheelhouse. He wanted to be sure of his own condition before being sized up by anyone else.

When Magruder walked on the deck of the enclosed veranda, he found Helen and Yazzie, his long-time Jewish friend, talking quietly with half-filled coffee cups resting on the classic Hanover oval glass table in front of them.   Helen, as usual, spoke politely and enthusiastically. She was an optimist at her very heart. Yazzie, a former U.S. Army strategist and secretly a proud member of the national military organization in the land of Palestine called the Irgun, was more pragmatic. He was a strategist, after all. He had already begun planning for the long-term strategy of national and international safety protocols to prevent the extinction of the human race. He was a deep thinker.

A third cup sat empty, waiting for Mac near the coffee carafe. Helen had bought that table at a second-hand store, despite his objections, because it suited her. It took three months more to find chairs that also suited her from an antique store in Alexandria, but in the end he had to admit it added a certain charm to the plain wooden deck of the enclosed summer porch. Besides, he had a hard time strenuously objecting to anything Helen did; he loved that she rejected pretense in favor of her own style and personal taste.

"So," began Helen, "How do you think it went?"

"About what I expected," Magruder answered tiredly. "They were completely caught off-guard and more than a little terrified. And who can blame them? This whole story of ours reeks like a bad Hollywood movie."

"Sit down, dear. You look exhausted," she encouraged as she observed him closely.

"They thought you were out of your mind," Yazzie declared. "I told you they would."

"That was to be expected, wasn't it?" Helen calmly replied. "It's not an easy thing to accept emotionally or philosophically. It would have been better if we didn't have to spring everything on them all at once, but personally I thought our first mission went splendidly, didn't you?" she prompted the two men.

"You make it sound like some kind of Boy Scout outing," Mac protested as he stretched his arms over his head and arched his back to counteract some of the stiffness. His stomach was still a bit nauseated as he carefully nudged his body to comply. "What do the Boy Scouts have to do with it?" Yazzie asked, somewhat perplexed.

Helen sipped her coffee and continued undeterred, "Pay him no mind, Yazzie. I think it went very well, almost exactly as planned." She exuded confidence that Mac and Yazzie simply did not possess right now.

Yazzie turned to look squarely at Mac. "What did they think about having a Jew on the team? Your last administration wasn't exactly friendly toward my people."

"You didn't come up," Mac countered as he pulled his arms forward and continued to stretch. Two pairs of raised eyebrows caused him to continue as his arms dropped to his side. "Okay, so I didn't mention you, but it wasn't out of spite or because you're Jewish. They weren't exactly on board with the whole alien invader taking over the earth thing, so I decided to keep mum about you. That way if they compromise Helen and me in some way, you'll be available to save the day."

"Well, if that isn't something…" Helen protested in feigned outrage.

"They already knew about you, dear one. You know I would never put you at risk," Mac said as he leaned over and kissed her forehead.

"There are certain advantages to being anonymous," Yazzie reflected. "Yes, being just a face in the crowd will work quite well for me I think."

"And if they get wind of you being part of a certain Palestinian organization, there's no way in hell we will ever get their support. As far as the White House is concerned they are nothing but trouble," Mac concluded, looking directly at Yazzie. "Good thing they don't know then, eh?" Yazzie answered stoically.

"Of course, we'll have to make you known at some point — just not right away. And then let them know that you are a loyal ally."

"Well, I've never been a part of a secret mission before, so I thought it was quite exciting," Helen added enthusiastically. "Besides technically we've only had these abilities for a few days, so I think we did quite well."

"A few days? It took six months for the, um, what should we call it?" Mac asked Yazzie sarcastically.

Helen inserted herself again. "Well yes, we were on the Greys' planet for six months, but we've only been back on earth a few days. It's different here. The disorientation alone takes some getting used to; at least I hope we get used to it."

"Is disorientation a polite way of saying we can't tell where the hell we are or how we got there?" Mac responded. "Walking from your kitchen into another world is not something any of us can ever take lightly. It seems surreal to say the least."

Mac never told Helen or Yazzie of the panic he felt at that first transition. It was the smell, like metallic sulfur and musty, rotting wood. It reminded him starkly of the ugliness of war. Seeing Yazzie there, crouched in a defensive position, reaching for the weapon in his boot didn't help.

"What just happened?" Helen had whispered as she sought the comfort of Mac's hand.

Mac remembered quickly pulling her behind his body as he backed the two of them into a position next to his tense Jewish comrade. "Yazzie, is that you?"

"What the hell, Mac, what's going on?" he responded with every nerve in his body on high alert.

"Do you have another weapon?" Mac asked tightly, regretting the moment he had removed his shoulder holster to help set the table.

"You will not be needing weapons," responded a voice that sounded like a scratchy vinyl record. "They are not allowed here. I am sorry for interrupting your existence, but it is imperative that we speak," the creature had stated as the monstrosity finally revealed himself. His unexpected appearance didn't help to defuse the situation.

They had to tilt their heads back to take in the sheer height of him. He was olive green in color and had thin, tough skin stretched tightly over a body of pure muscle and bone. His feet were more like hooves, with four toes on each foot, and his head looked like a helmet with eyes. But it was the four massive arms that had brought the smart ass out of Mac as he observed, "Well, the phrase, 'Toto, we aren't in Kansas anymore' just took on an entirely new meaning."

Mac pushed the memories aside and maneuvered into the chair next to Helen. He observed his wife and Yazzie as he poured himself a cup of coffee. His eyes surveyed the two and noted that they also looked physically drained.

"I guess it took its toll on all of us trying to keep those guys in stasis that long," he mused quietly.

"Did you notice the difference here? Like the difference between swimming in water and Jello, doable but more difficult," Yazzie observed as he straightened in his chair. Smoothing his already thinning hair, he quoted a familiar Psalm, "But it had to be done. Strengthen, O God, what you have done for us."

"He's right," Helen agreed. "This is important; beyond important. We've got to have their utmost confidence if we're going to succeed. After all, we're trying to save our entire species from enslavement. Our personal cost is negligible at best."

Magruder smiled to himself. Leave it to Helen to cut to the core of any situation without regard for self-preservation. The absolute ridiculousness of the situation would drive most people to the brink of insanity. But she was able to accept and react to most any situation with a calm resoluteness most did not possess. No wonder the other officers' wives trusted her counsel. She believed when no one else would; that was her secret strength.

"I know, I know," Mac acknowledged. "The whole world is counting on us, and they don't even know it."

"No different from our old jobs, eh, Mac," Yazzie offered.

"I gave up wanting to be appreciated a long time ago. You did, too."

"Jews have never been appreciated, especially now. But, yes, I understand the sentiment."

"Oh, I think you both try to put on a good show of your manliness, but deep inside it still feels good to be appreciated – or at least acknowledged. It's just human nature," Helen opined.

"But are we really human anymore?" Mac said, reaching across the table to squeeze her hand.

Yazzie watched Mac and Helen and enjoyed the moment between them as he thought of his late wife before he got back to business. "How long do you think we'll need before taking on another assignment like this? I'm drained…do you think it will get easier with time?"

"We're all exhausted," Helen answered quickly. "We can move inter-dimensionally with little effort but holding those creatures in stasis is altogether different. My energy level just collapsed at a certain point. That worries me. I mean, what would the consequences have been if we weren't able hold the Anakim in particular in stasis any longer?"

Mac wanted to disagree with her, but he knew his limits, as any well-trained operative would know. Helen was correct; they were all nearly out of juice from this morning's meeting with the President. He hoped they would not need to put such a display on again any time soon, for all their sakes. But that would ultimately depend upon how the President and Colonel Quinn reacted to his presentation in the Oval Office. He wasn't quite sure how it would go from here, but the Greys had assured them that presenting this real-time example was vital to Truman. Magruder hoped they were right. *Hell,* he thought to himself, *I'm praying they're right about everything.*

Mac looked intently outside of the enclosed veranda and made a slight motion to Yazzie that was also noticed by Helen. "What is it?" she asked apprehensively.

"That's the third time that black Buick has come past the house this morning," Mac answered her.

"Is that significant?"

"We're out in the middle of nowhere, Helen."

Yazzie added, "Not many government-issued black Buick's this far out of D.C."

"Oh, dear."

"My soul melts from heaviness; strengthen me according to Your word," Yazzie breathed out another Psalm quietly. He looked at his watch as he heard the car turn up the drive. "They made good time. We'll continue the debriefing at my place?" He waited for heads to nod before he vanished.

Helen sighed as she said, "I was hoping to tidy up before we had to leave," and then the veranda was empty.

CHAPTER 4

Truman sat in the Oval Office behind his historic desk and sighed as if the whole world were depending upon him to save them and, in a way, they were. They just didn't know it. "I don't know how you do it, Mr. President," Colonel Quinn remarked solemnly as he sat across from the man he had grown to highly respect over the past six months.

"Do what, Bill?"

"Your job. It's bad enough to be responsible for America; but now you have Europe, Japan, and the whole damn Pacific Rim. Then there's the Soviet Union looking over your shoulder every day of the week."

"It is. But like I always say, if you can't stand the heat…"

"Stay out of the kitchen," Quinn finished for him.

"Exactly." Truman rose from his chair and walked to the window. It was snowing again. "Right now, I'm pushing Congress for funds to keep Europe out of the hands of those damn Soviets. Stalin is convinced the time is ripe to grab the whole continent. He figures the rest of the world is sick of war and won't do a damn thing to stop him," he said without turning.

"He may be correct, Mr. President. The West is tired of fighting. They want peace. They want their husbands and sons to come home."

The president regretfully turned from the peaceful scene outside and returned to his desk. "And I don't blame them. Hell, I want them all to come home too. But not at the cost of allowing that commie dictator to put all of Europe in shackles. I just won't stand for it."

"Yes, sir."

The room was silent for a moment as Truman retrieved a piece of paper from his desk and read it. "George Marshall is coming on soon. Once he gets settled, I'll talk to him about getting a plan in place that will get those folks back on track and keep Stalin out of the mix."

"He's a good man. I'm sure he can develop a more than sufficient plan for reconstructing Europe."

"I have every confidence in George. MacArthur on the other hand, I'm not so sure about."

"Sir?"

"The man's a damn narcissist," the president said with disgust in his voice. "He's more concerned with getting his name in the papers than turning Japan around. He's spent four years trying to kill them and now he's responsible to get them on track for democracy. I'm not sure he has the best interest of their nation or ours in mind."

"Sorry to hear that, sir."

"Well, that's not your issue, Colonel," the president said, realizing he had been using the Colonel as a sounding board. Reigning his thoughts back in, he continued with the real reason for their meeting. "We have plenty of eggs to fry here in D.C. already and now we find out there may be little green men from Mars trying to take over the planet. As if the Soviets weren't enough of a problem."

"With all due respect, sir. How in the hell do you keep all this straight?"

"I wonder that myself sometimes, Colonel. Still haven't got an answer though. I guess I'll just keep muddling along until somebody better shows up," he said with a slight smile. "Now, what have your intel guys reported about our little green men? Except they aren't little, and they aren't green. They're big, ugly, and smell to high heaven."

"It seems that the odor is gone though," Quinn remarked, hoping to find a reason to doubt what he had seen with his own eyes just days before.

"That would be Rose's doing. She had them in here cleaning the rug that same day," the president said with a smile. "She thought someone came in with something unpleasant on the bottom of their shoe. She was quite put out about it."

Quinn returned the smile, then stood and restlessly paced before the President. He would rather be anywhere but here at this moment. But like the boss said, *I guess I'll just keep muddling along until somebody better shows up.*

"Your silence is deafening, Bill," the president observed, with no trace of his previous smile.

"Sorry, sir. I'm still trying to get a grip on that meeting with Mac the other day."

"You and me both. I need to know if we really are on the verge of an alien invasion or if we were deceived by some third-rate parlor trick."

"More like a first-rate parlor trick if that's what it was. But, yes, I've already selected someone to delve into this discreetly."

"Can he be trusted with this?"

"Absolutely. Curly is as straight and loyal as anyone in the CIG (Central Intelligence Group). He came over from the SSU (Special Services Unit) and before that the OSS (Office of Strategic Services)."

"Okay, he has impressive credentials, but do you trust him?"

"With my life, Mr. President. He's as tough as nails, Texan. Graduated from Texas A&M and enlisted in the Army when the war started. He'll probably be a lifer. An American patriot if there ever was one."

"An Aggie, huh?"

"A proud Aggie, sir. I think he bleeds maroon and white on game days in the Fall although I heard he still gets grief from his family that he didn't go to Texas Tech. They're Red Raiders all the way."

Truman smiled. "That's good enough for me. Where is he right now?"

"Germany. Ostensibly, tracking down escaped Nazi leaders."

"Ostensibly?"

"He uses information from those captured to find the German scientists Hitler had on his payroll. They were looking at nuclear energy long before we did."

"I thought we had enough of those guys. Didn't we complete the Manhattan Project because of them? Not that my predecessor bothered to keep me in the loop while it was going on."

"It's not just about nuclear research, sir. They had rockets and jets far beyond our capabilities. And we heard they were working on biological weapons and doing antigravity research as well with great success," Quinn stated. "There are hundreds of scientists still out there. We know the Soviets have been scooping up as many as they can track down."

"Dammit! We can't let those Soviets bastards get a jump on us with that technology! They would destroy the world just to say they are in power!"

"Yes, sir. That's why Major Hale has been working over there. He travels as an officer in our Army and that gets him in and out of nearly every place he goes."

"And when it doesn't?"

"He goes in anyway."

"I like this man already."

"Yes, sir. I do too."

"Has he been successful?"

"Yes, sir. He's tracked down several fanatical Nazi-loving ODESSA operatives and over the course of many interrogations received some solid leads on scientists trying to hide or escape Germany altogether."

"Those former Nazis trying to get their 'brothers-in-arms' out of Germany now that they've turned the whole nation into a garbage dump?"

"Yes, sir. He brought in a couple that he caught with their pants down, so-to-speak. They are still being questioned outside Nuremberg by Army Intel and CIG. A few other ODESSA members didn't like the idea of surrendering and resisted – strenuously."

"Meaning?"

"Curly buried them without honors, sir."

"Sounds like my kind of soldier. Bring him in," the President said solemnly. "I want to talk to him."

"Yes, sir."

CHAPTER 5

The six-foot two-inch Major Donald "Curly" Hale rode on the passenger side of his Army issue general purpose vehicle all G.I.s just called a Jeep. It was still dark and nasty cold as he and his driver bumped their way along the winding dirt road toward a farmhouse outside Fussen, Germany. Corporal Hedges along with Privates Cooper and Perez, veterans of these missions, followed in an Army GMC CCKW truck commonly called a deuce and a half. If their assignment went as planned, the deuce and a half would leave with more men than were trucked in.

Nazi bastards.

Hale hoped the information received about former Nazis slinking down from the nearby Tegelberg Mountain to reach Austria was spot on. Freedom was only about one kilometer from this old farmhouse to the border. The "unoccupied" house was well-maintained and stocked with food and supplies according to his source. It was easy walking distance to the border unless men like Hale and his team were there to stop the unrepentant murderers from utilizing prearranged escape routes.

The former Nazi SS members and Nazi sympathizers of the Organization Der Ehemaligen SS-Angehörigen (ODESSA) had begun getting high-level Nazi pricks out of Germany before the war had even ended. So much for loyalty to the death for the Third Reich. These war criminals, human butchers by any other name, had no desire to face justice for their deeds. Instead, they used stolen money gathered from all over Europe to fund their escapes and relocations to South America. Argentina seemed to be the nation of choice for ODESSA refugees.

But this dark morning Hale hoped to stop the relocation of at least three high-level former SS officers disguised as businessmen. Hans Bergmann, Claus Ricard, and Oskar Weber were on their way to the border according to intel gathered from various sources. Hale and his team were planning a slight detour in the trio's travel plans through the Pullach Compound outside Munich for interrogation.

Every time an ODESSA member was caught, more intel could be gathered to assist in locating even more fleeing Nazis and bring them to justice; at least that was part of Hale's assignment. His underlying mission was to use information gained to find and secure missing German scientists. Sources revealed that these scientists had been involved in producing an atomic bomb since 1939 and they would have succeeded had Hitler been smart enough to give them the proper resources to complete their work.

Fortunately for the rest of the world, Hitler was an idiot in that regard. He depended too much on his traditional war machine to win the conflict, and it all came tumbling down on his head. Hitler's scientists were brilliant but under-funded. They were on the cusp of developing rockets, bombs, and biological weapons with nuclear power that would have easily overcome every nation on the planet. The German Bell spacecraft under construction would have put an arsenal in outer space, giving them the ability to strike anywhere on earth at any time. His scientists were ahead of the rest of the world regarding the utilization of earth's outer sphere and Hitler would have unquestionably been the ruler of the world. But now, because of his own short-sightedness, he was only a bad memory; however, his scientists were still to be found.

Hale reined in his thoughts as they neared the farmhouse. *Focus on one step at a time; concentrate on the moment,* he told himself. Compartmentalization was a great trait when you were in Hale's line of work, and he was damn good at it.

As they rounded a low hill, light could be seen in the house. "Somebody gets up early," Sergeant McCann remarked as he slowed the jeep to a stop.

"Not a smart move to light up a place that's supposed to be deserted," Hale answered thoughtfully. "Damn, we were supposed to be ahead of these guys so we could take them down when they first arrived. Pull over and cut the engine. We'll go on foot from here. I don't want them to hear us coming and bolt."

After both vehicles were parked out of sight, Hale and his four men silently moved across the uneven ground toward the farmhouse, using the unkempt terrain and early morning shadows to mask their progress. Even with all their gear and armed with a couple of M-1 Carbines, two Tommy Guns, grenades, and Hale's Colt .45 pistol, they seemed to glide like shadows across the landscape. Their armory was a little light on this trip; however, it was more than enough to take down a few old men who couldn't outrun a dead dog, much less experienced dog soldiers.

Hale silently held up his hand, stopping his men about fifty meters from the house. Pointing toward what was left of the back door, he whispered, "Did you see movement over there, McCann?"

"Maybe. But my eyes could be playing tricks on me this time of the morning," he replied with the frosty mist of his words clinging to his eyelashes.

"I could have sworn I saw someone slide into the house. Better make sure we ease ourselves into that place quietly. I don't want to walk into a trap. Let's take our time."

"Yes, sir," his team quietly responded in unison, ignoring the biting cold. It wasn't like it mattered who was in the house. They had to go.

Hale signaled for McCann and Cooper to move to the back of the house. Hedges and Perez were motioned to the front, but before they could leave their current positions, a woman screamed as gunfire erupted from the farmhouse.

Hale and his men dropped flat to the ground and searched for targets as the interior lights went out. The gunfire continued for less than sixty seconds, with only two shots zinging through the front window in their direction. Then there was nothing but silence.

"Anybody hit?" Hale asked, with his chin still in the dirt.

"We're all good," McCann replied quietly after getting a thumbs-up from the others.

They cautiously lifted themselves off the frozen ground, keeping an eye on the rickety wood porch wondering if there was to be a round two. The seconds seemed minutes as they remained stock still to see if they had been made, despite the moonless night. Seeing no movement, Hale finally broke the silence. "All right, let's see what's going on in there."

"I got it, Major," McCann said as he took the lead in a crouched sprint to the back door with Cooper close behind.

Hedges and Perez quietly edged toward the front door with weapons raised.

A scant second after the two men reached the backdoor, Hale moved quickly to their rear facing away from the house to watch for an ambush.

"I'll go left," McCann started in a husky whisper. "You go right, Coop. Major, you come right up the middle once it's clear."

"You sure, Billy?" Cooper asked. "You went first last time."

"And the time before that. It's my job."

"You're a stubborn Irish prick, Billy."

"Aye, and I will be 'til the good Lord calls me home or back to Mother Ireland. Either one's good with me," the sergeant responded with a lopsided grin and a bit of Irish brogue for effect.

Hale smiled as he scanned the countryside. This argument happened every time they had to bust into a hornet's nest. "All right, Billy," Hale commanded. "You're up on three."

"Got it, Major. On three."

Hale began the count by silently raising his index finger, then his middle finger, and before he got to his ring finger McCann and Cooper were already up and charging into the house – as usual. Hale followed close behind after one last glance across the landscape to verify that an enemy wasn't hiding in the overgrown brush surrounding the old house, waiting to come up their six. Once inside, he moved swiftly into position in the center of the room.

Hale's team breaching the back door was the signal for Hedges and Perez, who instantly busted through the front door swinging their raised weapons back and forth clearing the room. Silence…nothing but the sound of their own boots on the old wooden floorboards.

Once inside, Hale and his men found themselves in the kitchen. The room was warm and smelled of sausage and fresh coffee. Three plates with the remains of a meal sat unwashed on the table with various utensils and a partial loaf of bread waiting to be sliced. The trio moved slowly to the only interior door in the room and found themselves in the living room with Hedges and Perez.

Hale noted the hallway to his right and was moving in that direction when his boot hit something soft and heavy that interrupted his forward momentum and caused him to stumble. He quickly extended a hand to catch himself and made contact with something warm and sticky on the floor. No one had to tell him what was now on his hand.

The lack of light, while an asset on their approach, made recognition difficult in the house. As their eyes adjusted, using nothing except the glowing embers from a dying fire, they could see the room had been a killing ground. Hale's boot had connected with one of two victims lying on the floor with blood seeping from their now soulless bodies. A third man, tied to an overturned chair with rough brown rope, was dead as well. He had obviously been tortured.

A sound from the back of the house caused all five men's heads to swivel away from the gruesome scene and raise their weapons toward the hallway. Hale was closest, so he took the lead absently wiping his bloody hand on his trousers to ensure his grip would not slip. Silently and swiftly the men moved down the short hallway, stopping outside each room to listen for any sound or movement, then opening each door and flipping on a light for visual confirmation that it was unoccupied.

Water could be heard running behind the second door on the right, and a slender light showed under the door. Hale gently tried the doorknob without success, so taking one step back he applied his heavy boot firmly to the door right beside the uncooperative knob. With his weapon ready, he immediately filled the entrance with his body as the door slammed into the opposite wall. A terrified dark-haired young woman was pinned beneath a nude dead man beside the bathtub, and she had tears running down her face as she desperately tried to push the heavy weight off her body. Her dress was torn from the neck to her midsection, and when Hale entered, she quickly stopped struggling with the dead weight and snatched up her dress to cover her exposed breasts.

"Bitte, tut mir nicht weh! *Please don't hurt me,*" she cried out as she raised her arm to shield her face. "Bitte, tut mir nicht weh!"

"Niemand wird dir wehtun. *No one is going to hurt you.*" He replied softly. He holstered his weapon and raised his hands as if in surrender as he slowly reached over and turned off the spigot. "Sprechen Sie Englisch? *Do you speak English?*"

"Ja. Yes," she whispered wide-eyed as she lowered her arm uncertainly while keeping a firm hold on her torn dress.

"Good. Listen, I'm Major Donald Hale of the United States Army," he said as he squatted to her eye level. "My men and I are here to help you. Do you understand?"

"Ja, thank you, thank you," she said submissively as her haunted eyes searched Hale's face. He shrugged out of his field jacket and wrapped it around her shoulders before rolling the naked body of her attacker onto the floor.

"Billy," Hale called out, keeping eye contact with the woman. She recoiled from even the touch of the dead man's skin as she pulled her legs under the large jacket still warm from Hale's body.

"Right here, sir," he replied as he stepped partially into the bathroom doorway.

"The rest of the house secure?"

"Yes, sir. The men got everything covered."

"Good. I want you to take this woman." He turned to the woman curled into as small a space as she could get and asked, "What's your name, ma'am?"

"Tamar," she whispered with her eyes darting between the two men. "My name is Tamar."

"Tamar. That's a nice name."

She smiled shakily in response as she tried to pull her bare feet even further under her covering.

"Billy, see if you can find Tamar some shoes, then take her to the jeep and make sure she's secure. I want to do a walk-through and see if I can figure out what the hell happened here."

"Yes Major. Then what?"

Hale smiled reassuringly at the tear-streaked face of the woman on the floor as he said, "Then we take Tamar back to Pullach Compound. Maybe she can fill us in on what happened here during the hour-and-a-half drive."

"Yes, sir," Billy said as his eyes shifted from the girl to the body. "Hell of a night, Major."

"Yeah. Hell of a night."

McCann guided Tamar down the hallway toward the living room and procured a pair of shoes from one of the dead Germans lying on the floor. Tamar glanced back at Hale as she slipped the over-sized boots on her slim feet and tried to secure them. Hale saw her look and felt protective of the young woman, although he knew her very presence here prohibited him from shielding her from the questions to come. He went back into the bathroom, both to do a quick analysis and to avoid Tamar's pleading eyes.

"Excuse me, ma'am," McCann started. "It's standard procedure to search anyone we are transporting. Just in case… you know."

"Ja. Yes, of course," Tamar whispered, nodding her head in resignation.

Tamar looked at the ceiling as the warm field jacket slid to the floor and unfamiliar hands slid along every part of her body. Her thick wool dress did not do much to protect her sense of dignity, however the soldier was quick and thorough and made the uncomfortable situation as painless as possible for her. "She's good," he said to two others in the room as he handed the borrowed jacket back to the shivering woman.

Hale looked back at the dead man in the bathroom and wondered how Tamar was able to extricate herself from such a large man. He searched the bathroom with what he hoped was a new set of eyes. Nothing stood out. The dead man couldn't tell him anything – if there was anything to tell besides he was trying to rape Tamar.

Did she get lucky? Was the man drunk? What the hell happened here?

Hale heard Sergeant McCann call out all clear and was relieved that nothing incriminating was found on the young woman. She had suffered enough at the hands of these Nazi bastards. Now all he had to do was gather as much information as possible. He would have Perez get on the radio and call for a clean-up team to come and gather the bodies. They could haul them back in the deuce and a half, but that may be traumatic for Tamar. *No sense in making it more difficult. She's been through enough for one day.* Cooper could stay with Hedges to keep the scene sterile.

Hale bumped the toilet as he walked around the dead German's body for an alternate view of the small room. Something scratched the back side of the porcelain tank and thumped to the floor. *What the hell was that?* He moved around the tank and toilet slightly to see a familiar object lying on the bathroom floor, a handcrafted icepick. He had seen ice picks like this before. Hell, he had used ice picks like this before…and there was blood on it.

CHAPTER 6

It was a typical cold January Washington, D.C. evening, so Mac decided to light a fire in the fireplace which had remained unused so far this winter in their absence. It was one of the creature comforts he particularly enjoyed, so he was happy when Helen and Yazzie agreed that the temperature in the living room was a bit lower than what they considered comfortable – even after the changes the Greys had made to their bodies.

They sat around an early American-style oak coffee table. Helen was cradling a cup of coffee in her hands, but Mac and Yazzie held glasses of a smooth Kentucky bourbon.

"I may have found a lead," Yazzie announced triumphantly.

"Seriously? He may actually exist then?" Mac said, a bit stunned.

"You didn't believe the Greys?" Helen asked, cocking her head to one side.

"No," Mac and Yazzie said in unison.

"Well, for heaven's sake, why did you look for him then?" she asked, nudging a plate of coffee cake toward Yazzie with an encouraging smile.

"Oh no, no. I must watch my figure to impress the ladies," he said, rubbing his flat, firm belly and smiling broadly.

"Let's just say that I'm still trying to get all this straight in my mind," Mac replied as he stood and went to freshen his drink. "The Greys gave us heads full of information, but I'm not sure they gave us everything."

"You think they held something back?" Helen asked as she settled back into the overstuffed sofa.

"I can't say for sure, but I'm absolutely certain they don't want us to know everything they know," Mac replied while pouring another two fingers into Yazzie's upheld glass.

"Or if we're even capable of knowing everything they know," offered Yazzie. "We know very little about them."

"We know what they told us, that's all," Mac answered simply as he returned the bottle of bourbon to its place.

"And yet, here we are trying to convince President Truman that he needs to mobilize for alien warfare," Yazzie added sardonically.

"We all saw the threat clearly while undergoing the transformation," Helen defended, taking another sip of her coffee.

"I'm not saying the threat isn't real, Helen," Mac explained as he detoured his return to the sofa to stoke the fire. Red sparks lifted from the logs as flames licked the sides of the exposed bark. "All I'm saying is that there may be more going on here than what we know so far. And maybe that's for the best."

"How so?" questioned Yazzie.

"If we knew all there was to know we may have declined to undergo the transformation. Where would earth be then?" Mac mused. He returned the poker to its stand and resumed his spot next to Helen. "Trust but verify, eh, Yazzie. Where is he? Are you positive it's our man?"

"There was a Makoto Fujita, Lieutenant Commander of an I-400 class sub who became a nautical engineer right here in the USA. He was drafted into the Japanese navy right after the war started," Yazzie reiterated. "But then I lost him. No record after that."

"Sure sounds like our guy. Of course, the Greys could have picked a name out of a hat. We won't be able to confirm until we talk to him. If he was in the Japanese military, are you sure he's not dead?"

"Could be," Yazzie answered. "Don't know yet. I'll keep looking."

The clock on the mantle sounded its steady tick, tick, tick, as they each sipped their chosen beverages in silence and stared at the dancing flames in the fireplace. After a moment, Yazzie leaned forward in his chair and placed his glass on the coffee table. "Do you think they're buying into this, Mac?" Yazzie asked seriously.

"I've known President Truman for a while and Quinn for far longer. They will take precautions and verify what they can before moving forward, just like we are doing."

"Even after seeing those creatures," Helen said with a sigh. "You would think that would be enough for anyone to believe you."

"The nation has just come through four years of all-out war, Helen. Even if they believe me, they still must consider the consequences of entering another conflict so soon. The American economy is still shaky, and the American people are tired of war."

"And politicians are already staking American claims to what's left of the world," Yazzie added cynically.

"Be that as it may," Helen interjected, as she rose and took the remainder of the coffee cake into the kitchen. She raised her voice to be heard as she covered the two remaining slices and put them in the refrigerator. "We all know what could happen if Truman doesn't heed the alien threat."

"Which threat?" Yazzie asked, raising his voice so she could hear. "The Shalanaya or the Anakim?"

"Aren't they the same?" Helen asked from the other room.

"Maybe, maybe not," Mac offered, not willing to commit either way.

The telephone rang, interrupting the conversation. Helen answered it in the kitchen, then called, "Yazzie, it's for you," placing the receiver on the counter before returning to her place on the sofa.

As Yazzie left the room, Magruder's posture became stiff and his voice tense. "Who would be calling him here? Who even knows he's with us?"

"The Post Office apparently knows," Helen responded, arranging her skirt as she sat. When she looked up and noticed her husband's change in demeanor, she asked, "Is something wrong?"

"Bad news?" Mac asked as Yazzie reentered the room with a furrowed brow.

"Probably," he responded with a sigh. "A telegram from Menachem, you know, George, in Palestine. Tamar is no longer with him."

"Tamar?" Helen inquired.

"Yazzie's niece. He was able to get her out of Germany into the Ukraine and then Palestine just as the wheels came off civilization there and the slaughter began," Mac explained.

"Oh, my God! What about the rest of her family; did they escape, too?" she asked Yazzie.

"No. Unfortunately, my brother was convinced that the situation would eventually blow over in Germany. He just sent Tamar as a precaution until the hostilities had subsided. I was already in Palestine and had enough connections to bring her to me."

"Oh, the poor girl, I can't even imagine," Helen said with her heart breaking. "She lives in Palestine?"

"She did. It seems since we've been gone she's made her way back to Germany," Yazzie said quietly, with his suspicions about why she had felt the need to return.

"And what does George expect you to do about it?" queried Mac.

"Sending me a telegram? I'm quite certain he expects me to go get her and bring her home."

"Who is this George or Menachem person? Why does he want your niece brought back to Palestine? I don't understand," Helen questioned.

Yazzie looked at Mac to see if he should answer Helen directly. Mac shook his head, then turned to face Helen. "There are a few things you don't know about Yazzie, dear."

Helen knew that look. That *I've-kept-this-from-you-for-your-own-good* look. It was infuriating! She was as much a part of this operation as the two of them now. "Like what, sweetheart?" she asked, dripping with sugar as she tried to keep her temper in check.

"Well, Yazzie works for some people over in Palestine. Important people."

"So, he doesn't work with you at the CIG?"

"No, no he does, however, he also works with an organization in Palestine. In fact, my organization works with his organization to gather information from Palestine," Mac replied smoothly, trying to head off the argument he could sense was coming.

"Alright, and what's the name of this organization you failed to tell me about?" Helen probed demurely.

It was like waiting for a volcano to erupt; watching sparks and smoke send up a warning. It was time to jump in. "We're called the Irgun," Yazzie inserted without a hint of reservation. "And George is Menachem Begin. I report to him. So does Tamar."

Helen digested the information for a moment, leaving only the ticking clock to carry the conversation. "Oh, my God," she finally breathed out. "The Irgun is a terrorist organization! What are you two doing working with those people?"

"It's complicated, Helen. But you know me well enough to know that I wouldn't be working with them unless I had approval," Mac explained quickly. "And the same goes for Yazzie."

"Besides, one man's terrorist is another man's patriot," Yazzie opined with a lift of his chin.

"You can't be serious," Helen said with open disbelief.

"Let's deal with one issue at a time, shall we," Mac suggested, rubbing his left temple as all the issues at hand tumbled through his mind. "Tamar will have to wait. I'm sorry, but we must stay on course."

Yazzie didn't flinch as he evenly replied, "I have an order from Menachem. He told me where she is, and I *will* go find her."

"You take orders from me, too, and I'm telling you Tamar can wait. She's not going anywhere. We have too much at stake right now, Yazzie," Mac replied sternly.

"Hear me, my friend, she is my only niece. She lost both parents to those Nazi bastards in Germany, and I will not leave her there to be murdered as my brother was. *I...will...not.*"

"I understand how you feel, but the aliens are the greater threat right now and you know it. Tamar is resourceful and can be returned to Palestine later."

"Bullshit!" Yazzie shouted in a rare display of anger as he vaulted from his chair. "You know nothing about the suffering of the Jews under Hitler! You expect me to leave her there when I have the resources to get her out? Tell me that if it were your son, if it were Munro, you would feel the same."

"The Nazis are not in power anymore, Yazzie," Mac returned as he shot up to face him and even the playing field. "We won. Remember?"

Helen could see the argument intensifying with no immediate end in sight, so she leaped from the sofa and squeezed between Mac and Yazzie. She put her hands flat on Mac's chest and took a few steps toward him, forcing him to retreat as she put a little distance between the two enraged warriors. "Okay, okay, let's just step back a moment and think. Both of you have valid points and I can see that neither of you are willing to concede, but we can't find ourselves fighting each other when we have more important goals to accomplish."

Mac looked somewhat triumphant as he said, "So, you agree. The aliens are the greater threat. Tamar can wait."

"No. Actually, I don't," Helen responded gently.

"What? Helen, the Greys made it clear time is short. We must act now."

"You're right, time is short, however Yazzie is also right. We don't understand what his people have gone through in Germany – in all of Europe for that matter. And if we don't care about the suffering of all human beings, why bother worrying about the alien threat? But perhaps we can accomplish both goals," Helen offered. "President Truman knows about you and me, Mac. He doesn't know that Yazzie is involved. Correct?"

Mac nodded his head in agreement.

"So, maybe Yazzie can take care of Tamar as quickly as possible, then return here. In the meantime, we can go try to explain our absence to Munro as well as my family."

Mac observed Yazzie's steadfast face before answering.

"I can't keep you from going after your niece no matter what I do or say, can I?"

"No," Yazzie answered simply. "You can't."

"I guess it's settled then. You go after Tamar, but I would suggest that you bring her back here – not Palestine. Menachem is not known for his patience nor mercy for those who do not follow his orders explicitly. Chances are Tamar could be in serious trouble over there."

Yazzie smiled slightly at Mac and Helen.

"You weren't going to take her back to Palestine anyway, were you?" Helen presumed.

"No."

"You wily bastard," Mac stated evenly. He knew Yazzie had a way of getting what he wanted while making the other side believe it was their idea. He always was the sly one.

"Okay, everyone has their assignment. Yazzie, watch your back in Germany. Helen, you and I will go smooth things over with our family. That is unless you need backup in Germany?" Mac asked hopefully. "It may be safer there than with my in-laws."

CHAPTER 7

Pullach, Germany, was a medieval-looking town complete with the Schwaneck Castle. The city was located just south of Munich and sat on the west bank of the Isar River. Its access to the river and the construction of the Isar Valley Railway right through town eventually caused an industrial boom in the previously small community. It also undoubtedly influenced the decision to locate the headquarters of the German intelligence agency, Bundesnachrichtendienst or BND, right in the middle of town. Because the Pullach compound was already set up for military intelligence work it had made an excellent location for U.S. assets to set up shop after the war.

By the time Curly Hale and his men had arrived back at the compound, the sun was up, and a winter mist was hovering over the river. A clean-up unit was ordered to the farmhouse and their lovely captive Tamar had been escorted to her assigned quarters. She had said little on the ride back from Fussen, fitfully dozing off and on as the jeep bumped along the rough road. Hale attributed that to the shock of the men killed there and nearly being raped by a Nazi thug. He had to question her again, of course, but figured it could wait until she had cleaned up and settled in and he had gotten a few hours of shuteye.

He was not overly confident that she had any useful information about ODESSA operatives, much less the missing nuclear scientists, but he had to ask. The fact was she had been there, in the farmhouse, with four dead bodies and he had to know why. Being the lone survivor of a massacre could be considered a huge, flaming red flag or simply an unlucky coincidence. All he could do now was ask more questions and see if any of the answers were plausible, perhaps even probable. Maybe.

Tamar walked into Hale's tiny office space, looked around at the sparse furnishings, and waited for him to ask her to sit in the old, well-used wooden chair across from his desk. He flashed her a smile and waved his consent for her to sit as he sized her up. It had been dark and there had been a few other things on his mind last night, so this was the first chance he had to get a good look at her. She was taller than he originally thought; about five foot seven or eight. Her dark hair, tied back last night, was now flowing freely down her back. The waves of softness framed her heart-shaped face and accented her delicate features, but her most striking feature by far was her emerald green eyes the color of deep, clear water.

"Have a seat, Tamar," Hale began the conversation casually. "Are you being treated well by the staff? I'm happy to see that you were able to repair your dress."

"Yes, the soldiers or… um, the staff have been very kind. They brought me a needle and thread and an extra blanket."

"Good. Good. Do you think you're up to answering a few questions for me?"

"More questions? But I told you everything I know at the farmhouse in Fussen," she said as she began twisting a loose thread around her finger nervously.

"There are just a few follow-up questions so I can complete my report. For my boss you see. The Army does everything by the book."

"The book? What book is that?"

"Oh, I'm sorry. It's an American saying. It means we follow the rules," Hale returned with an encouraging smile. His smile faded a bit as the subject turned more serious. "Now, I don't want to rehash some things that may be painful for you, but I need as many specifics as possible, you know, for my report. You told me that Hans Bergmann offered to help you get out of Germany. Is that correct?"

"Yes, I was foolish. I see that now," she said, raising her eyes from her lap. Tears were beginning to pool in her amazing eyes. "I thought he was a good man, you see. I was being attacked…robbed at the train station in Munich, when he intervened on my behalf. I thought he was a good man, a gentleman. He said he needed someone to cook and clean for him. A…um housekeeper, yes? In return, he would take me away from here, away from the war. He took me to the farmhouse from Tegelberg."

Hale took a handkerchief from his pocket and passed it across the desk to Tamar. She hesitantly accepted it, then began twisting it around and around as she had the thread. "Tamar," Hale said gently, "the war is over. Why were you so desperate to leave Germany?"

"The war is never over for my people. I am a Jew," she said quietly to the square of cloth in her hands. She then straightened in the chair and fastened her eyes on his. "Am I in danger from you now also?"

"No, of course not," Hale replied quickly, taken aback by the very question. He was here trying to catch the inhumane bastards! "Did Bergmann know you were Jewish?"

"Yes. I foolishly told him along the way to Fussen. He seemed very sympathetic –at the time. It all changed once we got to the farmhouse. He became angry and resentful. I have no idea why," she said as the handkerchief was twisted over and over in her hands. "Then when we got inside, those two other men were there. They were hurting this poor man. It was horrible. I tried to run away, but Bergmann grabbed me and tied me up. He made me watch as they tortured that man to death." A sob caught in her throat at the memory, and two tears rolled down her cheeks and dropped into her lap. "They cut him to pieces…he screamed and begged for mercy but…they just laughed at him."

"So, the two men who were dead on the living room floor of the farmhouse when we got there were the ones torturing the man tied to the chair?"

Tamar nodded silently. "I can still hear the man's screams. I can't get them out of my head," she admitted as the tears flowed.

"I can understand that Tamar. Many of us here have the same nightmares that we can't seem to overcome. War does that to you."

"But this wasn't war. It was just murder!" she exclaimed.

"You're right. It was murder."

Hale leaned back in his chair and held his questions to allow Tamar time to regain her composure before continuing. She finally remembered the handkerchief in her lap and used it to dry her tear-streaked face.

"We can stop if you like. I can have you come back later," Hale offered. At the negative shake of her head, he continued. "All right. Did Bergmann know the two other men in the house?"

"I think so. They didn't say anything specific, but they looked at one another as if…well, they didn't seem surprised to see Bergmann and he didn't seem surprised to find them there."

"Was it a prearranged meeting?"

"Maybe, I don't know," she replied with a shrug of her shoulders.

"Bergmann told you nothing on the trip there about meeting someone, about the other men in the house?"

"No. Nothing."

"And did the two men say anything to you while you were there? Did the men speak to Bergmann? Did they ask him anything? Did he ask them anything? Did the man being tortured say anything?" Hale peppered her with a new question at each negative shake of her head.

"I already told you they said nothing! Why do you keep asking me questions I cannot possibly answer?" she wailed.

Hale took it down a couple of notches when he realized he was taking out his personal frustration on her. After a couple of deep breaths, he continued. "Because it's my job, Tamar. I'm trying to find some very evil people and make sure they never do anything like this again. It's my job to find them. It's my job to lock them up and throw away the key."

"Do you not think that I hate them, too? I would be happy to tell you whatever I know, I just don't know anything!"

But Hale pressed on. "It may be something small. You may have seen or heard something that will help us. Please think, Tamar, we need that information."

"I understand that. Trust me, I would love to help you find these animals. They are a curse to our nation."

A new piece of information. Hale breathed slowly to keep his emotions in check before continuing the interrogation. "So, you must be German."

"Why do you say that?"

"Because you just said those people were a curse to 'our' nation. That would lead me to believe that you are German, and this is your homeland. True?"

"I was born in Stuttgart. Raised in Munich," Tamar admitted.

"So, you've lived here your whole life then."

"No. My parents sent me to the Ukraine when I was fourteen."

"Why did they do that?" Hale asked while jotting down a note.

"The Kristallnacht – the night of broken glass," she replied, with the memory clouding her eyes with pain.

"I heard about that. I'm sorry," he said with genuine compassion as he glanced up from his desk. "That was in 1938?"

"Yes. My people call it the November Pogrom. We had been through many pogroms over the centuries. This was nothing new, and we thought it would pass. My father thought it would pass. He was wrong…"Tamar replied, with her voice trailing off.

"So, your father sent you to the Ukraine?" Hale probed gently.

"Yes. He was concerned that it may get worse before it got better. He and mother decided to send me to be with family in Odesa."

Hale laid his pen aside and looked at Tamar intently. "You were pretty young. Weren't you afraid to go that far from home?"

"Terrified. As I said, I was only fourteen years old, traveling to another nation without mother or father. I cried most of the way there."

"And your father and mother stayed behind in Germany?"

"Yes. I never saw them again. I received word in Palestine that they had died in the death camps. Murdered by those Nazi bastards!" Tamar spat with her eyes, turning as hard as the gems they resembled.

"I can understand your anger…" Hale began.

"Can you? Were your parents taken forcibly from their home, put on a train, and sent to a prison camp where they were starved to death? Don't think for a moment that you understand, Major!"

"I'm sorry, Tamar. I don't mean to upset you. It must have been horrible for them. And for you being so far away and all alone."

"I wasn't alone. My father's brother uncle Yitzhak took me in."

"You just said you got word about your parents while in Palestine. How did you get there?"

"Uncle Yitzhak. Things were not much better in the Ukraine. Anti-Semites were everywhere. Uncle Yitzhak had some friends who got us out of there. We crossed into Palestine like thieves breaking into another man's house."

"I'm surprised you would choose to go there. Palestine is pretty much home to a whole lot of Arabs," Hale observed.

"It's our ancestral home. Where else could we go? It's the only home we have left in the world."

A knock on the door interrupted the conversation. Hale got up and went to see who was at the door. Sergeant McCann stood just outside the door and motioned for the Major to come outside. There, he handed him a small paper bag. They whispered briefly, then McCann saluted and walked away.

Hale looked in the paper bag thoughtfully as the pieces began to fall into place. When he reentered the office, the bag was deliberately placed as a center piece on the desk, then he paced briefly before turning his attention back to Tamar. "So, you and Bergmann entered the farmhouse. Two other men were already there, and they were torturing a third man who was tied to a chair. Is that what happened?"

"Yes, that's what happened."

Hale walked slowly around his desk to face Tamar; a look of displeasure ingrained on his face. "You know, you're very good at what you do. But I'm damned good at what I do, too."

"I don't understand. What are you talking about?" she asked with eyes wide.

"I found an interesting icepick with a hand grip in the bathroom at the farmhouse. You do remember the bathroom, don't you?"

Her eyes blinked ever so slightly, but enough to show she was startled at the change of direction the interview had taken. "Of course, I remember the bathroom. That evil man Bergmann tried to ravage me in there! You were there! You saw!"

"Apparently I saw what you wanted me to see. A terrified young girl fending off a brutal sex attack. That's what you had planned, right? You see, things just didn't add up for me. Bergmann was naked, lying on top of you. But you still had your dress on." He paused as if a thought had just crossed his mind. "You tore it purposely to make it look like you were under attack."

"Why are you doing this to me?" Tamar cried as she unconsciously gripped her dress as she had that night.

"Oh, there's more. The two men in the living room had both been shot multiple times as if in a shootout, but there was limited blood loss. That just didn't make sense to me. I've been in many battles in my time and there's always plenty of blood."

Tamar closed her eyes and turned her head away from him, still gripping her dress, as she rocked gently back and forth in her chair, murmuring something softly like a lullaby.

Unmoved by the display, Hale continued as he returned to his chair. "An examination of both men showed a small puncture wound behind the right ear. The size of an ice pick…your ice pick, I believe. That's what killed them. They didn't die in a firefight. I think you staged that as well as the rape scene in the bathroom. Hell, it may have been you who tortured the guy in the chair for all I know. How convenient to be able to place the blame on three dead Nazis."

"I don't know what you are talking about," she wept. "Why are you doing this to me?"

"Oh, but I think you do know. You see, Sergeant McCann just brought me a nice leather sheath. One that fits the icepick perfectly. One that was found in the farmhouse this morning."

Hale pulled the sheath out of the paper bag and showed it to her. Then he reached into his desk and pulled out the icepick. He showed her how the icepick fit snugly into the sheath. Even the wooden handgrip slipped nicely into place.

He held it up for her to view before continuing. "I know this weapon extremely well," he explained. He reached into his drawer again and pulled out another icepick quite like the first. "I carried one just like it for most of the war. I'm pretty sure you got yours from the same place I got mine. They're not given to just anyone. Only highly trained operatives carry one of these."

Tamar turned her tear-streaked face toward him with her brilliant green eyes wide. "Operative?"

"Oh, there's more, Tamar, if that's even your real name. A close inspection of the tortured man in the house revealed he had been cut to pieces; certainly, a slow and agonizing way to die."

"You're mad!" she cried out defiantly.

"Am I? What are the chances my men go back to that farmhouse and come back with a knife that perfectly matches the cuts made on the dead man? What are the chances that they find a sheath to go with it? What are the chances they find more evidence that it was you who staged the whole damn thing?"

"You have completely lost your mind," she said in amazement. "I could never do such a thing! How could I overpower one man, let alone all the others there?"

"I don't know, but until I figure this out you are to remain here under my care."

"I'm a prisoner, now? Is that what you're saying?" she asked with defiance.

"I'm saying you are my guest until I can sort out what actually happened at that farmhouse. Sergeant McCann will escort you back to your quarters."

"You bastard!" she exploded. "You're no better than the damn Nazis!"

"Frankly, I think I'm far better than the damn Nazis, and I just proved that by taking you into protective custody instead of having you shot," Hale responded with a hard edge to his voice.

Someone knocked briefly and then opened the door, interrupting the interrogation. Sergeant McCann looked apologetic as he said, "Sorry, sir. This man just showed up. He has orders and I couldn't stop him from coming in without shooting him."

"Maybe you should have. I'll take it from here, Sergeant."

"Sir," McCann replied and quickly left the room.

"Who might you be?" Hale asked tersely as a man entered the room.

"A superior officer here to take Tamar into my custody," the man answered firmly.

Tamar turned quickly at the sound of his voice to see him looking directly at her. "You," she gasped in surprise. "I thought you were dead!"

CHAPTER 8

Hale threw the custody release orders on his desk in disgust. He had the young woman right where he wanted her. He knew she would soon crack – at least enough for him to inch his way closer to the truth of what happened to Bergmann and the others in that farmhouse.

Of her complicity in the matter, Hale had no doubt. Whether she could have orchestrated what he and his men found was inconclusive, but all the evidence this far pointed to one person killing at least three of the four in that house. He had a hard time reconciling all those deaths to a five-foot-eight-inch young woman about the same age as his sister in Lubbock, Texas.

But if Tamar had done it, she was a hellcat on two feet, and she was not someone that should be released into an unknown stranger's custody. *What the hell is going on here? And why wasn't I given a heads-up that this guy was on the way?*

Hale had to admit that the orders were duly signed. He would recognize that signature anywhere. Colonel Bill Quinn was his superior officer and had assigned him to his post here. Hell, Quinn had been adamant that he scour Germany and all of Europe if need-be to find every last scientist that had worked for Hitler's nuclear program and ship them back to the states.

Hale's questions were stacking up as he pondered why Quinn would suddenly have an interest in this particular woman, and how did he even know she was here? After all, an After-Action Report hadn't been filed yet. *And who the hell was this guy who gets to waltz in here and walk away with my…my what? Prisoner? Guest? Interviewee?*

Hale called out for Sergeant McCann from behind his desk.

"Sir," McCann reported.

"Billy, I need to get a telegram to Colonel Quinn ASAP."

"Yes, sir. I can get it over to COMMS as soon as you get it ready. It will go out within the hour if you want."

"I want." Hale grabbed a paper tablet and quickly wrote his message, then tore off the sheet and handed it to McCann. "ASAP Billy. I want to find out who that guy was and what interest he had in our little lady from the farmhouse."

"Sir, do you think it's a good idea to demand that a superior officer explain what the hell their intentions might be?" he questioned, as he quickly scanned the note. "Officers generally don't take kindly to someone questioning their orders. No offense, sir."

"None taken. Okay, see if you can clean it up and make it pretty before I get myself in hot water. You were an English teacher before the Army got you, right?"

"Yes, sir. High School English."

"Then make me look good, Billy. I certainly don't want to appear insolent to the new head of CIG, now do I?"

"I'll take care of it, sir. Shakespeare's writings are one of my specialties. I'll make the request down-right poetic."

Hale smiled at McCann in genuine appreciation. "Just try to convince him that I need to know what's going on in my own house."

"Roger that, sir. What pray tell dost thou envision for thy servant, that I might give thee humble satisfaction…" McCann continued with his poetic license as he bowed his way out the door.

"Well, a little Shakespeare ought to get Quinn's attention," Hale mused quietly to himself. "Or get me sent to the medic for serious mental observation."

Yazzie wove the small, well used BMW he had commandeered for Tamar's rescue through the city streets in an irregular pattern, watching for any ambitious young soldiers that may have been ordered to follow them. Once convinced they were on their own, he jetted the little car down a couple of alleys to be one hundred percent certain before connecting with the road out of town. As they bumped along the dirt road, Yazzie finally felt secure enough to slow down a little and relax back into his seat.

Tamar had been stealing glances at her uncle as she placed both hands flat on the roof to brace herself for their break-neck speed escape. Driving as if the devil himself was chasing you was not that unusual in their line of work. In fact, it was the man currently in the driver's seat that had instructed her how to lose a tail when she was just 15 years old. The most important thing to remember was that sometimes it really was the devil chasing you.

Tamar continued to look at her uncle as if he was a ghost. Several times she started to speak, opening her mouth, but unable to put a complete thought together, she was forced to close it once again. Thinking she was beginning to look a bit like a fish in a pond, she stopped in frustration.

"I'm sure you have many questions, Plymenytse," Yazzie began using a familiar Yiddish term of endearment. "We can wait until I get you to a safe place if you don't feel like talking right now. But know, that I have many questions for you, too."

The landscape had changed from the gray buildings of the city to the winter snow-clad countryside as Tamar quietly stared out the side window. Her eyes glistened as she finally found the words. "I thought you were dead."

Yazzie heard the catch in her voice; it was not like her to be so emotional. After the loss of her parents she hated showing weakness, so he kept his voice steady and casual. "A reasonable assumption under the circumstances."

"You were supposed to meet me in Odesa. I searched the city for several days looking for you."

"You should not have waited at all, Plymenytse," Yazzie scolded gently. "You put yourself in danger."

She finally turned to look at Yazzie. "We are always in danger, Feter," she answered with the Yiddish term of endearment for her Uncle Yitzhak.

"That is true. But to extenuate that danger was not wise," he instructed as he patted her knee fondly.

"I could not just leave you if there was any chance you were in danger," she said earnestly. "I would never forgive myself if I knowingly left you in the hands of those communist bastards. They are every bit as ruthless as the Nazis and you know it."

"Yes, I know. Still, a day at the most should have told you that I would not make the rendezvous. You had a mission to accomplish," he responded as he keenly watched a black vehicle coming up behind them. When it slowed to turn down a side road, he relaxed once again.

"And I did. I infiltrated the commissar's office, planted the devices, and left without a trace. Exactly as Menachem ordered. I even identified a possible asset within the office." She turned her head to gaze at the bleak countryside once again and continued absently, "I forwarded the information to Tel Aviv. I don't know if they have pursued the matter."

Yazzie looked approvingly at his young niece and smiled fondly. She caught his look and returned the smile, and nothing more was said until they arrived at Yazzie's destination. A small stone house in an outlying village in a nondescript neighborhood that sat nearly fifty meters back from the worn dirt road. He followed the drive around and parked behind the house, out of sight.

They entered through the back door into a small storeroom. Uncle Yazzie drew his weapon and motioned her to stay in place, as he verified the house had not been compromised in his absence. As she listened to her uncle's progress and waited for him to give the all-clear, she noticed that it was well stocked with food and supplies.

"Come in," she heard from the other room. "All is well."

As she walked further inside the two-bedroom house, it seemed clear to Tamar that this house had been prepared for continuous use. The question was, by who? She looked through the house carefully, noting floor-to-ceiling panels spaced at regular intervals around the room. They appeared to be decorative in nature and must have been added after the original construction of the house. After running her fingers down the edge of one of the panels, she found the latch she had suspected was there. Behind the panel, she found both weapons and ammunition, along with a stash of currency and passports.

"Is this one of Menachem's safe houses?" she asked simply.

Yazzie smiled almost mischievously before answering. "No. Even the great Menachem Begin does not know of this place. And he never will."

"Is that wise?" Tamar asked as the panel was moved back into place.

"It is practical."

"Who runs this place, then?" she queried lightly as she moved a curtain aside a few inches to peer into the front yard.

"You do not need to know, Tamar. It is for your own good."

"Tamar it is now, hmmm?" she commented as she turned from the window. "Why so formal Feter?"

"Because we need to get down to business. I need to know what you were doing here in Germany and who else knows you are here. I need to know…"

Tamar interrupted before he could continue with his need-to-know questions. "Are you going to interrogate me, Uncle? Seriously?"

"You went outside the scope of your assignment. I want to know why," he said while forcefully tapping the table with his forefinger to make his point.

"And you disappeared for six months. I want to know why," she rejoined defiantly, with her hands on her hips.

Yazzie sighed, then walked to the front door and checked to make sure it was locked. When he turned to face Tamar he said, "You are much like your mother. She, too, demanded to be informed of all matters which she decided were in her best interest. Even family baking secrets could become a war of wits in the household."

"And she would win the war every time," Tamar added triumphantly.

"Yes. Yes, she did. It was one of the reasons I told your father to marry her. She was strong; extraordinarily strong," he said as he returned to sit at the small dining table.

"You told papa? I thought they had an arranged marriage by their fathers," Tamar exclaimed at this new revelation.

"That's what they told you. They didn't want you to get any ideas about selecting your own husband someday," Yazzie said with a twinkle in his eye.

"What! That's preposterous," she protested as she joined her uncle at the table. "They would not lie to me about their marriage."

"What's to lie about? They got married. They made you. That's all you need to know. But the fact of the matter is that your father was much too shy to even ask your mother for a late afternoon stroll around the park."

"Yes, mama told me. So, that's why their fathers made the arrangement."

"No. Both fathers did agree that it would be a good match. But it was me who pushed your father toward your mama. I threatened to date her myself if he didn't do something soon."

"You never," Tamar laughed. "I can't imagine you with mama!"

"I couldn't either. She was far too good for me," he claimed modestly. "But she was perfect for your papa. Anyway, he took the threat seriously since I had a certain reputation with the ladies in those days."

"Feter! You? I cannot imagine such a thing."

"That's because you have always known me as Feter Yazzie. Surprising as it may seem, your father and I were considered quite handsome in our youth. But I was the one willing to make advances toward the young girls in our village." Yazzie wagged his finger as he clarified, "And by advances, I mean strictly proper advances. I was very courteous and always came with flowers in my hand. It worked every time."

"Feter." Tamar giggled at the thought.

"Anyway, your father took the hint and asked her for a walk one day. And that led to courtship, and that led to marriage…"

"And that led to me," Tamar interrupted, like a little girl finishing a fairy tale.

"Yes, sweet girl. That led to you," he said, smiling softly.

Tamar left her chair and went to Yazzie and hugged him. He responded in kind and clutched her tightly.

Yazzie sighed slightly and said, "You are everything your parents could ever have hoped for and they would be so proud of you; of what you have overcome and what you now do for your people. They would be so proud."

"So, you are no longer cross with me for going outside the parameters of my assignment, Feter?" she asked hopefully.

"Oh, I'm still cross. It was a dangerous and foolish thing to do in this treacherous world. You are too reckless."

"This has been pointed out to me before," she confessed as she flipped the hair tickling her face behind her shoulder. "But I just do what is necessary."

"Ah, you refer to our beloved Menachem. He can be very forthright."

"*Your* beloved Menachem. I tolerate him so I can get what I want in the end."

"And what is that?"

"Justice. Justice for our families – for our people," she said with her emerald eyes like smoldering embers. "Justice for the millions of innocent lives throughout Europe who endured a cruel and unjust war. Why is that so hard to understand?"

"Oh, I understand, and Menachem understands. All of us who survived this nightmare understand."

"Then why not strike back now, while they are too unorganized to retaliate? We can take advantage of their current weakness!" she argued slapping her hand on the table.

"We are taking advantage, Tamar. Just not in the way you want," Yazzie returned as he stood and went to the window.

"What does that mean?"

"It means that we live in a very complicated world," he returned cryptically as he scanned the yard. "And a complicated world requires complicated measures to ensure the future. Those measures must be calculated carefully. You want to throw a brick through a window. That is not complicated."

"I want to put a knife in Nazi throats."

"Indeed. Not complicated," he admitted as the curtain was allowed to fall back into place. "But not effective either. Not now."

"Then when, Feter?" she implored, pacing the length of the room. "When? Do you know how many Nazis they executed at the Nuremberg trials? Ten! Only ten Nazi bastards were hung when there are thousands of these murderers still free. Others may not want justice for the millions killed by these madmen, but I do. And there are many just like me crying out for this justice. Who will give them justice, Uncle? Who?"

Yazzie paused and put his hand on Tamar's shoulder as he spoke softly to his niece. "It is a complicated world that we live in. It took years for these mad men to take power and it may take a while to get retribution against all those who brought such destruction. But with God's help, we will."

"I'm not so sure it's as easy as you make it sound. Not after what I saw in Berlin," she told him as a hint of defeat edged her voice. "I'm not sure the war is over."

"Berlin? What were you doing in Berlin? I thought you have been working here in southern Germany?" he asked, trying to keep his voice even at this new piece of information.

"I started in Berlin and made my way south. I had to see for myself that Hitler and his henchmen were killed or incarcerated by the Communists. You can't trust anything Stalin says. You know that."

"I do. But what about Berlin made you suspect the war continues?" he asked, with the implications of her observations spinning in his head. "Germany is an occupied nation. They have no more power to make war on anyone."

"Maybe not from Germany. But what if they have found a way to transfer their war-making abilities somewhere else?" she asked with a tilt of her head.

"I'm not sure I follow."

"I'll tell you everything I know, Uncle. But only after you tell me where you have been for six long months without contacting me," she said with an I-always-get-my-way tone.

"This is not a negotiation, Tamar."

"Of course, it is. You taught me that; you and Menachem. Anything can be negotiated if the leverage is right. Did you not tell me that after we arrived in Palestine?"

Yazzie stared at his niece with both agitation and pride. "Just like your mother," he repeated as he shook his head. "Just like your mother."

Yazzie paused momentarily and then seemed to come up with a workable compromise. "Since it was I who rescued you, why don't you go first? Tell me what you are doing here in Germany. How you made your way into Berlin through hostile Soviet Army occupying forces without identification. How you found yourself in a farmhouse with several Nazi war criminals several hundred kilometers away from Berlin. And how you managed to convince the Americans that you were a poor damsel in distress. Then I will remonstrate with what I know. Is that suitable?"

"I shall make us some coffee, Uncle. I'm afraid my story may take some time and I'm sure that your story will take just as long. We may as well enjoy some of the fresh coffee grounds in the kitchen, yes?"

Yazzie smiled approvingly at his niece. *She has come far in her training.*

CHAPTER 9

Hale was still fuming late into the day about losing his number-one witness in the farmhouse murders. Witness, hell, she had probably done it. But she had been whisked away before he could get her to confess, or at least tell him how in damnation she had taken on four men and survived.

And now, just as things were coming together, he was being recalled to Washington. *Damn!* He hated leaving anything unfinished. At this point he didn't even care if the dead men were Nazis; he just wanted to know what really happened and instinctively knew Tamar was a critical piece to that puzzle.

Hale was both agitated and concerned at the same time. *How does Quinn expect me to do my job when he allows my chief witness to waltz out of my office with somebody I never heard of before?*

He picked up the orders again and looked at them in disgust. *It's just not like the Colonel to yank a suspect out of my custody like that and call me home out of the blue without an explanation.* "What the hell is going on here?" he asked the empty room.

A knock at the office door interrupted his thoughts. Then Sergeant McCann's head appeared through the sliver of space created when he barely opened the door. "Looks like we got another mystery on our hands, Major. Just got a call from the field. Something about four bodies in a graveyard."

"There are a lot more than four bodies in a graveyard, Billy. What does it have to do with us?" Hale asked, with his mind still preoccupied with the recent change in events.

"The call came from Hedges. He was flagged down by a civilian and dragged to the scene. He says it's damn peculiar and definitely not usual."

"Define unusual."

"He said he had to puke before calling me. Something he saw there. I told him to stay put until I talked to you."

Hale smiled as he dropped the orders back on the desk. "Tossed his cookies, huh? Okay, sounds like we're going to have a long day's night again, Billy."

"Yes, sir. The sun's almost down. It'll be pitch black by the time we get there. It should add to the ambiance considerably," McCann said with a grin.

"Grab your gear. Let's go grave robbing."

"Yes, sir." Sergeant McCann returned as he swung the office door open before leaving to get his gear. Hale glanced once again at the orders lying on his desk, then placed them back in the envelope they arrived in, sealed it, and placed it in his desk drawer. This would have to wait until he got back from chasing ghosts.

The gray clouds, heavy with the promise of new snow, hung low in the sky, blocking any light the moon may have cast. A single light bulb by the church entrance valiantly worked to dispel the darkness, but they still needed flashlights after disembarking from the jeep. They made their way carefully along the uneven ground with their beams casting long shadows across the weary headstones.

The cemetery had probably been there for hundreds of years. That was not unusual in Germany, which had a several thousand-year-old culture. Who knew how many people were laid to rest there? Who knew how much history lay beneath their feet? But tonight, Major Hale looked into a freshly dug grave and had his own questions about the occupant. Who was he? How did he get here? And why in the hell did someone skin the poor guy?

Hale relieved Hedges as soon as he got his first look at the scene. Poor kid was still looking a little green when Hale and McCann showed up. The Corporal was battle-hardened, but he had never witnessed anything like what he had found here. The best thing for him was to get back to Pullach, take a hot shower, then head to the bar and down a few shots to clear these images from his head. At least that's how Hale intended to handle it once he was through with his cursory investigation.

"Major," a voice called out from a distance. It was Sergeant McCann.

"What is it, Billy?"

"We got more bodies over here, sir. Two of them. They look to be in the same shape as yours. It's damn disgusting. And there's a live one inside the chapel. Cooper and Perez are with him, but Cooper says the guy won't be with us long."

"Somebody survived this?"

"Opened his eyes when the preacher found him. Scared the crap out of him. Cooper said he doesn't know how he survived this long."

Hale shone his light across the skinless body in the grave once more, making mental notes as the exposed muscle was illuminated. He took a deep breath of the cold winter air to ease his roiling stomach, then walked purposefully to his First Sergeant and followed his nod to the bodies. They lay close together, just outside the doors of the cemetery chapel. There was a blood trail from inside the chapel and down the two steps to where they lay. They too had been skinned.

Two shovels and two picks leaned against a wood-framed wheelbarrow a few feet away. Blood in the wheelbarrow suggested that it had probably been used to move at least one of the bodies. Two sets of tracks marked the soft earth: definitely not civilian. Those were boot prints. Military?

The boot print mystery went on his mental to-do list as he quickly went inside to find Privates Cooper and Perez kneeling beside a bloody mess that was probably once a good-sized man. "What have you got?" Hale quizzed as he moved to stand over the body of the dying man.

Cooper and Perez had used all the sterile gauze they had in their medical packs to staunch as much bleeding as they could. It was too little, too late.

"He's in shock. Basically, he's got both feet in a grave he just hasn't laid down yet," Cooper responded.

"We did what we could, Major," Perez added apologetically.

"You did your job, boys. From the look of it, no one could have saved him." Hale's eyes scoured the darkened chapel. "Did you find anything? Did he say anything?" Hale asked.

Cooper spoke first. "He kept mumbling that he did his duty, then something about one General Kruger and scientists. I couldn't quite make it all out, but he kept saying that they had to get out before it was too late."

"Kruger. General Helmet Kruger," Hale said mostly to himself.

"I don't know, sir. Does it mean anything to you? And what about the scientists? What do you make of that?"

"If it's who I think it is…"

"Sir?"

"General Helmet Kruger was Waffen SS. He was last seen working with ODESSA trying to get German scientists out of the country. It was rumored that he may be trying to get a warehouse full of the guys so they could be auctioned off to the highest bidder."

"He's going to sell them? Who buys scientists Major?" Perez asked.

"Basically everyone," Hale responded absently. "The U.S., British, French, Soviets; we're all trying to get our hands on every scientist that had anything to do with the German nuclear program."

"Damn," Cooper remarked. "I had no idea."

Hale surveyed the room briefly to see if there was any physical evidence but saw nothing. He instructed the men to stay with the dying man until relieved, and then turned and left the building.

McCann was waiting outside. "Anything usable, Major?" he asked as Hale walked past him.

"Maybe. I wonder what the hell we may have stumbled onto here. Did you find any other fresh graves?" Hale asked with a frosty mist floating out of his mouth with the question.

"No, sir. Just the one. I'm thinking they were going to pile them all into the one grave and get out before sunrise."

"Makes sense. You said the parson was first on scene?" Hale asked.

"Yeah, some local preacher. Said he couldn't sleep so he decided to come in and prepare for a service to be done here tomorrow. He entered through a side door and found the guy inside, bolted for the front door, and slipped in the blood trail over there," McCann said, pointing. "He sure wasn't expecting to find anything like this. Set him back on his heels a little."

"Where is he now?"

"I think he's still puking up his guts on the south side of the chapel."

"Can't say I blame him. If I hadn't seen the remains at Bergen-Belsen and Buchenwald, I would probably be doing the same thing right now," Hale said, trying unsuccessfully to block the memories of that gruesome site.

"Yes, sir. I remember puking all day that first day."

"You and me both, Billy. The photographer here?" Hale asked, cramming those memories into a mental closet and slamming the door.

"Yes, sir. He's grabbing some extra film. Said he would get plenty of pictures for you, as usual."

"Tompkins?"

"From the Signal Corps. Yes, sir."

"He knows the drill. Make sure he gets shots of those boot tracks as well. Tell him I need the photos on my desk as soon as he gets them processed, will you?"

"Yes, sir."

"Well, guess I'll go see if that preacher's finished puking. You see a medic yet?"

"Yes, sir. He's puking next to the preacher."

"Oh boy," Hale said under his breath as he rubbed the back of his neck. "Okay, did you get his name?"

"Captain Jensen, sir. Just got here from Walter Reed in Washington. He's never seen combat, sir. I don't think he was prepared for this."

"I'm not sure any of us are, Billy."

"Amen, sir. Amen."

Hale flicked his flashlight back on and made his way around the chapel. He stopped a moment along the way to shine the light across the gravestones, looking for any movement. Maybe the jokers that did this were hanging around to see the show, but even the black silhouettes of the barren trees were as still as the tombstones they shaded. The German preacher and new medical doctor were still hunched over with their hands on their knees, trying to quell the dry heaves that took over once their evening suppers had been expelled.

Hale questioned the ashen-faced preacher long enough to know the man knew nothing about what had happened here.

No, he didn't know who the bodies were.

No, he didn't see anyone else.

No, he didn't hear anyone else.

No, he had no idea how they got there.

No, he didn't want to stay to find out.

Mostly he just wanted to get home to his family and try not to have nightmares for the rest of his life. So, Hale sent him home with an escort and turned his attention to Captain Jensen. The young doctor was finally able to stand up, although he did so by leaning on a large tree.

"I hear it's your first tour, Doc," Hale began conversationally as he rubbed his hands together against the cold.

"If General Reed finds out about this, it may be my last. And the end of my career," the young doctor lamented as he closed his eyes and tipped his head back against the rough tree trunk.

"You're not the first to empty his belly after witnessing something like this, and you won't be the last," Hale returned sympathetically.

When Jensen was able to lift his head, he saw that Hale was a higher-ranking officer, and he did his best to stand at attention and salute.

"Don't bother, Doc. Just clear your head. Your stomach's already empty."

The young man sighed heavily and gave an embarrassed, "Sorry, sir."

"No need, Captain. Go back to HQ and get yourself put together. I'll have Sergeant McCann escort you to your quarters."

"No sir, I have a job to do, Major," he returned in what he hoped was a strong and steady voice, but the shakiness gave him away.

"You can't do it in your condition. Besides, these guys are already dead. They aren't going anywhere, and you can't help them. But you can get me some autopsy reports once I have the bodies sent back to Pullach. You up to that?"

"Yes, sir. I'll get it done."

"Good man. I'll send McCann over here. Then I'll see you after you get the reports ready on the DOA's."

"Yes, sir."

"Doc?"

"Sir?"

"General Reed will never hear about this in the AAR."

"Thank you, sir," he said with relief evident in his voice. Jensen raised his head enough to read Hale's name on his uniform. "Thank you, Major Hale."

Hale patted Jensen on the shoulder. "Curly. My friends all call me, Curly."

CHAPTER 10

A knock at Colonel Quinn's door stopped his pen midair and took his attention briefly from the writing of his missive.

"Enter."

Lieutenant Hornsby entered the office and held up a dispatch for Quinn to see. "This just arrived for you, sir. It says urgent," he stated, as the item was handed to Quinn.

"Thank you, Jack," Quinn returned.

"Shall I stay, Colonel?"

"No," Quinn answered as he looked up from the delivered package. "That's all right. I'll read this and see if an immediate response is required or not."

"Yes, sir. May I get you a cup of coffee or anything else before I go?"

"No thanks, Jack. I've already had three cups this morning. I appreciate it."

"No problem, sir." And with that Hornsby efficiently exited Quinn's office, closing the door behind him.

Quinn ignored the letter opener in his desk and took out his Buck pocketknife to open the dispatch and get a look at what had just been sent his way. That knife had been a gift from his father when he left to begin his military service. He and that knife had been through a lot together; it kept him grounded. He hadn't read two sentences before he was interrupted by a polite cough. He instinctively reached for his sidearm but wasn't wearing one in the office.

"So, how's your day going?" John Magruder inquired calmly.

"Dammit, Magruder! You scared the hell out of me!" he exploded as he looked into the smiling face of his predecessor.

"Sorry, Bill. I'm still getting used to doing this inter-dimensional travel myself and I haven't quite found a good way to announce my arrival yet."

"Inter-dimensional? What the hell is that supposed to mean?" he asked with some of his annoyance at being caught unawares coming out in his tone.

Mac didn't answer but walked slowly away from the one window in the room, perusing his old office to see if anything had changed. It seemed a millennium since he sat in Quinn's seat, even though it had only been a few months. His mind did a fast forward through all that had transpired since the day his name was on the door. He took a seat in the single chair opposite the desk. It was enough to make his head spin.

Quinn sensed that he was not going to get a satisfactory answer, so he decided to move on to the subject at hand. "So, what's so important that you just turned up in my office? Without an appointment, I might add."

"Wow, you just cut right to the chase, don't you? No polite conversation, no inquiry about my health," Mac returned with a grin.

"What do you expect, Mac?" Quinn asked as he jumped to his feet. "You turn up two weeks ago, after abandoning the Central Intelligence Group for six months, with no plausible explanation. Then start talking about national security and aliens! You can appear and disappear at will, for God's sake." He breathed heavily for a span, then dropped back in his chair. "It's not normal, that's all I'm saying. It's just not normal."

"You act like I don't know that," Mac returned hotly. "Do you think this seems normal to me? I had a sweet life, a good life before all of this. My enemies, the ones who would like nothing more than to see me, *and now my family,* dead, have expanded exponentially. I didn't ask for this, Bill, I didn't ask for any of this."

The two men locked eyes for a time, then Quinn finally spoke. "So…how about this weather, huh?"

Magruder broke into a smile. "Cold. Lit up the fireplace the other night."

"Yeah, yeah, it's the season for it. And how's Helen?"

"Helen," Mac returned, shaking his head. "Well, Helen is insanely confident and upbeat. I worry about her…and Munro."

Quinn could finally see normal; a father and husband worried about his son and wife. He hesitated but then proceeded, as it had to be discussed. "Look at this from my point of view, Mac. Would you have believed me when you occupied this office if I told you aliens are real and they want to take over the world?"

"You saw them. You know they're real."

"But are they a *real* threat?" Quinn asked earnestly. "There has been no contact, no active attack. We don't even have proof that they are currently or ever have been here. How is the President supposed to get anyone to take this seriously?"

Mac stood and walked to the window. It was not the best view from the White House, but he had always liked it. "This was always our biggest concern," he confessed. "We're working on it, getting confirmation that is. There may be photographic evidence coming from Germany, and we're looking for an eyewitness," he said as he finally broke from the familiar view and faced Quinn.

"Eyewitness?"

"He's Japanese," Mac said ruefully. He put his hand up to deflect the coming onslaught. "I know, I know. We got his name from the Greys. We've been trying to find him ever since we got back."

"Go on."

"The Greys said the aliens were already up and running on earth before the war even started. We have reason to believe that some of the technology Hitler used did not come from his scientists, it came from them. Their people, if I may call them people, had already infiltrated the German scientific community. That's why they are so far ahead of everyone else in the world when it comes to lethal technology."

Quinn looked grim but didn't speak so Mac continued. "I have sources on the ground in Germany that confirm there are already plans to restart their operations; the third Reich wants to resurrect. We think the alien presence is both inspiring the move and aiding it."

"Restart their operations. What does that mean? What operations are you talking about?" It was Quinn's turn to stand and pace. "Do you have any idea how preposterous this sounds, Mac? My God, this sounds like lunacy."

"This is what they do, Bill. Do you remember when I said the Shalanaya were the greater threat? They look enough like us that they can infiltrate countries and study the culture. Then they appeal to nationalism or fanaticism or whatever will instigate war. We must find them."

"If what you're saying is true then, yes, they must be found and found quickly. However," Quinn said, holding up one finger at Mac's eager agreement, "there must be proof. You said photographic evidence is coming from your sources in Germany. Any chance you can tell me who those sources are?"

"Soon. But one of the sources doesn't even know he's a source – yet."

"How convenient," Quinn muttered under his breath as he returned to his seat.

"He's one of your men, Bill. Hell, he was one of my men at one time. He's competent, reliable; a damned bulldog when it comes to finding and securing evidence. He can bring the photographs with him if you recall him to Washington."

"Recall who to Washington? I don't even know who the hell you're talking about," Quinn returned as he leaned back in his chair and folded his arms. "So, who is your source that doesn't know he's a source, Mac?"

"Major Donald Hale. You have him searching for Nazi scientists right now. His office is at Pullach."

"I know where he is. I signed his orders. Are you telling me Curly Hale is one of your sources?" Mac nodded. "But he doesn't know it?"

"Not yet."

"How is that even possible? And just when the hell will he figure out he's one of your sources?"

Mac sighed, knowing how unusual his request was. "Listen, he may have inadvertently had contact with the handiwork of the Anakim. As soon as you bring him back to D.C. with the photographs, we can ascertain if our suspicions are correct."

"You realize Curly has not sent me one single communique about any such photographs."

"That doesn't surprise me, but you should be getting an After-Action Report from him about a strange occurrence very soon. Probably today. Might want to stay ahead of the curve, Bill."

"You can be a son of a bitch, Mac."

"I know," he said, unaffected by the barb. "But we can't afford to let the aliens get too far ahead of us like we did the Nazis and Japs. Look what it cost us. Hell, look what it cost the world. And this alien threat is exponentially greater."

"And these photographs you're talking about will confirm all this?"

"Well, the photographs and the autopsy reports."

"What autopsy reports?"

"The ones attached to the AAR Curly needs to bring here post haste."

"So, photographs and autopsy reports. Anything else you want to spring on me while you're here?"

Mac looked a little chagrined at the question, realizing his impertinence. "No, I think that's it for now."

Quinn shuffled a few papers on his desk and then responded, looking like the cat that swallowed the canary. "Major Hale is due in Washington the day after tomorrow. I recommended that he be assigned to this project a couple of weeks ago."

"Oh, okay. So, you just let me make a fool of myself to put me in my place, huh?" Mac asked, impressed with Quinn's move in spite of himself. "So, who's the son of a bitch now?"

Quinn casually shrugged. "I had some good role models."

Mac smiled and relaxed. "You still got that bottle of Kentucky bourbon in your top desk drawer?"

Quinn responded by opening the drawer and pulling out the bottle along with two shot glasses and placing them on top of his desk. Mac calmly picked up the bottle and poured the bourbon, then handed one glass to Quinn.

"You think I need this," Quinn questioned seriously.

"I think we both do."

Both men tossed their heads back and downed the bourbon in one gulp, then sat quietly engulfed in their own thoughts as the shot sweetly burned all the way down. Mac finally broke the silence. "I know this is not the way we usually operate, Bill. You and I have worked together for a long time and have developed a certain pattern that we are used to. We just can't fall back into those patterns or tactics anymore. We are entering a new frontier and we all need to pick up the pace in a hurry. Otherwise, we will just be picking up the pieces of the world we once knew."

"Be honest with me, Mac, am I signing Curly Hale's death warrant?" Quinn asked as he twisted the shot glass around in his hand, watching it reflect the overhead lights.

Magruder knew exactly what Quinn was feeling. If he were honest with himself, he felt the same way. "He's good, you know that. And it's imperative that we have very restricted knowledge of this assignment, so we need the best. But if you're concerned about sending him out solo, I know a female operative that…"

"Why would I put a female operative with Curly?"

"Because she's good. She's very good."

"One of ours?" Quinn asked.

"Well, she has worked with us before."

"So no," Quinn said succinctly. "No way, Mac. We don't even know what we're getting into here. I'm not going to risk it."

Mac nodded, then walked to the window to peer outside.

"You're going to fight me on this, aren't you Mac?" Quinn asked, knowing the answer before the question was out of his mouth. Mac said nothing; he just kept enjoying the view. "You know, there are times when you really are a son of a bitch," Quinn offered calmly.

Mac just smiled, as if given a compliment. And for him, it was.

CHAPTER 11

February dawned crisp and clear in the nation's capital. Mother nature had been busy leaving lacy patterns of ice on every window and a frosty blanket on all her domain. As the sun rose, the frost glistened and shone like diamonds everywhere one looked.

Tamar had risen and dressed quietly. She wanted to experience her first trip to America and see the city, but Uncle Yazzie had kept a close eye on her since their arrival, and she had been unable to slip away. Oh, they had driven around town and Uncle had pointed out sites, but she had found in all her travels that it wasn't the same as actually walking among the people.

She silently opened the door to her room and closed it behind her, then tiptoed down the hall and peeked into the kitchen. It was unoccupied. She slipped through the kitchen, carefully avoiding the floorboard that creaked, and tilted her head around the corner of the living room. Empty! Perhaps today she could make her escape, if only for a little while. She grabbed a baguette from the kitchen counter and the coat she had thoughtfully placed on the back of an overstuffed chair by the front door and slipped outside.

The baguette was placed in her mouth as she shrugged into her coat and scanned the landscape for any sign of Uncle. He had gotten quite stealthy in his old age, it seemed. Oh, he had always been light on his feet, however now it seemed he could appear out of thin air. Today, though, she had beat him! Today was hers to do with as she wished, and she intended to make the most of it.

She did not tarry but made her way to the street to mingle with anyone afoot. She broke off pieces of the baguette and ate along the way, taking in all the sights, sounds, and smells of a free nation that had not been ravaged by war. It was not aimless meandering that chose her path, however, as she was determined to see for herself if it was true. It had to be a silly tale her uncle was teasing her with as it was just too preposterous to be believed. She was going to see if the most powerful man in America, or perhaps in the world, really walked unaccompanied to work from the apartment the President and first lady were renting during some White House renovations.

The city was beginning to rouse as lights blinked on and open signs were placed in steamy windows. She returned the wave of a café owner as she walked and wondered if he had ever seen war. Would he be so friendly if he knew some of the things she had done? Indeed, the things that she was still willing to do to avenge her people. Did these people know of their good fortune? To walk streets without rubble, that had never seen a bomb; to have a city with buildings that remained intact rather than mere skeletons of what they once had been.

Tamar pushed these thoughts aside as she determined to enjoy this day, her day, to the fullest. She brushed the crumbs from her hands and the front of her coat, then picked up her pace a little. She threaded her way through back streets and alleys, unconsciously employing her training as she made her way to President Truman's temporary residence. Her pace slowed as she neared her target. Not wanting to cause alarm by lingering, she took a couple of steps leading down to a basement entrance where she could unobtrusively wait and observe. She felt a little silly peering over the steps leading to the street-level dwelling like a teenager, hoping to ambush an idol for an autograph.

She smiled at the thought as she rubbed her hands together against the cold. Not many people were foolish enough to loiter on the street in this weather, so Tamar didn't feel it necessary to change her location several times as she may have done if this were Irgun business. People bundled up with winter coats and heavy woolen scarves wrapped around their necks up to their eyes would exit their buildings and either quickly get into a vehicle or hustle on their way down the street. A woman in a black hooded jacket on the corner across the street seemed to be the only other person with no destination in mind.

Uncle had always said it wise to take note of two things; something or someone present that's out of place and anything or anyone that should be present that wasn't. This woman seemed to fit both criteria, and it made Tamar uneasy. Why was a woman out on a city street at this time of the morning alone? And what was worth waiting for in this blistering cold? Tamar told herself that this was not her business, and her imagination was playing tricks on her. After all, this was America, not Germany or Palestine. Maybe the woman worked in the area, or perhaps she was waiting for an illicit tryst. Tamar smiled ruefully. Perhaps Uncle was right, maybe she did need some time off.

Then the door she had been observing for the past half hour opened and President Harry S. Truman stepped onto the stoop. She noted his fashionable charcoal gray wool coat and his matching fedora hat as he paused on his front step to size up the day. He was trim and shorter than she had imagined. A bit fascinated by the man, it took Tamar a moment to realize that the woman on the corner had pushed the hood off her head exposing her fair hair as she crossed the street, then began walking directly toward the president.

Now? She decided to leave her conspicuous post on the corner at the same time the president appeared? Too much of a coincidence, Tamar thought as she closed her eyes and clearly heard Uncle Yazzie's voice, *"Above all things we must keep a low profile."*

But it wasn't right, and she knew it wasn't right. Running on pure instinct, Tamar hurried from her spot on the stairs deriding herself for letting her feet get so cold. She ignored the pain in her numb feet and picked up speed down the walk. The woman had locked eyes with the president; she dipped her head and smiled as Truman tipped his hat courteously.

When Tamar saw the glint of a weapon sliding from the woman's coat sleeve, her perception of time slowed. The city buildings lining the street faded into the background, traffic noise silenced, and the air stilled. She could feel her every breath and every step as she calculated her speed against the arc of the ice pick, ready to be thrust into the President's kidney. She brutally pushed him forward to his knees as she threw herself headlong into the would-be assassin's chest. The force catapulted both women past the president into the street, a tangle of petticoats, with the weapon flying from the woman's hand and skittering across the pavement.

A primal "Nooooooo…" came from the woman as Tamar grappled to gain control. The woman was slightly smaller than Tamar but was deceptively strong. She let out a piercing scream while her eyes went completely dark as if they were nothing but empty sockets. The sight unnerved Tamar to the point that about a bucket of adrenaline shot into her bloodstream so when the struggle found Tamar rolled onto the pavement with the assassin's hands around her neck, she slammed the heel of her hand directly into the woman's nose with as much force as she could. The momentary release of her throat allowed Tamar to roll the woman, and consequently herself, over to where Tamar sat atop her foe. The woman's feral screaming stopped only after Tamar slammed her head into the street and it lolled to one side. Mercifully, her hollow eyes closed when she lost consciousness.

Left panting, Tamar straightened up in time to see a man running up to Truman. He bent over the president asking, "Are you all right, sir? Are you all right?" as he assisted him to his feet.

She saw it too late, his posture, the curl of his hand. The woman had not been acting alone. There was a second assassin! "Look out!" Tamar yelled as she leaped to her feet, but her warning was never heard. Two shots rang out, reverberating through the street, the sound bouncing off the stone buildings, and the second would-be assassin was thrown backward from the force of the hits.

Tamar swiveled to see the shooter pounding down the sidewalk with his weapon still aimed at the assassin. Knowing the threat was over, she relaxed and used the back of her hand to wipe away the blood now flowing from her split lip. The shooter arrived on scene at the same time the D.C. police rounded the corner at a full gallop. As she took a step toward the President to check on his welfare, the shooter, having visually verified that the assassin was down, turned his gun on Tamar.

Suddenly staring down the barrel of a gun with adrenaline still pulsing through her veins set off an immediate reaction. No thinking was necessary as she swung her leg around and sent the weapon flying while drawing back her fist. The man turned, prepared to take her down, placing three fingers in position to stab her throat when Tamar followed up her kick with a punch in one smooth motion. Her fist landed right between his eyes on the bridge of his nose, causing his eyes to roll back in his head as he crumpled to the sidewalk.

Tamar assisted Truman to his feet and asked him quietly, "Are you okay?" Truman nodded mutely, his eyes only leaving hers a moment to glance at the would-be assassin's weapon lying unused in his hand. She raised her hands in surrender at the police's arrival.

"I'm okay, I'm okay," Truman insisted as a wall of uniformed protection formed around him. "No, no, she saved me. Let her go," he insisted as handcuffs were clamped on Tamar's wrists.

Once the cuffs came off and everyone was convinced that the split lip was the worst of her injuries, she walked to stand over the shooter. She shook her head in disbelief and wondered what God could be thinking as she said, "So good to see you again, Major Hale."

CHAPTER 12

Colonel Quinn rushed through the door of the Walter Reed General Hospital room to find Curly wide awake and already complaining to the charge nurse. He wasn't upset at his accommodations; he was upset that he was in the hospital at all.

"I'm telling you I'm just fine," he complained as he got up from the bed and started toward the small closet in the private room. "Now, get my clothes so I can get out of here," he commanded the nurse with the best 'I mean now' look he could muster while sporting a large purple goose egg on his forehead and battling a splitting headache.

But she was a veteran combat nurse herself and did not kowtow to orders from one of her charges. With hands on hips she commanded in return, "You do not give orders on this ward, Major; I do. And I'm telling you right now that you are under strict orders to remain in my custody until Dr. Westbrook says it's safe to turn you lose. So," she said turning on her best bedside manner as she pointed him back to the bed, "stop complaining, enjoy the room service and the lovely garden view outside your window."

"And who is the idiot that issued orders to keep me in this brig?" he petulantly rejoined as he stubbornly held his ground.

"Um, that would be me, Curly," Quinn interrupted as he approached the bed. "And if I were you, I would listen to Colonel Rodgers, here. Among other things she did a stint behind enemy lines in the Philippines waiting for MacArthur to come back as he promised. I'd say she's earned her place to issue orders in her ward."

Hale was surprised to see Quinn, as he had not noticed his entrance while squaring off with his captor. And he was more than a bit stunned to hear about the veteran status and rank of his charge nurse. His face reddened as he realized his error in recognizing her authority. "My apologies, Colonel. Obviously, I was unaware of your position," he offered haltingly.

"My combat status should be of no import here, Major. All you had to do was look at the insignia on my lapel. That should have told you everything you needed to know," she reprimanded sternly.

Colonel Rodgers was quite petite in stature, barely five feet tall, and her pale blue eyes and auburn hair belayed her inner toughness as a U.S. Army Charge Nurse. Her commanding voice was readily recognizable as an officer accustomed to giving orders and seeing those orders carried out.

"Of course, ma'am. Again, my sincerest apologies."

"Apology accepted. Now get back in bed. Your gown is flapping in the wind and your backside is going to catch cold," she said, smiling demurely.

Hale quickly grabbed his hospital gown and pulled it together in back to cover his naked posterior. "Ma'am!"

"Oh, calm down, Major. I have seen more than my fair share of Army butts. And I have served with more of those asses than I care to remember."

Quinn began to laugh and cough involuntarily in response to Rodger's candor. Hale looked at her with raised eyebrows and both surprise and respect. Hell, he might even grow to like a tough little gal like her.

After Rodgers made sure Hale was returned securely to his bed, she turned to Quinn. "He's all yours, Bill."

"Thank you, Nancy," he replied warmly, still smiling broadly.

Hale took notice of their familiarity immediately and called them out. "You mean you two know one another?"

"Oh yeah, I've known Nancy since she was a kid," Quinn admitted. "Our families were quite close. I played baseball with her brother Pete in high school."

"Pete played short-stop and Quinn was at first base," Rodgers added. "And I'm pretty sure I watched every home game and most of the away games growing up."

"You know, someone could have told me that earlier," Hale suggested in an exaggerated huff.

Quinn answered Hale with a knowing grin on his face. "And miss all this fascinating repertoire?"

"Well, fascinating as it may be, I have other patients who need my attention," Rodgers said as she headed out the door. "Press the bell if you need anything – anything other than a way out that is."

"Thank you, Nancy," Quinn said sincerely as she disappeared around the corner.

Hale sighed heavily as he looked up at Quinn from his bed. "I suppose I deserved that."

"Oh, you did," Quinn agreed.

Turning serious, Hale asked Quinn directly, "How is the President?"

"Just fine, thanks to you. He's already back in his office, taking care of business. He's a tough old bird."

A soft knock on the open hospital room door drew their attention to a uniformed police officer waiting at the threshold. "Pardon the intrusion, gentleman. I'm Captain Brewster of the District of Columbia Police Department. Do you mind if I ask a few questions about this morning's incident?"

Hale looked at Quinn, who nodded his head in assent.

"Thank you," Brewster continued as he walked to Hale's beside and pulled out a small notebook. He pulled a pair of glasses from his shirt pocket, adjusted them on his nose, then read from the notes. "It says here that you came upon a possible crime in progress this morning. A crime being perpetrated upon President Truman. Is that correct?"

"It is," Hale answered as the officer peered over the top of his glasses.

Brewster gave a little grunt as his eyes returned to the notebook. "And you intervened on behalf of the President?"

"I did."

He mumbled a little 'hmmm' as he retrieved the stub of a pencil from the opposite shirt pocket, touched the end of it to his tongue, and jotted a note. "And it says here you subdued the suspect with lethal force." The officer tipped his head forward and looked over his glasses again. "So, why were you armed?"

Hale stared at him with an open mouth for a moment, then glanced at Quinn. "You're kidding, right? I'm a Major in the U.S. Army; it's sort of a part of the uniform. Do you leave home without your weapon?"

Quinn knew exactly how Curly felt. After a time, your sidearm became a part of you. Its weight was comforting and leaving home without it was like stepping outside without your trousers.

"No reason to get riled," Brewster returned blandly, looking back to his notebook. "It just seemed a might peculiar since a witness said you weren't in uniform, so I thought I'd ask."

"Listen, if you're asking if I shot the son of a bitch, yes, I did," Hale said with the force of his convictions. "And put in the same situation I'd do it again with absolutely no regret. Hopefully, I killed the bastard."

"Well, almost," Brewster said as his glasses were carefully folded and returned to his pocket.

"Almost? I put two bullets into that prick!"

"And somehow he lived through it. At last report, he was just out of surgery and is now in protective custody. I'm told the Secret Service has already relieved my men and is securing the prisoner." He returned the pencil and notebook to his pocket as he continued. "Funny thing, isn't it? How his injuries were much more severe, but he lived, and the other assassin died. I guess you just never know, do you?"

"And what about the other woman, the one with dark hair? Did you get her?"

"Actually, we were hoping you could give us more information on that female Federal Agent," Officer Brewster replied. "We didn't get her name in all the hullabaloo. She said she was working undercover; that's probably why we can't seem to find anything about her."

"Female Federal Agent," Hale restated blankly. Hale and Quinn exchanged glances but kept their poker faces in place. Questions were mounting about the morning's events.

"Yeah, the one who saved you. The field report says she immediately took control of the scene after you were rendered unconscious; identified you as the one who saved the President's life. Then directed my patrolmen to escort President Truman to the White House while you were on your way to Walter Reed since you're military. She did a right fine job considering the gravity of the situation."

"Yeah, right," Hale said cautiously. "But how did you know to send me to Walter Reed? As you said, I was in civilian clothes."

"The lady agent identified you as an Army Major and personal guard to the President." Brewster looked at both Quinn and Hale silently for a moment, then asked, "That is correct, yes?"

Quinn cleared his throat and avoided Hale's eyes while answering in the affirmative. "Yes, that's correct, but not something we want widely known right now. Can we keep that under our hat for now?"

Brewster tapped the side of his nose as he nodded and winked. "Well, I guess that's all I need, gentleman. It looks like the Secret Service is going to take this case off my hands, but I still needed to dot my i's and cross my t's if you know what I mean."

Quinn and Hale both nodded in understanding.

"Thank you for your time, and Major Hale, thank you for protecting the President this morning. You did a hell of a service to your Country."

"Just doing my job," Hale muttered. Something was terribly off, but neither Hale nor Quinn was willing to discuss it with an audience, law enforcement or not. But both knew they would need to unravel this puzzle as soon as the D.C. Cop was finished with his interview.

Brewster walked to the door but turned to face Hale and Quinn before leaving. "Oh, the party line is that the President tripped and fell on his walk to the White House this morning. Passersby got a little excited in the process and greatly exaggerated the event to my arriving officers. But we sorted it all out and determined it to be a simple accident. Nothing more."

"Thanks for the heads up, Captain," Quinn responded appreciatively. After Brewster left the room, Quinn and Hale stared quizzically at one another.

"What the hell just happened here, Colonel?" Hale asked, wondering if the clout on the head had scrambled his brain a little.

"There was another woman at the scene? Other than the one that died?" Quinn asked.

"Yes, sir. I thought she was part of the attack. Maybe I misunderstood her intentions. It all happened so damned fast."

"That doesn't explain her identifying herself as a Federal Agent. I've never heard of a female undercover agent – in any agency around here," Quinn said with his mind reeling from the fact that there was a woman loose in the city impersonating a Federal agent. "Run through it from the beginning for me. What do you remember, Curly?"

"I was on my way to our meeting and saw two women fighting in the street."

"Two women?"

"Correct, one blonde and one brunette. They were going at it hard. I guess one of them must have been this supposed Federal Agent."

"Do you think you could identify her if you saw a photo?"

"I doubt it. She was in my peripheral and I was focused on the man with the shiv in his hand bending over the President. I fired twice, verified he was down then turned my weapon on her." Hale's eyes clouded over as the scene replayed in his head, wondering what he should have done differently. "She was an unknown. I didn't know whose side she was on so I turned my weapon on her, figuring I would hold her until it was sorted out." Hale grimaced as his eyes returned to Quinn. "But she had my number, boy. I wasn't even fully facing her yet when the gun flew from my hand. I drew back prepared to immobilize her hand-to-hand then the world went black."

"If she were a Federal Agent why not identify herself? What reason would she have to hit you? And hit you with what?"

"I can't say. She left me with a nasty lump on my forehead though," Hale said as he touched the spot tenderly. "I got a look at it in the mirror earlier. I'm going to have an impressive bruise on my forehead and two matching black eyes."

"So, to sum up, some unknown woman gets the drop on you while you're protecting the President, and that's quite a feat," Quinn offered Hale's bruised ego. "And we have absolutely no idea who she is..."

"Or who she might work for," Hale finished.

"Who the hell is this mystery woman?"

Hale looked at Quinn with concern before adding, "And where is she now?"

CHAPTER 13

Rose Conway arranged the coffee cups and filled the carafe on the tray in the Oval Office before leaving the room to the President and Colonel Quinn. She quietly closed the office door behind her to allow the men to freely discuss what actually happened earlier in the day. She had enough experience to know that when the President asks you to cancel the rest of his afternoon appointments something serious has happened. The rumor was that shots had been fired, but of course, she would unabashedly deny any knowledge of such an occurrence if asked. The two men were undoubtedly in the process of strategizing the White House response, but she didn't get to her current position by eagerly participating in office gossip – whether it was true or not.

"Are you sure you don't want Steelman to be here, Mr. President?" Quinn asked before they began the discussion. "He is your assistant, and you can bet he won't be happy to hear about this second hand."

Truman nodded in agreement to the assessment as he took several deep breaths in an attempt to dispel the adrenaline continuing to give him the jitters. It was a natural reaction to the morning's events, he knew. However, no matter how natural his reaction it was, it was not a good look for the person holding the nation's highest office. He turned from the window to face his desk. "John is a good man; probably better than I deserve, but I would rather keep everything under wraps until I know exactly what happened and why it happened."

"Understood, sir," Quinn assented, as he picked up the carafe and poured two cups of coffee. He slid one mug over to the President's side of the desk as he began. "Do you want to start or shall I?"

Truman looked resigned. Like so many of the unpleasant things of this job, it had to be done, so he pushed ahead. "What I saw was minimal and occurred swiftly, so I guess we should get that out of the way first. Then you can tell me what you have learned thus far." Truman sat down and lifted his mug. A slight tremor in his hand caused him to gently return the cup to its place, as he paused and looked thoughtfully at its contents. He raised his eyes to look directly at Quinn. "You know, I have been in combat before."

"Yes, sir. The Great War. You were an artillery officer, weren't you, sir?"

Truman nodded his head and chose to enjoy the enticing aroma coming from the cup without attempting another sip. "I suppose they will have to come up with another name since we seem to have had a recurrence of the first one," he said with a rueful smile. "In any case, I saw my share of combat, but it was always at a distance. It's just the nature of being artillery, you know. I never saw the enemy face to face. This morning showed me just how frightening it can be when you realize someone is intentionally trying to take your life. It's unnerving."

"Yes, Mr. President, it is," Quinn answered softly. He had been where the President was at this moment. Trying to bring your body under control, trying to shake off the unwanted weakness in your limbs. He completely understood the need to examine, reexamine, and analyze each moment leading up to such an event.

"Can I surmise from your dossier that you've had more than one such experience?"

"I have had the good fortune of surviving several such incidences, yes sir," Quinn admitted.

"If you're being modest on my account, Bill, it's not necessary. I am well aware of your sacrifices for this nation and am deeply indebted to you. To you and all the brave men and women who have sacrificed so much," Truman voiced sincerely with the memories of his own years of service parading through his mind. He could see the faces of the men who had become like brothers during those years, and he could name each one that hadn't returned home. "It's just that I have never come this close to someone who seemed to hate me so much that they were willing to kill me."

"It's not that simple, sir," Quinn said. "Not when you're President."

"No. No, I suppose it's not," Truman conceded as he took a sip of coffee, carefully holding the mug with both hands before continuing. "In any case, let's get back to this morning. I was walking from my apartment as usual when a young woman with fair hair approached. She looked as if she were going to exchange pleasantries so, I tipped my hat to her in recognition. Then suddenly someone forcefully pushed me forward, and I fell to the sidewalk. It's a wonder I didn't break an arm or leg when I hit the concrete."

"So, someone else came up behind you?" Quinn clarified.

"Yes, a dark-haired woman. She must have been the one to push me down, as there was no one else there. She and the other woman fell into the street and engaged in hand-to-hand combat. I've never seen anything like it in all my life!"

"Are you saying the two women, both women, seemed to be trained combatants, sir?" Quinn asked with a furrowed brow.

"Oh absolutely, they were directly on my left only in the street. I could see everything. There was nothing Hollywood about it, you know what I mean? They were not slapping at one another, pulling hair, or trying to scratch each other. They were throwing punches and kicking one another, modesty be damned. They both seemed very professionally trained in how to kill an opponent. Of that I am sure."

"And is that when the other assailant showed up?" queried Quinn as he jotted notes.

"Yes, as best I can remember. One of the women subdued the other, and then I heard a man asking me if I was all right. When I looked up to see who it was, two shots rang out and the man fell backward on the sidewalk right in front of me."

"Was Curly, my man in the hospital, was he the one who fired the shots?"

"To be honest, I have no idea who fired the shots or where they came from because of the damn echo. But I heard the shots and saw the man fall. I tried to get up when I heard someone coming up fast behind me. He called out to see if I was all right, then checked the man who had been shot. The police rounded the corner about that time and there was a lot of commotion. When I looked back, he was on the sidewalk clearly unconscious, and I wondered if he had been shot in the process as well."

"No, he suffered no gunshot wounds; just a concussion and a big lump on his forehead," Quinn informed the President.

"How did he get that?" At the shrug of Quinn's shoulders, he pushed on. "I see. Well, it's good to know that he's okay, anyway. So, to continue, while I was wondering about him, the woman came beside me and asked if I was injured in any way as she took my elbow and helped me stand. I assured her I was fine, apparently thanks to her and the gentleman now lying at my feet."

"So, you got a good look at this woman?"

"Oh, yes. She was quite striking. Young, Caucasian, dark hair, and quite under control if you know what I mean."

"She wasn't frightened or overly emotional after that confrontation?" Quinn inquired curiously.

"Nothing like that, even with her injury. A split lip," the President clarified Quinn's unasked question. "She was calm. Seemed to be assessing the entire situation even as we spoke. That's when a couple of police officers arrived and tried to arrest her. I spoke up for her, then she took control of the scene immediately. Very professional. Very well trained."

"What do you mean, she took control?"

"She immediately identified herself as a federal agent and then began to issue instructions to the police officers. She identified the two attackers when I thought there was only one and identified your man as the one who came to my aid and probably saved my life. She even pointed out the stiletto knife the man still had in his hand and another one in the street that fell from the woman's hand during the tussle as probable murder weapons. She had the officers usher me here to the office and the Secret Service took over from there."

"But she never gave you or the officers her name?"

"Not that I recall. What did you learn from your man in the hospital?"

"That would be Major Donald Hale. If you remember we spoke of him previously as possible personnel to be assigned to the other, uh, issue," Quinn looked to see if Truman recalled the conversation. He continued at his nod. "We call him Curly. He's as good as it gets in the field. I just transferred him here from Germany. In fact, he was on his way to meet me when all this happened."

"It would appear to be a quite serendipitous moment, don't you think?"

"I do, indeed, Mr. President."

"I prefer, however, to believe it was God's protection," the president said with conviction. "So, Major Hale was on his way to see you when he witnessed the attack. Is that what he told you?"

"Yes, sir. He saw the brunette woman come out of a stairwell and begin running down the sidewalk. It was such an unusual site he had picked up his pace a bit. Then he saw her plow into the other woman and knock her off her feet. It wasn't until then that he recognized you, sir." Quinn stopped for a moment and took a prolonged sip of coffee to put his thoughts together on how to approach what was next. Just how much should he disclose?

"Just spit it out, Bill, and I don't mean the coffee," the President said, looking at him keenly over the rim of his cup.

"Yes, sir, that's probably best. Well, Hale was familiar with the tactic they used; recognized it immediately and had occasion to use it himself in the field. That's when he pulled his weapon and began a full-out run. The blonde was the initial assassin. Attractive, non-threatening. Curly thought the man was probably the backup in case she failed."

"That's why he intervened," Truman stated quietly.

"Yes. Major Hale saw the women fighting and ignored them since they were otherwise occupied. Then he saw the man moving to kneel beside you and caught the glint of the weapon. His service pistol was already in his hand, so he fired two shots. They were hasty, but on target, and the man went down. Once he checked to make sure the man was no longer a threat, he turned his attention to the women, or at least to the woman who was still standing. He had no idea who she was or whose side she was on. But before he could get his pistol in position, his weapon went flying from his hand and he was knocked unconscious. He woke up in the hospital an hour later."

"So, who attacked Major Hale? Was there another person there? I don't recall seeing anyone else," the President reasoned aloud.

"I don't know, sir. It could have been someone unaccounted for, or it could have been the woman. Until we get her in for questioning, I'm afraid it's all just pieces of a puzzle."

Truman's gaze shifted past Quinn. "I was wondering when you'd get here," he said, quite pleased that Mac's sudden appearance had not caught him unaware.

"Sir?" Mac asked as Quinn swiveled in his chair to see who had joined them.

"I'm just fine," the President said, holding up his hand to stop the onslaught of questions he was sure was coming. "God was looking out for me, and the assassination attempt was stopped before any damage was done."

"Assassination attempt! Oh my God!" Mac exclaimed. "What happened?"

"You didn't know?" Truman inquired. "So, what brought you here?"

"I think we can assume that's irrelevant right now, sir," Mac said. "Who tried to assassinate you? What happened?"

"Well, one of the would-be assassins is in surgery, and the other is in the morgue. As to who sent them? I don't know. I do know that if it hadn't been for Major Hale and our mystery woman, I would most assuredly be the one currently in the morgue."

A blank veil lowered over Mac's face as an impossible thought entered his mind.

"Okay," Quinn said. "I know that look. What do you know?"

"What?" Mac innocently inquired. Knowing his attempt at innocence had failed spectacularly at the dubious looks on both men's faces, he said, "Okay, okay. What do I know? Nothing for sure, but let me ask you, was the mystery woman a pretty brunette that fights like a hell cat in a skirt?"

"That's an apt description I'd say," Truman returned.

Mac sighed, then looked at the ceiling while cursing under his breath. "So…do you remember the female operative we discussed the other day?" he asked Quinn.

"You turned a foreign operative loose on American soil without telling me?" Quinn asked with his eyes sparking outrage.

"No! No way! I'm surprised you would even accuse me of such a thing," Mac shot back.

The intercom buzzed at that moment, throwing ice water on the impending shouting match. Rose's apologetic voice came over the box. "I'm so sorry, sir, but the coroner is on the line and is quite insistent it's imperative that he speak with you immediately. Shall I take a message?"

"No, that's fine. I'll take it. It seems we could use a little break anyway," he assured her as he looked at the heated faces of the two men before him. "Hello…yes this is the President."

The voice on the other end of the line came out in a rush. "Mr. President, it's such an honor to speak with you directly sir and I wouldn't bother you if I didn't think it was important but I'm pretty sure you will think this is important, so I called." The man took a couple of breaths. "We have a problem here, sir."

"How so?" the President asked, wondering if the gentleman on the line was going to hyperventilate.

"Well sir…well I know how this sounds, but I've just got to come on out and say it. Regarding that incident that didn't happen this morning," the caller's voice dropped to a furtive whisper, "this here body your men left me isn't human."

CHAPTER 14

Tamar was more than a little relieved when Uncle Yazzie was otherwise occupied as she slipped back into the house from her highly eventful walk in town. She was able to change her clothes and tend to her injuries before his attention turned in her direction. Determined to stay out of any further trouble, she willingly complied with his suggestion that she spend the afternoon with Helen Magruder while he ran an errand.

So thankful that Uncle was blissfully unaware of all that had occurred, Tamar emptied the ice cube tray into a container at Helen's request with a small sigh of contentment. She marveled at the ingenuity that allowed her to get ice cubes directly from the small freezer portion of the refrigerator.

"You don't have ice cube trays in Palestine?" Helen asked with interest as she filled up two glasses.

"I have heard that the British do in their quarters. But I have never actually seen them. It's wonderful, isn't it? You don't need to wait for an ice truck to bring blocks of ice to your home."

"Oh my," Helen responded with a laugh as freshly brewed tea was poured over the ice. "That brings back memories. We had those when I was young. What a chore to chip off sections of ice from that big block. I can't tell you the number of times I got scolded for mishandling the ice pick. That poor table was stabbed so many times and ice wound up everywhere."

Tamar laughed with Helen at the memory as she accepted her glass. Helen pointed to a chair at the kitchen table and invited her to sit down. Tamar complied and tried to enjoy the woman-to-woman time so lacking in her life, but it set her on edge a little. Memories of sitting in the kitchen helping mama prepare evening meals kept overwhelming her senses. Oh, they would talk and laugh about everything! It was a bittersweet memory that had Tamar at a disadvantage with the effervescent Helen.

"You are most welcome to stay with us," Helen offered. "We are quite used to having long-term guests, and to tell you the truth, I would enjoy the company. The house seems so empty since our son went off to college."

"You are very kind, Mrs. Magruder," Tamar responded politely.

"Oh, please, just call me Helen. Mrs. Magruder is far too formal for friends."

"Thank you, Helen, but I think my uncle wants me to stay with him for a while at least; until I can find my way around the city on my own."

"Nonsense. Yazzie's place is much too small and has little ventilation during our hot and humid summers. You would be much more comfortable here," Helen insisted as she stopped to take a sip. She then looked at Tamar tenderly and continued, "But perhaps you've missed him as much as he's missed you. You know we have tried numerous times to get Yazzie to stay here with us, but he seems to prefer the bachelor life."

"Yes, he has always been a very private person," Tamar responded with relief that Helen had graciously given her a way out of being a houseguest. "I think he enjoys being by himself more than with anyone else since my aunt died; if that makes any sense."

"Oh, it does, and I think you're right. It's just who he is," Helen agreed. "Well, if you change your mind, dear, just know our door is always open for you. So now that the obligatory pleasantries are out of the way, I would like to hear about you. Yazzie is a typical man when it comes to details, there aren't any. So, tell me about yourself."

Tamar blushed at the request and seemed uncomfortable being the focus of Helen's undivided attention. Though she was enjoying the 'normal' female interaction Helen provided, after being on her own for so long in hostile surroundings, Tamar knew there was little genuine information about her life that she could share. Her in-depth knowledge regarding weapons or tactics was out. The training she had endured or missions she had been on were also a no. So, she pulled out one of the most often-used arrows in her quiver. A change of subject. "There is one thing I would like to do while I'm here," Tamar said brightly. "I would like to see a motion picture."

"Oh, I would love that!" Helen agreed enthusiastically. Then, perhaps sensing Tamar's discomfort, Helen picked up the conversation and ran with it. She shared a little Hollywood movie star gossip garnered from the local newspaper and made her case as to why Humphrey Bogart and Ingrid Bergman's movie *Casablanca* was still the best work either of them had done to date. Just as Helen was about to firm up their movie date, Mac and Yazzie were heard coming through the front door.

"We'll have to see what's playing…" Helen said as she and Tamar walked from the kitchen to the living room to greet the men. The expression on their faces stopped Helen midstream. "What happened?"

"Someone tried to kill President Truman this morning," Mac replied straight out.

"Oh, dear God! Is he all right?" Helen exclaimed.

"Let me make some iced tea while you talk," Tamar said quickly as she turned to leave the room.

"Hold up, young lady," Mac returned sternly as Tamar slowly turned her head back to see if her secret was out. It was. "Sit," he said, pointing to an armchair.

Resigned to the coming chastisement, she avoided her uncle's eyes as she sat down. Yazzie stopped his pacing and exploded at his niece. "Keep a low profile, that's what I said. How could you involve yourself like that? Do you have any idea what could have happened? Your impulses are going to get you killed one day!"

"Yazzie! That's quite enough," Helen ordered firmly. "You will not use that tone of voice in my home. You know better than that."

"What should I have done?" Tamar barked back. "Let him die?"

Mac stepped forward. Helen was stunned at her young guest's response but held her hand up to the men to stop another barrage at Tamar. The look on her husband's face was no different from Yazzie's and Helen knew he was upset. She had once seen him like this when his Executive Officer had made what he considered an egregious error in judgment. However, this was her home and not the Command Post and most certainly not the battlefield. She had maintained a set of decorum rules early on in their marriage, and it would not change now.

She looked at Mac and said calmly but firmly, "All right, I can see you're upset, but what does the assassination attempt have to do with Tamar?"

Yazzie walked to a living room chair and plopped himself down. Then gave Tamar a piercing look. "Would you like to explain? And please, don't even try to deny anything. This has you written all over it," he said tersely.

Tamar glanced at each of the others in the room with a contrite look, then sighed heavily before speaking to the only friendly face in the room. "I just wanted to see if the President of the United States really walked unaccompanied from his apartment to the White House every morning, as Uncle had told me. It seemed too incredible to me that a world leader would be so careless."

"Go on," Yazzie insisted with no sympathy. "Tell her the rest. All of Washington will probably know about this when the evening newspapers come out. Low profile indeed." Yazzie finished speaking in Yiddish, which meant nothing to Mac and Helen, but Tamar looked like a schoolgirl being scolded by the principal.

"What should I have done?" she asked, with defiance rising in her voice. "What would you have done? Can you tell me that?"

"You shouldn't have been there at all," Yazzie shot back.

"But I *was* there, and I knew what was happening. I could not just turn my back and walk away. I couldn't," Tamar returned passionately. "And I would do it again!"

"Tamar," Helen said softly. "Is that what happened to your lip?" At her quick embarrassed nod, Helen continued. "Were you hurt anywhere else, dear?"

"I'll be just fine," she answered with a jut of her chin. "I can take care of myself." When she saw Helen's crestfallen face, she immediately regretted her sharp reply and said softly, "Thank you for asking."

"It's a big damn mess, that's what it is," Yazzie said to Mac.

"No, Feter, no it's not," Tamar replied with relief in her tone. "I didn't forget what you said. I did keep a low profile. No one knows who I am; I slipped away once I knew the President was safe. No one knows who was there…except…"

Yazzie raised his eyebrows and lowered his chin at her hesitance. "Except?"

"Well…" she said, biting her lower lip.

"Oh Lord Most High, this can't be good," Yazzie lamented, wondering how things could get any worse.

"Major Hale was there," she confessed timidly.

"What?!" he exclaimed. *I tempted the Lord and He answered me*, Yazzie thought as he rubbed his forehead with both hands.

"He may not have gotten a good look at me, though," Tamar rushed on. "I think I knocked him out before he recognized me." Her eyes grew wide at her unexpected admission and her uncle's open-mouthed stare. "Well, it wasn't on purpose! He was going to shoot me!"

Yazzie held up his hand. "Stop. Just stop. I don't want to hear anymore."

"But…"

"No…uh-uh," he said with a wag of his finger each time she tried to plead her case.

"Major Hale, do I know him?" Helen asked the room.

"Possibly. He served with me in the SSU and CIG and now serves under Bill Quinn," Mac replied distractedly. "And how do you two know him?"

"Oh, this just gets better and better," Yazzie said to himself as he began to pace again. He stopped and looked at Mac directly. "I just met the man recently…"

Mac frowned at the obtuse reference, then when the connection was made said, "Oh, no way. No, that's just not possible." Then he started to laugh as he said, "Oh hell no."

"Wait, what?" Helen asked, totally confused. "You lost me."

When the men threw their hands in the air and walked away, Tamar answered contritely, "He was the man that arrested me in Germany. The one Uncle saved me from."

"You're the one that clocked him," Mac stated more than asked while still laughing. "It was nice of you to give him full credit for saving the President since you completely annihilated his dignity."

"Is he okay?"

"Concussion and the most beautiful set of black eyes you've ever seen," Mac said, drying his eyes. "But I've got bad news for you, kiddo. I gave the President your name."

"What?! Why?" Tamar gasped. "No one knew anything."

"C'mon I was standing in the Oval Office when he mentioned the pretty brunette that fought like the devil himself to save him. Who else could it be? And why the hell did you identify yourself as a Federal Agent?"

"She did, what?!" Yazzie shouted.

"Oh, my Lord," Helen added as she covered her mouth.

"I needed to get away. I thought that in the confusion it might be a good strategy to keep the local police busy with the President and Major Hale."

Mac, Yazzie, and Helen stared at Tamar, their mouths agape in disbelief, and maybe with just a bit of pride and appreciation for her quick thinking.

"Well, it worked," Tamar said under her breath as she contemplated her hands as they rested in her lap.

"So, what now?" Yazzie asked with a sigh. "How much trouble is she in?"

"Trouble? The President wants to give her a damn medal," Mac said with a grin. "One of the assassins is dead. The other is in the hospital recovering from surgery and all is well with the world."

"At least one of them is alive to interrogate," Tamar inserted, happy to be off the railroad tracks with the train barreling right at her. "Those shots were impressive, to say the least. The Major was running full speed when he fired and landed both. It's no wonder the man died."

Mac and Yazzie glanced at one another, then Yazzie spoke, "It was not the man who died, love, it was the woman. But don't be concerned, it was justified."

Tamar looked at them blankly for a moment. "No, no that is not possible."

"It's alright, dear," Helen said as she patted Tamar's hand.

"No, you don't understand. I didn't use enough force to do that. I know how hard I hit her; she should not have died."

"I'm sure it will all come out in the autopsy," Mac assured her, thinking of the findings already discovered that could not be disclosed. "She may have had a precondition no one knew about. Let's just be thankful the President is alive. He is also very appreciative. His secretary will be making arrangements for the medal presentation. It will be a closed ceremony, of course, and you will never be allowed to share this with anyone. Ever."

Tamar almost stuttered in her response to this unexpected and unprecedented event. "Of course. I understand."

"Oh, there's more, young lady," Mac added as he looked at Yazzie, who stood up and walked to Tamar. He placed his hand on her shoulder. She was suddenly wary and stared at her uncle in anticipation of some really bad news.

"What is it, Feter? What is wrong?"

"At the President's insistence, you may be redeployed so to speak," Yazzie said quietly.

"What does that mean?" Helen asked, now herself wary.

Yazzie patted Tamar on the shoulder and said calmly, "It means she may now work for the President of the United States."

CHAPTER 15

The dark and dank "dead room" of the D.C. morgue held up to ten bodies at any given time. Colonel Bill Quinn was only interested in one. The typical protocol to gain access to a body had been bypassed; there would be no signature on the visitor log nor any evidence that anyone had come to claim or identify 'Jane Doe'.

Barbara Martin's name would never be connected to Jane Doe or the rumors of an assassination attempt on President Truman's life, even though it was her body currently on the slab. The Secretary of War for whom she worked as a clerk would be notified by mail of an unfortunate illness in her family that required her immediate departure. She would extend her deepest regrets and wish everyone well.

Dr. Stanley Zimmerman was on edge and had been on edge ever since his call to the President. Well before that, truth be told. His nerves had been frayed the moment his lowly office was swarmed with Secret Service agents. He had been the only one in residence at the time as his assistant had left for a serendipitous dental appointment. Suddenly there were suits escorting a body, asking questions, demanding that he sign a non-disclosure agreement. They were a highly intimidating group that never had to straight out voice a threat; you just knew.

Quinn met Zimmerman in his office. They exchanged perfunctory greetings as Quinn displayed his White House credentials, then quickly moved to the concrete stairwell that led down to the holding area. All other personnel had been dismissed for the day on the pretext of a chemical leak in the building. Everyone had been instructed to remain home until further notice, as no one would be allowed entry until the inspectors declared it safe. The ruse ensured that Zimmerman and Quinn were the only two breathing people in the building.

The two men shared little more than a nod from the time they shook hands until walking into the "dead room" itself. Neither seemed inclined to initiate any type of obligatory small talk about the weather or share a joke to break the ice as they trod down the cold gray steps. They were both accustomed to the macabre when it came to death, one from war and the other by profession, yet neither had dealt with anything even remotely like this.

Doctor Zimmerman was the only son of Jewish refugees from Austria circa 1885. His parents had so wanted a doctor in the family that he had felt obliged to study to become a surgeon. He did his undergraduate work at the University of Virginia, then completed his graduate and doctoral work at Columbia University where he met the love of his life and future wife, Lucinda. They had never been blessed with children, due to Luci's childhood bout with mumps, but they still had led a happy, prosperous, and peaceable life together in Arlington, Virginia.

There came a day, as with all surgeons, where his hands were not as steady as they once were, and he knew it was time to retire. It was impossible to imagine life without a scalpel in his hand. He tried his best to hide the dread he felt at the loss, but his dear Luci was, as usual, way ahead of him. When she heard of a medical examiner leaving his post in Washington D.C. discrete inquiries were made and an interview was arranged.

He was both grateful and irritated at his wife for suggesting the move. The idea of going hat-in-hand to obtain employment seemed most undignified. Yet, he accepted the interview and then the position with a newfound purpose in life. While he would never perform life-saving surgery any longer, he could solve the mystery of 'why' for grieving families who had lost someone they loved. And as it turned out, he was exceptionally good at it.

His whole reason for uprooting their lives was to keep his wife happy and loved. He had done so for thirty-five years when suddenly she collapsed at their bedside one morning two months ago. In a single heartbeat, his beautiful Lucinda was gone. It felt as if a piece of him had died with her, and his life had become dull and without meaning - until today. Today his world had been turned upside down.

A man from the White House would come and instruct him how to proceed, he was told. The President himself said don't allow anyone else to access the body and to keep his mouth shut until contact was made. He had pretty much figured that much out on his own. That's why he called Truman directly. The real surprise had been when without a single moment's hesitation Mr. Truman believed him.

Quinn had seen more than his fair share of dead bodies in thirty years of military service. So, he had not hesitated when the President directed him to contact the M.E. personally. It seemed highly unlikely that seeing one more body would add to the nightmares already disturbing his sleep. He was wrong.

Zimmerman silently rolled the body in on a wheeled table. It was appropriately covered with a white sheet, as one would expect. Before lifting the cover, the M.E. spoke as gloves were tugged into place. "I figured whoever came would want to see for themselves, so I didn't stitch her up yet."

"Any chance she has something humans could catch?"

"Is she infectious? I can't say for sure. She looks healthy, but that doesn't mean much in this situation, does it? Do you know who she is, where she lived or worked?"

"We're looking into it," Quinn returned, unwilling to share any more information than necessary. "Why do you ask?"

"Examining where she spent the most time would be the best way to look for contagions. See if anyone she was in contact with is sick."

Quinn nodded, then Zimmerman peeled the sheet back so he could view the entire corpse. Quinn did his best to refrain from any outward emotional response as he scanned the would-be assassin from head to toe. The body was female, attractive, and looked to be early to mid-thirties, average height with very fair hair and skin tone. The skin had been folded back into place over the Y-shaped incision, however, the edges of the skin that had been cut were turning brown like an overly ripe banana.

"What's this?" Quinn asked, pointing to the discoloration.

"It's the darndest thing, isn't it? I have no idea. It seems to be corrosive in nature, almost like the flesh is rotting at a highly accelerated pace." He gently rolled one of the edges between his thumb and index finger, causing a brown residue to cling to the gloves. Quinn tried not to wretch as Zimmerman examined it under the overhead florescent lights and noted, "I could probably tell you more if I had more time."

The M.E. carefully folded the skin back, exposing her internal structure. *Yep*, Quinn thought, *absolutely not human*. "You tell anyone else about this?" he asked, with his eyes never leaving the corpse.

"No one," Zimmerman replied quickly. "Like I said, my assistant was out, and seeing how the body was delivered I assumed there was a rush on it, so I started without him. Once I saw the configuration of her internal anatomy, I just stopped. There was a notation in the paperwork dropped off with the body that only the Secret Service should be notified of my initial observations. I was to do nothing else until I contacted them."

"You didn't find that strange? Only notify the Secret Service?"

"Of course, I found it strange. But this is D.C. Strange happens here all the time. Just not usually this strange," Zimmerman surmised wisely. He looked at Quinn directly and asked, "Am I in trouble? For calling the President instead of the suits?"

"No…no, you did the right thing," Quinn assured him as he again surveyed the body on the table. "She does look almost human, doesn't she?"

"Almost," Zimmerman reminded him. "Not quite. You can see the outline of the rib cage that normally houses the human heart and lungs. But not her, her heart and lungs are below the diaphragm in the lower abdomen. Best I can tell without taking her apart any more than I have already, the kidney and liver are much higher."

"It's like a reverse of our physiology," Quinn said, almost to himself.

"Exactly. When I first got the body, I did some standard tests: x-rays, pulled some blood, and so on. They have all confirmed my initial observations. She is not human."

Quinn's head snapped around as his mind immediately went to the containment of information. "There were tests? Oh, sweet Judas priest, how many hands did those pass through?"

"Just mine," the doctor assured him. He looked a little embarrassed as he continued. "I taped the x-rays and other results under the gurney. I had to destroy the physical evidence, though. I didn't want anyone stumbling on it by accident." Quinn breathed a sigh of relief at the doctor's paranoia. "There is one thing maybe you should know," Zimmerman continued. "The blood looked normal enough when I pulled it, but by the time I went back to destroy it that stuff had turned blue."

"Blue?"

"As a jaybird."

Quinn heaved a sigh, then asked, "Do you know what killed her? I heard she took a blow to the head."

Zimmerman looked at Quinn with raised eyebrows. "You know I'm a *human* doctor, right? How am I supposed to know?"

"I had a roommate once that got the same look as what's on your face right now whenever he had an ace's high full house, Doc. What have you got up your sleeve?"

The M.E. leaned back against a table and folded his arms. "Okay, this is strictly off the record because I can't say for sure. But if I had to guess…asphyxiation."

Quinn was confused. That diagnosis didn't line up with Curly's eyewitness account at all. "Where did you get that?"

Zimmerman's face lit up just a little as the thrill of discovery broke through his professional demeanor. "Well, when I couldn't get any deeper into the autopsy inside, I took another look outside. Her eyes…oh well, I probably shouldn't go into her eyes," he said with a physical shiver. "To make a long story short, her toes and fingertips show indications of oxygen deprivation. And," he said with relish, "Her finger and toenails are fake as in surgically implanted fake."

This was getting to be more information than he wanted to know, so Quinn decided to get on to business. "All right, here's what we're going to do. Make sure she is locked in isolation and I'm going to send some men down here to take custody of the body."

"Sounds good to me," the doctor replied as he pulled the skin flaps back into position. "I don't want her…it…in my morgue any longer than necessary. Should I close up the incisions?"

"Yes, absolutely. No sense in tempting fate," Quinn responded. "The body will be removed and relocated. I guess I don't need to tell you that this is very restricted knowledge. No one – I repeat, no one is to ever know this woman was here. Am I clear, Dr. Zimmerman?"

"Perfectly. Who would believe me anyway?" he asked rhetorically as he retrieved the supplies to sew her up.

"Who is your number two around here?" Quinn asked casually.

"Dr. Finney. He's second in charge of the morgue and generally does the daily administrative work here."

"Do you trust him?" Quinn inquired as the doctor threaded the needle to mend the gruesome wounds created in a standard autopsy. "Umm…could you possibly finish that up after I leave, Doc?"

"Completely. He is…what's that?" Zimmerman asked, as his mind registered the request. "Oh certainly, certainly. He's one of the finest men I have ever met. I don't think I could run this place without his able assistance," he finished as the thread was laid aside and the sheet temporarily pulled over the body.

"I have an offer for you, Doc," Quinn said as he walked from the room. He had seen enough and was ready to put some distance between himself and that body. "I checked your dossier before I got here. You're a widower for two months now. I am genuinely sorry for your recent loss. No children. No family within the borders of the United States. Retired from a successful surgical practice. No money problems, meaning your second career was probably just to have something useful to do. The District of Columbia and the United States appreciate your dedication and professionalism by the way."

Zimmerman froze as he heard Quinn rattle off his life history as if written in an obituary. An involuntary shudder went up his back as he tried to clear his throat and then tried unsuccessfully to wet his suddenly dry lips as he parroted, "An offer?"

"I need someone to escort Jane Doe to her final destination. Since you are already aware of the delicate nature of this task, it makes perfect sense to me that you would accompany her."

"Oh," Zimmerman breathed in relief. "Yes, I could take a few days for a trip. Doctor Finney is more than capable to fill in."

Quinn smiled a sardonic grin and stared directly at the doctor. "Good to hear. He will be a great replacement for you if, or when, you decide to make the move permanent."

A flush of color crept up Zimmerman's neck as he tried to contemplate what Quinn had just said. "Permanent? Do you even have the authority to make such an offer?"

"What do you think?" Quinn answered with a banal smile.

Zimmerman thought of what it was like going home to an empty house every night; of thinking he heard Luci in another room, only to remember that she was forever gone. He thought of his match-making neighbor that said it was time for him to reenter the dating pool. It wasn't fair to stay single when there were so many ladies looking for good husbands, she said, and oh by the way she had a friend that would be perfect for him once he was ready.

"My home. My furnishings..."

"My people would take care of all that for you, Doctor." At Zimmerman's hesitation, he continued. "'You would be a highly valued resource of the Government of the United States of America. This is an honor that isn't offered to just anyone."

The Colonel was correct that nothing was holding him here. He could escape the pitying glances and constant sickening advice from every person he met as if they knew what it was like to lose the one person that meant more to you than anything. Actually... he had loved doing research in his college years. Is that what this was? Where was this final destination? Did it even matter? And if he said no, knowing what he knew now, would his life ever be safe again?

"When do we leave?"

Quinn smiled as he checked his watch. "Midnight. My men will pick you up and escort you to the Naval Air Reserve. You are not to speak to them about anything. You will be met there by Captain Ralph Jenkins. He is escorting another non-human body from Germany. You two will get to know each other quite well I'm sure as you figure out what we're dealing with here."

"Another non-human! What the hell is happening?" Zimmerman's mind was racing as he tried to take in all that Quinn was saying. After losing his dear Luci he had wondered what was left for him in this life, but nothing like this was ever imagined. This was surreal. This was crazy!

"How do you feel about Nevada?"

"Nevada? I'm assuming we're talking about a military installation. There are several much closer," Zimmerman mentioned. "Why move the body clear across the country to the middle of the desert?"

"Because that's where the Nevada Test and Training Range at Groom Lake is located."

"Groom Lake?" Zimmerman asked with a frown.

"Yes, Groom Lake. An installation known for its high-level security and active participation in nuclear testing…and your new home for the foreseeable future."

"Oh, my God."

CHAPTER 16

The Greys' edict to provide only minimal information was annoying enough but sending what little information they were willing to share in vivid technicolor just set Mac's teeth on edge. The message would sit in one's mind, flashing like a bright neon sign until it was acknowledged and deciphered. The process reminded him somewhat of Germany's Enigma system for sending coded messages. He and Yazzie had spent some time discussing the possibility of Enigma being alien technology.

Translating what was sent was a two-step process. First, the message had to be translated into English, then it had to be translated into something that made sense. The latest message was a perfect example:

> *Your enemy's footprint is visible in high places.*
> *The treacherous ones whisper in high towers,*
> *And place spears in unsteady hands.*
> *A trail of deception cannot be erased.*
> *The righteous have wings upon their feet.*

Mac was deeply perturbed at the latest message received from the Greys. The telepathic message, while astonishingly vivid, was deliberately vague. Their culture prohibited interference with other races as history was expected to play out on its own. However, since human history and the Grey's personal history were at a crossroads, they had, after a considerable amount of discussion, decided that a minimal amount of assistance would be offered in their own self-interest.

The truth was that most of the time their information was of little to no use. It was like being given the clue that a particular piece of straw was in one of twenty-five haystacks. Knowing this to be true, Mac had attempted to ask for a few more specifics but had been cut off. The Greys considered themselves morally superior to any species that continued to engage in war. So even if they were the catalyst behind the impending bloodshed, they felt that their decisions and methods should not be questioned.

While Mac was certainly unhappy about the lack of clarity in the recent transmission, he was not surprised at their response to his query. He, Helen, and Yazzie had spent enough time in transitioning their physiology at the hands of the Greys to know that they were all about dispensing precise bits of information nothing more, and certainly not responding to questions from those considered to be lower-life forms. They expected yes or no responses to their transmissions and became offended at any inference that the information provided was inadequate to make informed decisions.

That the Greys were not omniscient, nor immortal was made clear during Mac, Helen, and Yazzie's time on their planet both through personal observation and the Grey's own confession. They watched and observed other species and made prognostications based on their observations of culture and behavior but could not deliver prophetic disclosures as to future events. In other words, they didn't know what was going to happen with the Anakim.

Their expectations of Mac, Helen, and Yazzie, as much as could be determined, were that the barbaric human race stood the best chance of victory over the Anakim. The hope was that the trio, with minimal physical changes, would carry out a diligent investigation based upon the scant information provided and determine a course of action that would ensure a complete and total defeat from which the Anakim could never recover. Earth would survive and the Greys would never have to stoop to personally engaging in war to protect their own planet. And, of course, their arrogantly assumed predestined path to the heavenly tenth dimension would remain undeterred.

Upon realizing that their agreement to accept assistance from the Greys, no matter how minimal, had made them inter-dimensional targets, Mac, Helen, and Yazzie immediately set about to find a few safe houses upon their return to earth. The log cabin Mac and Helen had purchased several years before as a retirement property had become one of them. Being a General's wife had taught Helen that nothing was truly private anymore, but she longed for at least a semblance of privacy if possible and that desire had caused her to use a legal pseudonym on the title deed to keep away prying eyes during their retirement years. Her fortuitous decision had given them an invaluable place of solitude and safety.

The cozy cabin and spectacular wooded views made the decision to buy this property easy. Purchasing the real estate from a long-time family friend who had decided to move from this remote location in the Poconos to a more urban area was what allowed the completion of the transaction to be done quietly. They had jumped at the opportunity at the time and now they were both beyond pleased with their foresight, as the log cabin had become a reliable sanctuary.

The three compatriots sat around the small banquette in an alcove just off the kitchen. The three-sided alcove had a four-paned window in the long wall opposite the opening to the kitchen. The kitchen's peninsula, in turn, opened into the front room, creating a large roomy living area from which all three spaces could be viewed. The ceiling had been left with open rafters displaying the height of the tall, slanted roof. Two bedrooms and a bath were on the opposite side of the house. Its construction was all wood, both finished and unfinished, making it appear quite rustic, however, it was equipped with all the modern conveniences.

"How do they expect us to find proof if they don't give us more information than a silly riddle?" Helen pouted as she rinsed dishes at the farmhouse sink.

Yazzie agreed as he assisted with clearing the table. "It's like playing an Agatha Christie mystery game with these people. If I can even call them people. I'm still not sure exactly what they are."

"They are the Greys," Mac reminded him absently as he read the cryptic message again. "That's all they told us and according to them, that's supposed to be enough. It's damned irritating. How can they expect us to convince our leaders of this imminent threat when they only give us minimal information to work with?"

Helen held up the coffee pot. "Anyone?" At the negative shakes of their heads, she filled her own cup. "Did you get the impression that they felt we should have already had some kind of discovery that would verify their communication?" Helen asked no one in particular as she sat back down. "It's like they were indignant that we had not used the information we were already given."

"Okay, let's look at it again," Mac said. Helen and Yazzie groaned. Their minds had been lit up with the same information at the same time as Mac, and their responses were similar. Two hours into this discussion, they were all frustrated.

Helen picked up the sheet of paper the Grey's transmission had been recorded on with a sigh and read it aloud again.

> *"Your enemy's footprint is visible in high places.*
> *The treacherous ones whisper in high towers,*
> *And place spears in unsteady hands.*
> *A trail of deception cannot be erased.*
> *The righteous have wings upon their feet."*

"Your enemy's footprint is visible in high places. The enemy has got to be the Anakim," Mac stated, recapping their discussion so far. "And the treacherous ones are the Shalanya. The righteous are hopefully the three of us."

"Yes, those are the players," Helen agreed, brushing a wayward crumb from the table.

"High places and high towers are probably related," Yazzie added. "If you remember, their Council of Elders convened in the glass tower on the Peak of Enlightenment. So, I'm assuming here on earth it would translate into government or governments."

"Okay, so if 'spears' refer to the military then we've got the Anakim walking around governments most likely through the Shalanya, who are influencing the military. Not good," Mac replied. "Then deception cannot be erased."

"More precisely, dear," Helen interjected, "A *trail* of deception cannot be erased. In other words, there is evidence of their deception and if we're righteous, we will find it."

"I would translate the last line as so get up off your *tuchus* and find it," Yazzie said, utilizing his Yiddish for one's posterior. "Other than that, I would have to agree."

Helen and Mac laughed, but the levity was short-lived. "The Greys let us use the stasis of real Anakim and Shalanya to convince Truman and Quinn of their existence," Mac said. "But they were never clear about the extent of alien infiltration already on earth. I guess I just assumed the alien presence was minimal, you know just starting, and we were being recruited to stop them before they got established."

Helen stood to take her half-empty cup to the kitchen sink. "We have to remember that the Greys cannot lie. It is just not in their makeup. They must tell the truth if they want to get to their heaven. If that is the case, we now also have to assume there are indeed Anakim and Shalanya currently operating in the world."

"We know they *said* they cannot lie," Yazzie inserted. "We have yet to determine if that is a fact."

Mac joined Helen at the sink and retrieved a glass to get a drink of water. "I just can't imagine them lying to us after going to all the trouble to change our physiology to make communication and dimensional travel possible for us. What purpose would that serve them?"

"We just met these creatures, Mac," Yazzie responded. "We don't know for sure if their intentions are as they say. Perhaps we took them at their word too soon."

"I got the impression they know we know something. But I have no idea what we know that they know."

"Don't make it an Abbot and Costello routine, dear," Helen reproved her husband gently. "Let's try to figure out what we have learned so far and see if any of it may relate to the Grey's message. They said that the Anakim and Shalanya were instrumental in starting both world wars, but they never said how. Not to me anyhow."

"This message seems to say they didn't incite and run. They may have embedded themselves and not just in one government, 'high places' was *plural*," Mac emphasized.

"This only makes matters worse for us, since we have no idea how many of these creatures may already be here. Much less what damage they may be doing," Yazzie stated.

"Well, we know at least one worked in the White House," Helen added quietly. "Did Tamar say anything useful? She did do hand-to-hand combat with one."

"No, she just insists that her blow was not lethal. But then she doesn't know what we know," her uncle replied. "One of my sources told me that an ambassador was sent to Menachem requesting her reassignment to Truman immediately. To say that he was unhappy doesn't begin to cover it. But how can he say no to the President of the United States?"

"Begin may not be happy, but we need her. I suspect she is already unknowingly involved if what happened in Germany is any indication," Mac said. "She's certain that the German officer had diamonds?"

"Our family has been involved in the diamond trade for generations. If she said there were diamonds, you can trust her on that. That's why she followed him to the farmhouse. She was hoping to find a trail for the diamond's dispersion. That could have helped lead to who is providing the uncut diamonds and how they are converting them to cash."

"It was a good plan, Yazzie," Mac said, admiring Tamar's instincts. "Quinn will want to know if those diamonds are still at the farmhouse or if they have been moved."

"She said she hid them in the root cellar of the farmhouse just before Major Hale and his men arrived. Whether they are still there, however, remains to be seen."

"Do you think the diamonds have anything to do with the Shalanya?" Helen asked innocently.

Mac and Yazzie turned to stare blankly at Helen. She became aware of their looks and decided to continue. "Even aliens would need money to function here on earth. If these are financing their operations, then finding the source is imperative. Disrupt the money, disrupt the organization."

Seeing the logic in Helen's assertion, Mac responded quickly. "That will be Curly and Tamar's first assignment. We'll tell them to find the diamonds. If the diamonds were supposed to be used to finance ODESSA operations to restart the Fourth Reich, it makes perfect sense."

"And the alien connection," Yazzie added quizzically. "How do we explain that?"

"We don't," Mac responded. "First, let's see if the diamonds are still there. If so, then we'll determine if the Greys are trying to tell us that the Shalanya are using high-level government and business professionals to convert diamonds to working capital. If that's the case, then they will be forced to attempt a retrieval of the diamonds because of the disruption to their financial network."

Mac looked at his wife and added, "Helen, you're a genius."

"It's nice of you to think so," she responded sweetly.

"If we are truly blessed, then finding the source may also lead us to the Shalanya using it," Yazzie said with a whispered prayer seeking success. A sly smile lit up his face as he continued. "A double blessing would allow us to use the gems to finance our own operations."

"Do Tamar and Curley know they will be working together?" Helen asked.

Mac and Yazzie both grinned.

"Not yet. It should be really interesting," Mac responded. "I'm pretty sure it will be like boxers in opposite corners of the ring. We'll have to keep a close watch on them until it's certain they won't kill one another."

"It might be said that the safe money should be on the man," Helen said, "but I don't know. My money might be on Tamar in that fight."

CHAPTER 17

Elizabeth Truman, better known as Bess, did a quick final inspection of the living room of the residential quarters in the White House. She trusted the maid service to keep the area clean, however as her mother had always said "it's not what you expect but what you inspect that gets done." So, as was her custom, she walked slowly through the room and gave it a close visual once over. Once a pillow on the sofa was plumped up a bit, she was completely satisfied.

President Truman and Bill Quinn walked into the room just as Bess concluded it was suitable for guests. She smiled at both men as they entered, and they returned the smile warmly.

"Bill," Bess said politely as she extended her hand. "So good to see you again."

Quinn took her hand and replied, "Always a pleasure, Mrs. Truman."

"Now, Bill. No need to be formal here. This is our living quarters, after all. Just call me Bess, please."

Quinn looked to the President for guidance. Truman just smiled and shook his head. "I never argue with my Bess. You would do well to do the same to remain in her good graces."

"Yes sir," he responded graciously.

"Bess dear, Bill and I will need some privacy this morning. I have two other guests arriving shortly. You understand, of course."

"Of course," she replied easily. "I'm due for tea with some old friends in the dining room as it is. Just ring the bell on the reading table if you need anything at all."

"Thank you, dear."

Truman kissed his wife on the cheek, and she left the room to join her guests at the tea party, softly closing the door behind her. Quinn pulled two small boxes from his pockets and handed them to the President. He opened the boxes to see the Legion of Merit medals he would present today, then handed them back to Quinn and nodded.

"Secret Service will usher them here, Mr. President," Quinn remarked. "When we're finished, they will be escorted out."

"And then?" Truman asked.

"And then we put them to work, sir," he responded directly.

Truman nodded his head gravely. It looked as if he was going to make another comment, but a knock on the door interrupted the conversation. "Enter," Truman called.

Major Hale, smartly dressed in his Army-issue officer's uniform, came in closing the door behind him. He snapped to attention as soon as he saw the President.

"At ease, Major," Truman said casually.

"Yes sir," Hale responded. Then he walked across the room to shake hands with his Commander-in-Chief and Colonel Quinn.

"Glad you could make it, Curly," Quinn said as he shook his hand. "I'll bet Colonel Rodgers was happy to see your release come through. Your black eyes are coming along nicely. How's the head?"

"Better thanks and yes, she was over the moon to get rid of me," he answered with a smile. Then clearing his throat, "I'm not exactly sure why I'm here, Mr. President. No thanks are necessary as I was just doing my job, but the Colonel here made it seem like an offer I couldn't refuse."

"You didn't tell him?" President Truman asked Quinn.

"No sir, he would have hopped the first transport out of town if I did."

"Colonel, what's going on?" Hale asked with suspicion. "I'm beginning to feel my fight-or-flight response kicking in."

A knock on the door interrupted the conversation once again and once again the command to enter was given. All three men looked up to see a Secret Service agent guide an emerald-eyed beauty by the elbow into the room and then quietly withdraw. Hale's mouth fell open before the door had even closed behind her as he saw his one-time interviewee standing in the living quarters of the President of the United States.

Tamar looked uncomfortable at best with her back stiff and chin slightly raised. She hated ceremonies and felt completely out of her element here. Uncle Yazzie said that she could not refuse. To do so would be a great insult. Then he had reminded her, again, that it was her own rash actions that put her in this situation. However, every nerve in her body was acutely aware that she was at a distinct disadvantage in this place. It was, after all, a virtual fortress in a foreign nation and that was never a good place for an agent to be.

Hale's face was one of complete confusion as President Truman broke the awkward meeting by walking to Tamar and taking her hand. "So good to see you again, my dear." As they joined the two others in the room, he continued, "I can see by the look on each of your faces that you did not expect to see one another here. Good, that was by design."

"You!" Hale directed at Tamar. "It was you? You were the one fighting the other woman at the scene. How? Why were you even there?" Tamar remained mute as the light went on. "You hit me!"

"You were going to shoot me!"

"How was I to know whose side you were on?"

Truman interrupted the outburst with a wave of his hand as Tamar muttered under her breath, "You deserved it." Hale ceased his questions and looked embarrassed to have made such an outcry in front of the President.

"My apologies, sir."

"Of course. Of course. Quite understandable under the circumstances." Then he gestured to Quinn to explain.

"You were both responsible for saving the President's life. So, he felt both of you should be rewarded for your brave and unselfish efforts to protect him. You were brought here to avoid the normal White House chatter. You are to both receive a medal for your actions that day. You can never wear them or even disclose that you have been awarded them. Do you understand?"

"Sir," Tamar protested, "I am not an American citizen and should not be here receiving this honor."

"I was only doing my job…" Hale began at the same moment.

"Too late, it's already done," Truman said, effectively cutting off their appeals. He held out his hand to Quinn, who returned the small black cases to the President. He opened each box to display the handsome metals to Hale and Tamar. "It is with great honor and appreciation that I present the Legion of Merit medal on behalf of the American people to you Major Donald Hale and you Tamar Shimon for acts of heroism above and beyond the call of duty on February 1, 1947. A grateful nation thanks you." And with that, the boxes were presented to Hale and Tamar with each appearing a little chagrined.

"Thank you is simply not enough," Truman continued. "You both have my eternal gratitude. We have no idea how dramatically our nation may have changed had the assassins succeeded. So once again thank you for myself, my family, my friends, and our country."

"Thank you, Mr. President," Hale began. "I don't know what to say."

"Thank you is more than sufficient, Major. And it is I who thanks you."

Tamar looked up at Truman, tears glistening in her eyes. "I can't possibly accept this, Mr. Truman. I only did what anyone else would have done," she explained in a voice just above a whisper. "Awards like this should be reserved for Americans like Major Hale."

"You can and you will," Truman corrected her. "That medal represents the gallant action of the person receiving it. It is no respecter of race, creed, or national origin. The world would have changed drastically had you not intervened on my behalf and the assassins succeeded. History would have been forever altered for our children and our children's children. Now, please tell me that you will receive this honor on my behalf."

"Of course, Mr. President. I am honored," Tamar said, finally succumbing to his wishes.

"Wonderful," Truman said with a smile as he clapped his hands together. "Now, I had better get back to the Oval Office before anyone notices I have exceeded my free time. Just remember that everything you two do from here on out is a vital part of the history of America and the world."

"Sir?" Hale asked politely, as the comment caught him off guard.

"Colonel Quinn will fill you in on the details." And with that the President left the room, closing the door behind him. Hale and Tamar both turned their gazes on Quinn, looking for an explanation.

"I'm sure you both have questions but let me save some time and answer a few of them right now." To Major Hale he said, "Curly, you probably wonder how and why Tamar is here?"

"Well, yes sir. I mean, she was taken from my custody by…"

Quinn held up his hand to stop Hale before he could continue.

"I am well aware of how and why she was released from your custody. And no, it wasn't my signature on the paperwork, however, that's another story for another day. She was on assignment for one of our allies in the Middle East when you found her. I'm certain she can give you the particulars later."

"Yes sir," Hale responded accordingly while thinking there was no chance in hell she was going to tell him anything.

"Tamar, you don't know me, but I have been appraised of your work from an impeccable source. Therefore, I have agreed to accept your qualifications for the task ahead."

"Task? What task?"

"You now work for me. More succinctly you now work for President Truman, and he has put you under my command."

"Excuse me," Tamar stammered. "I work for no one. I'm just…"

Quinn once again interrupted and put up his hand to silence her protest. "We are well aware of who you are. You work for Menachem Begin of the Irgun in Palestine."

Hale looked as surprised as Tamar at this news. Tamar was stunned and tried quickly to cover her shock. "I do not know who this person is, nor the organization you speak of," she said firmly.

"Don't bother, Tamar," Quinn said. "An ambassador was sent by the President to Begin. He is most pleased to offer the services of one of his agents to assist the United States of America in whatever capacity the President, or I, see fit."

"I am confused," Tamar admitted, unconvinced.

"I am too, Colonel," Hale added anxiously. "The Irgun is a terrorist organization. Why would we be dealing with them at all?"

"They are patriots, fighting to regain the rights to their Country," Tamar shot back quickly.

"They are blowing up buildings that are the property of the British government —our allies throughout the war," Hale retorted hotly.

"That's enough, both of you," Quinn ordered.

"Yes, sir," Curly responded, trying to cap his animus.

Quinn handed each of them a small envelope. "I want you both to report to the address in these envelopes at 1800 hours this evening. You will meet the other members of your team and your orders will be assigned at that time."

"Team? What team? What are you talking about, Colonel?" Tamar asked impatiently. "Until I hear from my people, I don't work for you and even if they confirm what you are saying, I never work with a team!"

"You do now," he said in a voice that brooked no argument.

Hale jumped in. "And I already have a team in Germany, Colonel. Am I being reassigned?"

"Everything will be explained tonight. For now, all you need to know is that you two will be working together until further notice."

"You can't be serious, sir. We don't even know what her involvement was at that farmhouse," Hale protested. "We investigated two bloodbaths within twenty-four hours of meeting her. That can't be a coincidence."

Tamar was nonchalantly checking her nails as he spoke until he hit on some new information. "Two? What are you talking about?"

Hale ignored her interest. "Who's going to carry on the work I was doing? We were close to something, Colonel, really close." At Quinn's silence he added, "Besides, she's a woman, sir!"

"Thank you for noticing," Tamar remarked cynically.

"Trust me, it wasn't a compliment," he replied irritably. "Women, as you have already proven several times over, are nothing but trouble."

"You're just angry because I got the better of you. Imagine that a mere woman getting the better of an invincible Army Major."

"You had to be *rescued* from me in Germany, sweetheart, by a man, as I recall," he reminded her sarcastically. His voice lowered, and he leaned forward so he was in her face. But Tamar didn't give an inch. "What happened in that farmhouse? Tell me that. Why were you there?"

"Why were you there?" she shot back, undeterred.

As tempers flared, the two of them looked as if they were about to engage in a full-fledged brawl. *I would have loved to have been a fly on the wall of that interrogation,* Quinn thought. *Mac's friend may have saved Curly from the brig by removing her when he did – method notwithstanding.*

"That's enough! Have you forgotten where you are standing right now? This is the living quarters of the President of the United States. He has given me explicit orders to put you on a team of special investigators. You *will* accept those orders and you *will* comply with those orders. Do I make myself clear?"

"Yes sir," Hale answered, breathing deeply. "Crystal clear, sir."

"Yes Colonel," Tamar responded, quietly seething. "I understand. I will check with my employer to verify my orders."

Quinn inwardly smiled at her tenacity. "Good. Now take the rest of the day off until this evening. I expect both of you to be there on time and with proper attitudes. Informal civilian attire. Understood?"

Hale and Tamar both begrudgingly acknowledged the order, even though their expressions clearly indicated they were not pleased with this unexpected turn of events. At the moment, Quinn was not sure he was pleased either.

Tonight's meeting will certainly be interesting, he thought to himself. *Interesting indeed.*

CHAPTER 18

Curly pulled the collar of his coat up against the biting cold, then checked his watch. He was early. Per the sealed instructions received from Quinn (at the medal ceremony that never happened) he was waiting on the designated corner for his contact. He had done a walk by the address earlier in the day, just to check it out.

Quinn had made arrangements for the meeting to be held at a newly acquired (if the bright red sold sign was to be believed) property off Maryland Avenue just outside the downtown area of Washington, D.C. Curly knew the CIG had several such properties, but they were constantly being bought and sold to ensure that their purpose would remain under wraps. Hale had heard it rumored that J. Edgar Hoover had his agents seeking out these same assets, necessitating the need for the constant changing of properties.

Hoover's FBI owned an extensive array of strategically located apartments and homes throughout the city that served as a very sophisticated system of observation points. This system negated the need for FBI agents to physically follow suspected individuals while they were in the Capital. They were simply observed from the shadows and passed from one observation point to the next along the way. The suspects were anyone Hoover deemed a threat to his power as Director of the Federal Bureau of Investigation.

While under the authority of former OSS Director William "Wild Bill" Donovan, many homes and apartments had been used to make sure his people were not being monitored by either foreign assets or the FBI. When the OSS was disbanded to make way for the SSU and eventually the CIG, Magruder and then Quinn carried on the practice and made certain new unknown properties were routinely acquired. If it was suspected that Hoover's people had discovered one of these properties, it was immediately sold, and a new location purchased. It was a constant cat-and-mouse game between the CIG and FBI.

Hale was checking his watch again when he heard a breathless. "Oh darling, am I late?" His disgust for what he could only assume was Quinn's warped sense of humor was at an all-time high as Tamar approached, putting her hands against his chest, and leaning in for a soft kiss that lingered a few seconds too long. She pulled back slightly and said, smiling slyly, "I'm just working our cover."

A bit annoyed that this woman seemed to have a talent for getting under his skin, Hale decided that if that's how she wanted to play it, he was one hundred percent on board. So, he wrapped his arm around her waist and pulled her close, planting a warm seductive kiss on her lips.

"Do that again," Tamar said as she tucked her hand in the crook of his arm and turned to walk to the rendezvous point, "and die."

"Just working our cover," he said with a broad grin as he patted her hand.

They walked up to the door of the mid-town house arm in arm five minutes before the assigned time of 1800 hours per Colonel Quinn. Curly was about to knock when loud animated voices were heard inside, stopping his hand in midair. He was not amused when he saw Tamar immediately lean in and put her ear to the door. She was eavesdropping on whoever was already inside.

"What do you think you're doing?" he whispered fiercely.

"Shhhh. I'm trying to hear," she replied firmly.

"Are you out of your mind? We do not listen at the door when our superiors are in discussion," he stressed angrily.

"Then how in the world do you ever find out what they don't want you to know?" she shot back at him.

The argument inside grew louder until Curly and Tamar could both clearly hear Quinn say, "Do you have any other surprise information you haven't told me about yet?"

They did not know who he was questioning, but it was apparent he was furious. Hale had seen Quinn in such situations, and it was never pretty. He expected full disclosure from his men and demanded full revelation of any information attained so it could be utilized efficiently. How could he make intelligent decisions, he reasoned, without all the information? After all, any withheld information could be the difference between life and death for one of his agents, and that was simply unacceptable.

The door suddenly swung open, and Quinn found Tamar stumbling backward at his presence. Hale caught her before she tumbled from the porch, and both now looked at Quinn like children caught with their hands in the proverbial cookie jar. Both were desperately searching for something to say in their defense; however, Quinn did not wait.

"It's about time you two got here," he said irritably. He looked at his watch and noted that it said 1805 hours. "When I say 1800 hours, I mean 1800 hours. Or have you forgotten how to keep time, Major?"

"My apologies, sir," Hale stammered.

"It was my fault, Colonel…" Tamar interjected.

"I don't care whose fault it was. Get in here."

Hale was somewhat stunned at Tamar's sudden defense but decided to remain quiet. He had no desire to make the situation any more uncomfortable with his superior officer. But he did throw a glance at Tamar, wondering what she was up to.

"Take off your coats and get comfortable then I'll introduce you to your new team."

Tamar stepped inside, then stopped dead in her tracks as she immediately recognized Mac, Helen, and her uncle standing in the living room. She was left speechless as she attempted to hide her complete and utter surprise. Hale, however, did not try to suppress his feelings when he recognized Yazzie in the room.

"Colonel," he said to Quinn. "That's the man who illegally took Tamar from my custody!"

Yazzie stepped forward and offered Hale his hand. "Yitzhak Shimon at your service, Major."

Hale left Yazzie's hand hanging as he proceeded to berate him for his illegal activities. "You forged those transfer papers, didn't you?"

"Yes. It was done in a hurry, but it was a rather exceptional job if I do say so myself," he replied proudly.

"Yazzie is remarkable. Such attention to detail," Helen beamed.

"I know who he is," Quinn interrupted before Hale could protest any more. "And before you go any further, no, I was not told of the subterfuge until after it had taken place. No, I did not appreciate it. No, I would not have approved it, but after a full briefing by Mr. Shimon and Mac I understood its necessity."

"You're defending his actions, Colonel?"

"Not without significant consternation, Major," Quinn admitted.

"I hear we are on the same team now, Major. Perhaps we can dispense with prior distrusts that we may move forward for the common good," Yazzie added. Then he turned to Tamar. "I am certain you are as surprised as the Major, Plymenytse," he said.

"I am, Uncle. I do not understand."

Hale suddenly understood why Tamar and Yazzie had the same last names. They were related! "Oh, this just gets better and better," he lamented. "Keeping secrets is a family tradition with you two!"

"Keeping secrets keeps us alive," Tamar replied hotly. "We were fighting the Nazis and their reign of terror years before you Americans decided to grace us with your presence!"

"That's enough," Quinn barked at them. "I don't want to spend another second playing referee to your incessant squabbling! Do I make myself clear?"

"Yes, sir," Hale responded begrudgingly.

"Yes, sir," Tamar echoed.

Mac had followed the conversation with interest. The idea of pulling this disparate group into a cohesive unit seemed highly unlikely at the moment, but stranger things had happened of late…much stranger.

Mac stepped forward and offered his hand to Hale, who accepted and shook it graciously. "I have followed your career, Major. It's quite impressive."

"Thank you, sir. And you are?"

"This is Brigadier General John Magruder. He was my predecessor at the CIG," Quinn explained.

"Oh! Of course, sir," Hale responded, more than a little embarrassed that he didn't recognize his former commander. "I have heard a lot about you. My pleasure, sir."

"And this is Helen, my wife, and partner in espionage," Mac added with a smile as Helen stepped forward and offered her hand. Hale took her hand gently and inclined his head slightly.

"My pleasure, ma'am."

"Helen is just fine, Major. Or may I call you Curly, as Colonel Quinn does?"

"Curly is perfectly acceptable, ma'am…I mean Helen."

"Wonderful. Now that we're all friends, perhaps we should get down to the reason we're all here," Helen suggested as she sat on a sofa with a protective sheet still draped over it.

The rest of the people gathered in the room assented to Helen's suggestion and found places to seat themselves in the disheveled room. When everyone seemed at ease, Quinn started the conversation.

"All right. Tamar, I know you're already familiar with Mac and Helen. I understand they have been your hosts since you arrived in Washington. Curly, you and I are the late comers to this group. While I will be your primary contact, Mac here will call the shots in the field. Is that understood?"

"Understood sir. But may I ask what we are expected to accomplish as a team?"

Quinn waved his hand to Mac, who stood up and began to pace back and forth in the room. "Curly, we believe that you and Tamar may have come across vital information in Germany that needs to be investigated further."

"I don't understand," Tamar related hesitantly. "What does my investigation have to do with Major Hale or with you? I was on a different assignment for a different entity. I do not understand the mutual interests," she said honestly.

"And we don't expect you to," Mac answered directly. "Let me explain. Major Hale has been on assignment to find any remaining German scientists who were working on the Nazi nuclear program and return them to the United States as soon as possible. It is imperative that these scientists not fall into the hands of the Soviet Union. If they were to develop an atomic bomb such as we have it could be catastrophic for us and the rest of the world."

"But if you already have a bomb and have shown that you are willing to use it, why should you fear the Soviets?" she questioned rationally.

"Stalin willingly sacrificed millions of his people to achieve victory over Hitler in the war. If he is willing to continue that trend, we could expect him to use that weapon despite our possible retaliation. The numbers are greatly in favor of the USSR. We, however, are not willing to put millions of American lives in that kind of sick mathematical equation."

"What do you want us to do, sir?" Hale asked.

"You're to return to Germany as a team."

"To what end?" Tamar inquired.

"I have been informed by Yazzie that you hid something of special interest at the farmhouse outside Fussen."

Tamar did not withhold her displeasure with her uncle for divulging the information she had provided him. "That is the property of the Jewish people," she protested. "I found it. I claimed it in the name of my people."

"A reasonable claim," Mac admitted. "However, we have reason to believe there is more at stake here than a few uncut diamonds."

"Uncut diamonds," Hale blurted. "What uncut diamonds?"

"Tamar," Mac said, yielding the floor to her.

With all eyes on her, she grudgingly spoke. "When I was in Berlin, I saw Herr Bergmann stash the diamonds in his satchel. I decided to follow him to see where it would lead."

"That was wise thinking," Helen complimented her.

"Thank you, Helen," she answered.

"How did you even recognize uncut diamonds?" Hale asked, almost dismissively.

"My family has been in the jewelry business for generations," Yazzie intervened. "My brother, Tamar's father, owned a jewelry store. If she said she recognized them as uncut diamonds, you can, what is the American term? Take it to the bank."

Hale seemed somewhat mollified at the explanation. He then turned back to Mac. "So, you want us to go pick up the diamonds."

"Correct, that is if they are still there. If the premises have been searched by other interested parties, then they may already be gone. That would be most unfortunate."

Quinn then stood and handed Hale and Tamar each a large packet of documents. "You two go find out about those diamonds. The rest of the team is looking into something else."

"Something else?" Hale questioned.

"Need to know, Curly," Quinn replied evenly.

"There has to be a reason Bergmann was carrying those diamonds," Mac inserted. "We need to know where they came from, where they were going, and what they were to finance. But first, we need to acquire the diamonds themselves. Are you two up to the task?"

"Yes, sir," Hale answered affirmatively.

"Of course," Tamar agreed.

"You know," began Mac, "during the war, the allies bombed a production center that halted the German's ability to make jet rockets that could have reached London. Had they succeeded in producing those rockets we would have most certainly lost the war. The Germans were so far ahead of us in every scientific field. We had no idea what their true capabilities were back then."

"As I recall," Quinn added, "it wasn't until we captured the property that we found out what they had been doing deep underground. Those V-3 rockets never got the chance to be fully implemented because we accidentally bombed the site thinking it was something else entirely. That accident saved thousands if not millions of lives."

"This is the first I've heard of it," Helen enjoined.

"The point is," Mac continued, "that we stopped the total destruction of London, and it was an accident. We had no idea what they had or what their capabilities were."

Yazzie stood up and looked at Hale and Tamar before stating, "I believe the hope is that you two may have such an accident. Perhaps God himself will be on our side and we can prevent innocent deaths once again."

Mac looked at Hale and Tamar, sighed, and said, "I don't relish putting you in harm's way. But it seems we are still in a war of sorts and need information. You will need to rely on one another. God's speed."

Quinn added, "You leave on a military transport tomorrow at 1200 hours. You will make connections in London before going on to Frankfurt. Transportation will be waiting for you there. Do what you need to do," Quinn instructed. "Oh, and you are to work as a team, understand? If I find out you've gone your separate ways, there will be hell to pay."

With that, Quinn dismissed Hale and Tamar from the meeting. "Make sure you're not followed," he advised, as the door closed behind them. He turned to look at Mac. "You didn't mention the aliens I noticed."

"I did not. If this is truly connected, they will find out on their own. It's better that way. Why waste time trying to convince them when 'seeing is believing' is more to their liking?"

"That's certainly true of Curly. Tamar, I don't know."

"My niece has always been very inquisitive," Yazzie mentioned. "If there is a connection, she will find it."

"I still don't like the idea that you sprang this on me tonight, Mac. You should have told me earlier that untold numbers of aliens were already interfering in human affairs. And the fact that one of them was working in the White House is nauseating. President Truman has made the investigation into White House infiltration our number one priority."

"As I told you, Bill, we didn't know ourselves, or I would have told you. You said the female killed in the assassination attempt was working in the War Department. That shows clear intent to interfere with our military response. That's not good, but it gives us a place to start."

"I went to the morgue personally and spoke with the M.E. I saw the body," Quinn said. "There is no question she was alien. No doubt whatsoever. The man is as human as you or I. He worked in the same department but in a different division. Why he would agree to work with her is still undetermined."

"Well, I am told he should be available for questioning tomorrow. He came through surgery and is recovering. We can ask him ourselves," Mac advised. "I want to get as much information out of him as I can before we have him executed for treason."

CHAPTER 19

Colonel Quinn arrived at the Oval Office precisely thirty minutes prior to his scheduled meeting with President Truman. If the President's current meeting ended early, Quinn wanted any extra time he could get with the Commander-in-Chief. Truman's secretary, Rose, made Quinn comfortable and served him a cup of coffee while he waited.

Not one to waste time, he had brought a dossier to occupy the half hour before his assigned time just in case. The intelligence community seemed to be moving even faster than it did during the war, and he needed to keep abreast of any new pertinent information that might become available. And, of course, now there was the other thing.

As if scouring all of Europe locating Nazi scientists that could upset the global balance of power if they fell into the wrong hands wasn't enough. Now he had to worry about hostile aliens infiltrating the nation. The idea that two members of the War Department were working for hostile powers sent chills down his spine. He wasn't certain what was more disturbing, finding that one of them was indeed an alien or that one of them was human. Why would someone side with an alien race whose goal was presumably to conquer the planet? That question would be one of many asked when Quinn interrogated him later today.

The doctors had assured him that the man, now identified as George Piper, would be coherent enough for questions after noon today. He was certain Truman would want all available information as soon as possible. They had to find out just how long this had been going on, who else was involved, and what their ultimate goals were. It was not going to be a pleasant interrogation for Mr. Piper.

Rose looked up from her desk and nodded at Quinn as she responded to the intercom. He was hopeful the President was available already. It would give him an extra fifteen precious minutes with Truman, and that was significant.

"The President will see you now, Colonel," Rose invited pleasantly. "Would you like another cup of coffee? I can bring it to you."

"No thank you, Rose. I think I'm wired enough already."

And with that Rose opened the door to the Oval Office and Quinn went inside. The President was on the telephone dealing with an obstinate senator – as usual. They all wanted inside information as to the President's plans. But Truman knew only too well that any information shared could wind up in the Washington papers as front-page headlines. Unfortunately, some congressmen thought getting their name in the limelight for a short spell was well worth the risk to national security.

Truman waved Quinn to the chair in front of his desk as he promised they would discuss the Senator's issues at length later, then hung up. "It's no wonder Americans don't like politicians," he remarked offhandedly. "I don't like them either and I'm one of them!"

Quinn nodded in agreement as he sat down opposite the President.

"What have you got for me, Bill?"

"His name is George Piper. He also works in the War Department here in the White House which is damn scary. I plan to question him this afternoon. The doc just wants the drugs to wear off enough so he can hear and understand. He says it does no one any good if he's still out of his mind on pain medication."

"Understandable," Truman replied as the gravity of the situation weighed on him.

"Mac's team is going to search both of their living quarters, unofficially of course, to see if there are any leads as to who was holding their leash. Lt. Hornsby will be working with Secretary of War Patterson to quietly investigate what each of our assassins was working on. Neither Patterson nor Hornsby has been read in on the full story with Miss Martin. They were just told that we had been unable to contact her since she left and because her sudden departure was so close to the incident, they should look at her work with extreme prejudice."

"Very good," Truman said. "Has Miss Martin's body been dealt with?"

"Yes, there's no evidence she was ever in the morgue. The paper trail shows the unidentified female body delivered by the Secret Service was accidentally cremated – a paperwork error by the grieving Doctor Zimmerman. They were not happy by the way. The error is what caused him to retire and move to parts unknown."

"And Zimmerman is on board?"

Quinn shrugged. "He met the transport as instructed. He and Captain Jensen both seem a little shell-shocked at the sudden turn their lives have taken, but they and their packages made it to Nevada without incident. I'm attending to the sale of his house and transport of his belongings personally."

"It's damn unsettling that two traitors could be walking the halls of the Capital with us, and no one had a clue," Truman said as he leaned back in his chair. "It certainly gives my critics some validity. Of course, they are only referring to being soft on the communist threat but in light of what we now know, I'm thinking that checking the backgrounds of Federal employees might be a prudent move. Without question, I'll have to limit J. Edgar and the FBI's involvement."

The President was silent a moment as the details of such an endeavor sifted through his head. Then realizing time was passing, and he hadn't yet expressed the reason for this meeting, he sat forward and continued. "Listen Bill, with all that has been going on I am more convinced than ever that changes are needed in our intelligence operations."

"I would concur with that, Mr. President. What do you have in mind?"

"You know J. Edgar believes all intelligence services should be under his authority."

"Yes. He fought President Roosevelt tooth and nail over Bill Donovan's appointment to head the Strategic Services Unit. He doesn't like sharing intelligence duties."

"Exactly. He tried repeatedly to stop the formation of the OSS. And did his best to convince FDR that there was no need for any intelligence service besides his FBI. Fortunately, the President disregarded his advice. The OSS proved to be a major contributor to our victory over the Axis powers."

"I understand that he approached you as well about disbanding the Strategic Services Unit before we became the Central Intelligence Group. He still thinks his organization is better qualified for foreign intelligence gathering than we are."

"I wholeheartedly disagree, Bill. In fact, I have been drawing up plans for another separation of intelligence powers in America. I've been working on this since September of '45 and it's still a work in progress. The reality is that we need an entire intelligence community, not just one intel group. Even though I don't fully trust J. Edgar, I do believe we need an intelligence gathering service stateside. In my estimation, that should be the FBI. Do you agree?"

"I have no reason to disagree, Mr. President. Hoover seems to have his finger on the pulse of everything going on in this country and that's certainly needed for domestic surveillance."

"My thoughts as well. However, in the face of what we now know to be a viable new foreign enemy, I think we need a better division of intelligence duties."

"What do you have in mind?"

"I am convinced we need competitive intelligence services."

"I'm not sure what you mean, Mr. President," Quinn admitted.

"Basically, it means we need the division of intelligence services so they can keep one another honest so to speak. This will also make it much harder for any one of the agencies to be misled."

"So that we're not depending on just one source," Quinn reasoned.

"And we'd have more than one intelligence director. If Hoover had his way, he would be the dictator over all related intelligence operations in America. I cannot let that happen. It's far too dangerous to have only one man in charge of such sensitive material. We need separate agencies with separate leadership. No one person should be in charge of all intelligence gathering. It's safer that way."

"You won't get any arguments from me, Mr. President. The OSS fought Hoover over every bit of information we obtained. He was adamant that he be informed of all our operations. Frankly, Wild Bill never trusted Hoover and after dealing with his various shenanigans for four years, I don't trust him either. He seems prepossessed with personal power. That's dangerous, in my humble opinion."

"Exactly. When Igor Gouzenko defected to the Allies, he showed us where our intel services lacked cohesiveness. Hell, he knew before we did that Russian spies were working on the Manhattan Project. Spies who were filtering information to Stalin about our new secret weapon! Our secret project was leaking like a sieve!" Truman exclaimed.

"And he brought proof that Russia was no ally. Stalin had his mind set on world domination. He was no different from Hitler in that respect, Mr. President."

"And when Lt. General Gehlen gave up his Nazi intelligence, he showed us photographic evidence of the Soviet's infiltration of the project. Didn't you work with Bill Donovan on that info?"

"I did, sir. It was damned frightening what that ex-Nazi general provided to us. At the time it was decided not to reveal the information to President Roosevelt for security reasons."

"Because of Vice-President Wallace, I know," Truman admitted. "When I was read in on the account it was shocking to see what the Soviets had been able to steal from our program. I was not as shocked to learn that Wallace was suspected as a Communist sympathizer."

"More than that, sir. Several members of the OSS were convinced Wallace was acting as a Soviet asset in the White House. We couldn't let him know what we had learned from the Nazis at that point."

"May God help us, Colonel. We just can't let ourselves be duped that way again. But I think I have a way to strengthen our intelligence position against both the Soviets and our new alien enemies. The American public can never know we are still fighting on two fronts."

"I agree, sir. But how do we do that effectively?"

"I want the FBI to keep to the domestic side of intelligence services. But our foreign strategy needs some revamping to accommodate our new alien threat. We're already facing the onslaught of the Soviet Union. Stalin has it in his mind to rule the world just like Hitler did as you mentioned before. There is no doubt in my mind about that."

"Agreed," Quinn replied. "But what can we do to keep the Russians under the microscope while simultaneously trying to assess the alien threat? We're already spread very thin, Mr. President."

"I know you are, Bill. That's why I want to create new agencies that can cover all areas identified as threats. The key is to keep the American public from knowing we have this new threat. They're already worried we may wind up in another world war because of Stalin. Any new threats could prove disheartening right as the economy is beginning to recover."

"I don't have to tell you that we can't possibly maintain intelligence superiority with what we have," Quinn asserted. "What new agencies do you propose? And how do you view the division of duties?"

"First, we need an agency to guard our communications. Leaps and bounds are being made in this area and as technology increases this may become vital. Secondly, someone is needed to monitor our own military intelligence so we can stay ahead of all foreign adversaries. Lastly, we need to continue collecting data from our enemies and assessing their strategies so we can adapt and prepare adequate defenses for the nation. This group would be responsible for keeping senior officials appraised of any new foreign threats. Right now, that's what you do as the CIG."

"Yes, sir. How would that change, if I may ask?"

"I'm still working on it, Bill. This plan is still on the drawing board right now. But I think we need an organized and efficient intelligence community to battle the forces ahead of us. We want to be as proactive as possible, so the United States doesn't find itself behind the eight ball again. Luck may have been on our side with Germany and Japan, but I don't want to assume we'll have the same good fortune with the Russians. And then there are the aliens. They are a huge unknown. We must move and move quickly."

"Question, sir. How do we pay for all this? We're on a shoestring budget as it is. As you say, the economy is on the upswing, however, I can't see Congress allocating new monies when the country is still in debt from the war. And it's been my experience, sir, that most of Congress doesn't see or understand the importance of funding the intelligence community."

"I have been questioning that myself, Bill. Franklin had a knack for acquiring and spending money from dubious sources throughout his career. I'm afraid I'm just a simple businessman at heart and have no predilection for such activities. And it's not just funding for intelligence operations at stake. Many European nations have been decimated by the war and need help. Mac was right when he said that destroying a nation through war was a good way to weaken their defenses and ready them for a takeover. And I fear that the aliens aren't the only ones looking at this as a golden opportunity." Truman stopped and looked keenly at Quinn. "I'll have to deal with Congress on appropriations but I'm certainly open to suggestions."

"Well, sir," Quinn said with a sly smile. "How would you feel about financing our activities with an enemy's money?"

Truman laughed. "Well, that sounds promising. But just exactly how are we to obtain this windfall from our enemies?"

"This may be a long shot, but what do you know about converting uncut diamonds to cash, Mr. President?"

CHAPTER 20

Mac and Yazzie surveilled the area around George Piper's home with interest. It was nothing like the cheap apartment at the address listed on his personnel form with the Department of War. However, information garnered at the apartment led them here, thanks to a meticulous examination of the rubbish can in the hallway by Helen. A scribbled note from the attorney that handled Piper's recent divorce indicated he did not know which address to use for correspondence. The attorney had been very apologetic, but his office's small oversight provided their clue to the existence of a second residence. It was a far cry from the compact studio apartment.

The exterior of the old two-story Victorian home was in immaculate shape. It looked as if it had recently been painted and the ornate gingerbread metal trim newly refurbished. The grounds seemed perfectly manicured, with plentiful plants and trees even though they were now mostly dormant. Mac and Yazzie both wondered how a man holding a low-level job in the War Department could afford a place in this upscale neighborhood. It would be the first of several questions pondered before they left Mr. Piper's home.

Helen walked up to the men and showed them a house key. She proceeded up the seven front steps onto the wraparound porch. There she easily opened the front door. Mac and Yazzie smiled in approval of her ability to finagle the key from a next-door neighbor who had revealed that it was she who sold the house to Piper a couple of years ago. Helen could be very convincing as a mother looking in on her son. Mrs. Pettigrew was more than happy to help, especially since Mr. Piper had never mentioned his simply lovely mother before.

Helen noted the historic Victorian interior was pristine. Antique chandeliers in the entry way and dining room lent authenticity as well as warm subdued lighting. Decorative wall sconces and Tiffany lamps were in each room. Rooms were dressed in rich floral wallpapers and heavy brocade draperies. Beautiful tapestries adorned the walls and only served to enhance the glistening, well-polished parquet floors. This was not the home of an entry-level worker on a budget.

"Did Piper come from money or did a rich relative leave him a boatload of cash?" Yazzie asked.

"No," Helen answered. "I did a pretty thorough background check on him. I couldn't find any relatives, living or otherwise. He's originally from Saginaw, Michigan according to his birth certificate. There were death certificates on file for both parental names listed, but not much else."

"Well, something's not right," Mac observed as he wondered if the oil painting to his right was authentic. "There's no way he could afford a place like this on his modest salary."

"Makes you wonder where he got the money, doesn't it?" Yazzie asked sarcastically. "At least we can now assume he was in it for the pay off and not the cause."

"Hmm, it's strange, isn't it? This home is over the top ornate and the lady assassin's place was simply stark," Helen observed. "Complete opposites. I wondered when we were there if someone had cleaned it out before we got there. And I'm absolutely certain I've seen a key like the one we found before."

"One odd-looking key from an alien's apartment is not much to go on," Yazzie returned.

"That's why we're here," Mac responded. "He managed to hide his collusion with an enemy like a pro. So, if he's hiding something here we need to find it. Look for anything out of the ordinary that may lead us to his handler."

"Handler?" Helen asked.

"The person that was in contact with him and gave him his assignments. Like we do now for Major Hale and Tamar. We need to find this person and work our way up the chain of command."

"I've never thought of myself as a handler before. I'm not sure I like the responsibility. I don't like the idea of giving someone an assignment that could be dangerous. What if they get injured, and it's all my fault for putting them in that situation?"

Mac and Yazzie looked at one another and then back to Helen. Both men knew the consequences of sending operatives into harm's way. It was a burdensome responsibility that was never easy. And knowing what could happen, it never should be easy.

"Yazzie and I will take that responsibility, Helen. Your job is purely administrative right now; like obtaining the key to this house. It's a necessary function that Yazzie and I are not as well equipped to do."

Helen seemed agreeable to the division of duties. Yazzie smiled sorrowfully because he knew that even administrative obligations could be dangerous in certain circumstances.

As they walked through the house opening cabinets and rifling through drawers, Mac reminded them to track what they touched or moved and to be sure to return it to its original state. If someone else was maintaining a watch on the house, they didn't want to alert them to their presence. Yazzie simply smiled at the word of caution. He had done this many times in far more dangerous surroundings. But the prudence was still appropriate.

"I feel like I'm Basil Rathbone in a Sherlock Holmes movie," Helen remarked with a slight smile. "All I need is a large magnifying glass. Oh, and maybe the hat. A hat would be good."

"But you're not," Mac reminded her gently as they continued their methodical room-by-room search of the large premises.

On the second floor, Yazzie noticed a slightly crooked seam in an otherwise perfectly appointed walnut-paneled study. A closer inspection showed minute scratches along one side as if it had been moved or replaced at some time. He called for Mac and Helen to join him as he ran his fingers along the edges of the board. They watched as he pressed and prodded without success. Then he spied what he was looking for, an unused electrical outlet with a small, imbedded button. A press of the button produced a soft 'click' as the panel released and a door revealed itself. There was a single item inside, a locked metal box. Yazzie pulled the metal box out and set it on the desk.

"Now we're in a pickle," Helen observed. "I doubt Mrs. Pettigrew has a key for this."

Mac and Yazzie both smiled as if sharing an inside joke. Yazzie then reached into his jacket and removed a small pick from a black pocket-sized tool pouch.

"Just in case you weren't able to get a key from Mrs. Pettigrew," Yazzie explained to Helen with a smile. In less than five seconds the steel metal box lid was open and sharing its secrets. Inside were several documents and a small soft leather bag about six inches long with a draw string pulled tight to contain its contents.

Yazzie placed his handkerchief on the impressive oak desk, then opened the bag and emptied its contents. Out poured a sparkling stream of beautifully polished diamonds. All eyes were on the gems, winking up at them from the starched white material.

"They're beautiful," Helen admired. "But where would Piper get his hands on diamonds like this?"

"That's the ten-thousand-dollar question," Mac answered.

"More like a million-dollar question," Yazzie corrected as he selected one and held it up to the light. "I have never seen this many polished stones in one place, and my family's business was diamonds. Such clarity. I would need my glass eye to be absolutely certain, but I don't see a single flaw. This is simply inconceivable."

"Well, now we know how Piper got paid and how he could afford this house," Mac stated with surety. "There's no way he got these on his own. Somebody paid him with these diamonds, and you can be sure they don't want it widely known."

"But who?" Helen inquired.

Yazzie looked at Mac and said, "If they are not aware that Piper is in the hospital, they may not know these diamonds are at risk. That may explain why no one has come looking for them yet."

"My thoughts exactly," Mac confirmed.

"We need to know how he got them and how he turns them into cash," Yazzie observed. "But most importantly, we need to know their origin. Where they were mined may identify who's behind this."

Helen reached inside her purse and pulled out several envelopes. "I found this bank statement in his desk drawer at the apartment," Helen offered. "He has a small amount of cash in this account; nothing that would suggest he was anything but a paycheck-to-paycheck employee."

Then she held up three other envelopes for Mac and Yazzie to see. "But these accounts are quite different. I found them here and they are from three separate banks in the D.C. area. There are several thousand dollars in each account and each account is under a different name but with the same Post Office box address. He's hiding these accounts for a reason," Helen surmised.

Mac and Yazzie looked at Helen and smiled. She might be a female Sherlock Holmes, after all.

"Do any of those banks have a lien on this place?" Yazzie asked.

"Not that I can see. Just checking and savings accounts."

"Chances are he paid for this place in cash," Mac observed. "He could have done it himself or used a second person to handle the transaction."

"Like the mysterious lady assassin," Yazzie surmised. "They may have been working as a team, and who knows for how long."

"That's disconcerting," Helen said with a frown.

Mac straightened and went to look at the serene upper-class neighborhood from the study window as he thought. He stood to one side and pulled back the ornate silk drapes, scanning for anyone who might be monitoring Piper's home.

"You think someone else is watching the place?" Yazzie asked as the precious stones were returned to the leather bag.

"I think there's a good chance. And so, do you."

Yazzie nodded, admitting his thoughts.

Helen seemed disturbed and asked Mac, "What do we do now? If someone saw us come in here…"

"I know," Mac answered before she could finish. "We didn't bring the car, so no one can follow us home. But someone should stay here to see if anyone else is lurking about."

"I'll stay," Yazzie volunteered. "I'll take up a position in a corner of the property. I saw a good place on the way in. It's a little overgrown which will provide some cover, but I can see both the front and rear entrances from there.

"Okay, and I'll go meet Bill at the hospital," Mac said while checking his watch. "I told him I'd join him there when Piper was cleared for questioning. I don't want someone else to get there before we do."

"I'll return the key to Mrs. Pettigrew, then take the diamonds to the cabin," Helen declared as she carefully secured the small bag down the front of her dress. "We can decide what to do with them later."

Mac would have been amused at Helen's selected hiding place, but he was too concerned about leaving her on her own. "Don't linger. Don't get delayed with small talk. Return the key and get out. Transport the second it's safe."

Helen placed her hand on his wrist to calm him. "I'll be fine," she said quietly. "I'm not as foolish as you may think."

"All right," Mac agreed reluctantly as he came to grips with the fact that this was their life now. "Let's see what we can find out then we'll meet at 1600 hours. Agreed?"

Yazzie and Helen both nodded their ascent.

"That's 4:00, dear," Mac clarified to Helen with a grin.

"I know what it is, John Magruder," she said as she tweaked his arm. "I've been an army wife for nearly thirty years. I figured that time thing out long ago."

Then all three disappeared from the room.

CHAPTER 21

The hospital personnel at Walter Reed General Hospital had been given no information on George Piper. They didn't know his name, where he worked, or any other background information that Quinn had obtained thus far. This was strictly a need-to-know patient and quite frankly, they didn't need to know. Their only task was to keep the unfortunate gunshot victim alive long enough for Quinn to get some answers. This security wing was off-limits to the public and unauthorized hospital staff. Guards were on duty at the elevator to keep watch. No one got on this floor without identification proving they belonged there.

Quinn was already in the hallway by the nurse's station when Mac arrived. Both men had provided military I.D. to the guards and were allowed onto the wing without question. As usual, Quinn appeared agitated at having to wait for someone else to get something done.

"Have you been waiting long?" Mac asked Quinn.

"Too long, as far as I'm concerned. Some uppity second Lieutenant nurse told me to wait here until she got the doctor's approval for visitors."

"You think she's pulling rank on you, Bill?" Mac responded with a wry smile.

"You know better than that. I just spoke with the doctor not more than an hour ago, and he assured me Piper would be ready for us. He said he left orders with the nurses, but she acted like she had no idea what I was talking about."

A nurse looking to be in her late thirties or early forties with her dark hair swept back into a severe bun walked up to the men carrying a clipboard and looking very officious. "Have you been helped yet?" she asked.

Quinn jumped at the chance to get some answers. He looked at her I.D. badge and responded quickly. "Captain Miller, we're here to see the patient in room 225. Dr. McCallum told me on the phone that he would be awake and ready for questions by now. But when I tried to go to the room the short blonde nurse that bathed in a vat of perfume before her shift stopped me and said she needed to check with him again."

The Captain frowned and suddenly changed in demeanor. She looked quickly through the papers on her clipboard and then asked, "Did you get her name, sir?"

"I'm Quinn. Colonel Quinn," he responded. "And no. I didn't get her name. She came and went in a hurry. That was ten minutes ago, and she hasn't come back," he complained.

The Captain stepped behind the nurse's station and looked at the personnel roster. "I know every one of these girls," she announced. "And none of them would be wearing perfume on duty. It's against hospital regulations because of possible allergic reactions by the patients. I'd better go…"

The words weren't out of her mouth before Mac and Quinn went barreling down the shiny linoleum hallway to room 225. Captain Miller was right behind them, charging into the room. The heavy smell of sweet perfume still hung in the air.

One look at Piper's glassy-eyed stare and they all knew he was dead. "Oh my God," she breathed. A quick visual survey showed no physical signs of struggle or physical trauma. The nurse picked up a small broken vial from the floor.

"There's no label on this," she said, trying to contain the panic rising in her voice. "I have no idea what it is!"

Mac looked at the IV still in Piper's arm and surmised that the mystery nurse had injected something into the line, causing his death. The autopsy may provide a more precise answer but that did them no good now. He was dead, and the assassin was nowhere to be seen.

"Damn," Quinn cursed, as he ran his hand over his head. "Damn, damn, damn!"

"I need to get the doctor," the charge nurse exclaimed with her voice shaking as she rushed from the room.

"Where exactly did you run into this perfumed nurse?" Mac asked Quinn.

"A couple of rooms down from here," he answered while mentally kicking himself. "I told her I was here to see patient John Doe. She took me by the arm and led me back to the nurse's station and said to stay there until she came back with the doctor's approval."

"Damned clever girl," Mac observed. "Didn't panic, just delayed you long enough to do the job and waltz out of the hospital free as a bird. Professional."

"She played me for a fool," Quinn fumed while pacing the room.

Out of habit, Mac continued to check the room for any clues while waiting for the doctor. There wasn't much hope of finding anything after all the deed was done. The murderer had already come and gone, leaving nothing but the scent of her overpowering perfume behind. He opened the drawer beside the bed, empty.

"Well, at least now we know we're not on a wild goose chase," Mac told Quinn as he turned to the patient's closet. "Not that it's any comfort to…"

Mac's train of thought was abruptly shattered when a twist of the handle caused the door to slam open and a body to tumble out landing on his feet. He automatically jumped back from the corpse releasing his person from the touch of death. It was a young female, barefoot and dressed only in underclothing. Mac knelt down and checked for a pulse. Nothing.

"Dammit," Quinn said as he watched Mac shake his head in the negative.

Captain Miller reentered the room with Dr. McCallum on her heels. She screamed when she saw the body lying in a heap on the floor.

"Janet! That's Janet Baker! Oh, dear God!" she wailed as she rushed to the lifeless body. She gathered her in her arms and rocked back and forth while she wept aloud. Mac and Quinn stepped away, knowing there was absolutely nothing they could say or do to ease her pain.

Dr. McCallum tried to take in the horrific scene before him. His formerly recovering patient and a member of his staff both found dead in the same room. He automatically turned to rush from the room to call security when Quinn hooked his arm and stopped him.

"Doc," Quinn said quietly, "I've got this. Block off this corridor. No one enters. Where is there a phone I can use?"

The doctor choked out an order to the closest nurse to take Quinn to a phone before turning back to room 225. He was shaken to the core, no doubt about it, but he tried his best to maintain his composure in the crisis. He was aware that this patient was of special interest to the powers that be. However, he never expected two murders, not in this hospital.

"I have to call her husband," the distraught woman moaned. "I think I have his number. I have to let him know," she told Mac vacantly as he helped her from the floor.

"No, ma'am," he responded gently. "We'll take care of that."

"No, no I have to call him," she insisted, with the shock of the situation preventing her from comprehending his words.

"No Captain. You will not," Mac said with more force as he restrained her from leaving the room.

"Hey, there's no need for that," Doctor McCallum complained.

Quinn sprinted down the hall as he saw suspicious glances at the raised voices coming from room 225. He assured a curious young girl collecting lunch trays that all was well as he blocked her view with his body, then closed the door.

"What the hell? I leave for two minutes."

"Containment," Mac said with a shrug as he released the woman from his grasp.

Quinn took over command of the scene as Mac exited the room. Quinn explained to the doctor and his nurse that this was now a matter of national security, and the CIG was taking charge of the investigation. Autopsies would be performed on both bodies to determine the cause of death with the results forwarded directly to Quinn's office. They were no longer involved. His office would make any and all notifications and inquiries, and they absolutely would NOT speak of this event to anyone including friends, family, or the press under threat of incarceration.

Mac loitered in the hallway, smiling and nodding at hospital staff until Quinn's security team arrived. He barked a few orders, and they instantly obeyed. A man was posted at the door of room 225 to ensure the scene was completely sealed until further notice. The guards at the elevator would continue to monitor the corridor and deal with any unauthorized personnel seeking access.

Hospital staff were to be placed in isolation and questioned. Quinn instructed his men that any visitor present on the floor should also be detained if needed. The assassin's overuse of perfume might work in their favor in this case. Maybe someone would remember her through that factor alone. That damn woman got on this floor even with security, and he wanted to know how.

Transportation was quietly arranged to move the bodies from the hospital to the morgue and precautions were taken to ensure that the whole it-never-happened event was smoothed over. A car was dispatched to collect Mr. Baker from his place of employment and bring him in immediately. Quinn's staff was tasked with creating a plausible explanation for the sudden and unfortunate death of Lt. Janet Baker that would satisfy her shell-shocked husband.

Above all, it was to be kept out of the papers. Nosey reporters continuously watched the hospital, hoping to get a juicy bit of information on a well-known war criminal being brought in for treatment or some other event that could be spun into a sensational story. Anything to get tongues wagging about the tragedy, the family's suffering be damned.

"No one in without my written approval. And not a word to anyone," Quinn ordered the Sergeant now stationed outside room 225.

"Not a problem, sir," the Sergeant responded without uttering a single question.

It had been exactly 28 minutes since Mac had left George Piper's lovely Victorian home.

After the long flight to Frankfurt, Germany in a military transport plane both Hale and Tamar were exhausted. Little had been said on the trip as both agents were still adjusting to the idea of a partnership. Neither had much faith in the other yet both instinctively knew that to work as a team there had to be an element of respect and trust if they were to be effective. Working without it could mean the difference between life and death in their world.

As they exited the plane onto the tarmac Hale spotted a jeep parked on the side of the airfield waiting for them. His able assistant and friend Sergeant William McCann was leaning comfortably on the jeep with his long legs crossed at the ankles. He grinned broadly and walked from the jeep to Hale, saluted smartly, then shook Hale's hand.

"Would you be needing a ride, Major?" he asked jokingly.

"It's damn good to see you, Billy. Did the old man put you up to this?"

"Colonel Quinn thinks of everything, sir. I got my duty papers three days ago signed by the Colonel himself. I'm your personal escort for the duration."

"Three days ago," Tamar said in surprise. "That's before he even told us about the assignment!"

"That's the Colonel for you," Hale responded. "Always thinking ahead."

McCann hadn't zeroed in on the person that exited the plane with Hale until that moment. He was more than a little taken aback when he suddenly realized who was standing behind Hale on the tarmac. His bewildered look did not escape either of the travelers.

"Well, it's nice to see you again, Sergeant," Tamar stated conversationally. "It's always good to see a familiar face."

No explanation was offered as she politely held out her hand for McCann to shake. Then she pointed to her luggage as if McCann were a hotel concierge and walked directly to the jeep. She climbed in the back seat and waited for the two men to follow.

"It's probably none of my business, sir, but what the hell?"

"I'll fill you in later," Hale said with a heavy sigh. "It's a long story."

"I'll bet," McCann agreed. "Where to first, sir?"

"Let's go to Pullach and get billeting for the night. I'll need to grab a few things. Then we will head to Fussen first thing in the morning."

"You got it, boss," McCann answered lightly as he picked up Tamar's bag and tossed it in the jeep. Hale stowed his own rucksack and then slid into the passenger side.

Hale and McCann did all the talking on the ride to Pullach. Hale revealed as much about the assignment as allowed to let McCann know where they may be going. The sergeant took it all in and asked questions sparingly. It appeared to him they were resuming their search for Nazi nuclear scientists, although he could not figure out how Tamar fit into the puzzle.

"Have you guys had any incidents since I left?" Hale asked after McCann was caught up with everything on his end.

"Just the usual renegades that pop up from time to time. Perez and Cooper nabbed a guy a couple of days ago."

"What was that all about?" Hale questioned.

"The local Polizei called us into a suspected resistance site. Turns out the guy was holding an old couple hostage trying to extort cash from their banker son in Munich. Perez was trying to talk him down while the guy strong-armed the lady and waved a gun around. I was told the old gal was feisty and looked like she was ready to spit nails. Anyway, negotiations weren't going very well, so Cooper just up and shot him in the foot," McCann said with a grin. "That was that. The intel people have him now trying to sort things out."

"What about the old couple?" Hale asked.

"Good as gold, sir, once American soldiers raided the place and grabbed the guy. The mayor even said the town would pay for the damaged door and window that got broken in the process. He said it was the least they could do to support the fine Allied forces protecting them from those evil Nazis still lurking about." McCann smiled as he tried to imitate the German Mayor's accent and profuse gratitude.

"All those newsreels of the cheering Nazi crowds idolizing their Führer and when we get here, you can't find a single Nazi anywhere," Hale remarked.

"Funny how that works," McCann acknowledged sarcastically.

Tamar listened to the conversation between Hale and McCann but added nothing. She was content just to remain isolated in the back seat while trying to make herself as comfortable as possible. Jeeps were made for military use, not civilian comfort. But she had been in far less comfortable modes of transportation while escaping Germany several years before. In Palestine things were even more primitive, so her current slight discomfort was of little consequence.

They pulled into Pullach after 2100 hours. Both Hale and Tamar were ready for a hot shower and a good night's sleep. McCann made sure they were billeted promptly and told Hale he would be outside his quarters by 0600. Hale let him know that 0700 would be preferable, using the excuse that Tamar was probably going to need the extra hour of sleep. McCann assented accordingly, then left to get the jeep serviced before the next day's trip to Fussen.

In the morning McCann drove Hale to a storage locker to retrieve his camera and briefcase. When they returned to quarters to pick up Tamar she seemed a bit irritated that the men had left her behind while they ran their errand. She was suddenly feeling like the little sister who was forced to tag along with her big brother at her parents' insistence.

She was no longer a little girl and definitely no one's tag along. She had more of a right to be here than either of them. Her parents had died at the hands of those bastard Nazis. It was all she could do not to take up arms and hunt them down one by one. She fantasized about holding a pistol to their head while they cried out for mercy, but there would be none. Not for those sons of the devil himself. But they were only dreams – for now. The mission had to come first.

Sergeant McCann suggested they eat breakfast at a nice little neighborhood gasthaus on the way to Fussen. It specialized in traditional German meals and catered to both Germans and Allies, who were stationed in the area. Hale and Tamar both agreed that it would be preferable to the standard Army chow at Pullach.

After a hearty meal of ham and brötchen with butter and jam and some thinly sliced cheese, their stomachs were full and their appetites satisfied. Then the trio continued to Fussen. It did not take McCann long to locate the farmhouse. Hale noted that Tamar's demeanor changed as soon as they drove onto the farmhouse grounds. She was more alert and apprehensive. Her eyes darted from one end of the immediate farmhouse property to the other, scanning and searching. Then her eyes settled in on the root cellar several yards from the back door of the house.

Hale exited the jeep and then offered Tamar a hand to help her out of the back, which she ignored. Her recon of the site had begun, and she didn't want any distractions, chivalrous or otherwise, in the way.

"Nice boots," Hale said, remembering his sister saying complimenting a woman's shoes would gain him favor in their eyes.

"You were expecting high heels?" Tamar returned as she left Hale and McCann and began walking straight away to the root cellar, ignoring the weeds and briars catching the hem of her skirt.

"She seems a might on edge, Major," McCann observed.

"Yeah, I noticed."

"You want me to go with you, sir?"

"No, hang back. Just get the camera ready. We'll need to snap a few pictures down there. Stay here and keep an eye out," Hale directed.

"You expecting trouble, sir?" McCann asked.

"Always, Billy."

"Well, I just gotta say knowing what happened when we were here last time, I'm sorta glad she's on our side this time." At Curly's look, he shrugged his shoulders and said, "Just sayin'."

Hale turned to go after Tamar. Realizing she was already halfway to the root cellar he went double time to catch up. When he stepped beside her, she didn't react to his presence. Hale did not know a lot about women, but he was pretty sure her icy demeanor meant she was upset with him.

"You know, I don't like this any more than you," he stated in annoyance. "But the mission has to come before personal feelings. You understand that, right?"

Tamar stopped in her tracks and swiveled on her heel to face him. Hale was suddenly greeted with emerald eyes that could have cut glass. "You really think you are dealing with an amateur, don't you Major? I have been trained to work with Hasatan himself if necessary, to meet my objective," she replied, using the Hebrew name for Satan. "I am professional and will work with you as long as I am ordered to do so. But not a moment longer."

"So, you think I'm the devil?"

"No. But I'm pretty sure you work for him," she said distractedly as she turned away to scan the landscape again.

"I work for Colonel Quinn. Are you calling him the devil?" Hale asked mockingly.

"Oh, there it is. Your smug American attitude. You believe the whole world revolves around your United States of America. You are arrogant as well as obnoxious," she said with a shake of her head. "I have no idea why Menachem authorized me to work with you."

"Well, if I had to guess, and I do, I suspect we have corresponding objectives of some type. But we are not high enough in the food chain to be told what that objective is."

"Why are you talking about food? We just ate an hour ago."

"It's not about food, Tamar. It is a colloquialism. It means we don't have the security clearance to know what the corresponding objectives may be," he explained.

"Do you mock me, Major?"

"No. I was just trying to explain something to you."

"Your arrogance precedes you. If you think this poor little Jewish girl needs an education from a big strong Army Major. I do not," she said defiantly.

Hale could see this conversation was going nowhere, so he decided it was time to get back on task. The mission must come before personal feelings. He knew it to be true but sometimes found it hard to take his own advice.

Tamar resumed her trek to the root cellar with Hale at her side. He felt more like her bodyguard than her partner. His team had been cohesive. They worked and moved as one. Hell, it seemed like they could read one another's minds sometimes. This thing with her was different. They were always at odds and it made him uncomfortable. How were they to work as partners if they couldn't even joke with one another?

Hale and Tamar noticed a flash of light skitter across the bottom of the root cellar door simultaneously as they drew close. They stopped dead in their tracks and looked at each other, knowing that someone with a flashlight was below ground in the dark room. Each drew their .45 caliber pistols.

Hale took the lead, despite Tamar's visual disapproval, and reached for the latch at the exact moment the door slammed open. Hale was hit solidly in the face with the edge of the door causing him to stumble backward as a man dressed in black rushed past him and glanced off Tamar. His flashlight narrowly missed Tamar's head as he thrashed wildly at the unexpected company, but the blinding light shining directly in her eyes gave him a moment to regroup.

Tamar saw dots dancing in the air as the assailant swung his arm around, trying to shoot Hale point-blank in the chest. She threw herself into his back, nearly knocking all three of them to the ground as the weapon discharged over Hale's shoulder. The deafening sound rocked him, but he was able to fire back as the man in black rolled off and ran but he couldn't tell if he hit him. Tamar jumped past Hale and fired two quick rounds at the man as he disappeared behind the house.

"Are you injured?" Tamar shouted at Hale.

"No. Just my damn ears ringing. Where is he?"

Tamar pointed toward the rear of the house just as Sergeant McCann came running full steam with his Thompson sub-machine gun, ready to engage. "What happened? You two all right?" he shouted.

"We're fine," Hale responded louder than necessary as the ringing in his ears affected his hearing. "I'll go right, Billy."

"I'll go left, Major," he answered, as he had many times before in combat.

Tamar did not wait for instructions. She sprinted for the tree line behind the house. She kept low and had her pistol in firing position. Hale and McCann went left and right, hoping to outflank the intruder if possible.

Hale and McCann emerged from their positions at approximately the same time. They did a quick head check at the corners of the house and when neither received any gunfire, they both moved quickly and decisively to new positions. They were scanning the area, looking for their target, when a flurry of gunshots came from the area where Tamar had gone.

Both men broke into a run toward the sound. They silently searched with weapons still in position for a confrontation as they closed in on her last known position. She finally came limping toward them through the brush. Hale got to her first, then motioned for McCann to locate the shooter, but Tamar waved them both off.

"He is gone," she said, grimacing. She held her left thigh and they could see blood running down her leg and into her boot. "I hit him before he got in a waiting car. There will be a blood trail, but he is long gone by now."

Her colorless face and lack of fighting spirit told the men she was in serious trouble. Hale picked her up before she could protest and carried her toward the farmhouse. McCann ran ahead and busted through the door with his weapon, ready to greet any other visitors that may have been in residence. Finding none, he swept several items from the kitchen table with his arm so Hale could gently lay their fierce lady combatant down on the table. McCann grabbed a small sofa pillow from the living room to place under her head as she struggled to remain upright.

Tamar began to describe the man as McCann bolted from the room. "He was not a large man. Slender build. Light hair. Dressed in a black or navy-blue suit. The car headed east on the dirt road," she said quietly.

"We'll get him later. Where are you hit?" Hale asked urgently.

"Thigh. High above the knee," she replied weakly as she leaned back and tried to brace herself on her elbows.

Hale quickly raised her dress to find the wound. All rules of modesty were ignored as he found the bloody hole and quickly applied pressure, causing Tamar to groan in pain as he did so. McCann's boots hit the wooden porch alerting them to his return.

"I got the med kit," he shouted before he even entered the kitchen. "Did you check? Is it a through and through?"

"Not yet." Hale returned as Tamar's elbows gave way and her head dropped to the pillow. Maintaining pressure on the wound, they bent her knee and lifted her leg hoping to find a matching bullet hole in the back of her thigh. An audible sigh of relief was heard when they spotted the exit wound.

"She's losing a lot of blood. We're going to have to get her to the hospital. I can't do this here," McCann said as he grabbed supplies from the medical kit. "I can clean it up enough to transport her to Pullach. They'll probably transport her to the 97th General in Frankfurt once she's stable enough for the trip."

"Got it," Hale confirmed as they deftly worked to staunch the profuse bleeding.

"The cellar," she whispered, with the pain evident on her face.

"Don't worry about the cellar," Hale returned. "We need to get you to the hospital."

"Behind three boards. South wall," she continued as if he hadn't spoken. "Don't leave without the satchel," she ordered before falling unconscious.

"I'll get it," Hale assured her, even though she would not hear him. Then he added softly, "You just can't help yourself, can you?"

CHAPTER 23

Tamar woke with a start, surprised to find herself in an unfamiliar place. Her memories from the last thirty-six hours were sketchy at best, but she did remember being shot and the bumpy, painful ride to the field clinic in Pullach that sent her in and out of consciousness. She had vague dream-like recollections of being airlifted from Pullach to Frankfurt flipping through her mind like random photos flashing by in no particular order. The crisp white sheets, white walls, and IV bottle hanging from a metal ring connected to the shiny metal headboard said she was now recovering in a sterile hospital room. Her left leg was propped up on a couple of pillows, and she noted with pleasure that the pain was minimal. Evidently, the pain medication administered was working and she was content with that.

She raised her head slightly to see Hale slouched in a chair at the end of her bed. His head hung down in exhausted sleep with his chin resting comfortably on his chest. His soft snoring was actually a bit comforting, which she found peculiar since he hated her. Didn't he? Yet here he was, keeping guard over her in the hospital room. It was so odd, but her head was still fuzzy, and she wasn't thinking clearly. Obviously, the medication easing her pain must be affecting her cognitive faculties. It made her nervous; the sooner she could think clearly, the better. She made a mental note to request less pain medication to keep her mental capabilities sharp. Better a little pain than for her reactions to be slowed should she unexpectedly need them.

Her only concern at the moment was how long this injured leg would keep her from her duties. The Irgun would have her back in action as soon as she felt ready to walk with little pain. She had no idea what the American's view of ready for duty would be. She only knew that the urgency to track down her attacker and find out what he knew about the diamonds she had hidden in the root cellar was returning at a rapid rate.

She groaned and dropped her head back to the pillow as she suddenly felt an urgent need to relieve herself. The leg could be managed, she thought, but having her arm tethered to the bed by an IV would definitely complicate this normally easy process. There was no bathroom visible from where she lay, so that meant she must venture from the room to find relief.

A glance at the sleeping Major Hale and she determined that the steel bedpan on the table next to her bed would be a last resort. The indignity of using a bedpan was bad enough, but with him in the room, whether he was awake or not was out of the question. She managed to sit up without issue, however moving a leg that felt forty pounds heavier than it should proved to be more difficult than expected. Even the unsuccessful effort to shift its position was causing a noticeable throb.

After several futile and painful attempts to reach the IV bottle, she resigned herself to the fact that the hated steel bedpan would have to do. However undignified, it was the lesser of two evils when she considered the alternative was wetting the bed. That simply would not do. So, she leaned back on one elbow and reached across her body to the other side of the bed to get the steel pan. The unanticipated increase in pain at such a move found her yelping in pain.

"Let me help you with that," Hale said softly as he instantly appeared at her side.

"You will do no such thing, Major," she replied forcefully through her agony.

"Then let me get a nurse."

"I can certainly manage this without assistance, thank you very much," she said irritably.

Hale just picked up the bedpan and walked out of the room. "Hey! What do you think you're doing? I need that," she managed to yell as he disappeared around the corner.

Less than a minute later, a young nurse entered the room carrying the bedpan and closed the door behind her. "Oh my, it's so good to see you're feeling better," she said with a genuine smile as she cranked the backrest into a sitting position. "Major Hale was quite insistent that I get this to you immediately. I know this is embarrassing and uncomfortable, but it is quite necessary, dear."

She assisted her into position and continued chatting to ease Tamar's discomfort as she straightened the room. "You shouldn't be cross with the Major. He's just concerned about you. We've been pumping fluids into you. That's undoubtedly why you felt the urge. You lost quite a bit of blood, but your color looks much better now than when you first got here."

"I still don't like it," Tamar complained, hating to be at a disadvantage.

"I wouldn't either, I assure you," the young nurse empathized. "What I wouldn't mind is Major Hale standing guard over me all night," she admitted with a smile. "He and his escort drove all night to get here, and he never left your side. The Sergeant is in the waiting area sleeping on the floor. He refused to leave the ward until he knew you were awake and secure. You must be pretty special to these soldiers."

Tamar was both pleased and confused. Why were they showing her such concern? It was apparent to her that neither man thought she should be involved in 'Army work'. Yet, they treated her quickly and professionally after the shooting and made sure she received medical treatment immediately. But driving all night to ensure her safety here seemed to go above and beyond their duties.

"I don't understand," she admitted to her nurse.

"Just be grateful, honey. I certainly would. Now," she said as the dreadful bedpan was deftly removed. "I'll get your pain meds. You're due for another injection and by the look on your face, you really need it. By the way, the nice Sergeant McCann put a change of clothes for you in the bottom drawer when you are cleared to leave. I'll be right back." And with that, the nurse promptly left the room.

By the time Hale returned, Tamar had been given a sponge bath and her wounded leg redressed. She had to admit she felt refreshed. It felt like a week's worth of grime had been removed from her exhausted body.

"Well, you certainly look better. Can I get you anything?" Hale asked as he walked into the room. The softness in his voice surprised her. The genuine look of concern and relief was not even remotely what she had expected. If anything, she thought he would be ecstatic to leave her here in the hospital and continue the mission without her. She was genuinely perplexed.

"Did you find it, the satchel, I mean?"

"That's what you want to know? After all of this, your first question is about the mission?"

"Of course," she replied, a little flummoxed that he would expect anything else. "What else would I want to know? So, did you find it? Oh, and where am I?"

"Yes, I retrieved it as Sargent McCann tucked you into the jeep for the ride back to Pullach. It wasn't our first priority, however, we both knew you'd give us hell if we left without it. And you're at the 97th General Hospital in Frankfurt. It's a military hospital and you're safe here."

"Sergeant McCann?"

"I sent him to find us quarters. Once he secures billeting, we'll clean up and come back."

"Don't you have reports to file or something? I'm pretty sure Colonel Quinn will want to know how I managed to get myself shot while on a simple search," she said, embarrassed at her failure on their very first recon together. "He may reconsider having me on his team."

She waited for Hale to agree or possibly even go so far as to say he wanted her off the team as well, but he said nothing. He seemed to be thinking of a response, and she was sure it would not be to her liking.

"The report's been filed. Don't worry about it," he finally responded. "You get some rest. I'll be back later. There's a guard outside your door."

"Wait...what? Do you honestly think I'll attempt an escape...like this?" she asked.

"It's not your leaving that I'm concerned about," he responded without a hint of humor as he left the room. There was a conversation outside the door, but she couldn't understand what was being said as the medication began to do its job. She found herself feeling lightheaded and weary. She didn't remember falling asleep.

Then there was a presence. There was someone in the room. She fought her way up from the darkness of medicated sleep. Whoever it was, they had their hand on her thigh, touching her bandaged wound. Struggling to pry herself from sleep, she could only imagine who would take such liberties. The medical personnel always woke her before dressing the wound. Then her imagination took a turn when she suddenly concluded that there was only one person it could be.

"Major Hale, remove your hands or die," she mumbled as her eyelids fluttered open.

"Shhhh," a calm, familiar voice answered. "It's only me Plymenytse."

She thought it a product of her medicated state as Uncle Yazzie's smiling face came into focus. "Feter? How…how can you be here? Am I dreaming?"

"You are not dreaming, Tamar. I am here. Of course, I am here. Where else would I be?" he asked. At her confused silence, he continued. "What happened? Were there bad guys, or did you annoy Major Hale until he shot you?"

"He has not known me nearly long enough to want to shoot me yet," she returned with a groggy smile as she motioned for him to crank up the bed. "What are you doing here, Uncle?"

"I had to see for myself," he said as he sat beside her. "And say a prayer, of course. I thought a Psalm might help. The Lord builds up Jerusalem; He gathers together the outcasts of Israel. He heals the brokenhearted and binds up their wounds," he quoted as he reached to cup her cheek with his hand. "That and I hoped to borrow your great-great-grandmother's healing hands."

"I don't understand. I never knew my great-great-grandmother. What healing hands? What are you talking about, Uncle?"

"We did not talk about it in the family. Oh no, it was forbidden, you see. There was a time when such gifts were considered witchcraft."

"I never heard anything about this," she persisted. "Tell me about her."

"We will speak of it at length once you have recovered," Yazzie offered. Then he leaned in and slipped a Colt 38 revolver under the sheet. "Six shots. It's clean and loaded."

Tamar's face grew serious. "Feter, I don't understand. Why are you giving me this and how did you get it in here? In fact, how did you get in here?"

Hale walked into the room and was visibly stunned when he saw Yazzie sitting next to Tamar. The smile he entered with quickly faded as he said, "They didn't tell me you were here."

"I'll explain later," Yazzie offered to Hale without being asked.

"I'd rather you explain now. Did you show the guard some forged papers like you did me in Pullach?"

Yazzie had hoped to get in and out without Major Hale's knowledge, but at his entrance, Plan B needed to be initiated. "I received word about Tamar while I was enroute to see my friend Samuel Gassan in Amsterdam. He has an import-export facility there," he explained.

"For what?" quizzed Hale.

"Diamonds," Tamar answered. "He is probably the best procurer of diamonds in the world."

"Yes," Yazzie agreed, as he deftly turned the conversation away from questions regarding his arrival. "There were cut diamonds found at George Piper's home in Virginia. You made quite an impression on him in Washington when you were last there, as I recall. Anyway," he continued as Hale recognized the obtuse reference to the would-be assassin. "I was going to talk to Samuel about their authenticity and place of origin."

"Diamonds," Hale repeated. "More diamonds. What the hell is going on here?"

"That's what we're hoping to find out, Major," Yazzie replied. "As near as I can tell they are flawless, so I was hoping Samuel could give me information that might help trace their supply chain. There has to be a connection."

"Yes." Tamar agreed, then cocked her head to one side. "But Frankfurt is a long way from Amsterdam, Feter. What are you not telling us?"

Yazzie's face didn't give away anything as his niece tried to stare him down with her emerald eyes. "Suffice it to say that I was on my way to Amsterdam…" he started again.

"To check with your friend about the diamonds you found," Hale finished. "But you never said how you found out about Tamar's injury in the first place. You never said how you diverted an aircraft to come to Frankfurt. You never explained how in the hell you got onto a secure hospital ward at a military installation. Shall I go on with unanswered questions, Yazzie?"

"And you never explained how you got this up here," Tamar added, as she slipped the Colt pistol from under the sheets. Hale's face went from pale to crimson red in about two seconds.

"What in the hell is going on? And don't give me another one of your cockamamie stories. I have the authority here to toss your ass in the brig and I'll do it if you don't give me some pretty damned convincing answers. Answers that I can verify!"

Yazzie raised his hands in surrender to both Hale and Tamar. "Just because we are assigned to the same team doesn't mean you are to be read into everything I'm doing. I must receive permission to brief you. If," he said, silencing their interrogation with an upraised finger. "If and only if I receive authorization, we will need to take this conversation to a more secure location, Major," he stated.

"We're in a hospital room with a sentry at the door in a secure hospital located on a guarded military base. How much more secure do you need to be?"

"I see your point however it's non-negotiable. When you hear what I have to say, you will understand the need for specialized security. Perhaps we can get your Sergeant McCann to chauffeur us to a quiet residence I have access to here in Frankfurt?"

"You're not going without me," Tamar announced emphatically as she nearly fell out of bed trying to retrieve the clothes Sergeant McCann had thoughtfully brought for her. "My leg is feeling much better. Great Grandmother must have heard your prayer."

"Great, great grandmother," Yazzie corrected.

"Who? What are you talking about?" Hale asked.

"Get the nurse in here to remove the IV, okay?" she directed as she stood up straight and looked at her uncle and Hale. "Are you going to turn around or not? I have no problem dressing in front of you if necessary. I have endured enough humiliation already to make me immune to any other indignities."

Hale and Yazzie quickly turned their backs so she could dress. Both men's faces turned red in embarrassment. They looked at one another, trying to figure out how to handle this situation.

"She's your niece," Hale accused Yazzie.

"She's your partner," he responded in kind.

CHAPTER 24

Neither Mac nor Quinn relished the idea of trying to explain to the President how a foreign agent infiltrated a military hospital to kill their only witness. To admit the agent was most likely an alien made it even worse. Helen seemed a bit less apprehensive. Her thought was that they now knew more than they had a few days ago and the President would be pleased to note they were making progress.

They met at the Willard InterContinental Hotel in a private room the concierge had provided at Quinn's request. The Willard, as it was known to locals, was tastefully opulent, with lots of carved dark wood trim and drippy chandeliers hanging from tall ceilings. It also had a formidable history of the rich, powerful, connected, and moneyed doing business within its walls. The elegant ambiance was certainly a draw; however, the complete discretion of the staff was far more desired by the power brokers of D.C. The thick carpets and finely upholstered furnishings were just a bonus.

There was a quiet side entrance clientele of a certain status were directed to if they desired to avoid undue attention. Quinn and the President used this access directly after the Secret Service quietly surveilled the area and checked the proffered room for listening devices. Truman had thought this a bit much even after the assassination attempt, but the men charged with protecting his life had been on edge ever since the incident. Doctor Zimmerman "accidentally" incinerating the assailant had only served to deepen their fears.

After the Secret Service had vacated the room, Mac and Helen "showed up" as only three people in the whole world were able to do. Their method of entry was still a bit unnerving to both Truman and Quinn, but both men understood the value of an untraceable entry if they were to remain outside the purview of prying eyes, particularly those of one J. Edgar Hoover.

A morning tea had already been prepared and delivered to the room on a linen-covered cart. The coffee, tea, and pastries prepared by the resident chef with all the necessary accouterments would provide a light mid-morning snack and also serve as a suitable cover for a simple presidential chat with a longtime friend. There was nothing unusual to arouse suspicion from any interlopers.

"I thought Yazzie was going to be here, too," Quinn said to Mac as they shook hands.

"He had an urgent, unexpected appointment to attend to," Mac explained.

"Nothing serious, I hope," President Truman offered, as he signaled everyone to the sitting area. "I had hoped to meet him today."

The gentlemen waited for Helen to place the silver tray from the cart on the coffee table before seating herself, then they joined her in the gold and white brocade chairs.

"Nothing he can't handle, Mr. President," Mac said, offering no other explanation. A glance in Quinn's direction let him know that his briefing would come later. Quinn nodded discreetly as Helen began to pour coffee as the meeting started.

"So, what happened at the hospital, Bill?" President Truman asked pointedly as he declined cream and sugar with a shake of his head, then accepted a cup of black coffee from Helen. "How does someone gain entrance to a secure facility like that undetected?"

"My evidence team theorizes she got in disguised as a window washer. They found an open window on the tenth floor with the platform they use right outside. A pair of coveralls had been left on the platform. She undoubtedly had other clothes on underneath which would allow her easier access to Piper's room." Quinn accepted a cup from Helen, then added cream and sugar as he continued. "It makes sense that those clothes may have been a nurse's uniform. Nurse Baker may not have been part of the original plan, I don't know. If she happened to walk in on the assailant while she was killing Piper, she may have been collateral damage. Whether the second death was planned or not, she then exited the building dressed as a nurse. She may have acted alone, but it is reasonable to think an accomplice was waiting for her."

"So, a woman… do we know if she was a citizen or a foreigner?" Truman asked, using the jargon he and Quinn had agreed upon. At Quinn's negative shake of the head, he finished his original thought. "So, a woman gained access to the hospital dressed as a man and then left dressed as a nurse?"

"Yes, sir. That's what we believe. I have men working to locate her right now, but the prospects are not good at this point. An ambulance was reported stolen about the same time, but that report was later retracted. The vehicle was found off-post filthy, but undamaged a few hours later. It had been thoroughly cleaned by the time we found out about it."

Truman's mind whirred with the implications as he silently took a sip of coffee. "Okay, well, what else do you have?"

Mac pulled five passports from his pocket and fanned them out on the antique coffee table as Helen pulled the coffee tray to one side. The President leaned forward in his chair to view the display as he asked, "Am I to assume these items have something to do with one or both of the assassins?"

"Yes, sir," Mac responded. "These all came from the *foreign* asset. Six American passports with the same picture but different names. The genuine article is under the name she used here; the others are superb forgeries, according to Yazzie. He said there are only a handful of forgers in the world that could produce nearly perfect work like these. He'll be looking into it while overseas. It looks like each passport was used for a different country when she traveled. None of the passports were diplomatic. She also had a forged letter stating that she was an American government employee working in Japan."

"Japan," Truman stated flatly as visions of Pearl Harbor ran through his head.

"Are there stamps in any of them?" Quinn asked.

"Yes. As I said, each one was used for a different country. She made trips to Great Britain, Germany, the Netherlands, Egypt, Argentina, and Japan. Holland and Germany had the most stamps by far and we will be concentrating on the days of her visits to trace the rat lines the enemy is using to transport people and property, specifically diamonds, from nation to nation," Mac answered.

"Where did you find these?" Quinn asked as he examined one of the forged passports.

"Helen obtained them from Miss Martin's safe deposit box."

"Miss Martin?" Truman queried.

"She is the, uh, foreigner," Helen said with a grimace. "Oh my, I'm not at all accustomed to these kinds of meetings, as you can see. My apologies."

"None needed," he replied genuinely. "But just how did you get access to this woman's safe deposit box?"

"She returned daily after our search to monitor the woman's incoming mail without my knowledge. She then visited the bank listed on a renewal notice for the box," Mac stated, obviously still a bit displeased with his spouse of over thirty years.

"By herself?" Quinn blurted out in surprise.

"Well, we found next to nothing the first time we were there," Helen said defending her actions. At the men's astonished stares and continued silence, she continued, "I am quite capable you know. A simple meeting with the bank manager by a dithering, flustered middle-aged lady telling him of a family illness and a lost key did the trick. He was quite understanding."

"That's not the point, Helen," Quinn started.

"You're not going to give me the same lecture Mac did about operating without backup, are you, Bill? He was most disagreeable about the whole thing," she added off-handedly.

"Yes of course he's going to give you the same lecture, Helen. You didn't have any backup," Mac said in near exasperation. "You didn't let your team know where you were and when to expect you back. It's dangerous to operate that way. You cannot go off on a lark without notifying your partners!"

"Oh, Mac, really," she rebuffed her husband.

"I'm afraid I must agree with Mac and Bill, Helen," the President added sternly. "No one should have to tell you that this is a dangerous business. Please, do not ever do that again. I must insist."

"Of course, Mr. President," she said contritely. "You're right. I certainly defer to your expertise in these situations. Never again, I promise."

Mac and Quinn's jaws dropped as Helen outmaneuvered them. They may have been experts on the battlefield, but she definitely had the upper hand in the parlor. She had at once made President Truman the gallant hero with sage advice, while at the same time dismissing the same recommendations from her husband and Colonel Quinn. She smiled sweetly at the two men, then lifted the tray and offered, "Pastry?"

Mac and Quinn shook their heads in mock disbelief as the President smiled at her deftness of political maneuverability.

"In any case," Mac went on, "even though it was a completely reckless move on Helen's part, it paid off. We now know Miss Martin had passports for several nations indicating she had contacts or at least possible contacts worldwide."

"And we know from Dr. Zimmerman's report that she had been surgically altered to look human," Quinn added. "His detailed reports from Groom Lake are quite helpful. And all information thus far indicates she was an extremely valuable asset. The broad daylight assassination attempt was a risk. But if she had succeeded you would be gone, sir, and she would have continued to be their eyes and ears in the White House. That they were willing to accept that risk means one of two things; either they were supremely confident they would succeed without interference, or the situation had become desperate. Either way, her loss is undoubtedly huge for them. That's a big benefit for us even though we don't yet know what caused them to make their move at this time."

"It would have taken extensive training to make her able to survive unnoticed in a very foreign world and culture," Mac explained. "The assimilation process may have taken months, perhaps years to modify and then train for this type of work. Add to that the extensive period to get her a position at the correspondence desk in the War Department and you can surmise how great her value was to the enemy. This does not happen in a few weeks."

"Astonishing," Truman remarked. "What about the other assassin?"

Mac answered first. "Well, we know he was a planner and courier for the War Department. His work and that of Ms. Martin crossed paths regularly so we can easily see how they maintained contact without suspicion. He had a small office right in the White House as well as one over at the War Department."

Truman's face went flush at the news of him being in the White House. "So, which one was the lead?"

"Probably her," Mac ascertained. "She would have taken the longest to train and was the one with all the passports. She probably seduced him to get him to pass classified information."

"Most likely," Quinn agreed. "Frankly, she was way out of his league. His ego and greed led him like a lamb to the slaughter."

"That probably explains his divorce," Helen concluded.

"No doubt," agreed Mac. "She probably convinced him that he was doing his country a great favor as she offered him significant benefits and lots and lots of money."

"Don't be profane, dear," Helen admonished from her seat.

"My apologies, sweetheart, but it is a well-known method to turn men against those who trust them. Make them feel stronger, smarter, and above all unappreciated, and the trap is set. Men are often led by their self-image rather than their intellect."

President Truman rose and walked to the marble fireplace, as he processed this information. It was a damn mess, and it happened on his watch. The Secret Service was busy discreetly reviewing federal employee files, and he had already decided to produce an executive order to establish a federal employee loyalty program. It was a slow start, but the information that passed through these hands could determine the fate of the nation. It had to be secured.

They had to find a way to restrict the flow of knowledge to only those who needed it. The military already had standards in place, perhaps those standards could be expanded to include federal employees. If that could be coupled with the division of intelligence duties, he could seal the wanton flow of information from the White House for good.

He then turned to face the others. "So, we have two would-be assassins accounted for. A third killer murdering George Piper and a nurse at Walter Reed tells us we're not out of the woods yet. Do we have any idea who is running these agents? I assume someone is in charge."

"We came to the same conclusion, sir, but we don't know who's calling the shots yet," Mac admitted. "It's clear that someone ordered Miss Martin and Piper to kill you. We might have concluded that the two were in it alone if it hadn't been for Piper's assassination. He must have known the handler's true identity."

"Why would you assume that?" he asked curiously.

"Because," Quinn interrupted, "there's no other reason strong enough to expose the fact that additional players exist."

"Listen, sir," Mac chimed in, "they're getting bolder. No operator in their right mind would choose to take out a world leader using hand-to-hand on a public street instead of by long-range rifle *unless* they felt they couldn't fail, or they had no choice. They have reason to fear you, Mr. President. Possibly because of what you did at Hiroshima and Nagasaki or maybe because they think you might be inclined to do it again. It's well known that you are a decidedly different decision-maker than your predecessor, or maybe it's about something else entirely. There is no way to know right now."

"I see," he responded thoughtfully. "So, what do you recommend we do next?"

"A couple of things," Mac answered. "First, I think Bill informed you about the diamonds found at Piper's house."

"He did."

"Well, since Mr. Piper has caused so much trouble, why don't we let the traitor finance our operations? Bill thinks, and I concur wholeheartedly, that you should use that contraband to help start up the intel divisions you've been working on. We all know Congress is not likely to release the funds necessary to adequately support such a mammoth overall."

"Not bloody likely," Truman agreed. "Dealing with them is like slaying a dragon some days. But what do diamonds have to do with funding the new agencies?"

Helen, who had returned the remnants of their beverages to the cart, came closer to the President and said, "Actually, Yazzie is already working on converting the diamonds to cash, Mr. President. That's one of the reasons he's not here this morning. He's on the way to Amsterdam to meet a friend we think can help facilitate this work."

"Do I want to know how all this works?" he asked carefully.

"Probably not, Mr. President," Mac answered honestly. "But hypothetically speaking, let's just say that someone, like Bill maybe, would set up an import/export business in New York City. That business could work hand-in-hand with an import/export business in Amsterdam, well known for handling jewels. There would be no connection to the White House."

"I see," Truman replied thoughtfully. "And you're sure this man would be willing to work with us hypothetically speaking, of course?"

"Absolutely sir. He is a Jewish patriot for Palestine and as it happens, our goals and theirs currently align."

"And he can be trusted?"

"He would be monitored the same as any asset, of course. But you have to understand, sir, that our involvement in World War II created a group of what you might call American patriot nomads in the Jewish sector. They are working hard to create a Jewish Palestine so their people can have a permanent place to call home. As long as we don't betray them like some other countries and our goals remain consistent with their goals, men like Yazzie and his friend will deal honestly with us. It's most assuredly in their best interest to remain allies with the most powerful nation in the world while they are pursuing a homeland of their own," Mac assured the President.

"All right, back to this strictly theoretical process. How would this businessman in Amsterdam turn diamonds into working capital? And are you absolutely certain there would be enough money to facilitate the startup of my plan?"

"Yazzie confirmed that there are more than enough cut diamonds from Piper and uncut diamonds from Germany to get us started, sir. His friend can authenticate all the uncut diamonds and make sure they are given Certificates of Origination indicating where they came from. All will come from various mining operations in Africa. No one will be the wiser."

"And then?" the President pressed.

"Then he will act as broker of the diamonds for us. As a broker, he will take a percentage for his work. He will probably send a portion to Palestine, then wire the business's portion to a bank in New York. Distribution of funds may filter through several other unrelated businesses prior to finding its way to D.C.

Congress never has to know where the money is coming from or how it's being used."

"Hmmm, well that's something to think about, isn't it?" Truman said as he returned to his seat. "Well, if that concludes our business for today…"

"Oh, my goodness," Helen exclaimed. "I almost forgot about the key! It was taped under a table in the *foreigner's* apartment. I got it right that time, didn't I?" She twinkled as she produced the large rusty key from her pocket. "And I figured out where I saw one like it before, the National Museum. I took Munro when he was just a boy, but I can't remember what it was used for."

"The very fact that it was important enough to be hidden in her place means that we'll have to investigate," Mac said.

"Oh wonderful, I was hoping you'd say that," Helen said, clapping her hands. Then she asked with a wink, "during museum business hours or after hours?"

"After hours?" Quinn said, wondering how he would cover up the break-in.

"Don't worry, we won't get caught but if we do, I learned from a sweet church secretary that it is often easier to get forgiveness than it is to get permission."

"A sweet church secretary," the President repeated with a smile. "Well, who can argue with a sweet church secretary?"

CHAPTER 25

Hale and Tamar were dropped at the gate of the appointed meeting place arranged by Yazzie. Sergeant McCann was told to return for them at 2100 hours. No other information about the clandestine meeting was given, nor did he ask for any. He understood that certain information was classified "above his pay grade." And, as a good soldier, he respected his orders and would reappear at the appointed time to retrieve his charges. However, an itch on the back of his neck had him running a continuous grid search around their meeting place until the pair was back under his protective wing.

Once inside, Hale and Tamar found a comfortable fully furnished residence. A burgundy leather sofa and chairs flanked a glass coffee table already laden with trays of fresh bread and fruit. Two carafes with everything needed to have a nice cup of tea or coffee sat next to the fruit tray. The room had a decidedly masculine air to it. Amateur landscape and still-life paintings on every wall hinted at a hobby enjoyed by the owner and they wondered if maybe Yazzie had an easel in the back room.

The pair slipped out of their winter gear and placed them on the coat tree by the front door, then helped themselves to coffee but passed on the food. They silently sipped their beverages and walked the length of the room examining both the décor and artwork. Clearly this place was designed to hold meetings. It was upscale and at the same time held a homey quality that would set both higher-level guests and those unaccustomed to such elegance at ease.

When Yazzie entered the room, he already had a cup of coffee in hand. He smiled broadly when he saw Tamar, then waved his hand to his guests to find a seat as he spread a teaspoon of jam on a piece of homemade bread. Hale chose the sofa while Tamar chose the eastside chair so she could keep her eye on the front door. Yazzie smiled as he guessed the reason for her choice of seats. He watched her movements. She seemed a little stiff, but all things considered, she was moving well.

"I'm happy to see you two are punctual," he began. "Finding young people who know how to tell time seems to be getting harder these days," he mused as he took a bite of bread and jam, then closed his eyes in ecstasy as he chewed.

"Chit-chat isn't necessary, Yazzie," Hale rebuked. "Just tell us what the hell is going on." Tamar nodded her head in agreement, then wondered why she found herself agreeing with Hale. It felt strange.

Yazzie raised his eyebrows at the sharpness of tone and lack of respect it insinuated but refrained from commenting. "Always straight to the point, aren't you, Major? Very well, let's get started. First, let me say that my being here is no accident."

"We already gathered that, Uncle," Tamar interrupted. "Why don't you tell us how you got here so fast? It is a two-day trip from Washington to Frankfurt by air. You could not have received word of my injury in time to make such a commute. That seems like a good place to start to me."

Hale watched Tamar, then nodded his head in agreement to present a unified front. "She's right, Yazzie. There is no way in hell you could have gotten here in the time frame you indicated. Even by air, you couldn't make it here that fast unless you got on a flight that left directly after ours. Are we not trusted? Were you sent to shadow us?"

"Well," Yazzie responded, as he paused to take another bite. "Mmmm, you really should try this. Heavenly, just heavenly. Well, you are both correct about the flight time. A fine piece of detective work there. A standard flight from Washington D.C. with its connections would not have gotten me here as quickly as I suggested in the hospital."

The pointed little shot of sarcasm was not lost on Hale. Yazzie seemed to be deliberately baiting the two of them, and it was getting under his skin. Tamar, however, seemed unaffected by his maneuvers.

"And what about the hospital?" Tamar interjected. "What kind of trick did you use to accelerate the healing of my leg? And don't tell me another story about great, great grandmother. A gunshot wound should take far longer to heal. Yet, I am able to walk reasonably well without any assistance. Explain that!"

"The Shimon's have always been fast healers," Yazzie returned unruffled as the last bite of bread was popped into his mouth. Tamar rolled her eyes.

"You arrived in Frankfurt before I had even filed my report to Colonel Quinn. Hell, he may not have that report on his desk even now! Something doesn't add up here, Yazzie, and I want to know what it is. If I am not trusted just say so," Hale demanded.

Yazzie rose to refresh his coffee before continuing calmly. "Let's start with the obvious, shall we? You are still searching for Hitler's most talented engineers and scientists, correct?"

Hale tamped down his impatience. "Correct."

"Before the war ended those people were able to produce some incredible scientific marvels. Rockets and jets that could move at speeds the allies could only dream of. Weapons that, if deployed, could have won the war for Hitler in a matter of days. It would have cost the allies hundreds of thousands more lives had they been implemented."

"I am well aware of that," Hale reminded him. "What does any of that have to do with you?"

"So, do you honestly think you were the only American searching for these assets?" he asked as he returned to his seat. Yazzie looked pointedly at Hale. "Some of them were only too happy to begin working for the other side immediately. We are still inspecting and re-engineering some of their creations. Obviously, if we can get more of those remarkable men to work with us, the process would be much faster. The Russians are doing their best to capture all these engineers and scientists for exactly the same reason. We simply cannot allow that to happen. World War Three would erupt overnight and Stalin would take Hitler's place as world dictator."

"We don't need a history lesson, Uncle," Tamar said irritably. "We know the stakes are high. Just answer our questions and stop obfuscating. We are not children."

"No, you are not, despite your petulant behavior of late," Yazzie scolded. "Both of you have already lived lives of too much danger. And it is not over yet. The fact of the matter is that we are already experimenting with some of the Nazi inventions. Our engineers coupled with the willing defectors have done a fairly good job thus far; at least with a few of the inventions."

"Such as?" Hale inquired with renewed interest.

"Such as this." Yazzie opened a paneled door so Mac and Helen could step into the living room. Hale and Tamar both jumped to their feet with mouths hanging open as if they had seen a couple of ghosts.

"What the hell?" Tamar yelled in German and English.

"No need for profanity, dear," Helen corrected Tamar sweetly. "We know this is a shock for you, but we felt this was the best way to tell you. After all, seeing is believing, especially since Yazzie was determined to visit you in the hospital."

Mac stepped in front of Helen and Yazzie and took over the conversation. "Frankly, I shouldn't have to explain myself to subordinates," he growled. "I expect you to accept your assignments and carry them out. I don't expect you to question why and how we do things on our end. Do you understand?"

"Yes sir," both Hale and Tamar responded automatically.

"Then let me make this simple and to the point. We now have technology you are not privy to. We are utilizing that technology to keep those Communist bastards from taking over the world."

"No profanity, dear," Helen rebuked her husband gently.

"My apologies, Helen. I will do my best to chasten these two pups without my usual blasphemous tirades before the troops."

"Thank you, sweetheart."

Mac sighed heavily, then looked at his shoes as he counted to ten. He could not believe his wife would correct him in front of the team, especially subordinates. He would have to speak to her about this later.

"As I was saying, some of the specialized technology smuggled out by those defectors is currently being tested. It may be far above our intellectual abilities at present, but just because we don't understand it doesn't mean we can't use it. Understanding will come later as more data becomes available. So, I don't want to hear another word from either of you about how I conduct *my* team. Am I making myself clear?"

Perfectly, sir. Absolutely, sir came from the two agents, now more than a little embarrassed and uncomfortable about their arrogant behavior. Helen tried to lighten the mood by offering food and drinks around, but Hale and Tamar remained subdued as the meeting continued.

"Now, since we're already here, let me catch you up on what's been happening in D.C. The would-be assassin Curly took down has himself been assassinated."

Hale and Tamar's heads both shot up at the surprise news from Washington.

"Someone secreted themselves into Walter Reed and killed him before we could question him. It's a bloody mess back there, and the President is demanding answers as to our lack of security in a supposedly secure hospital ward."

"My apologies, sir, I should have stayed. I should have…" Hale remarked.

"No need for apologies, Major. You had nothing to do with it. Frankly, Colonel Quinn and I are responsible, and we will take the heat. The only thing we know about him thus far is his name was George Piper, and he worked for the War Department. He had an office in the Pentagon and another in the White House."

"Oh my God. That can't be possible," Tamar said in surprise.

"Apparently it is possible. We are, of course, taking strong measures to ensure this never happens again."

"But if he was in the White House, General, isn't it possible that other enemy agents are in there as well?" Hale observed with concern.

"That is the assumption, Major Hale. Colonel Quinn is already conducting a clandestine review of the personnel records of every employee with access to the White House looking for evidence of any other possible agents. It's going to take time, but that's our issue. Yours is following up on what happened in Fussen. It can't be a coincidence that someone else was there looking for the diamonds you found."

Hale and Tamar were both speechless at the realization he already knew they had retrieved the diamonds. However, after the previous dress-down, neither verbally responded to the news.

"Yes, I know all about the diamonds," Mac admitted at their surprised expressions. "Technology, remember? Anyway, cut diamonds were found at Piper's second residence. His reward for treason we assume. It seemed like too much of a coincidence, so Yazzie visited the farmhouse before coming to Frankfurt."

"How could they possibly be connected, sir? I mean, yes, it does seem too coincidental to be random, but how can the two possibly relate?" Hale asked.

"That's what we're trying to figure out, Curly. We need to prove or disprove the theory either way."

Yazzie stepped forward and looked directly at Tamar. "By the time I arrived, there was no sign of anyone using the house since you were there. The place had been trashed, possibly by the person that shot you. There were some blood stains on the living room floor, but they were old. The only thing unusual was a substantial amount of blue ink splattered on the floor and wall."

Yazzie, Mac, and Helen all watched intently to see how Hale or Tamar would react. There was no apparent surprise on either face, so Yazzie continued. "As for the .38, after what happened at Walter Reed General Hospital, I thought it prudent to bring you a weapon for defense. Just in case, as it were."

"Thank you, Uncle," Tamar said appreciatively.

Mac picked up where he left off. "Now Yazzie is headed to Amsterdam to check out a lead there and solicit some help from a friend of his."

Tamar looked at Yazzie and blurted out, "Samuel?"

Yazzie smiled and nodded his head.

Mac continued with his instructions to Hale and Tamar. "You two head to Berlin." He looked at Tamar and said, "You said you found Bergmann in Berlin, then followed him to Fussen. If there's even a remote possibility he picked the gems up there, I want to know where he got them and who he got them from. I want his contacts. You will wire me any pertinent information unless you deem it classified. In that case, use the appropriate military channels. Understood?"

Both respectfully responded with, "Yes, sir."

"Good, it's 2100 now. So, get out of here and have Sergeant McCann get you up to Berlin ASAP. Hopefully, the information you uncover there will determine if our two sets of diamonds are connected. Be damn careful, these guys are good."

With that admonition, Mac opened the front door and ushered Hale and Tamar out of the house. They moved quickly down the walkway to the street, where McCann was pulling up right on time. Inside the residence, Yazzie kept his eye on the two of them from the window. Once they left with McCann, he turned to Mac and Helen.

"Do you think they bought it?" he asked Mac.

"I hope so."

"Did you have to be so gruff with them, Mac?" Helen asked. "They were only doing their jobs. There was no reason to be cross with them."

"Major Hale would have expected nothing less from me, Helen. He's an officer in the U.S. Army. He knows how these special briefings go."

"And Tamar?"

Yazzie smiled wryly at Helen and said, "Oh, this was a tame dress-down compared to what Menachem Begin does with his agents, I assure you. She will respond accordingly."

"I still wonder if we shouldn't have just told them the truth," Helen said wearily.

"The Greys wouldn't authorize it," he reminded her. "They were adamantly opposed to letting them in on our secret. Besides, it takes a lot of energy to do what we did for the President. We had no time to prepare, and the rest required afterward would have set us back from our other duties."

"I know, dear. But it seems as if we have sent them on a dangerous assignment without knowing all the facts. That doesn't seem fair."

"Fair? Nothing is fair in war, Helen. You should know that after all these years. And as for the facts, we're still learning them ourselves. When I am convinced they need to know, then I will tell them whether the Greys approve or not. Until then, this is still very restricted knowledge. There is no other way to keep the enemy from discovering the Grey's involvement, what skills we have, or what we know about them at this point."

"I still don't like it," Helen said with concern.

"They are both highly trained, Helen," Yazzie offered in comfort. "They know what they're doing. They will complete their assignment or die trying."

"That's what I'm afraid of."

CHAPTER 26

Hale and Tamar were chauffeured by Sergeant McCann to a small but popular German konditorei in the western sector of Berlin. It was off the beaten path and virtually unknown to tourists but a favorite among locals, making it a good source of information with its busy crowd of movers and shakers in the city. In fact, it was over a cup of espresso in this very shop that she first noticed Bergmann making contact with his associates. While Bergmann's eventual end (before providing essential information) was unfortunate, she and Hale had decided to start at the beginning and hoped for an unlikely repeat performance of former Nazi communications at the eating establishment.

Tamar had learned that the husband and wife's family who owned the konditorei were actually very anti-Nazi but had played the part of loyal Hitler supporters throughout the war. Maxwell and Gertrude Wagner hated Hitler. They hated everything he stood for and had surreptitiously provided a steady stream of information to England's MI5 unit from overheard conversations about the goings on around Berlin from their well-heeled and highly placed business clientele.

Maxwell would have preferred to take a more physical approach to deal with the Nazi scum, but his wife and a very pretty British agent named Dorothy convinced him otherwise. Dorothy insisted that information gained about the financial district was just as crucial as any other form of destabilization and far more valuable than a single assault. Maxwell reluctantly complied but was always convinced that a good confrontation or two would have been so much more satisfying.

Tamar smiled brightly up at Hale and caressed his arm as they entered the eatery and said, "Ooh, there's a table, Curly darling. I'll get it while you order."

The Konditorei was located in the Hotel-Pension Savoy in the Berlin Kurfuerstendamm which is quite similar to the popular Broadway area of New York City. Americans just called it the Kudamm for convenience's sake. It was frequented by the elite members of German society who seemed to have survived the war fairly unscathed. They were anxious to get their city and nation back to normal as quickly as possible so that any atrocities they may have participated in could be buried forever.

Curly brought two espressos and a slice of kuchen with two forks to the table. He smiled warmly and quietly asked, "When did we become a couple?"

"It will allow us quiet conversation without raising eyebrows, Major," she responded in a whisper as she scooted her chair around the table closer to his. She played her role as the smitten kitten to the hilt as she flirted and laughed coyly with her paramour. "I was first sent to Germany by Menachem Begin on behalf of the Irgun. I spoke the language and was somewhat familiar with the area from my childhood," she continued as she raised a forkful of kuchen and fed it to Curly.

He accepted the bite and smiled as he brushed the hair back from her face and let his arm rest comfortably on the back of her chair. "When was this?"

"Hmmm, about a year ago," she responded after a delicate sip from the petite cup. "My contact worked at the Deutsche Bank and it was through him I learned of Bergmann's questionable sources of revenue as well as the dealings of several other prominent businessmen."

A veil clouded her eyes as they darted from his and took in the room at the last revelation. He took her chin in his hand and turned her face back to his, gently running his thumb down her cheek. Their foreheads came together as they smiled. "I was told you went off mission here. Do you want to tell me what happened?"

She shrugged casually and took another sip. "Information of a personal nature came to my attention." As Hale's eyebrows raised in question, she continued. "My contact oversaw property transfers during the war. It seems he facilitated the sale of my parent's home to our disgusting Nazi neighbors within days of them being taken. I visited our house and asked if any photographs had survived. The bitch that answered the door pretended to know nothing, but she was wearing my mother's brooch."

"What did you do?" Hale asked as he softly took her hand.

"I returned that night and burned the house and everything in it to the ground," she responded with a warm smile. "I slept so well that night that I tracked down several others during my time here. Each of them had profited handsomely from the slaughter of my people. I decided to send the self-righteous bastards on their way to eternal judgment the same way they did my parents. It was truly amazing that they thought their past would simply fade away and no retribution would come their way."

Curly took a sip of the bitter coffee as he thought this new revelation through. "Did the family get out?"

"I don't know," she returned as a piece of the coffee cake was broken off and popped into her mouth. "And I can't say that I really care. They were Nazis."

"You could just kill innocent civilians without remorse?"

Tamar tossed back her head and laughed as if he had just said something amusing. "Innocent? They were anything but innocent. In fact, they were probably the ones who turned my parents in and had them put on the train to Auschwitz. Actually, it's easier to kill people like that than one would think."

"So, how many houses did you burn down with the families still inside?" He asked with a tinge of accusation in his voice.

"Don't be silly, Curly. You don't use the same method every time. It would be too obvious," she answered coolly, with a small smile on her lips.

He was unsure how to respond. How this beguiling young lady could be so ruthless while appearing so charming was almost frightening. Yet, knowing what she had lost in the war, he could understand her becoming a one-woman vigilante.

She took her napkin and wiped an imaginary crumb from Hale's face. He then brought her fingers to his mouth and kissed them. "Tell me what happened at Fussen," he whispered in her ear.

She pulled back coyly and looked up at him through her lashes. "Ever the romantic, aren't you? Well, I was sent to determine how Bergmann was smuggling people and money out of Germany without getting caught by the Allies. My contact had worked with him at the bank prior to his steady rise within the Reich so we knew he already had established contacts." She paused to sip the last of her coffee, then entwined her fingers with his. "He came to this café every day and met a wide variety of people. That's why I followed him here. I saw many drops; mostly envelopes, papers, things like that."

"Which direction were they going?"

"Both ways, sometimes from him, other times to him. I assumed he was selling information. It was only when the satchel was passed to him that I stopped watching and followed him to Fussen."

"Did you kill him?"

She raised her deep green eyes to his. "Only in self-defense," she responded quietly.

"Am I honestly supposed to believe that?"

She pulled back and wagged her finger at him as if he had been naughty. "You don't understand, Major. I wanted him alive. You see, dead men can't tell me their secrets." Tamar laughed and said aloud, "Not yet silly boy, I want another espresso," as the waiter approached. The waiter smiled knowingly as he cleared the dishes and hurried off to bring two more coffees.

Hale nuzzled her ear and asked, "So, what happened?"

"I wanted to see what was in the satchel," she responded, as she teasingly pushed him away. "You see, the object was never to kill him. It was always about the money. We knew huge amounts of money and valuables were being smuggled out of Germany, all assets confiscated from Jews. We plan to reclaim those assets to help with the work occurring in Palestine."

The waiter returned with the coffee and Hale gave him a quick 'Danke' along with a couple of bills. They each took a sip of the fresh coffee before Hale continued. "So, Bergmann was a link in the rat line."

"Rat line?" Tamar asked.

"Whenever a bad guy wants to move something of value, whether it's information or a physical asset, from one point to another without detection it is rarely moved in a single straight line. As you probably know, it is passed through several hands as invisibly as possible to hide the point of origin and the final destination. But the rat will always leave a trail if you know what to look for."

"Yes, I see what you mean. You are correct. He was not working alone that we knew for certain, but I had to know for sure if my instincts were correct. I watched closely for an opportunity to check the bag, but it never left his side. So, I snuck into the farmhouse when they were arguing."

"What were they arguing about?"

"Bergmann was angry because they had accidentally killed the man being tortured. He had information Bergmann needed and he was furious at their mistake. I was in the backroom when it went quiet. After a few minutes, I heard him coming and tried to get out, but I was a few seconds too slow. He caught my foot as I went through the window."

"Wait, it went quiet?"

Tamar smiled as her index finger gently traced an imaginary pattern on the back of Hale's hand. "Yes, the ice pick was his, you see. Bergmann killed the other two before he caught me. He recognized me from the café, so there was no talking my way out of it. He had disrobed to bathe, to get the blood off I suppose. That's what saved me, he had left the pick in the bathroom."

"How did you overpower him? He had fifty pounds on you at least."

"It was not me; it was God Himself that saved me. Bergmann had me by the hair, dragging me to the bathroom to retrieve the pick he'd left in the sink. As I struggled, he slipped on the wet floor and hit his head. It gave me the only opportunity I needed."

They both remained quiet for a moment as Curly placed his arm around Tamar and pulled her close. Tamar suddenly flinched as a familiar face arrived at the gasthaus. When she tensed under his touch, he released her as he spoke into her hair, "Just staying in character, darling."

"No, no. I know that man, the American over there," she said in a hoarse whisper. "He met with Bergmann."

"Are you sure?" Hale asked as he turned from her and took his cup in hand to get a look at him. "How do you know he's American?"

Tamar smiled up at him, keeping the ruse going. "Are you kidding? He's completely out of place here. He would never pass as a local. His clothes, his shoes, and even his glasses are all wrong. I'm positive he's the one I saw with Bergmann."

"Do you see the bag he has with him?"

"Oh yes, it's very similar to the satchel Bergmann used. Unfortunately, the gasthaus was very busy that day and I couldn't see if they exchanged bags. What is he doing back in Germany?"

"Well, either the gentleman has multiple customers here or Herr Bergmann has a replacement. We need to follow him." Hale checked his watch. "McCann is stationed down the street in a pub. He'll see us when we leave."

As they contrived a plan, a tall pale man with sandy blonde hair entered the café and stood a moment surveying the clientele. His thick wool sweater did little to hide the fact that he was muscular and fit. The American quietly folded his paper, then casually stood to leave. He motioned to the new arrival, pointing him to the seat he was vacating as he shrugged into his coat. The blonde made his way through the small seating area and thanked him as he dropped his bag to the floor and sat down. His accent sounded Nordic or Scandinavian, maybe.

"No problem," the American replied as he retrieved the bag just dropped and put it over his shoulder at the same moment the new customer tugged the American's bag beside his chair.

The pretend love birds watched the exchange, then rose to leave with Hale pulling the chair out for Tamar. "What about him?" a smiling Tamar asked with her eyes darting over to the newcomer.

"No jurisdiction there," Hale replied while placing his hand on the small of her back to guide her out the door. "Besides, he doesn't look like an intelligence officer. I want to know what an American businessman is doing here making a live drop."

Tamar slipped past an elderly couple just entering the café, leaving Hale to hold the door for them. He smiled and nodded to cover his impatience while taking a backward glance as he edged toward the exit. The blonde weightlifter stood and moved toward the counter, deftly pushing the satchel with his foot from his chair to rest next to the seat directly behind him.

"Danke, danke," the white-haired couple said repeatedly at Hale's kindness.

"Bitte," Hale responded as the new owner of the satchel used his receipt as a bookmark, placed the book in the satchel, then stood to leave. Hale stopped just outside the door and searched for McCann across the street. He used his index and middle fingers to point to his eyes, then pointed at the American sauntering down the street opposite his position. McCann nodded and turned to follow.

Holding his hand out to Tamar, Hale delayed giving the third person involved in the drop time to exit. A dark-haired Asian man about five feet four in a dark wool coat and expensive leather shoes exited and turned left as Tamar took Curly's hand. He tucked it under his arm and patted her hand as he said, "The gentleman has a very handsome bag, yes?"

She looked at him quizzically. When her attention shifted to the man walking briskly ahead of them, her eyebrows went up in recognition. "Hmm, very handsome indeed. Perhaps we should ask him where he bought it. After all, it's exactly what we've been looking for. A target of opportunity?"

"Hell yes, it is."

CHAPTER 27

Randall Smithers III was in his element. The trip from Washington D.C. to New York City to London to Berlin had been successfully navigated, and he was now getting ready to take the opposite route for his return home. The exchange had gone beautifully. It really was a shame that no one could know of his prowess at undercover operations. He had accomplished the task of retrieving a substantial amount of cash in exchange for some select classified documents specifically requested by his counterpart from Tokyo without raising an eyebrow, just as he had done several dozen times before.

His former contact, Hans Bergmann, had disappeared without a trace. Undoubtedly, he had taken his last diamond cache and fled the country to live in luxury at an undisclosed destination. *That's the problem with those Nazi bastards,* he thought to himself. *Always trying to enrich themselves without a thought of the greater good. Never understanding the need for personal sacrifice from the lower classes.*

Smithers never liked working with Bergmann, anyway. The thought of working hand-in-hand with that fascist made his skin crawl. The common street trash insisted on calling him Smitty, which made Smithers grit his teeth in disgust. However, the finances the pompous ass provided to help the cause were worth the momentary nausea of being in his presence. Maybe his new contact would be more agreeable. Perhaps, given the chance, he could even recruit the thus far unnamed Japanese courier to his side. The right side. The inevitable worldwide victors.

Smithers had come from "old money". His New England family had been one of the earliest British families to settle in the Colonies. They had prospered in the new world and eventually had become highly sought-after by those within the political arena. His ancestors knew how to get things done, things that men running for office couldn't do. Of course, his family's unerring support carried a hefty price tag, and they always collected. Always.

He had grown accustomed to the privileged lifestyle afforded him and enjoyed extensive travels to Europe as a part of his education at his grandfather's insistence. Contacts made during those travels later became useful in his adult years. He had been a Rhodes Scholar who did his undergraduate work at Harvard. Following graduation, he crossed the Atlantic to further his education at Oxford and earn his graduate degree in Policy Studies, the English version of Political Science.

It was while at Oxford in 1930 that he met a gorgeous young woman named Mistaya Andropov. She was the most beautiful and intoxicating woman he had ever met, and she was a devout communist. They had many fascinating conversations about capitalism versus communism, which convinced him beyond any doubt that she was as brilliant as she was captivating. Her passion for him and her country eventually won him over completely. Under her tutelage, Randall Smithers III betrayed his family's proud American heritage and became a confirmed communist. She was most persuasive as she lay naked beneath him panting what a true communist leader he would be for the people of America. Who was he to argue with such a beautiful and astute Russian graduate student on loan to Oxford?

His thesis arguing that the United States, Great Britain, Russia, and Japan should form an economic alliance was lauded greatly at University. Their combined economic strength and military power, he theorized, would allow complete domination of the rest of the world. The socialist mindset could then be adapted to unite the four nations into a single functioning communist government. That government would in turn organize other nations economically under their strict control, of course, to enhance and further their own strategic worldwide goals.

After his time at Oxford was complete he intended to take up permanent residence in Russia with Mistaya at his side. He still remembered the wicked fight they had at her insistence that he must return to the United States to further the cause. After all, he could infiltrate America like no foreigner possibly could. Her vicious accusations that he was nothing more than a spoiled rich boy on holiday from his controlling parents and that he was not a true believer steeled his determination to prove her wrong.

His paramour had warned him of the lies the American government would tell about Mother Russia. She prepared him well for the grueling interrogations he would endure as they attempted to keep him from his rightful inheritance as a communist leader in America. He was supremely confident that he could beat them all. With his talents, he would pass every interview and convince even the most ardent adversaries along the way that he was a changed man and just the person they needed working in the United States government.

He planned to survive the scrutiny of his communist leanings as a student by claiming to have "seen the light" when he became aware of Stalin's atrocities upon his people. The slaughter of nearly 30 million, even before the war, was proof of his maniacal tyranny. Oh yes, he had an answer prepared for every question that might be asked. However, Randall Smithers III Rhodes scholar and Oxford graduate was bypassed several times in favor of other candidates. He immediately surmised that the obviously far less qualified interviewers were intimidated by him and his credentials. He had played his part perfectly, so it couldn't possibly have been him. It had to be jealousy on the part of the interviewers, plain and simple.

In the end, family intervention was required to net him a position in the War Department. His claim of being a devout American citizen was weighed with skepticism, however, by calling in a few favors his father finally secured an entry-level Planner position for his only son. It took twelve long years of insincere flag waving and spouting of capitalist propaganda to work his way up to Lead Planner in 1943, and even after all that time, there was still much consternation about his promotion among his peers. But no one could deny his remarkable acuity when it came to data analysis. Thus, he was able to position himself to be directly involved in setting new economic policies with America's former enemies, Germany and Japan.

Smithers considered himself to be a true Renaissance man. He was well-educated, sophisticated, knowledgeable of worldwide politics, and a lover of the arts. He also had no trouble attracting the ladies. His communist paramour actually encouraged him to increase his proclivities for women and use them to advance the communist cause. She was instrumental in teaching him ways to seduce almost any woman of almost any age and obtain their full confidence and support. She had been a wonderful teacher and he a most willing student.

Once he became the teacher rather than the student, his eyes were gradually opened to the realization that Mistaya had targeted and then used him. His anger at the thought quickly diminished as he conceded that his extreme value made him a prime target. How could she possibly have ignored him? He was the whole package; intelligent, connected, well-traveled, and committed. Of course, he was far more intelligent than they knew and far more committed to rising to the position of power he was born to than any ideology. Still, recognizing her subterfuge made it easier to abandon the communist mantra when a Shalanaya temptress came his way. Under communism, he would have been a prince, with the Shalanaya he would be king.

He had gone so far as to take a wife of the proper social structure to fulfill civic appearances. She was attractive enough to pass the scrutiny of critical social icons, yet vapid enough to believe anything he told her to believe. This made it easy for him to carry on many affairs over the years. He had netted consorts in America, Europe, and more recently Japan. The Shalanya had made it clear that his most ardent desires of sex, power, and money were unlimited for the would-be King of America.

The only thing he did not excel at was the intricacies of spy tradecraft. Its value was highly overstated in his opinion and didn't even seem necessary, not for him anyway. The ability to travel unmolested throughout the world for the War Department gave him a sense of superiority and security that negated any qualms about the discovery of his duplicity. Paranoia was for the weak and unconnected. He was neither.

He failed to recognize that his open disdain for the skills that kept clandestine operators alive and undetected left him vulnerable. Today it was the reason he never noticed Sergeant William McCann tailing him from the gasthaus at the Berlin Hotel-Pension Savoy in the Kurfuerstendamm. Nor did he realize McCann was patiently waiting outside the Hotel Adlon Kempinski as he quickly retrieved his suitcase waiting by the concierge desk. And one astute glance out the back window of his taxi as it drove to the Berlin Airport may have made him aware of Sergeant McCann continuing to follow at a discreet distance.

As Smithers made his way through the airport, he was completely unaware of his surroundings, including McCann's presence ten feet behind him just out of his peripheral vision. He flashed his U.S. government I.D. at the desk and retrieved his waiting ticket without realizing that his every move was being watched and scrutinized.

McCann was the third person in line behind Smithers as he checked in. He noticed the federal emblem on the target's I.D. and wondered just what he had done in the gasthaus to draw Hale and Tamar's attention. The leather bag's similarity to the one they had retrieved from the farmhouse where Tamar was shot did not escape his notice. As Smithers voiced concerns over connecting flights, McCann made note of the itinerary. And as the arrogant statesman settled in the waiting area for his flight, he still had not made McCann or recognized the fact that he had been followed.

McCann slouched down in his seat and folded his arms over his chest, then pulled his cap down to obscure his eyes. He watched the American intently and rose to follow him into the latrine the only time he left his seat. There was no funny business as he simply used the facilities, then returned to his seat. McCann stayed and personally watched to make sure his target boarded the plane, then watched it take off.

Smithers' itinerary was the same as always. Berlin to London. From there he would fly on to New York and then Washington, D.C. But this time information about his flight status would be conveyed to Colonel Quinn at the White House. By the time the last leg of his journey was complete, CIG personnel would have his name and full background. His face will have been memorized, his work analyzed, and his many travel destinations would be under investigation. Quinn would have men in place to continue surveillance when Smithers touched down at the Washington-Virginia Airport.

Yes, his lack of tradecraft would now be his undoing.

CHAPTER 28

Hale used his military credentials to get the two of them aboard the PanAm flight to Tokyo. The arrangement to be seated in the back of the plane with crew members provided them a low enough profile so the Japanese operative involved in the dead drop at the German café would not see them when he boarded. Hale felt it imperative to take every precaution to ensure that he and Tamar were not recognized on the flight. The manifest identified the window seat in row five as passenger Okada. They knew nothing more of their target than that, but that was enough for the moment.

It was going to be an excruciatingly long trip. The only route currently available had six stops in total. The route went from Berlin to Frankfurt, then across the Atlantic to New York City, from there to Seattle, on to San Francisco, across the Pacific to Hawaii, then on to their final destination, Tokyo. The DC-4 aircraft they were currently on was actually a C-54A military plane that had been remodeled for civilian use. Hale was familiar with C-54A aircraft from the war. The military version had reduced passenger seating to accommodate the extra fuel tanks, hoists, winch, and large cargo area. Not nearly as sexy as the DC-4, but overall, a reliable ride. However, regardless of what model plane you were on for five or six days, it would be a long and uncomfortable trip. The advantage was that Hale and Tamar had plenty of time to observe and investigate Okada.

The former military aircraft would fly from mid-morning to mid-afternoon, stopping in each city for a night of rest in a comfortable hotel. Each stop allowed the passengers continuing on the journey at least a semblance of a complete night's sleep before re-boarding again the next day with new passengers just joining the flight. It was long and cumbersome, but it was still the best mode of travel after the seemingly endless world war.

Tamar watched from her seat in the back as Okada was seated. He carried the satchel with him and stowed it under the seat in front of him where it could be guarded against tampering. An offered blanket was accepted and fastidiously tucked around his legs shortly after takeoff. Those seated near him were closely observed until it was determined that none of them seemed to have any connection to him. She saw a few passengers flash looks of disgust at their former enemy. The horror stories of Japanese prison camps were by now well known. His presence on the plane was not appreciated by some of the occupants, and they saw no reason to hide their displeasure.

For his part, Okada seemed oblivious to the stares and glares of the other passengers. He occupied himself with a German newspaper and other reading materials. He never opened the satchel to peruse anything within, nor did he store any personal items in the case. His reading glasses were carried in his pocket and once an item was read, it was discarded.

He portrayed a typical businessman very well. However, the two tailing him noticed discrepancies. He dressed the part, but his actions did not match a successful businessman's routine of continuous unending paperwork. He was also far more aware of his surroundings than the diligent worker that was consumed by his task. His vigilance was surreptitious, of course, but he was always watching.

His acuity made Hale and Tamar careful to stay out of Okada's line of sight throughout the trip. Who knew what would happen if he were to recognize them from the restaurant in Berlin? It was an unpleasant task that required constant vigilance and ridiculous patience, but it was necessary. The satchel was key, and they would do what was necessary to determine what information had been purchased by their enemy.

Each time the plane landed, Hale and Tamar were always the last off and the first on the next morning. The flight crew was only told to stay out of their way as much as possible and to never mention they were on the flight. The operative phrase was "national security" and that's all the patriotic crew needed to know to cooperate fully with the two agents.

Hale and Tamar used a different hotel than the rest of the passengers to ensure there was never an accidental meeting with Okada. The help of the pilot, a former Army Air Corps Captain, was enlisted to keep an eye on Okada while at their sleeping quarters. He was more than willing to continue his military service for this flight, knowing that their final destination was Japan. Each evening they would call Quinn in D.C. to report their progress, or lack thereof, and to receive any instructions the Colonel may have for them.

All three agreed that surveillance alone was the best course of action until the final leg of the trip. Since there had been a double-blind dead drop in Germany, there was the possibility that another dead drop may occur enroute. If Okada remained in possession of the satchel, they would make their move on the flight from Hawaii to Japan. It was never easy to get the drop on a trained agent however, even agents were human. A boring uneventful trip and exhaustion may bring down his guard a little, and a little was all they needed.

Tamar suggested an approach she had used successfully in prior assignments for Menachem Begin and the Irgun. A vile of extremely potent sedative she just happened to have with her (you never knew when you might need it, she insisted) would be used to render Okada unconscious. She assured both Hale and Quinn that it would be more than sufficient to put Okada to sleep for the majority of the flight, and it was hardly ever lethal.

So, despite the men's raised eyebrows regarding its lethality, the plan was made. They rehearsed the proposed scenario in their Honolulu hotel room. Although the seriousness of the situation was not lost on either of them, they too were tired from their days of surveillance and became punchy during practice. So, when Tamar accidentally poked Curly in the eye, she giggled.

"That's not funny," he said as he held his watering eye and pushed her back toward the bed.

When she bounced off the bed and hit the floor is when the laughter started in earnest. Both found themselves laughing indiscriminately while attempting to get back on task to perfect their technique for tomorrow's flight. It was liberating and broke the tension that had been building for the past few days. They were grateful for the release, as there would be no laughing tomorrow.

About an hour out of Honolulu beverage service began. That was the cue for Hale and Tamar to go into action. They had to be fast and efficient, or this could end up an international incident. Timing was key, and both knew they needed to be in place exactly as practiced. Movements needed to be fluid and casual, not drawing attention, and it was imperative that they remain out of Okada's direct line of sight, even though they were going to be in close proximity. There was no room for mistakes. Tamar was confident. Hale was pretending he was.

As the stewardess poured a drink for Okada, Hale bumped into her in the narrow aisle. "Verzeihung, verziehung" he apologized with his best German accent as he bent down to assist with the mess. Hale kept the young server sandwiched between himself and Okada as she expressed her mortification for spilling the drink. While she apologized and attempted to pat down the expensive suit with a cloth to absorb the moisture, Tamar slipped several drops of the sedative into a new drink. She quickly handed it to the young stewardess with a smile as an act of kindness to assist her. The beverage was quickly placed in Okada's hands as Hale and Tamar retreated to the rear of the plane.

The stewardess had not been informed of the ruse and was red-faced and flustered after the incident. She had not noticed when Tamar came up behind her and did not see the liquid from the vial added to the proffered beverage. It was only after completing her task that she saw the backsides of Hale and Tamar as they disappeared into the rear crew quarters, and she wondered why the mystery couple had decided to come out of hiding.

For their part, Hale and Tamar returned to their positions in the crew cabin and smiled as they blew out sighs of relief. It had worked. Well, at least getting the sedative into Okada's drink had been accomplished. All they could do now was wait and see the effects of the narcotic.

"I have to admit," Hale began quietly, "I wasn't sure this would work. At least work as easily as it did."

"I don't want to say I told you so, but…"

"Thank you for not being smug."

"Oh, I am being smug. I don't mind the confirmation."

"Uh, huh. You said you have used that technique in Europe. How many times has this worked for you?"

"Counting today?"

"Yes, counting today."

Tamar closed her eyes and seemed to be mentally counting. When she opened them, she said smartly, "Exactly two."

Hale's face went pale.

Tamar waited five minutes before walking quietly down the aisle toward Okada. She was busy as the minutes ticked off. Her hair was twisted into a knot and pinned at the nape of her neck. A white sweater was buttoned into place over her dark blue blouse, and dark-rimmed glasses were retrieved from her bag and slipped on. It wasn't much of a disguise, but in situations like this most observers took note of things like clothing and glasses rather than looking at the person wearing them. It would be sufficient.

He was fast asleep as she approached, his snoring heard for several rows. The smiling stewardess was busy chatting with customers, asking if anyone needed a refill, or perhaps a blanket. The timing was perfect. While the passengers were distracted, Tamar slid into the empty seat beside Okada.

The question that had been left to her discretion was whether to take the satchel back to the crew cabin for inspection or to search it immediately in place. There were risks associated with each option. The lock on the bag made the decision for her. A key, hopefully the correct key, was located in Okada's inside jacket pocket and spirited away along with the satchel to the rear of the aircraft where Hale had been anxiously waiting.

"I still don't understand why you insisted it be you to retrieve this," he whispered cantankerously to her when she sat down.

She responded as the key was placed in the lock. "Because everyone knows that women are less likely to attract attention when moving from one seat to another. Those seated nearby would just assume I was a hard to please woman trying to find a more comfortable seat and would not think anything of me sitting down briefly then changing my mind and looking for another open spot."

The gentle click of the lock was music to his ears as he said, "I've never heard anything like that before and I've had extensive training. I think you're making it up."

"We must have gone to different training facilities," she answered with preoccupied assurance as the lid was raised and they got their first look inside. "Besides, I knew you would give in to my demands rather than risk an argument being heard up front."

"Well, the mission does come first," he returned in annoyance, knowing she was correct.

"Here," she said as the now opened satchel was passed to him. "Pull out one document at a time. I'll use my Minox Riga camera to get photos. As soon as we're finished, I'll replace the satchel. Most of the passengers are taking naps, so it should be easy to return without suspicion."

"You're becoming a major pain in my…"

"Ass," she finished for him. "I am well aware of the American euphemism."

"I was going to be polite and say my neck, but since you mention it, yes you are."

They withheld further dialogue as they concentrated on quickly removing one item at a time, taking a picture, then returning it to the same location in the satchel. Hale took note of the way each document, photograph, or map was positioned and was careful to return it to exactly the same position within the case. It would not be unusual, if Okada were experienced, for him to fastidiously arrange the contents to detect tampering. The attention to detail would hopefully ensure that his suspicions were not aroused, and their intrusion went undetected.

As soon as they finished the satchel was locked, and Tamar casually returned to the seat beside Okada to set it in place. As the key was returned to his pocket, Tamar froze when Okada snorted, coughed then with a sigh returned to a deep slumber. She gently slid out of the seat and quickly hurried up the aisle to rejoin Hale. Mr. Okada would have no idea his documents had ever been out of his possession. Just as it should be.

Neither Hale nor Tamar had taken any real time to read the documents while securing pictures. Their interest at the time was in being fastidious in replacing said documents exactly as found. There were some aerial photographs of unspecified land masses and islands, but they had no way of knowing whether the photographs would link to their investigation. That would be determined at a later date but given the circumstances, it was a pretty good bet that they did. It appeared all the written documents were encrypted so they could not determine if any of them pertained to the photographs.

As they waited for the aircraft to land in Tokyo, Tamar released her hair from the bun and removed the sweater and glasses returning the disguise to her bag. Passengers began to rouse, stretching and yawning as the plane descended. They gathered their belongings and readied themselves to disembark. Except Okada. His head remained tilted back on the headrest, with his mouth sagging open. Hale observed as Tamar returned to her old self, trying to determine if he was still breathing.

"Just how much knock-out juice did you give him?" he whispered hoarsely.

"What? Why?" she asked.

"Were you serious when you said he could die?"

Her eyes widened as she joined him, peeking through the curtain. The plane touched down, bouncing several times before smoothing out on the runway. Okada's head tipped to one side, but he did not rouse. They taxied to their gate and passengers began bumping their way down the aisle to greet waiting friends and family and still, he did not come to. As the last passenger disappeared out the door, a stewardess gently shook Okada's shoulder.

"Sir? Sir, we've arrived at our destination." Tamar and Hale held their breaths until he finally started with a snort and looked around at the empty plane. "You must have been exhausted, sir. I'll bet you're glad to get home," she said with a smile.

Temporary panic registered on Okada's face until he saw the satchel resting at his feet. He patted his pocket for the key, then in confusion rose from his seat and labored down the aisle.

Hale and Tamar fell back in their seats with collective sighs of relief and just grinned at one another. They gave Okada ample time to leave the airport, assuming that Quinn had assigned someone to tail him as planned. Their only priority right now was to get the camera to MacArthur's temporary headquarters to have the film developed. Then the photos could be analyzed to see what information had been spirited out of the United States to their enemies.

Quinn had provided the name of someone trustworthy on MacArthur's staff to hand the film off to for development, but they now knew an encryption specialist was needed as well. Hale's first call was going to be to Colonel Quinn to report on the success of their operation and to inform him of their new need. He was hoping Quinn would have an asset available that would not be tempted to shoot his mouth off about the particulars of their findings to those who were not allowed to see this VRK information. Plus, Hale greatly preferred to deal with people he knew or, as a second option, at least those his superiors had confidence in.

It wasn't intended to be a knock on MacArthur or his people, but Hale had been burned before. The fact was, he didn't know any of these people. This information was highly classified and far too sensitive to be released into the wrong hands, even though they may wear the same uniform.

"Do you think there is someone available with the ability to decode the encrypted papers?" Tamar asked as they hailed a taxi.

"I think there's a very good chance," Hale answered. "As long as there's an American presence in Japan there's sure to be an intelligence team here. No way MacArthur would be foolish enough to leave communications unmonitored while occupying a foreign nation. I wouldn't be surprised if we were getting assistance from our allies in this area."

"You think the Americans would trust outsiders with this type of specialized work?" Tamar asked as she slid into the back seat of a cab.

"Yes, in fact, we learned a thing or two from the Brits about decrypting. They are very skilled in that area."

"How so?"

"They broke the German's code fairly early on in the war. The Germans never knew that they were transmitting information directly to London where it was deciphered and taken to Churchill."

"Did he use it?"

"Of course. All is fair in love and war, Tamar. Especially in war."

"I hate that saying," she responded bitterly, thinking of her parents. There was nothing fair about innocents being killed. "So, he was able to prevent German bombings over England, yes?"

"Yes, and no."

"What does that mean?"

"It means he wasn't able to respond to all the information they received without revealing that they had cracked the code. Some lives had to be sacrificed that could have been saved to protect their secret. It was a necessary strategy to win the war."

"I don't understand. Why wouldn't he? He was responsible for all their lives."

"Yes, all their lives. That meant he had to make hard decisions about what information to utilize immediately and what needed to be saved for later. There were instances where he could have saved some British lives, but it would have been at the expense of losing even more lives later."

"That doesn't make sense."

Hale breathed in and then exhaled slowly before continuing. "Although disputed by some, it is believed that Churchill was aware of a coming attack on Coventry, England. He elected to allow the attack to continue. He was not willing to risk future victories at the expense of one community. Hundreds died in the bombing raid."

"That's horrible! How could he do such a thing? All those people!"

"Whether or not the story is completely true, Churchill probably made the right decision. If the Germans realized their encryption codes had been compromised they would have changed them, rendering intelligence gathering impotent. By allowing the raid, he was able to use future enemy transmissions to help set the stage for Allied missions. The attack on Normandy, for example, turned the tide of the war in favor of the Allied forces. If the Germans had changed their encryption code the invasion could have been delayed or even canceled. That may have meant the war continuing for several more years with thousands more casualties."

"So, he sacrificed some in the hopes of saving even more," Tamar reasoned aloud.

"Does that make sense now?"

"Yes. But I still grieve over the hundreds of lives lost at Coventry."

"I'm sure Churchill did as well. Leadership carries heavy burdens. That was one of his."

"I pray I never have to make such a decision. I don't know if I could forgive myself."

"I hope you don't either. The burden of those lost lives never leaves you," Hale said sadly.

Tamar hesitated before quietly asking, "You have made such decisions, haven't you?"

Hale did not respond other than the pall of grief set on his face and the tears welling up in his eyes. She did not need to question him any more.

CHAPTER 29

Helen let out an indignant huff as she watched everyone leave her at the door as they continued down the tunnels. Oh, it was so infuriating! After all, she was the one that recognized the key found at the alien's house. And it was she and Mac that had discovered its use through the highly knowledgeable docent at the museum. The white-haired, elderly gentleman had, by his own admission, volunteered at the museum for several decades and was a wealth of information.

Helen had been certain he didn't at all mind being pulled away from the class of inattentive and uninterested students he was herding through the exhibits to answer their questions. Surprisingly, he remembered the exhibit of keys a decade or so earlier as it had been a particular favorite of his. Of course, the scandalous pilfering of several of those keys while on display also added to the memory. Things like that simply did not happen here, he had explained. All museum personnel and volunteers had undergone extensive questioning at the time but to his knowledge, the missing items were never recovered.

The wizened old man could have knocked them over with a feather when he related that the items stolen were supposed to be original keys to the grid of tunnels rumored to be under Washington, D.C. It was all D.C. lore, of course, but it had made for a delightful story to add to the intrigue and history of the display.

At the docent's revelation, all protocols had been laid aside as they drove directly to Colonel Quinn's office and asked to see him without an appointment. Mac's former clerk was absolutely stunned to see them. Helen stepped in and shared how Mac had quietly whisked her away to deal with a serious health issue. They had been quite unable to make contact and unaware of the fuss they had caused. Upon their return, they were quite embarrassed at the whole situation. She was much recovered now, thank you, she gushed as Quinn returned from his meeting and they were ushered into his office.

"It's a good thing you returned when you did, Colonel, any longer and I would have had to have been at death's door the past seven months in Siberia as Mac walked through a raging sandstorm to get my medicine."

Quinn attempted a smile, then looked at Mac. "I'm surprised you came through the front door instead of your usual entrance."

"I didn't know if you had people in with you and this couldn't wait," Mac responded. "The key, you know the mystery key found at the apartment, we identified it."

"Let me guess, it goes to one of the founding father's horse stables," Quinn quipped as he sat down.

"Close, try the entrance to the tunnels under the city - you know, the ones under the White House."

Quinn laughed, then paled when Mac and Helen did not join in the merriment. "Are you serious?"

"There were several stolen from the Museum of Natural History eight to ten years ago," Mac confirmed as he paced.

"Did you actually try it? Did it work?"

"No, not yet. We came straight here. I was hoping to have a team and maybe a plan before we breached. Do you have any guys that are up for hand-to-hand with aliens?" Magruder asked, with his adrenaline beginning to surge.

"You mean there really are tunnels under the city?" Helen exclaimed.

Quinn was silent for a moment, then stood. "I have to brief the President before we do anything. Helen, do you think you could find Yazzie and get him back here in say…two hours?"

"Of course," she replied.

"Mac," Quinn said, turning to face him. "Are you up for a visit to Groom Lake? There's something I need to be done that can't wait and your particular training may come in handy."

Mac's head snapped up as he felt a twinge of outrage that he would be relegated to a contrived task when all hell could be breaking loose at any moment. "Groom Lake can wait. I need to be here."

"Really dear, you just lectured Curly and Tamar about questioning *your* command," Helen said primly. "Besides, the Colonel was referring to our current six months of training in all things alien. Only two other people in the whole world have that particular degree."

Mac looked at his shoes as his wife's scolding hit home.

"Colonel, we can switch places if you like. Mac can go round up Yazzie and I'll complete the other task. I'll need coordinates to translate…"

"Alright, alright, point taken," Magruder said to his wife as he squeezed her hand. "I'll do whatever needs to be done, Colonel. You're in charge. Besides, I hear Nevada is lovely this time of year," he added sarcastically.

Helen couldn't help but smile at the memory of that meeting as she craned her head around the corner of the dark musty tunnel the men had walked down. Mac would be furious if she followed and, quite frankly, she didn't want to go it alone down here. It was dirty and rather creepy. Even with a flashlight, the dark clung to you like wet clothes and she just knew there were rats down there!

She shifted back to her original position where a sliver of light shone overhead and thought how pleased she was that her first assignment from Colonel Quinn had been completed in record time. Yazzie had been located, and they returned home in just under an hour. Her successful operation had been sweet, but not nearly as eventful as Mac's assignment.

Before she left to find Yazzie, Quinn had told Mac how his suspicions had led him to enlist both doctors Zimmerman and Jensen to bait a trap. Since they now knew positively that there had been spies working within the War Department and, even with all of their advanced security, spies had infiltrated and passed on information regarding the Manhattan Project; was it unreasonable to think that spies may be present in Groom Lake? And now with the intelligence Mac, Helen, and Yazzie had provided regarding new enemies, Quinn found it more probable than ever. He had to know for sure, and what better way to catch a rat than with a trap?

Helen flicked on her flashlight and shone it around her feet. The very thought of rats made her shiver. Once satisfied that the vermin must be deeper in the tunnels, she clicked the light off and resumed her watch. Her fingers felt for the whistle in her pocket that she would blow if anyone approached the hidden door. Once certain of its presence, she took a deep breath to steady her nerves then resumed her reminiscing.

The three of them (she, Mac, and Yazzie) now had an uncanny sense of one another. They had found that the alien modifications had connected them in an almost telepathic way. Using this connection, she had no problem finding Yazzie in the business district of Amsterdam in the Netherlands. He had sensed her arrival and greeted her warmly upon exiting the building where he was conducting business.

"Helen, to what do I owe the pleasure?" he asked, kissing her cheek.

"I've been sent to fetch you," she responded. "But first, perhaps a cup of hot cocoa? I've heard about their chocolate and can't resist the opportunity."

"An excellent idea. I know just the place," he returned. "We can indulge while we catch one another up."

The little café was warm and smelled delicious. They found a small table in a back corner by the kitchen. It was not a much sought-after position due to the wait staff hurrying back and forth and the inability to enjoy a bright window view, but it suited their needs quite well.

"Have you had much success?" Helen inquired as she settled in her seat.

"Indeed," Yazzie replied. "My inquires have taken a most interesting turn."

"How so?" Helen asked as steaming cups of cocoa were delivered.

They both smiled and thanked the waiter, then waited for him to leave before continuing. "Metallurgy," Yazzie confided. "Or more specifically, titanium and uranium. There has been an uptick in the availability of extremely high-grade metals in the last few years. The Irgun in Palestine had heard rumors to that effect and verified them but as far as I know, they have as yet been unable to find the source."

"Oh my," Helen sighed as her cup was returned to its saucer. "That's not good. Who's purchasing it?"

Yazzie sipped, then quietly responded. "As you can imagine, there are no shortage of buyers. My friends are fearing another Hurban…that is, the destruction of our people. However, a very thin connection was recently made between the abundance of heavy and precious metals and a diamond route."

Helen's eyebrows raised in question. "Is it related to our diamond search?"

"It is quite a coincidence, is it not?" Yazzie leaned back in his chair and savored the exquisite flavor of the rich, dark chocolate. They were lost in their own thoughts for a moment before Yazzie asked, "Why have you been sent to find me and where is Mac?"

"Mmmm, the key obtained from *her* apartment," Helen began after a sip. "You know which one, of course. It seems that it may be attached to a door or doors to…" she leaned in and lowered her voice, "an entrance to tunnels under the White House."

Now it was Yazzie's turn to raise his eyebrows.

"Quinn went to brief the President while Mac was sent on an…um, unrelated errand to an exclusive little place in Nevada. We are to meet back in D.C. where a plan to determine the truth of the matter will be concocted together."

As Helen and Yazzie were sipping hot cocoa, Mac had been given coordinates that landed him in a small utility closet in the Groom Lake facility. A rough hand-drawn map of the building as well as a lab coat complete with a security badge, clipboard, and a pair of shoes with rubber soles had been left for him there. '10:45 coffee break' had been written on the back of the amateur attempt at schematics. He checked his watch, 10:40.

His instructions were to meet one of the good doctors and conduct a quiet interview on recent developments, then return home. That's all. Quinn did not want to draw attention or for any of their findings or observations to be transmitted in writing or over the phone lest they be intercepted and the lives of these two men be put at risk. The code word the three men had agreed upon while loading the would-be assassin's body on the plane for the trip to Nevada if an in-person meeting was required had been received by Quinn that very morning.

Mac slipped off his shoes and put on the ones provided. They were about a half size too big, so he cinched up the laces tighter than usual to compensate. He hid his shoes behind some supplies, then shrugged into the lab coat, picked up the clipboard, and carefully exited the room.

He turned left and casually walked down the long corridor as the arrow on his hand-drawn map had indicated. The floors were polished concrete, with white walls that were accented by the overhead fluorescent lighting. Even the hallway seemed sterile as he passed four rooms with solid steel doors with signage declaring them to be sealed environments. After the fourth door, he turned right into another hallway. A pair of similarly clad men in lab coats and rubber-soled shoes passed by Mac, nodding their heads in his direction as they continued on their way.

He picked up his pace as he passed two large laboratories with windows open to the hallway. Several dozen people in white coats were visible in each lab, hunched over brightly lit workspaces intent on their tasks. The stairway up to the cafeteria where they were meeting was on his left about ten feet ahead when suddenly sirens started screaming and pandemonium ensued.

Speakers were blaring instructions as a herd of lab coats began pouring from the stairway, nearly plowing Mac down in their haste. A young man broke off from the stampede and flattened himself against the wall opposite the stairwell. Looking both ways, he caught sight of Mac and made eye contact.

"How do you like your coffee?" he yelled over the loudspeaker.

"Black as tar and just as thick," Mac yelled back.

"This way," he motioned with his voice getting lost in the confusion.

Mac followed him down several hallways, dodging in and out of people who were fleeing in the opposite direction. They stopped short when they rounded a corner and saw a wide-eyed crowd of white coats and what appeared to be security personnel in a dense knot about twenty feet down the hall. An older man standing on the periphery glanced back at their appearance, and a visible look of relief flooded his face.

"Thank God!" they said simultaneously when the older man approached. They embraced while heartily slapping one another on the back.

"What happened Zim?" the young man shouted in his friend's ear to be heard over the din.

"Is this him?" Zim yelled back with a nod of his head in Mac's direction. At the positive response, he gave Mac a good once over, then signaled them to follow. They approached the now dispersing crowd and looked down a dark hallway at a misshapen steel door. "I was called away to Doctor Ismann's lab. I know I locked up before I left," he shouted right before the sirens went silent. "Thank God, I was about to go deaf."

"What did Ismann want?" the young doctor Jensen asked quietly.

"That's the thing…once I got there, he claimed he never called."

"Doctor Zimmerman?" a security officer asked.

"Yes?"

"We need to ask you a few questions."

"My work is highly classified. I doubt I will be of much help."

The security guard didn't seem put off or agitated by this reply. *I guess when you work in one of the most highly classified facilities in the nation*, Mac surmised, *you expect answers like that.*

"We just need to know if anyone else was working in that lab. There is a pile of ash in the general shape of a body. We're just trying to determine if there were any casualties."

"I work alone, young man. If anyone was in there, they were unauthorized and broke in while I was out," Zimmerman stated firmly.

"A pile of ash?" Mac couldn't help but interject. "So, thermite then."

The security guard looked at Mac as if seeing him for the first time. "What makes you say that doctor?"

"A steel door wouldn't be sagging on its hinges if it were just a regular fire, not hot enough. Only thermite could do that. We're damn lucky the fire was contained in just one lab," Mac said, including himself as one of the employees. Sensing the emergency worker's growing interest, he extended his hand. "Zim, so relieved you're okay. I hope they can figure out what happened."

Doctor Zimmerman shook his hand as he replied, "It's a damn mess. I'll have to waste my time setting up a new office and start all over again. It's a good thing all my research wasn't in the lab."

Clever man, Mac thought. *He told me everything I needed to know without skipping a beat.*

"Doctor, coffee another day? Unfortunately, I have to get back," Mac said, putting a hand on the young man's shoulder.

"Of course," Jensen replied. "Let's make it soon."

Mac turned and briskly walked down the hall, away from the scene.

"Hey! Hey, wait…" he heard as Doctor Zimmerman interrupted.

"When will I be able to get into my office, young man? There's classified information in there and I need to see…"

The voices faded as Mac turned the corner. He walked as quickly as possible without drawing attention as he tried to recall the path they had taken to get to Zimmerman's lab. He wanted to avoid any further questions, and he was afraid the conscientious young investigator might try to chase him down. Mac found the stairs to the cafeteria where they were originally to meet and slowed his pace.

Small clusters of lab coats were huddled together in the hallways, discussing the day's excitement. His slower pace allowed him to overhear snatches of conversation as he made his way to the utility closet. Speculation abounded. Self-righteous individuals spoke of safety protocols and the lack of discipline of some of their colleagues. Others discussed the horror of what could have happened had the fire not been contained and, of course, everyone was wondering who was to blame for the whole episode.

Mac slipped into the utility closet and retrieved his shoes, careful to straighten the supplies after, then left with shoes in hand, leaving nothing behind. Helen and Yazzie were already in Quinn's office when he arrived. Helen remembered her exuberance at being the first one back from their assigned tasks. She had looked up at his return to proclaim her victory when she saw his face.

A chill shook Helen's body, partly from the damp frigid air of the tunnels and partly from remembering the haunted look on Mac's face in the office earlier in the day. Deciding to focus on getting her blood circulating and deal with Mac's findings later, she moved from her stationary position and walked in a circle, stomping her feet in the dirt that had found its way down through the opening over the years.

Her stomping suddenly stopped, and she listened intently. Her hand instinctively closed around the whistle when she realized that the sound was not coming from the door, but from the tunnel. Hallelujah, they were returning at last! A broad smile filled her face as she stepped around the corner to greet them.

A man in a dark suit skidded to a stop about fifteen yards out at her appearance. Her smile quickly faded as she realized he was not one of her party. He glanced back, and she looked past him to see lights bouncing off the tunnel walls some distance behind him. His course was clear as he turned back and bounded toward Helen with every intention of sprinting past her to the exit.

She only had to delay him, she thought; the others were on the way. So, she positioned herself in front of the door, forcing him to go through rather than around her. Her maneuver didn't deter him in the least. He never slowed, that is until she planted the palm of her hand with all the force she had under his chin, snapping his head back as he ran at her. He flipped onto his back in the dirt and lay still.

Helen blinked several times at this unexpected outcome as Mac, Quinn, and Yazzie barreled around the corner. "Well, what do you know, it worked," she said with awe.

The men stared at her, then at the man on the ground. Finally, Mac said, "Where did you learn to do that?"

"Yazzie taught me," she beamed.

Mac turned to glare at Yazzie, who only shrugged his shoulders and smiled.

CHAPTER 30

The iron bar clanged into place, securing the handcuffs to the metal table sitting in the middle of the plush room. Randall Smithers III squinted and blinked several times as the black hood was swiftly removed from his head. Footsteps retreated behind him, and a door closed out of view. He shivered as his eyes adjusted. A middle-aged woman sat across from him in a richly upholstered chair, serenely sipping coffee.

The room was richly appointed with tapestries and artwork. Dark wood trim abounded with matching beams cutting across the high ceilings. A large chandelier hung overhead and a fireplace with a massive marble mantle sat empty at the end of the room, leaving the large space cold and uncomfortable. Light blue wallpaper with velvety swirls of cream lined the walls, giving an elegant richness to the room. All the furnishings, except the metal table and chair in which he sat, spoke of wealth and privilege.

"You have no idea who you're dealing with," Smithers spat.

"Neither do you," Helen replied quietly.

The oversized mirror behind the woman and directly across from himself reflected his image. Wet unkempt hair on a pale man with the beginning of dark circles under his eyes sitting soaking wet in his underclothes. An impressive bruise was beginning to form on his jaw. *The mirror was undoubtedly strategically placed*, he thought. *Hoping to intimidate me, no doubt.*

"What? Do you think you can torture me and get away with it?"

"Torture?" Helen replied with innocent surprise. "What makes you think I wish to torture you? Do you know something worth those extremes?"

He tried to sit up so his height would tower over hers, but his wet underpants caused him to slip back into a slouched position. "Where are my clothes?" he demanded. When Helen failed to respond he jumped to his feet, pushing the chair away with the back of his legs, and then attempted to overturn the table onto Helen's lap, using the handcuffs as leverage. The table didn't budge but the strain on the cuffs caused his feet to slide under the table, leaving him dangling from his extended arms lying flat on the metal surface.

Helen didn't flinch. "Perhaps you failed to observe that the table is secured to the floor," she said as she sipped her coffee.

"Help me up! Help me up, damn it!" he yelled as he struggled to rise.

Helen placed her cup on the saucer as if to assist, then instead procured the silver coffee pot on a side table and refreshed her coffee. "My father always used to say that if you got yourself into a mess, you should get yourself out. Character building, that's what he said."

"You bitch! Help me up or so help me when I get loose, you'll be sorry!" he snapped as his elbows strained to hold his weight.

"What were you doing in the tunnels, Mr. Smithers?"

He stopped struggling at the question. "Who are you?" Helen sipped and remained silent. "Okay, okay just help me up and get my damn clothes and I'll cooperate."

Helen smiled and replied, "You'll cooperate regardless."

Behind the one-way mirror, the men laughed.

"She's a natural," Yazzie said appreciatively.

"I told you she's tough," Mac replied. "I hated throwing her into the deep end though. She's never done anything like this before and a couple of hours of coaching only goes so far."

Yazzie touched the microphone. "You're doing great, Helen. Now he knows you're in charge." He took his finger off the button and turned to Mac. "She's the only one he saw in the tunnel; it makes sense for her to do the interrogation. You know it's to our advantage if he doesn't know who else she's working with."

They watched as Smither's eyes shot daggers Helen's way as he struggled to get his knees together underneath him. He then awkwardly managed to get to his feet but due to the handcuffs remained unable to stand completely erect. His left foot slipped on the wet floor, sending him face-first onto the table. After panting into the tabletop for a moment, he lifted his head to his captor with hatred in his eyes. A trickle of blood flowed from his cheek where it had made violent contact with the iron bar. He said nothing as he pushed his leg back to feel for his chair, then, hooking it with his foot, pulled it forward so he could sit.

"So, where were we?" Helen said as if all was right with the world now. "Oh yes, what were you doing in the tunnels, Mr. Smithers?"

"I need medical attention," he stated flatly, trying to stare her down.

"And I need answers," she returned matter-of-factly. "Let me make this perfectly clear, *Randy*, you're in a hell of a mess."

His face went red as she used the common short version of his name as if *he* were common.

"You should know from your Harvard education, if not your Oxford studies, that treason is punishable by death, *Randy*. And don't think for a moment that your father will be able to save your ass from the electric chair!"

A corner of Colonel Quinn's mouth curled into a smile behind the mirror. "I think I'm in love."

"Back off, buster. That firecracker is all mine," Mac said with pride.

"I've never heard Helen swear before," Yazzie observed. "Well, if ever there was a time for it, it's now."

Helen sat back in her chair. "Of course, we could just make you disappear without a trace. Poof, like you were never here." She smiled. "So, tell me, what were you doing in those tunnels?"

Smithers turned his palms down and cupped his hands on the table, then glanced away. The hesitation activated Yazzie. "You're about to hear a lie, Helen."

"It was my first time down there, I swear. I was doing a favor for a friend in the War Department. George asked me to retrieve a gold watch he thought he may have lost down there, but I never found it. It was just a lark, you know. George found the door and went exploring. He didn't hurt anything."

"George who?"

"Piper, George Piper."

"Mr. Piper is dead. Try again."

"What? He's dead?" Smithers asked as he processed the revelation. "I heard he was in the hospital…I guess he took a turn for the worse. I didn't know."

"He was assassinated," Helen stated without emotion. "By the same people you work for, I believe. I guess he outlived his usefulness. Like you perhaps."

Smithers blanched at the thought, then decided to go on the offensive. "I work for the State Department. Are you saying the United States government killed him? Why that's outrageous!"

"What were you doing in Germany a few days ago?"

"What? What does Germany have to do with George?" At Helen's lack of response, he sighed as if bored. "Germany was just a business trip for the War Department. I had several meetings while I was there."

"Uh-huh. I see," Helen said, never breaking eye contact. "And what documents did you hand off to a foreign operative? Or perhaps you'd like to tell me what was in the satchel you received in return?"

Smithers was thoughtful for a moment. He looked down and shifted in his seat. "You've been following me." When he lifted his eyes, he was smiling. "Well, I guess I've been found out…you're good, you know. No one else ever caught on."

Helen's posture relaxed, and she smiled back. "Are you surprised because I'm a woman?"

"Oh no, no," he said playfully, trying to hold his hands up in surrender. "Personally, I find women to be much smarter than men." At her dubious look, he said, "No, really. You're much more intuitive, you know? Always two steps ahead of every man in the room."

In the hidden room, Mac's eyebrows went up. "What the hell?"

"Don't worry," Yazzie said. "I think she's got this."

"Is he honestly making a move on my wife?" he said, with anger beginning to rise.

"C'mon Mac. Do you think this is the first guy to flirt with Helen when you're not in the room?" Quinn asked.

Mac turned to stare at Quinn. "You're not helping, you know, you're really not helping," he returned, as Yazzie shushed them.

Helen laughed and shook her head. "Do you expect me to believe you, Mr. Smithers, given that you're the one in handcuffs and I'm the one asking the questions?"

"Hey, I know when I'm beat," he said with a humble chuckle. "I don't stand a chance against a woman like you." Smithers fairly smoldered with sensuality.

"Well, you certainly didn't *stand* against me in the tunnel, did you?"

"That was you?" he asked in mock surprise. "It doesn't surprise me in the least. It really doesn't. I was a fool to think you wouldn't be able to stop me. But men underestimate women all the time, don't they?"

"It's one of the things we count on," Helen returned with a wink.

He laughed out loud. "I like you. It's crazy, I know, but I've always been attracted to strong women. Maybe after all this is over, we can go out for a drink. I'd really like that," he said as he leaned over the table and looked deeply into Helen's eyes.

"Mr. Smithers…"

"Call me Randall, please."

Helen laughed shyly. "Okay…Randall…tell me, what were you actually doing in the tunnels? Were you meeting someone?"

Suddenly Randall Smithers III knew he'd been had. His smile faded, and he dropped back into his chair. "You have no idea who you're up against, lady. Trust me, you don't want to get involved with them. If you're smart, you'll just walk away."

"Well," Helen said, propping her chin up with her fist, "women *are* smarter than men, according to you. So, how long have you been a traitor, Randall?"

"Well," he parroted back to her, "I guess it depends on your definition of a traitor, sweetheart."

"Mr. Smithers be aware that torture is not completely off the table as yet," Helen warned, with every bit of geniality gone. "Since you've formed such a strong affinity for the Nazis, I'm certain we could find something suitable from their handbook to, let's say, enhance your willingness to cooperate."

He was silent for a moment as he decided it was time to make a deal. "You think the Nazis are bad? Well, who I work for is a hundred times worse than the Nazis, but hey it's your neck. So, what's in it for me?"

"You're willing to turn just like that?"

He cocked his head to one side. "You seem to know a lot about me. So, if you did your homework, you know about my family. We're survivors, every last one of us. I do what I have to do. I'm not afraid to get my hands dirty if it's profitable, and that's what this was, profitable. And you know what? I'll come out on top of this too; I always do. So, what do you want to know? Because I'm all yours now."

Helen gave a Mona Lisa smile as Yazzie said in her ear, "Okay, his body language isn't reflecting submission, so let's see if he's going to be honest with us."

She looked at her captive with his fingers interlaced, resting comfortably on the table. He was relaxed and confident in his position. He reminded her of a child willing to parrot an insincere 'sorry' if it allowed him to play outside again.

"Did you work for George Piper?"

"George worked for *me*," he emphasized, a bit piqued that she didn't recognize his superiority. "In fact, I recruited him."

"Did he come up with the plan to assassinate President Truman?"

"Is that what he told you? Ha! What a laugh. George did what he was told, that's all. He was at the bottom of the food chain. Why do you think he was given that assignment? He was expendable if something went wrong as it obviously did."

"Good, Helen," her earbud chirped, "he just told you that he knew about the assassination plan ahead of time and that he wasn't the one in charge."

"Hmmm, well, okay," she said, adjusting the blanket in her lap.

"What does that mean?" he asked testily.

"Well, it seems to me that you're not what I would call an extremely masculine man, having seen you unclothed as it were," Helen responded, casting a glance down his chest. "A man that occupies a desk, I believe," Helen surmised. "I suppose that's why I thought you were passed over for the assignment. He was simply more physically capable when it came to tasks requiring strength and raw courage."

Smithers' eyes narrowed at the insult. "Brute beasts can be found anywhere for a price. Someone of my caliber with my talents and abilities is rare. You need to recognize my importance and show a little respect, woman."

"Who is your handler, Randall? Who is calling the shots?" she asked quietly.

"What are you talking about?" he asked with an arrogant lift of his chin. "I'd think someone as intuitive as you would have figured out by now that no one runs me, I'm the one in charge."

"Randy, Randy, Randy," she sighed. "A lie so soon? I thought we were friends."

"No, no, you don't understand," he said, as his eyes lit up with self-importance. "A horse may be bigger than the rider, but the rider is the one that determines where they go. You see, I'm the rider."

"Are you saying that you suggested they assassinate the President?"

"Oh no. Hell, I advised against that. All it did was bring unwanted attention. That's why I'm sitting here, am I right?" At Helen's nod, he smiled. "You see, I'm an analyst. I take mountains of information and synthesize it down to a recommendation. That's the bridle. But no, the assassination was pure revenge.

Ever since Harry blew their communications center in Hiroshima to hell, they've wanted him out of the picture."

Helen could sense the stunned silence behind her. No direction came from Yazzie, but since Smithers seemed talkative, she just let him continue.

"He's got them running scared alright. FDR, now he was predictable," he said, falling comfortably into his analyst mode. "Truman, on the other hand, is a wild card. I mean, who could have predicted that he'd actually drop the bomb? It set them back a couple of years or more. I heard it was chaos. That's when they sought me out. That was the smartest move they made; don't you think? Rebuild on an island, that's what I told them, but I've found them to be kind of stupid at times so who knows if they took my advice."

"Don't spook him," Helen heard in her ear.

"You're influential in setting U.S. foreign policy, are you not? Is that why they recruited you?"

"You're catching on," he said, pleased that she was beginning to see his value. *She'll be eating out of my hand in no time.* "The one that holds the reins is the one with all the power."

"Who recruited you?"

"Now that we're on the same side, do you think I could get dressed and have a cup of coffee like civilized people? I could catch my death in this cold. Then where would you be?" he asked smugly.

Helen smiled and looked down at the soft, warm blanket that covered her legs. "Who recruited you, Randall?"

He sighed deeply at her persistence. "It really doesn't matter now because they have been pulled out of D.C. You'll never find them."

Helen recalled a conversation she had with a chatty neighbor when she was checking the alien's mail every day after the cover story regarding her sudden departure was released. Could it be? She decided to take a chance. "How long was Barbara Martin your mistress?"

The shock on Smithers' face was unmistakable. "How?" was all he could get out. Helen's gaze didn't waver as mentally she heaved a great sigh of relief. His shock melted into fear as his most closely guarded secret was exposed. *Who were these people, and how did they find out?*

"I…I need to use the facilities," he stammered.

"Of course, we wouldn't want you to have an accident," Helen replied courteously. "I'll have someone bring a bucket. We're just getting started."

"A bucket?"

"Were you aware that Miss Martin was not human?" Helen asked with a tilt of her head.

Smithers' blood ran cold. *They knew.* They knew much more than his handlers dared to imagine.

CHAPTER 31

Enough information had been extracted from Smithers to know that the tunnels underneath Washington D.C. and the White House were extensive. The labyrinth of crisscrossing underground trails had been in use in one form or another since the Civil War and had been expanded over the years as particular needs arose. However, by the time the nation began to emerge as an industrial giant at the beginning of the twentieth century, the secret maze fell out of use and was all but forgotten.

When the tunnel system was no longer considered useful, since the cost to fill it in was prohibitive, the entrances had simply been camouflaged or disguised and locked up permanently. However, years later, a group unable to work in the open discovered their existence and deemed them ideal for their purposes. They managed to obtain keys to the netherworld of the tunnel system and began to use it clandestinely for their own ends. Working quietly and studiously, they had built for themselves an ideally located underground storage facility and technology center.

A very impressive array of rooms had been cleared out since their infiltration. Various supplies and provisions, enough to last a lifetime if needed, had been spirited down into the darkness right under the nose of their enemies. Personnel were assigned to the location and their secret work was able to continue safely without fear of interruption for years while they methodically moved toward their goal of subjugating the humans living just above them.

Until now.

In Colonel Quinn's office the day before they were scheduled to return to the place where Smithers had been unexpectedly encountered, Mac, Yazzie, and Helen had presented their plan. The three had discussed the situation at length prior to the consultation and had determined they should be lightly outfitted with enough firepower to hold their own if it came down to a gunfight. Though they hoped the recon mission would be a quiet one, they reasoned it was always prudent to be prepared.

Mac had taken point in laying out the plan to Quinn. When Mac balked at the idea of Helen joining them and began to enumerate the reasons for her exclusion, she interrupted to present her case with forceful determination.

"If Virginia Hall could handle herself behind enemy lines in France fighting the Nazis, then I can handle myself against whoever or whatever is hiding underneath my nation's capital." She took a breath and continued quickly to thwart any rebuttal by Mac. "You know she escaped through the French Pyrenees mountains during the winter – with only one leg? She carried 'Cuthbert', her prosthetic leg, with her when it became too difficult to use in the deep snow!"

"I know," Mac painfully admitted. "I worked with her under Wild Bill Donovan. I told you this story. But this isn't the same situation, Helen," he reminded her, knowing he was unlikely to convince her otherwise.

"I can wear a pair of dungarees as well as any man," she had gone on.

"Better," Yazzie had chimed in with a certain amount of amusement as he watched Mac.

"You see?" she had declared proudly to her husband. She turned her backside to him and asked rather coyly, "Do you think they make my bottom look too big?"

"Oh, for heaven's sake, Helen!" Mac responded with an embarrassed sigh.

"I think they make your bottom look marvelous," Yazzie had complimented.

"Shut up, Yazzie," Mac muttered uselessly.

"Leave him alone, dear," Helen defended. "Yazzie has an eye for things like this. Don't you, Yazzie?"

Yazzie smiled at Helen's insistence to goad Mac. "What can I say? I'm a Jew of many talents."

"I hate to break up the light-hearted repartee," Quinn had finally interjected as the meeting began to run long. "But I need Helen to work with our Groom Lake contacts. Doctors Zimmerman and Jenkins are busy setting up the new lab, but they have questions. Knowing with certainty that we have a traitor there; I don't want them to use any traditional means of communication. Helen, you've had more training in everything alien than any of us, so we need help in determining how to prepare for the future study of alien bodies. Oh, and of course alien technology if any comes our way. I'll brief you on your assignment while Mac and Yazzie go to the tunnels. Four of my best men are going with you – just in case."

Helen was heartbroken. "But what about Virginia Hall? You let her go behind enemy lines," she protested, barely restraining a pout.

"Ginny was behind enemy lines because that's where we needed her at the time," Quinn explained dourly. "You are needed in Groom Lake and that's where you're going to go," he concluded firmly.

Helen looked to Mac for support but immediately saw the look of relief on his face and that he was in complete agreement with Quinn. She sighed heavily, then turned back to Quinn. "Can I at least wear these dungarees to Groom Lake? I really do think I can pull it off."

Yesterday's conversation with Quinn was only a memory as Mac, Yazzie, and Quinn's men started the second recon of the tunnels the next morning. It took Quinn great restraint not to take the lead himself, however he knew his presence might be missed on the Hill and compromise the plan. So, with his ego firmly reined in, he assigned four of his own to the detail. If his men questioned why he insisted they go into tunnels under D.C. with enough arms to meet a small army, they didn't give voice to it. Their main goal was to obtain information not to get into a gunfight, but Quinn knew better than they what could be waiting, and it was better to be prepared than dead.

They each carried a short 10-gauge double-barreled sawed-off shotgun under their left shoulder holster and an M3 submachine gun without stock with a twenty-round magazine was slung under their right shoulder. An M1911 .45 caliber pistol was holstered with a Secret Service cross-draw holster on their left hip and their left forearms had a sharp Fairbairn-Sykes knife nestled in its sheath. Two fragmentation grenades dangled from their shoulder holsters to complete their personal arsenal. That should be more than enough for any close-quarters engagement.

"You men know what you're here for?" Mac asked as they prepared.

"Two-legged rat hunt, sir," the sergeant had responded. "Vermin living under the city. That's all we need to know."

Mac and Yazzie nodded appreciatively at the response.

The set of stairs they used in the Capital Building had been blocked from public use in anticipation of this exercise. Large sheets of plywood strategically tacked in place shielded them from view as the six men in full gear slipped from a conference room tucked away in a corner of the building to the stairwell. They trekked past the basement to the sub-basement where overhead pipes ran side-by-side the length of the buildings, making the ceilings seem low and the lighting dim.

Nothing except the shuffle of their rubber-soled boots was heard as they approached the faded green door exactly 120 feet from the stairs. They opened the door Smithers had been instructed to use by his handler, then took the grimy hallway to a storage room some twenty feet further. Yazzie and Mac found the hidden sliding door behind a shelving unit just as Smithers had indicated, then they each descended the iron rungs affixed to the solid rock into the tunnel.

Yazzie was the last man through, so he carefully closed the overhead opening before dropping the remaining ten feet into the dirt. A single flashlight with a red lens was clicked on and it remained pointed at the ground as they allowed their eyes time to adjust to the black interior. They were surprised to find the length and breadth of the tunnels and wondered among themselves if there were just a few "rats" down here or an entire community. The tunnel walls had rudimentary signs indicating direction at irregular intervals, but little else of note from where they stood. The air was frosty and still.

Although Mac expected to be in charge, Quinn had made it clear that his four men would lead. Mac and Yazzie would offer backup if necessary. So, Mumford, Collins, Shepherd, and Case took off down the tunnel in tight formation, with Mac and Yazzie bringing up the rear.

The slight click of Yazzie's tongue stopped the entourage in its tracks about ten minutes in. Mumford first bristled at the careless sound during an intense operation, but quickly realized it was not inadvertent. Yazzie motioned for the team to remain in place as a long, slender tube was extracted from a small canister he had in his pocket.

Yazzie walked several feet ahead as Mac quietly explained. "A sensor mounted to the wall up ahead. Liquid nitrogen will neutralize it. No worries."

"How the hell did he see it?" Mumford asked, voicing the question his whole team was thinking.

"He's Jewish," Mac replied as if that answered the question.

As they continued, Mumford held the flashlight at waist level, keeping it close to the floor to make sure they didn't trip over any type of explosive device that may have been set. A slight ambient light was seen up ahead, but the source couldn't be determined. So, when they came to the corner, Mumford laid flat on the ground and used a dark periscope to get a look down the adjoining tunnel. The scope had a 90-degree angle, so he could see several yards ahead from that position.

After nearly thirty minutes of slow but steady progress and a second stop to neutralize another sensor, Mumford held up his right arm and the recon party stopped. He made a couple of quick signs to his team, and they took prearranged positions behind him. Mac and Yazzie were motioned to stay where they were.

"Smell that?" Yazzie asked Mac.

"Damn, perfume and stink. Not good." Mac returned. "Smithers didn't say anything about Anakim being here though, just Shalanaya."

"I guess he isn't as high on the food chain as he thinks he is," Yazzie commented. "So, do we turn back now or continue on, old friend? These young men don't know what they're facing."

A security guard had been spotted standing outside one of the rooms. He held an M-1 carbine and had a Colt .45 strapped to his hip. Clearly, he wasn't there just for looks. Mumford knew Mac wanted prisoners for further interrogation, if possible, but not at the cost of the mission. He briefly thought several scenarios through to see if there might be a way to take out the sentry without deadly force but could see no way to approach him without being seen. If he or one of the others tried to get close, they would most certainly be met with gunfire. The decision was made, and he signaled Collins to come forward. He whispered something to him, then Collins moved against the far wall and waited for Mumford.

Chapter 31

The Master Sergeant took another look through his periscope. There was something distinctly different about this guy. The ambient light was enough to show he was a male, maybe five-six and a buck thirty, but there was something off about him. Long white hair just past his shoulders and a casually slouched posture at his post. Not military. And his features were, well, different somehow.

Mumford shook off the details now racing through his mind. They were vulnerable, and he needed to get this job done and done quickly before anyone else showed up. There would most certainly be a changing of the guard at some point, but he had no way of knowing where they were on that timeline.

The periscope was lowered, and he signaled Collins just as the guard turned his back to look in the other direction. Collins quickly slipped around the corner and out into the tunnel from the other side and fired two quick shots. Pfft, pfft. A silenced .22 caliber automatic did the trick. Both bullets found their way to the back of the guard's head, and he dropped to the ground without a sound.

The recon team moved forward as one to the door where the guard had been standing. Shepherd skillfully removed all weapons from the dead sentry and placed them well out of reach. Case grabbed the body and drug it to their former position, out of sight from this part of the tunnel. Then Mumford checked the door. It was unlocked, but they had no way of knowing who or what was inside. Mac made his way to the front to get close to Mumford.

"I'll do the breach. I know what I'm looking for," he said quietly to the Master Sergeant.

"No can do, sir," was the whispered reply. "The Colonel made it abundantly clear that you were to remain out of the line of fire."

"You do realize that I once commanded Bill Quinn. He took orders from me."

"Not today, sir. With all due respect get to the rear as ordered, sir."

Mac appreciated the man's dedication to his orders, but he didn't have to like them. He went back to Yazzie and groused quietly, "Damn sergeants think they run the Army."

Yazzie smiled knowingly. "They do."

Mumford again signaled for Collins to get ready. Shepherd and Case were right behind them. A four-man breach was a standard maneuver for each of these men and they had successfully completed them many times during the War.

Mumford pushed the door open forcefully and immediately moved to his right. Collins followed and moved to the left. Shepherd and Case followed behind, using the same pattern. All four men were inside the room, weapons at the ready in less than three seconds.

A very stunned young woman's head jerked up from her desk, shocked at the forcible intrusion. The white-blonde hair and the grey, almost translucent eyes could have made her the sentry's sister. Were they related? What in the hell were they doing down here? Was their albino-like skin from spending too much time down here? Something was going on that Mumford and his men didn't understand and didn't currently have time to work out. But their job was not to understand, it was to complete the mission successfully.

The young woman's eyes went dark as they watched in stunned silence. Then she suddenly dove for a hand-held device on a table beside her. She didn't reach the device. Collins pumped two .22 caliber rounds into her skull as he had done to the sentry outside the door. She collapsed in the same manner, without a sound.

Mac and Yazzie were right on the heels of the four others. They both grimaced as they saw the woman drop to the floor. Not because they were offended by the violence, but because they had wanted a chance to interrogate her. There was no doubt in either of the two men's minds that the woman and the sentry outside were Shalanaya. What were they doing operating underneath, if their calculations were correct, the White House?

A quick search of the room turned up nothing they could use to determine what she was doing there. This area was sparsely outfitted with just a desk, a table, and three or four chairs. What appeared to be a communication console was sitting on the table. There was not enough time to determine with any certainty exactly what it was or how it worked in the time they had.

"We'll come back for it later," Mac said. "Let's see what else we can find down here."

Mumford, Collins, Shepherd, and Case all noticed the black vacant eyes of the dead Shalanaya lying on the floor. It was clear they wanted to know more about what was going on here, but they were trained to do their jobs without asking questions that were above their pay grade. Still, the men were wondering who or what they had just encountered.

"When we get back on the surface, we'll explain what this is," Mac offered the men. He seemed to understand their questions without being asked. The men nodded, accepting Mac's offer. That was enough for now.

Mac pointed to the tunnel outside the room. "Your lead, Master Sergeant," he said to Mumford.

"Yes, sir," he replied and without hesitation led his men back into the tunnel with Mac and Yazzie following.

The tunnel dead-ended into a tee another twenty feet ahead. Mac signaled them to go right. Mumford continued sweeping the red beam back and forth to check for traps or unforeseen obstacles. Another turn had Mumford back in the dirt, using the periscope once again to surreptitiously check around the corner.

A burly, dark-haired man wearing a military police uniform was posted at this door. He was similarly armed as the first sentry, but the uniform changed the game. Unwilling to shoot one of their own, Mumford hesitated.

"Problem?" Mac breathed into his ear after making his way forward.

"Maybe one of ours, sir," Mumford returned quietly, offering the periscope for confirmation.

"He's not," Mac stated flatly, with no need to see him with his own eyes. "Take the shot, Master Sergeant. He's working with the enemy."

Mumford nodded, then signaled Collins who once again got off two muffled shots before the sentry was even aware of their presence. Pfft, pfft. His body crumpled.

They silently approached the room in formation, becoming keenly aware of a very pungent odor as they approached. Whatever was inside this room smelled like raw sewage. In fact, Mumford wondered quietly if they had simply come to an underground sewage relay point.

"You ever known an armed guard to be at a sewage relay station?" Collins asked him quietly as both men found themselves laboring to breathe.

"Can't say that I have," he answered pointedly, pulling the kerchief around his neck up over his nose.

Mac and Yazzie recognized the odor immediately and knew by its strength that Anakim were currently in residence. Before Mac could reach Mumford to call them back, voices were heard coming from the room speaking an unknown language. Suddenly, in the midst of the indecipherable conversation, an ominous low growl was heard. Mumford and Collins looked at each other quizzically.

"What the hell is in there?" Collins questioned, with the hair on the back of his neck standing on end.

The door suddenly jerked open, and gunfire erupted from the room into the tunnel. The six-man team automatically dropped to the dirt as bullets ricocheted, and the gunfire almost deafened them. Shepard and Case were the first to return fire. From crouched positions, they used their M3 submachine guns to spray opposite sides of the room.

Mumford immediately grabbed one of his grenades, pulled the pin, and tossed it inside. The second grenade followed in seconds. The explosions added pain to their already ringing ears, but the gunfire from within stopped immediately, and there was an eerie silence.

The three men leaped through the doorway and took up their standard positions. This was a much larger room than the previous one. A quick scan estimated it to be about twenty-foot by twenty-foot, with a ceiling at least fifteen feet high. The debris in the room let them know that this was their operations center.

Mumford counted six bodies lying on the floor. Four of them looked like the ones they had encountered earlier. Pale skin and hair, slight frames, and eye sockets that looked empty in death. The two other bodies did not look like anything he or his men had ever encountered. They were more 'things' than human beings.

As he surveyed the room, he realized someone was missing. "Collins?" He turned back to see Mac and Yazzie crouched over the still, lifeless body of his teammate and friend. A dark halo of blood soaked into the dirt of the tunnel floor around his head. As Mumford turned to move toward his downed man, a sound stopped him in his tracks. The "things" picked themselves up off the floor, temporarily stunned but certainly not dead. They were massive creatures that stood ten feet tall and were growling and howling like deranged animals. Except these animals were armed.

Mumford and his men emptied their 10-gauge shotguns into the creatures, catapulting them back into the rear wall. They dropped the shotguns and swiftly pulled their machine guns back into firing position, holding their ground, stone still, until the death of the creatures was verified. Surely, they must be dead. What could survive such injuries? Then both creatures grunted, cried out, and pushed themselves off the floor once again.

This time Mumford, Shepherd, and Case emptied their M3 submachine guns into the center mass of both creatures, determined that they would go down and stay down. As impossible as it was, they watched the creatures begin to move steadily toward them with hatred shining in their eyes as round after round left their machine guns without effect. The two creatures retrieved weapons from the mess and were drawing them into position when Mac and Yazzie stepped from behind and shot them twice in the head with their Colt .45s. It was only then that the creatures dropped to the floor and did not move again.

Quinn's men stopped firing, breathing hard. They cautiously stepped closer to the creatures, staring at them in disbelief. "What the hell are we looking at, sir?" Mumford asked Mac.

"That," Mac declared firmly, looking each man in the eye, "does not exist. Understand?"

"Yes sir," they all said in unison.

"These other bodies look like the ones from our first breach," Shepherd observed.

"Yeah," Case added. "They look similar to us but they're a couple of ticks off, huh? I'd lay money that they aren't exactly human either."

"I'm genuinely sorry, Sergeant. We weren't expecting them to be here, or we would have warned you," Mac said, understanding full well the grief and outrage being suppressed right now as Mumford went to stand by his friend.

"You knew about these…these monsters? You knew," Mumford accused vehemently. "How long have you known?"

"The rest will be covered in the debrief," Mac interrupted sharply, understanding how quickly the light of this new knowledge could jeopardize the remaining team members. "For now, we need to secure this room. Two men will stay until a team can be sent to retrieve the enemy bodies and anything else that might be of value. It will all be taken back to HQ for testing. Collins will go out with us now. Give his gear to whoever stays, they may need it. I'll leave mine too."

The men all replied with a respectful "yes sir" but the shock of the situation was clearly reflected in each of their faces.

"Master Sergeant, you good to lead?" Mac asked gruffly.

"Damn straight."

"Then I'll leave you to it."

"Look at that," Yazzie said, drawing Mac away from the situation meeting coming to order by the door.

An unfamiliar device had slid off a table and was now projecting a large map at a crazy angle into the south corner of the room. Even with the angle, you could see it was a picture of the Pacific Ocean. Mac recognized the land mass of China and Japan and thought he recognized the islands to the southeast of them. When they walked to the corner to get a closer look a series of colored lines on the map jumped out at them.

Yazzie looked at Mac before asking quietly, "RAT Lines?"

"Looks like it," he replied. "This island seems to be a focal point. There is a line here that extends from what looks to be the Marianas Trench. All the other destination lines start there."

Yazzie looked at the map again before continuing. "Some of these lines have been greyed out. I assume they are no longer in use."

"Why would you say that?" Mac asked.

"We, that is, some people I know in Palestine use a similar system to keep track of Arab supply lines in and out of Palestine. The bold lines would indicate the focal point. Everything starts there. The ones greyed out have been discarded and are no longer in use."

"That would make sense considering those greyed-out lines go from the Trench to the island to Hiroshima and Berlin. Those two cities were obliterated during the War. Whatever was going on there came to an abrupt end."

"Forcing them to find alternate routes," Yazzie continued. "It's a pretty good bet that's why the new bold lines go to Tokyo. The line from Tokyo branches out to Moscow and Washington D.C. among other places."

"Holy crap," Mac groaned. "Those damn Greys were right. These guys are working right under our noses, and probably have been for years!"

"But why are the lines beginning in the middle of the Mariana's Trench?" Yazzie wondered. "There's nothing there but deep water. No island or land mass of any kind."

"I don't know. But those lines always go through that island," he said, pinpointing with his finger the place on the wall projection. "There has to be a reason."

Mac glanced away from the map and looked over at Quinn's men, knowing their lives had just changed forever. "So, what's the plan, gentlemen?"

"Kill as many of the big bad as we can, sir," Mumford said with all three of their faces set like stone.

CHAPTER 32

Tamar wrinkled her nose at the strong scent of lilacs emanating from an office as they walked by. "Does General MacArthur know we're here?" she asked Hale with a sniff as they continued to their destination.

"I doubt it. He's got a couple of thousand people working here."

"Good, easier to blend in," she said, with exit scenarios and defense plans running through her head. "High-rise office buildings make me nervous. There's no way around it, you have to go down eventually and the enemy knows it. That limits your options."

Hale raised one eyebrow as they stopped at room 827. "You know we're in an American-occupied building, right?"

"Piper was in an American-occupied building in D.C. and they still got to him," she reminded Hale with an I'm-just-sayin' glance.

Hale considered her statement and had to admit she had a point, but he wasn't going to admit it to her. "We're not in D.C.," he finally answered as he rummaged in his pocket for the key.

"No. We're in Tokyo with thousands of enemy combatants all around us," she insisted, twisting her head around to take in every detail up and down the hallway.

"The war is over, Tamar."

"Maybe for you, maybe not for them. And definitely not for people like me."

The key Quinn had arranged to be delivered to them at their quarters allowed entry into the room, and they realized at a glance that it would be a fine place to set up their little headquarters while in Tokyo. The two bathrooms on the floor were shared, but that was a minor issue. The office itself was nearly 600 square feet with two large windows overlooking the city skyline.

Much of Tokyo was still in a rebuilding phase, and signs of the allied bombing raids that had decimated the city remained in evidence from the windows. The Emperor's Palace, directly across the street from the office building, which had been purposely spared in the raids, was still beautiful. There had never been any doubt in the mind of Americans that they would defeat the Japanese, despite the ominous beginning at Pearl Harbor. So, special care had always been taken to avoid leveling the Palace and its immediate surroundings in anticipation of its use after the war. It turned out to be the safest place in all of Japan as the war raged on for four years.

Despite bleak areas of black and gray dotting the landscape where bombs did their work, the view was beautiful. The office building sat in a commercial area of the city, however, the view from their windows included much more than just the hustle and bustle of commerce. Not only the manicured gardens surrounding the Palace were in view but the sparkling blue rivers and bay upon which the city sat painted an ironic picture of tranquility and peace.

Hale noted that the office was already furnished with three desks accompanied by chairs, a new Royal typewriter, and a serviceable no-frills sofa with a coffee table set in front. How Quinn had found this little gem for them was a mystery, but he was very thankful their time could be spent on tasks other than finding a secure place to work.

A knock on the door brought both Hale and Tamar to instant readiness. Tamar looked directly at Hale and whispered, "American-occupied building? They have already found us in a supposedly secure location."

"I don't think an invading force would knock on the door," he replied sarcastically in a low voice. Still, he pulled out his Army-issued Colt .45 and let it hang by his right thigh, ready for action if necessary.

The second knock was a bit harder and louder than the first. Hale moved Tamar out of the line of sight from the door. She grimaced at his assumption that she needed his protection, but gave way to the gentle push anyway. Then Hale walked to the door, keeping his body at an angle and to the side of the door just in case it opened suddenly.

"Enter," he said in a firm, military tone. The door opened and there stood Sergeant William "Billy" McCann. Hale immediately relaxed and holstered his weapon, a little embarrassed at how he had reacted to the situation. He blamed it all on Tamar's perpetual insecurities.

"Billy," Hale called out heartily. "What the hell are you doing here? And how in the world did you know where to find me?"

"Colonel Quinn, I presume," Tamar answered for him as she slid over to stand by Hale.

"Right as rain, ma'am," McCann answered jovially. "He had me sent here priority express. Said you needed a loud-mouth Irishman to chauffer your ass around Tokyo. Begging your pardon, ma'am," he apologized to Tamar. "I didn't mean to speak…"

"It's perfectly fine, Sergeant," she replied lightly. "I've been carrying the Major's ass for nearly a week and I'm already tired of it."

McCann burst out laughing, and even Hale had to smile at Tamar's candid response. There were times when he almost thought she could be a damn good field agent.

McCann's transition from Germany to Japan was explained as simply as possible to Hale and Tamar. Colonel Quinn had made it clear that he was to keep his hands on the wheel of Hale's transport vehicle and his eyes on everything around them. Nothing that seemed odd or out of the ordinary was to escape his attention and he was to report it to the Major immediately, if not sooner.

"That sounds like the Colonel," Hale said after McCann's report. "Leave no stone unturned and no detail left out."

"He sounds more and more like Menachem in Palestine," Tamar concluded with no indication of whether that was a good or bad thing.

"Anything else?" Hale asked McCann.

"He gave me a list of acceptable contacts here in MacArthur's compound. But he made it clear that we were not to interact with the General or his people unless absolutely necessary. He said they have enough on their plates, and they don't need us piling on anything else. That's about it, sir."

"Okay," Hale acknowledged. "You can take that desk with the Royal on it. I assume you can still type."

"It will give me great practice for when I begin to write memoirs of my historic and brave victories over both the Germans and Japanese during the Second Great War."

"You never fought in the Pacific, Billy."

"They're my memoirs, Major, not yours. A few rounds of Guinness in me and I will have defeated those pesky Russians as well!"

The two of them laughed at the good-hearted Irishman's bravado.

"Well, you'll probably wind up being a jack of all trades, but for now I just need you to type up any reports needed for the Colonel. We'll have to get them encrypted before they leave the office. I'm taking no chances with anything sent to D.C."

"Well, that explains a few things," McCann said to himself.

"What?" Hale asked.

"The Colonel said he would have a SIGABA delivered ASAP. He gave me the name of one of his men here who knows how to operate it."

"That should do nicely," Hale agreed.

"SIGABA?" Tamar questioned.

"It's a cipher machine used for encrypting messages, but it takes great skill to operate the machine proficiently. So, a technician will be required to operate and maintain it. We need to ensure that our messages and reports reach the ears of Colonel Quinn and no one else," Hale explained.

"That sounds reasonable," she approved.

Hale opened the satchel he had laid on the first desk as they entered the room. The pictures they had taken on the flight to Tokyo of the documents in Okada's satchel were extracted and held up for McCann to see. "Any chance he can decipher these?"

"I don't know, boss. I only know he can work the SIGABA. But I'll ask as soon as I find him," McCann responded.

"Then let's go find him. Can you procure us some transportation?"

"Already done, boss. That's how I got here."

"How in heaven's name did you already get orders to procure a vehicle, Sergeant?" Tamar asked in wonder. "We haven't been able to get anything done even with an appalling amount of groveling. Everyone seems so preoccupied with rebuilding the city that they have no time for anything else."

"Well ma'am, I do have a wee bit of leprechaun in me family roots," he deadpanned in an old Irish brogue. "That may explain it," he said with a wry smile and a wink.

Hale choked back a bit of laughter. He had seen McCann's leprechaun magic at work on more than a few occasions during the War.

Tamar smiled agreeably and said, "You would do well in Palestine with the Irgun. We could use an Irishman like you."

"Don't be recruiting my Sergeant, Tamar," Hale said in mock disapproval. He knew very well how valuable McCann was, and secretly admired her ability to recognize a worthy asset when she saw one. But she was not going to get this asset. This one belonged lock, stock, and barrel to the U.S. Army.

"Well, it was worth a try," she smiled coyly. "And Sergeant, please stop calling me ma'am. It makes me feel old and you're probably older than I am. My name is Tamar."

"As you wish, darlin' Tamar. And my name is Billy. May I regard you as my younger sister?"

"You may."

"Well then, welcome to the family, sis," he said, throwing his arms wide and catching her up in an unexpected bear hug.

The three laughed, enjoying a brief respite of joy and stress relief. There would be little of either in the days and weeks to come.

CHAPTER 33

McCann was as good as his word; he found Quinn's man, who was experienced in encryption and decoding. Surprised wouldn't begin to describe his reaction to the news that he was being pulled from the six-man team with whom he currently worked. Once shown the orders from D.C. he was more than willing to help on a new project, however, he made it clear that someone else was going to inform his superior officer. The removal of one of his best men *and* one of his Enigma machines caused the Lieutenant Colonel's color to go from pasty white to beet red from his neck all the way to the top of his shiny bald head. *So much for not bothering MacArthur's staff*, McCann thought.

Captain Geoffrey Farnsworth was a quick study with a brilliant mind and a passion for puzzles. That passion and his prior top-secret work at Bletchley Park in Buckinghamshire, England deciphering German codes for the British government made him a perfect fit to join the listening post in Japan targeting the Russians who were using a confiscated German Enigma machine and conscripted technicians. His mother was British and his father an American, providing him with dual citizenship in both England and the United States. But after being raised primarily in England, when the war started he decided to serve in the British Army.

When England began to draw down their military forces once the war was over, Quinn had been able to scoop him up and add him to his team. The Brits had hesitated at first, after all, Farnsworth had been working with high-level government information. However, dual citizenship afforded him options they couldn't deny. So, the Brits decided to make their sacrifice clear; they were going above and beyond the call of duty to cooperate with their staunch ally, with the explicit understanding that reciprocal cooperation was expected in the future. Once released into Quinn's custody, he was promptly whisked to Tokyo to work with MacArthur's staff.

Farnsworth was suitably impressed when McCann wheeled the government issue army green Dodge WC51 three-quarter ton four-by-four truck into a supply depot and picked up the SIGABA with virtually no difficulty. In London, it would have taken most of the day just to clear security, much less pick up controlled intelligence machinery. But he had learned Americans were impatient and accustomed to moving things along quickly in times of war. Since the military personnel under General MacArthur still considered themselves at war with Japan accommodations were made to hopefully hurry the process of complete subjection of the enemy along.

Arriving back at the office at 2:17 a.m. McCann and Farnsworth were met by Hale and Tamar at the loading dock in the rear of the office building. All three men were needed to load the 94-pound encrypting device and 172-pound safe in which the SIGABA was housed on a dolly they had pinched from a warehouse a couple of blocks down the road. The maintenance lift groaned when the 266 pounds of precious cargo was loaded, but it was able to drop them at their destination without issue.

Hale hadn't been keen on bringing the highly specialized equipment upstairs midday through the lobby in front of prying eyes where it was certain to invoke unwanted questions. Thus, the clandestine caper was hatched. The three men were to load and unload the equipment while Tamar went ahead to clear the path of any security personnel or overachievers working late. When she held up her hand, they obediently stopped while panting and wiping their brows.

"Oh, my goodness," they heard her say with a giggle, "I thought I was the only one silly enough to be here at this time of night. Oops, I guess it's morning already, isn't it?"

"What are *you* doing here?" a male voice asked as if he had just sat down next to a pretty girl at a bar.

"I had to finish some work. My boss doesn't like me very much," she said with a pout. "She said if I was late again, I'd be in trouble. I can't seem to do anything right for her."

"Oh," the man said sympathetically, "I'm sure it's not about your work. You're just too beautiful. I'll bet she's just jealous."

"Oh brother," Hale muttered under his breath as he chanced a peak around the corner.

Tamar glanced down shyly. "Oh, you're so sweet. I like your tie, by the way," she said as she leaned in and rested both hands on his chest.

"He's a goner," McCann said with a grin.

"Say, I know a bar that's still open. Would you like to go for a drink?" he asked hopefully, rubbing the back of his fingers down her arm. "It'll help you sleep."

"Poor shmuck is gonna get himself hurt," Hale said, shaking his head.

"I don't know…it's kind of late," she said with a husky sigh as her emerald eyes locked with his. "Well…we can ride down in the lift together and we'll see. Okay?"

"What's happening?" Farnsworth whispered.

"They're gone, let's go."

"Wow, she's really good at that," Farnsworth commented as they grunted the uncooperative dolly through the door.

"You have no idea," Hale responded, giving McCann a look. "We can drop the dolly at the warehouse on our way back to quarters and meet back here at, say, ten hundred. Okay?" At their nods, he said, "Lunch is on me tomorrow. Burgers, fries, and a cola sound good?"

"I usually have a pint of Guinness with traditional American fare," McCann suggested gingerly.

Before Hale could respond, Tamar walked into the office with a yawn. "Are we ready yet?" At their open stares, she gave them a wide-eyed look of innocence and said, "What?"

*****

"Billy, I need you to check on the agent I assigned to watch the import/export business," Hale said after they reconvened later that morning. "He's in civvies, of course, but he's due for a break. Just relieve him and take his notes. See who has been coming and going."

"You got it, boss. Anything else?"

"We were told Okada went directly there from the airport," Tamar added. "There may be a very practical reason it's located only two blocks from MacArthur's headquarters. We need to find a way in that won't arouse suspicion."

"Yeah, my thoughts exactly," Hale agreed. "It's an upscale business. Not exactly in a GI's price range. Well, we'll think of something."

"A perfect front for illegal operations," McCann observed. "We saw that in Germany, too. Nazis love to hide out in the open."

"I'm guessing the same is true here, Billy. Since we already have copies of the contents of his satchel in hand, we've let approaching him go until we can get set up here and find out what we've got. These documents are our first priority. Once this is sorted out, we can get a plan in place to see who Mr. Okada's associates may be."

McCann pulled the truck keys from his pocket and started toward the office door. Hale intercepted him just before he opened the door.

"Eyes on all the time, Billy. Just because Okada looks like a lowly Japanese businessman doesn't mean he – or his associates aren't trained killers."

"As always, Major," he replied firmly.

"Please be careful, Billy," Tamar said from across the room. "I wouldn't want anything to happen to my big brother."

"Luck of the Irish, little sis. Luck of the Irish." And with that, McCann walked out the office door.

Farnsworth had followed the conversation between the three as he set up the equipment, and though he tried not to show it, he was a bit confused as to the dynamics of the team. Tamar picked up on his state of mind as she began to organize the documents that needed to be deciphered.

"Sergeant McCann is my honorary older brother. I am a little sister," she remarked easily.

"What does that make the Major?" he inquired politely as his fingers continued with the task at hand.

"If you say I'm the father," Hale warned Tamar in jest, "I will most certainly send you to the corner for the rest of the day."

Tamar brought the first stack of prioritized documents to Farnsworth and stood beside him as she observed Hale. "Oh, Major Hale is my *much* older brother."

"Really? Much older brother?" Hale retorted with feigned offense.

"I don't quite understand you Yanks," Farnsworth conceded, as his head disappeared under the SIGABA momentarily.

"You're half Yank yourself," Hale reminded him.

"But raised in merry-old England, Major," he said as his head reappeared. "Ah, that's better. So, Miss Shimon, what does that make me in our clever little family?"

"Isn't it obvious? You are our distant cousin, newly arrived from across the pond." Then she laughed at her own joke.

"Which pond would that be?" he asked light-heartedly as a button was pressed, causing a red light to blink on. "We're in Tokyo, remember? Not New York or Washington D.C."

"I wouldn't argue with her, Captain," Hale advised as he thought of her interrogation in Pullach. "Sis can become quite cranky when she is closely questioned. I have been in that unfortunate position, so I know from practical experience."

Tamar smiled innocently and shrugged her shoulders as if she had no idea what he was talking about. "All right, I think we're ready to roll," Farnsworth said, rubbing his hands together in anticipation. "Are these in the order you want them processed?"

At Tamar's affirmative nod, he turned back to his new side-by-side encryption machines and began. Family time was over, it was time to get serious. Farnsworth made it clear that this was not a quick and easy process as he tried to manage their expectations. A cursory review of the documents from Okada's briefcase left the man who had seen thousands of similar documents 99% certain that they had been encrypted by the Enigma. This was not exactly an unexpected revelation as the Americans, Russians, and other countries had filled the airwaves with Enigma transmissions.

Twenty minutes into the process, the setting was determined. Then he went to MacArthur's version of Enigma and started decoding. An hour later, the first documents were ready for review. The information revealed was well worth the wait.

The first page processed was part of an analysis of the Truman presidency. The first few paragraphs were basically a disclaimer as to why he or she shouldn't be blamed for any incorrect assumptions. The author labeled Truman as a wild card and said his religious beliefs influenced his decision-making in unexpected ways. The days of predictable FDR where his actions could be anticipated with a great deal of accuracy were gone. Truman didn't have a long consistent history in government or international politics to provide a solid starting place for any kind of in-depth analysis.

After asserting his lack of responsibility if things went awry, the writer indicated that Truman's decision to use the atomic bomb on Hiroshima and Nagasaki was proof that he was a man of action, willing and able to make the hard decisions, and would take the advice of his military leaders. Would he drop the bomb again if he felt it necessary? The writer surmised that the notion shouldn't be dismissed.

As each page of the document they dubbed the "Truman Dossier" was deciphered and reviewed, it became clear that someone was not happy with the current President of the United States. The seriousness of Roosevelt's illness had been downplayed and was a closely held secret, the author insisted. Only a handful of his closest staff had any inkling that Roosevelt might not fulfill his last term in office. The presidency of Truman was an aberration and their failure to predict it was certainly no reflection on their abilities or organization.

"This guy is a bit of a toady for sure," Farnsworth commented.

"At this point, we can see that whoever wrote this material was not aware of the imminent demise of FDR," Hale said as he read the transcript provided by Farnsworth a second time.

"But everyone knew he was sick," Tamar offered. "Even in Palestine, we knew his time on earth would not be much longer. Of course, Menachem did not mourn his death as you Americans did. Your President had made a promise to the Arabs that he would never allow the Jews to have a homeland in the Middle East in return for cheap oil for your American industry."

"Whether he did or not," Hale began, "once he died, any verbal promises were unenforceable with a new President taking charge. Thus far, we don't really know how Truman will handle the Middle East oil situation."

"What else is there?" Tamar asked, opting not to engage in a debate about the late American President. "I am curious as to what our Japanese businessman was carrying that needed to be transported by hand from America to Germany to Tokyo."

Farnsworth handed another page to Hale without comment. Nothing needed to be said to show he was concerned about the text. Once Hale had it in his hands, Farnsworth sat back in his chair and waited for the Major to read it. He seemed to hope that Hale would have some insight as to the nature of this latest information.

Hale perused the paper in front of him and grimaced. "I haven't heard about any of this," he remarked at last. Then he looked directly at Farnsworth and said, "Fire up that SIGABA. This goes out to Quinn immediately. If it's true, then we have a problem with a leak in the White House."

"Care to share, Major?" Tamar prodded.

"Well, it looks like President Truman has some major changes planned for the intelligence community in America."

"Such as?"

"New and separate agencies to provide counterbalances of intelligence gathering. The author claims the new intelligence agencies will be billed as necessary tools to stop communist Russia from taking over the world."

"That doesn't sound strange to me at all," Tamar responded seriously.

"No. The intriguing part is that the author says he believes the changes are solely in response to the Cold War and are in no way related to *us*."

"Just who is *us*? Who is he referring to?"

"I have no idea. But the author goes on to say that a change of that type would definitely require a modification in their strategy and could impede ongoing infiltration activities at the highest levels of the American government."

"Geoffrey, is there any way to confirm the author of these documents?" Tamar inquired thoughtfully.

"Not as yet," Farnsworth offered. "At least not in what has been deciphered thus far. We may get a clue the more we uncover, but I would seriously doubt he would put his name on the document. He would not be very clever if he just assumed his documents could not be intercepted and decoded. From what I have seen thus far, this man is unlikely to take such a risk."

"Agreed," Hale chimed in. "And if the rest of the documents are anything like this, we're going to find we have a very savvy enemy who has no intention of being discovered."

"Of course, the Germans thought so as well, Major. Perhaps lightning will strike twice, and we will have the same good results as with Enigma."

"Don't get your hopes too high. At least not yet. Let's see what else this clever bastard has for us before we get too far ahead of ourselves."

"Right-o. Let me get cracking and see what other treasures are to be found here," Farnsworth said as he returned to his machine.

By early evening approximately one-third of the documents had been deciphered, most of which were part of the analytical Truman Dossier. Toward the end of the document, the tone changed from informational to advisory. The author indicated that although diamonds and other gems were usually highly effective as a worldwide currency, some governments and other entities they were looking to do business with would be more inclined to make a deal for precious metals. There was no mention of where the gems or metals were coming from, but indications were that supply was not an issue.

One standalone page mentioned missing assets that Hale assumed meant agents. He couldn't be sure, of course, but the language suggested as much. Whoever was missing was of great concern. Another asset was missing for a short period but eventually located and "dispatched without recall." That sounded ominous to all three reviewing the files.

The third document dealt specifically with the U.S. military. That caught Hale's attention immediately. The author spoke of deployment and strategies worldwide, but the section regarding Japan had one comment that caught their attention. Analysis was given then the writer indicated that his intel was not nearly as good as theirs when it came to Japan because "it's always better when you have a direct source." He then went on to disclose the rumor that the Pacific Islands were going to be placed under the Trusteeship of the United States by the United Nations Security Council.

"Direct source?" Hale questioned. "What does that mean? Do you think they could be intercepting classified information from MacArthur's offices? And if they are, how are they doing it? And how long has it been happening?"

"They could be tapping their phones, but what good does that do them?" Tamar asked no one in particular. "If the messages are encrypted, they have no way of knowing what is being sent," she reasoned.

"Not all messages are encrypted," Hale explained. "Simple telephone calls or telegraphs thought to be non-essential would not be encoded. It's too time-consuming for small talk."

"And you would be surprised how much information can be pieced together from basic communications," Farnsworth added. "A good analyst team can recreate a very good narrative from seemingly unrelated ongoing communications."

What they were doing with the intercepted communications was unclear. But it was obvious that they were primarily interested in American troop movements in the Pacific. *But why? The war was over. What possible reason would they have for knowing the location of our troops?*

"And the naval patrols," Farnsworth interjected once more. "They seem very keen on knowing where your Navy is at any given moment. That can't be a coincidence."

Hale's mind was reeling. Just the thought of classified American intelligence falling into enemy hands was unbearable. The damage that could be done was beyond imagination. "Who are these guys?" Hale called out in exasperation. "We don't even know who we're dealing with here!"

Tamar stood up from her desk with her notes in hand. She looked carefully at what she had written. "The analyst talks about where troops are located around the world, but about the U.S. military in particular. His handlers want to know about naval patrol routes and are worried about President Truman's future plans for Japan. He indicates that they know more about MacArthur's command structure than he does. What does all that tell us?" she asked herself.

"It tells us that whoever these people are, they're already far ahead of us. And that scares the hell out of me," Hale commented worriedly. "I don't like playing catch-up, especially when I don't even know what the game is."

"Really? Because it tells me that we're in the right place at the right time," Tamar said with a lift of her chin. "We need to contact Quinn and see if he has a trustworthy Japanese contact that can give us ideas on how MacArthur could have been compromised. Maybe a native will know things we do not."

"Makoto Fujita," Farnsworth said, as his fingers moved over the keyboard.

"If we can find out what kind of technology they're using to get information from the General, we may be able to backtrace it to its origin," Hale added.

"Fujita, you need to talk to Makoto Fujita," Farnsworth repeated, never slowing his pace. "He's the go-to guy around here. Smart as hell and in the know about absolutely everything."

"I think we heard about him when we first got here. What does he do?"

"Hmmm," Farnsworth said as he hit a button with finality then turned to face them. "Well, he's a combination of things; negotiator, planner, advisor, liaison between MacArthur and the Emperor. A very highly placed jack of all trades if you will."

"Can we get to him?"

"Yeah, I think so. He's always in demand, but if you were able to get to me, you should be able to get to him," he said as the newly deciphered page was snatched up. "I could set up a meet if you like."

Hale and Tamar sat silent for a moment with all the pros and cons of trusting someone new running through their heads as Farnsworth scanned the new page. Tamar was the first to speak. "We have to start somewhere. We just have to be careful what we disclose. I'm in."

"At least we know he's been vetted if he's working here. That's…"

"What are the odds?" Farnsworth said to himself with a chuckle.

"Are we boring you here?" Hale asked sarcastically.

"What? Oh, sorry, I just was reading some names listed here and there's a Shimon. I never heard that name before I met Tamar and here it is twice in one week. What are the odds, right? Yeah, we've got a Yitzhak Shimon."

CHAPTER 34

Magruder retrieved the small wooden chair from behind the desk and moved it to face the cot Fujita was lying on. His eyes were closed, and his breathing was even as he stretched out on the narrow bed with his hands comfortably behind his head. Mac waited patiently for him to rouse.

Perhaps sensing a new presence in the room, Fujita's eyelids fluttered open. He started slightly when he saw Mac in his peripheral vision. "I'm sorry," Fujita said as he moved to sit on the edge of the bed, "I didn't hear you knock."

"Maybe that's because I didn't knock," Mac responded with a smile.

This response caused Fujita's whole body to stiffen as he thought of what had happened to him many other times before he came to work with the Americans when his superiors had not felt it necessary to knock. "I needed to speak with you privately… off the record," Mac explained. Fujita did not respond but sat at attention with his hands carefully in his lap, waiting for what was to come next.

Mac pulled a pack of cigarettes from the front pocket of his shirt and tapped the edge of the pack until a single cigarette emerged. "Smoke?" he asked as he tipped the pack toward Fujita as if this conversation was taking place at a bar over a couple of beers.

"I don't smoke," Fujita responded after a moment.

"Neither do I," Mac said with another warm smile as he deftly pushed the cigarette back inside the pack while returning it to his pocket. "I recently found out that it's bad for me."

"Why carry them if you don't smoke?" Fujita asked, with a hint of interest in his voice.

"Well, they can be great conversation starters," Mac answered with a grin as he shifted his weight in the uncomfortable little chair. "Besides, I feel like something's missing when they aren't there. I was a smoker for many years before I was forced to quit," he admitted.

"They are not a temptation to you?" Fujita queried.

Magruder looked intently at the floor for a moment then raised his eyes to the man sitting across from him and replied, "Not when you know what's at stake." Fujita looked puzzled at the response but remained silent. "I suppose that smoking is forbidden in a submarine, yes?"

Fujita nodded silently. When Magruder didn't immediately continue Fujita stated more than asked, "You know of my past then."

Magruder stood and flipped the little chair around, so the back faced the bed, then straddled it. "Damn chair wasn't made for someone my size."

"Who are you?" Fujita asked quietly.

Magruder laughed and said, "Who am I? Well, that's an interesting question nowadays. Some days I'm not sure, but right now at this moment it's not really germane." Mac sighed as he looked at the man sitting as still as a stone across from him. He looked as if he was expecting to be backhanded at any moment. "I'm not here to hurt you. I just need information. You see, I heard about your time on the island…"

"I was delirious," Fujita interjected before Mac could finish. "I didn't know what I was saying then. I'm better now."

"That's the thing," Mac said solemnly, locking eyes with him. "I believe every word you said is true."

They silently stared at one another for several minutes as their minds whirred, each of them sizing up the other. Fujita was the first to break the silence. "Why would you believe the rantings of a crazy man?"

"Just because you've experienced something that others have not doesn't make you crazy. You may feel a little crazy at times," he said with a humorless smile, "but you aren't, and trust me I should know."

"So, you have been viewed as insane also?"

"Oh, without a doubt," Mac responded as he tried placing his forearms on the back of the chair. He then cursed under his breath as he stood and rearranged the uncomfortable chair once again. "Listen, I need the truth. It's important. What happened on that island?"

"I don't know what you expect to hear," Fujita said carefully. "I was weak. I lost my mind because I was weak. I had…hallucinations, but they were not real. I know that now. There's nothing to tell."

Magruder looked at him blankly, then suddenly burst out laughing. "Weak… you? I don't believe that for a second."

"It is to my great shame that I say this but it's true."

"Bullshit. Does that translate into Japanese?"

"Yes, it translates very well," Fujita said with a half-smile.

Mac leaned forward in his chair and rested his elbows on his knees while looking at the face of this one-time enemy before him. "You were educated in the United States and yet you fought against us in the war."

"Yes," he confirmed with a lift of his chin.

"Stuck between a rock and a hard place there, for sure. I don't suppose you were given a choice," Mac said, more to himself than the man sitting across from him. "Commander of an I-400 class submarine, yes?" At Fujita's lack of response, Mac continued. "Having a sub with an airplane must have been a real hoot. You ever get to fly it? You being a pilot couldn't have hurt when they were selecting the commander."

"Who are you?" Fujita asked with a piercing stare. "Have *they* sent you? If so, just get on with it. I am not afraid to die."

Yep, Mac thought, *this is our guy.* "I'm looking for information, not blood. So… who is 'they'?" Fujita was silent for so long Mac thought he had lost him. "Listen…"

"Would you like to hear a story?" Fujita suddenly asked, flashing a toothy smile. "I know some good ones." Mac wasn't certain where this was going, but hey the guy was talking so he nodded. Fujita stood and began to pace. "There once was a beautiful island with long beaches and lovely palm trees. The sun was warm, and the people were very happy there. Then one day giants came." Fujita cupped his hands like claws and stood over Mac, growling for effect.

"Oh no, what happened next?" Mac asked, getting into character.

"They were giant, ugly, evil, smelly beasts that stole women from their villages and killed anyone who stood in their way. They would come and make everyone afraid, then leave for many days. No one knew when they would come or when they would go."

"Where did they go?"

"No one knew. They would just disappear into the sky, poof," Fujita said, making a small firework with his hands to illustrate. He then sat on his cot and leaned toward Mac as if he were going to share a secret. "One day strangers in a big boat followed a sparkling bird to the island, but they didn't know about the giants. They made a mistake, you see, but they didn't know about the giants; not yet."

"And?" Mac encouraged when he hesitated.

"The strangers had a little bird, but they lost it. It left the boat and flew over the island, but never returned," Fujita said as he cupped his hands like a nest. "So, ten of the strangers went ashore to find the little bird because it was all alone. They couldn't abandon it, so they went to find it and bring it back home. Then suddenly a sword of light came down from the sky and cut their boat in half!"

Fujita's imaginary sword sliced through the air in front of Mac's knees, and Mac raised his eyebrows in genuine surprise. *What was this?*

"They watched with tears as their boat broke in two like a twig and sunk down, down, down into the depths of the sea. Ten men, just ten, were left. Nine of the ten men were hunted down and killed by the beasts. Only one of the men remained. One small man. The only survivor."

Fujita looked up at Mac to see if he was still following his story, then went on. "Oh, they were not all killed at once, no, but one by one they were caught and murdered in the vilest of ways. The little man felt very, very small and helpless as he watched from his hiding place and could do nothing as the giants peeled the skin from his friend's bodies and burned them."

Fujita's narration stopped as his eyes clouded over and he stared into space, lost in his story.

"What happened to the small man? Did he find the bird?" Mac prodded gently.

"What?" Fujita asked with a start. "Oh," he said, standing to pace once again. "Yes, he found it. Sadly, the beautiful little bird had broken its wings and would never fly again. The small man knew his time was near, so he set a trap for one of the giants and cut off his hand," he said dramatically, drawing his imaginary sword once again and swinging it at Mac's wrist. "He grabbed the hand and ran through the jungle jumping over logs and splashing through streams until he reached the hollowed-out tree where he lived. The giants looked and looked for him, but they couldn't find him. They didn't find the hand either," he said with a sly smile.

"Wow," Mac said with enthusiasm. "So, tell me, how did the man get off of the island?"

"Oh," Fujita shook his head sadly. "He never left the island. You see, he still lives there in the hollow of the tree..."

A knock on the door startled both men as someone called out, "Hey Makoto, you in there? Get it in gear buddy, you're needed in the conference room."

Mac turned to Fujita and expressed his regret. "I'm sorry, I must go the way I came. I hope my coming and going will not prevent us from being friends." And as the door swung open, Fujita was alone.

CHAPTER 35

"We lost a good man, sir." President Truman's eyebrows furrowed at Mac's news. "Our source apparently didn't know the Anakim were in residence. Once we stumbled on them, they opened fire before we could pull our team back."

"Anakim. Those are the massive beasts you showed us at our first meeting, correct?" Truman asked.

"Yes sir," Mac confirmed. "Two Anakim and seven Shalanaya were taken down. Unfortunately, no opportunity to capture. All bodies have been transported to the Groom Lake facility along with the tech found."

"Were you able to provide secure transport?" Truman asked Quinn. "After the destruction of Doctor Zimmerman's lab, we need to be even more vigilant in our efforts."

Yazzie grinned. "You have two men and a lady transport services in the house. The good doctors went to bed one night and walked in the next morning to find their new lab populated. Don't worry, Helen covered for us."

The President turned his gaze on Helen. "Oh, is it my turn?" she asked, turning a little pink. Briefing a president was not currently in her wheelhouse, but it felt good to be included in the process. "Yes, I filled the doctors in on everything alien I could without coming right out and telling them about the three of us," she said, motioning to Mac and Yazzie.

"How did it go?" Quinn asked.

"Well…better after I told them how and where the information came from was none of their business." Eyes widened in the room, and Mac coughed to hide a snort of laughter. "Well, of course, I didn't say it exactly like that. You know very restricted knowledge, above their security clearance, and so on." She folded her hands primly in her lap before continuing. "Well, it worked."

"Do they have what they need?" Quinn questioned, trying to suppress a smile.

"They weren't expecting quite so many bodies at once. However, this new lab is better equipped, they said. They found that the Shalanaya bodies degrade quickly, so they went to work on them right away. And both of them working together is a big plus as far as they're concerned. They will need help with the examination of the clothing and technical items. That's not where their expertise lies."

Truman turned to Quinn. "Find out who can be pulled in. Thoroughly vet them before giving them any access whatsoever, oh, and it might be a good idea to bring in a person or persons from the outside."

Quinn nodded as he jotted notes.

"They did look over the clothes the Anakim were wearing at my request," Helen added. "You and Mac were right, Yazzie. It is a lightweight fabric lined with an unknown alloy that seems to act as a non-penetrable shield against bullets. Doctor Zimmerman theorizes that when the bullet hits the cloth, the alloy instantly hardens to protect the wearer. It will require more testing to be sure. They have cataloged the other items, but it will be months before they can look at them without help."

"Okay, the enemy is secure, so what happened to our man?" Truman prodded solemnly.

"He's at Fort Belvoir, sir," Quinn assured. "Officially, he died overseas on an undercover assignment. He had no wife or kids; his parents have been notified. My men know to keep their mouths shut and after seeing the Anakim firsthand they are 100% on board. They were briefed after the incident and have been instrumental in clearing the remaining tunnels."

"Was anything else found?"

Mac spoke up and took the lead. "The encounter happened at what appears to be a communications hub."

"The second time you've interfered with one of their communication relays," Yazzie interjected. "They're going to hate you even more if they find out you were behind that incendiary bomb."

"The second time? Incendiary bomb?" Truman puzzled.

"Our source indicated that the primary Anakim communications center was located in Hiroshima, sir. That is, until you blew it all to hell," Mac replied. "That decision was more important than any of us ever dreamed."

Truman silently stared at Mac for a moment. Then his eyes misted up, and he removed his glasses to rub away the tears. After he situated the wire-rimmed glasses back on his nose, Helen reached over and put her hand on his. "You saved us all, Mr. President."

Harry Truman, the man, placed his other hand over Helen's and smiled gratefully at her words. The healing silence was broken by Yazzie commenting, "About that other thing, you may want to have the foundation of the White House checked."

Mac put his head in his hand as he shook it back and forth. "Can't you see that we were having a moment, rabbi?"

"For you who fear my name, the sun of righteousness shall rise with healing in its wings. You shall go out leaping like calves from the stall," Yazzie quoted from the prophet Malachi. "Yes, I see, however even a calf must have a solid foundation lest his foot slip, yes?"

Truman regained his composure and smiled. "Yes. So exactly why is the White House in peril?"

"An incendiary bomb…" Quinn wagged his index finger at Mac as he spoke. "Uh…I mean, a nasty gas leak ignited and destroyed any evidence of our foray into the tunnels. We believe it may have been situated close to the President's residence. Better?" Mac asked Quinn. At his nod, Mac continued. "Further investigation revealed the entrance we believe the Anakim have been using. Two large shipping containers were positioned over one of the access points to the tunnels. Each container was outfitted as living quarters with a reclining chair, a powerful air conditioner, and what we believe to be a monitor along with a stockpile of food, fluids, and supplies."

"Motion detectors found in the tunnels have been mounted in the containers, sir. They are being monitored 24 hours a day. We're hoping someone will be sent to see why transmissions from this location have ceased," Quinn said. "With any luck, we'll catch a canary willing to sing."

"This source you've mentioned," Truman directed to the room in general, "who is this? What do we know about him or her? Are they reliable?"

"His name is Randall Smithers III," Quinn responded.

"And, no, he's not trustworthy at all," Helen interjected.

"Smithers, Smithers…should I know that name?" the President asked, with his mind trying to place the connection he was certain was there.

"The Smithers family is old money and have been active in the sleazier side of politics for years. The patriarch was friends with FDR. In fact, despite Randall's dip into communist activities at Oxford, the Sphinx personally approved his hiring in the War Department as a favor to the old man," Quinn supplied.

"The War Department!"

"Yes, he is an analyst there and was recruited by none other than your female would-be assassin," Quinn affirmed. "He has been placed on a very short leash. One of my men is posing as his assistant and where Smithers goes, my man goes."

"Where do his loyalties lie?"

"With himself," Mac answered ruefully. "The Shalanaya promised him virtually unlimited sex, money, and power under their regime. It's all a lie of course, but he's too vain to think that they could dupe him. He was the American operative Hale and Tamar picked up on in Germany. We've been investigating him ever since."

"Germany?"

"He performed a dead drop. He's been doing it for quite a while," Quinn said with disgust. "Helen grilled him on what was exchanged. He doesn't know we have copies of everything. Of course, we'll verify to see if he's being honest with us. She told him that if he was caught in a lie, we'd audit his entire family."

"Brilliant, by the way," Yazzie said, making Helen blush.

"And what did he get to betray his country?" Truman asked.

"Nothing," Mac said, causing Quinn to jerk his head around. "Just several receipts from a newly incorporated import/export business in New York City. No ties to D.C. I believe Yazzie has a friend that does business there. He's going to check it out."

"Oh yes, yes," Yazzie replied, nodding his head compliantly. "I doubt I'll find much, though. Ownership of those things is hard to trace."

"I see," the President responded dryly. "Apparently Mr. Smithers is extraordinarily bad at treason."

"One thing of great importance, Mr. President," Yazzie interjected. "A map in the enemy camp seems to set out their supply lines. We'll need to verify, but Tokyo seems to be of primary importance."

"How are Major Hale and Miss Shimon doing? I assume they arrived safely."

"Yes sir," Quinn responded. "It seems Mr. Saburo Okada works for an import/export business located two blocks from MacArthur's headquarters."

"An import/export business, you say? Quite a coincidence that," Truman deadpanned as he leaned back in his chair. "I would expect their location is not a coincidence, however. What do we know about the proprietors?"

"Working on it," Mac said. "Oddly enough, they did turn up one piece of unexpected information. The Greys gave us the name of one Makoto Fujita as an eyewitness of the occupation of the Anakim on earth. Yazzie had traced him to Hiroshima where the trail went cold so we assumed the worst."

"Curly and Tamar ran into him, of all things," Quinn chimed in. "He's working as a high-level interpreter for MacArthur's group. Well, he's a bit more than that. He's a liaison between MacArthur and the Emperor, as well as a negotiator, planner, and advisor."

"I went to see him," Mac confirmed. "He's definitely our guy, but our meeting got cut short, so I need to talk to him again. I got the feeling he received a lot of grief from his people for claiming to have seen aliens so he's denying everything, but I think I can bring him around."

Truman was silent for a moment as he absently shuffled a few papers on his desk. "It seems our focus has shifted to Japan, gentleman, and lady," he said, nodding in Helen's direction. "Colonel Quinn, do you have everything you need here? Can you spare these three for a while?"

"I've got it covered, sir."

"Helen, if you're uncomfortable with the situation, traveling to foreign lands, I mean…"

"Oh," she laughed. "My father traveled extensively during his lifetime, and I had the pleasure of accompanying him often to the Philippines, Greece, China, and Germany. I will be quite alright, Mr. President. And besides, if you remember we're only a moment away if you need us."

CHAPTER 36

"So, are you new here? I mean, I've worked here for a while now and I've never seen you before," the attractive little brunette asked with a coy smile.

"Uh, yeah. I just got transferred in." Farnsworth managed to get out while trying to hold his allergies at bay.

"It's not like I try to scope out all the attractive guys or anything," she said with a flirty little laugh. "Well, okay, so I do a little."

The doors of the lift opened, and he practically ran out of the enclosed space to catch his breath. Remembering his manners, he swung his left arm back to prevent the doors from closing and made a sweep of his right arm, welcoming her to disembark. The female attention was not unwelcome by any means. It was just her liberal use of fragrance and his severe allergies were never going to mix.

He could already feel his sinuses beginning to clog. "Unfortunately," he said nasally, as they walked down the hall. "My assignment here is only temporary."

"Oh, that's too bad," she responded with disappointment. Then her face brightened with hope as she continued. "But there's no reason we can't have a little fun while you're here."

Farnsworth smiled while concentrating on taking as few breaths as possible without passing out. "Uh…we'll have to see. I sort of have to feel out my new boss, you know, just to see what's what."

"I get it," she sympathized. "It's always hard when you're new. Well, this is me," she said pertly as she pulled a key from her pocket. "Number 811. Come by and visit anytime. Maybe we could go to lunch or something. You've got to eat, right?"

"Right, right," he said, smiling as he edged away from her. "Great, just great," he muttered to himself as he continued down the hallway alone. "Now I can't breathe. Gonna be blowing my nose all day." He glanced back down the hall as he stopped at the office and saw her leaning in her doorway. She gave a little finger wave as his key slipped into the lock. He lifted his chin and gave her a raised hand in recognition, then she disappeared into her office.

"Bugger," he muttered. "She's going to be a problem." He knew the work he did was highly classified. He also knew that honey traps were set for mugs dumb enough to fall for them all the time. And after what he had decoded the past few days, paranoia had become a constant companion whispering caution into his ear day and night.

It was the paranoia that caused him to hesitate at the door to the office. It was also why he refused to turn the key until a couple of ticks after she went inside to start her day. The equipment in this office was valuable, and the information deciphered even more so. And if someone wanted the equipment, they would need a technician to run it, right? A couple more people got off the lift as he sneezed into his handkerchief. Only when they had disappeared into offices down the way did he feel comfortable turning the key to enter.

When the door swung open, Farnsworth stopped dead in his tracks. An unknown man was sitting at the desk with an MP40 submachine gun lying on the grey metal desktop in front of him. Fear gripped him as he raised his hands in surrender and took a step back.

"Here you go, dear," a woman said as she placed a cup of coffee on the desk in front of the man with the gun. She turned a sunny smile toward Farnsworth, intending to ask if he would like coffee when she stopped - confused. "Why does he have his hands up?"

"I don't know," Yazzie said as he gently ran a brush over the disassembled parts of his weapon. "Ask him."

"What in the living hell are you doing?" Mac asked as he put his hand over the mouthpiece of the telephone he was speaking into. "Put your hands down and get your ass inside."

"Uh, no, I don't think so," Farnsworth got out before he violently sneezed again.

"Oh dear," Helen said with concern as she took him by the arm and coaxed him to the sofa. "I was going to ask if you wanted coffee. I went out and bought a percolator the moment I saw you didn't have one. The electric percolator is one of the most wonderful modern conveniences, isn't it? But if you're feeling poorly maybe you'd prefer tea instead?"

At that moment, Tamar and Curly filled the doorway with weapons drawn. Tamar went low and Curly high. "Oh, good morning. Would you like coffee?" Helen chirped.

"Uncle!" Tamar exclaimed as her weapon was holstered and she ran to embrace Yazzie.

"What in the hell kind of outfit are you running here, Major?" Mac asked as he extended his hand and smiled at Hale. "Jittery bunch, aren't you?"

"We saw Geoffrey with his hands up, so we assumed the worst," Tamar explained as she pulled away from her uncle. "When did you get in?"

"Bloody hell!" Geoffrey exploded. "You know these gits?"

Tamar and Hale both began to speak at once until Helen brushed away their concerns with, "Oh, it's alright he's just a bit under the weather." Helen patted his shoulder warmly. "You'll feel better after a cup of tea."

Geoffrey blew his nose. "No, no I'm not sick, it's just my allergies. You're perfectly lovely, thank you, but I'm fine. It's just I rode the lift up with the girl down the hall that uses quite a bit of cologne. That's all it took to get the allergies going."

Helen, Yazzie, and Mac all glanced at one another.

"Of course, being greeted by a man with a gun, an MP40 no less, when I opened the office door didn't help," Farnsworth continued.

"The gun is in pieces," Hale said as he closed the door.

"Well, I didn't notice that at the time, mate," Farnsworth shot back.

"You never clean a weapon without another within reach," Tamar said off-handedly as she went to hug Helen. To make her point, Yazzie pulled a Colt .45 from an unseen holster in the middle of his back and smiled. Farnsworth paled.

"What are you doing here? Why didn't you tell us you were coming?" Tamar asked.

"Because we're sneaky," Yazzie said dryly.

Tamar laughed. "Everyone, this is Geoffrey Farnsworth. He has been invaluable in decrypting the documents we retrieved from Mr. Okada, the businessman we followed here. Geoffrey, this is General Magruder and his wife Helen. And this is my uncle…Yitzhak Shimon."

Farnsworth had been smiling and shaking hands until she introduced Yazzie. "What?" he asked in confusion. "Oh, I get it. Let's get one over on the new guy. Yes, yes I see. Well, you were quite a success. Good for you."

Mac, Helen, and Yazzie were at a loss. "Your name was one of five we deciphered from the recovered documents," Hale told Yazzie grimly. "It's unclear at the moment why you were mentioned."

"You mean he really is your uncle?" Farnsworth asked Tamar. "I thought you were joshing with me."

"We sent the information to Quinn, encrypted of course. I thought maybe that's why you're here," Hale said.

"No, this is the first we're hearing about it. We must have been in transit when he got the information," Mac responded. "No, actually we're here because of information we dug up in D.C."

"Uncle, you shouldn't be here," Tamar said urgently. "We can work this end. You need to leave immediately."

"Shouldn't we figure out why Yazzie's name was in the documents before any decisions are made?" Helen asked as she filled several mugs with coffee.

"Agreed," Mac responded. "Has everything been deciphered?"

"No, not yet."

"Well then, Tommy here should carry on with his business, and we'll get on with ours," Mac said.

A smile spread across Geoffrey's face. "You've spent some time with we Brits, have you? I haven't been called a Tommy since I left England."

"I served in the 112th Field Artillery Unit in the American Expeditionary Forces in the Great War. We worked with a few Brits along the way," Mac explained. "Heard all about Tommy Adkins. I guess it stuck."

Geoffrey unlocked the box and went to work decrypting the remainder of the treasure trove of information copied on the plane as Mac continued. "What else was in the documents?"

Hale took the lead. "A dossier on Truman, complete with an analysis of possible future decisions. The good thing is the analyst considers the President a wild card and didn't offer much hope of predicting what he'll do next."

"A wild card, eh," Yazzie commented as he reassembled his weapon. "I guess we know who wrote the dossier."

"Really, who?" Hale asked in surprise.

"Helen interrogated one Randall Smithers III, brilliantly I might add, and he used that exact phrase to describe the President," Yazzie explained.

"He was the American involved in the dead drop in the gasthaus in Germany. We had him followed once he left you," Mac added.

"I would have followed him a bit longer to see who his contacts were," Tamar commented. "But hopefully you got what you needed."

"Well, the decision was taken out of our hands when he accidentally ran into Helen. Once he identified her, just following him was off the table," Mac said.

"There wasn't anything accidental about it," Yazzie commented with a grin as he clicked the last piece into place.

"What do you mean, Uncle?"

"I flattened him," Helen said, beaming.

"The boastful shall not stand in Your sight; You hate all workers of iniquity," Yazzie said to Helen. "That Psalm sums it up very well, don't you think?"

"Yes, it does. Now we just need to know if he was completely honest with me. He's an analyst in the War Department and the most arrogant and egotistical person I've ever had the misfortune of meeting," she replied.

"The War Department!"

"Yes. As of right now, he has been persuaded to work with us. However, he's on a *very* short leash," Mac said with emphasis on very. "What brought us here came from another source. An enemy nest actually. We found maps believed to detail the RAT lines being used by the bad guys to transport diamonds, precious metals, personnel, and weapons. We're here to verify that assumption."

"There are three key points on the map: Tokyo, one of the Mariana islands, and a particular point in the ocean close to the Mariana Trench. Everything branches out from those three points," Yazzie added. "Tokyo makes sense. This is probably their new communications hub. Suppositions can also be made about the island. But lines emanating from a point in the middle of the ocean with no land mass for miles? That's more of a puzzle."

"That does explain one thing that turned up in the documents," Hale said thoughtfully. "They seem to have an unhealthy interest in the movements of the U.S. Navy ships in the area."

"Hmm, and what do we know of the courier from Germany? What role does he play?" Mac asked.

"Actually," Tamar said, "I'm beginning to think he's not a big fish. Courier is probably a good word to describe his function. The fact that he went straight from the airport to the business tells me that he may be reporting to someone inside."

"Yeah, we've had eyes on the place ever since we got here, but we've discovered nothing pertinent so far," Hale confirmed. "We've identified a few people coming and going, but it all seems legit."

"Well, with all the tunnels under the city, you'd be a fool to use the front door, right?" Mac murmured as he thought. "Rabbi, with your newfound interest in the import/export business, maybe you should pay a visit. You know, feel out the owner and find out if he's looking to do business in New York City."

Yazzie smiled. "I do love to talk about making money and I could introduce him to my niece who is looking to get into the business."

"I can do it. There's no need for you to go. They have your *name*, Uncle."

"Exactly, my dear. That's why I'll get a meeting with the boss. I'm the cheese needed to bait the trap."

CHAPTER 37

"I will take the lead," Yazzie said with finality to Tamar as they walked down the street. "McCann said Okada went inside the business with his satchel but left several minutes later without it."

"Which means Okada is most likely simply a courier, as I suspected. Not the person we need to find," Tamar added. "I know. I know, Uncle. We have covered this ten times since last night. I know what I am doing," she insisted.

"And, if we could, I would cover it another ten times," he answered firmly. "This is not a game, Tamar. We have no idea who may be waiting inside or what their intentions may be. It is imperative that we carry out the assignment as professionals looking to expand our customer base. Nothing more, nothing less."

"And I am your loving niece trying to learn the business from her doting uncle," she added petulantly. "I know my part, Uncle. Please, let's just get inside and find out who runs this place and follow the ratlines to the next rat hole."

Yazzie stopped in mid-step and held Tamar's hand tightly. He stared at her intently. "You are young. You are impetuous. I understand that. There was a time when I was as well. But you must learn to trust the instructions of your elders and follow them fastidiously. If you don't, someone you know, or care for deeply, maybe injured or killed. There is no room for error, my little sheifale, my little lamb. The pain of losing someone because of one's negligence never leaves your heart. Do you understand?"

"Of course, Feter," she responded with her Yiddish term of affection for her uncle. "I am sorry. I did not mean to upset you and I promise to keep you safe."

Yazzie smiled at his young niece and shook his head. "I appreciate your being so protective of your ancient Uncle Yazzie," he returned with a grin. "How have I survived all this time without your escort?" he continued with a laugh.

"Don't mock me, Uncle. I am deeply concerned for your safety."

"As I am for yours. Now, let's get inside and see what we can find, eh?"

"Of course, uncle," she answered obediently. Then, "Uncle?"

"Yes?"

"Will you tell me who was injured or killed because of your negligence when you were young?"

Yazzie turned away and began to walk toward their destination without saying a word. Clearly, there would be no answer today.

They entered the upscale business office confidently as if they had been invited and were expecting to be met by their host. The office interior was sharply decorated with traditional Japanese décor on the walls, but the furniture was more of a western design.

A substantial walnut desk sat in one corner of the room with an ornate chair made for someone with a large frame stationed behind it. A small intricately carved table sat beside the desk with a modern electric lamp that appeared to be more for decoration rather than function. Two comfortable padded chairs covered with a brightly colored silk fabric featuring swimming koi fish faced the desk, probably there for preferred customers.

But it was the two delicate teacups still on the desk that drew Yazzie and Tamar's attention. Both cups were at least half-full, and the smell of tobacco hung in the air even though the room was currently unoccupied. The two inquisitors looked knowingly at one another as they casually continued to scan the room.

"Perhaps we have caught them at a bad time, Uncle," Tamar said softly as she demurely lifted the long scarf draped around her neck to cover her hair.

At that moment, a beautiful young woman with black shoulder-length hair as silky as the lavish curtain from which she appeared entered the room to greet them. She was careful to pull the curtain completely closed behind her before turning to acknowledge them. She was petite, as one would expect of the Japanese, and wore a fashionable dress that could have been designed in Paris and probably was.

"Good morning Americans, how may I help you?" she asked with slick professional courtesy.

"Wir sind Deutsch," Yazzie replied smoothly. "However," he continued in English, "we are fluent in both German and English. We can conduct business in which ever language you like."

"You have my apologies," she replied without a hint of remorse. "There are many Americans in Tokyo at the moment. I just assumed. How may I help you?"

"Are you the owner of this business?" Yazzie asked.

"Oh no," she replied with a shy laugh. "I'm not nearly that important. I am just a clerk here."

"A clerk will not do. I would like to speak to the owner if you please."

"Oh, I am so sorry. The owner left on a business trip just this morning. He will be gone for an undetermined amount of time."

"Most unfortunate," Yazzie sighed. "Do you have a card with your telephone number on it? That way next time I can call ahead and make an appointment to avoid another wasted stop."

"Of course," she replied, as she went to the desk and opened a drawer.

"I have no cards, but perhaps you can tell him that Yitzhak Shimon will be calling to set up a meeting."

At the mention of his name, her hand involuntarily paused midair for a moment before reaching into the drawer and withdrawing a crisp white business card. "Of course," she replied with her smile again widened in efficient cooperation. "Is there anything else?"

"Yes," Tamar responded hesitantly. "I wish to buy tea. Could you direct us to a geschaft…er, I mean a shop where a purchase could be made?"

Directions to a local store several blocks away were quickly provided as the two prospective customers were walked to the door with several more perfunctory apologies as they were ushered out. Once outside Yazzie deliberately paused in front of the window and checked his watch.

"Benjiro Hayakawa," he said as the business card was tucked away in his coat pocket. "At least now we have a name."

"She's no clerk," Tamar said as she took her uncle's arm, and he patted her hand. "She recognized your name. A clerk would not be privy to information from the courier."

"Agreed. Is she still watching us?" he asked as they started in the direction of the tea shop.

"Oh yes," Tamar returned with a smile. "I don't think I will buy tea for Helen from the shop she recommended. She's probably on the phone right now, telling them to lace the leaves with something unpleasant. Poor Geoffrey would undoubtedly take the brunt of the attack."

"Very wise," Yazzie agreed as they turned a corner and stopped. "You go buy Helen's tea. I have some sightseeing to do. Many lovely canals to view."

"The tea can wait, Uncle. I will walk with you."

"Mr. Hayakawa is out of town, remember?" Yazzie said with a smile. "Don't worry, I will be careful. You do the same."

"I will go with you," Tamar said, firmly crossing her arms in rebellion. Her green eyes hardened like the jewels they resembled as her resolve set like granite.

"You always did love the water," Yazzie said in surrender, after realizing her stubbornness would not be overcome without a scene. Satisfied, she tucked her hand back into the crook of his arm as they continued. "Did you know that Tokyo has more than one hundred canals and rivers flowing beneath the city?" She shook her head in the negative as he continued. "The Uda and Onden rivers cross below the busy streets above. It is literally a city built on water."

They walked on, stopping to point and admire the various sites occasionally as they went. The entrances to underground waterways were nearly invisible, having been carefully integrated into the architecture of their busy commercial city.

Once a grid around the import/export business had been completed, a stop was made to procure the tea Helen had requested before heading back to the office.

The shop was very small and crowded, so Tamar went inside to make the purchase while Yazzie remained outside on the walk. He paced in front of the window, mentally reviewing the events of the day, glancing through the glass periodically to ascertain her progress. He breathed an impatient sigh of relief when she finally stepped to the counter to be served. Turning from the window toward the street, Yazzie stepped back against the glass to allow a knot of pedestrians passage when a small Japanese woman with grey streaks throughout her dark hair began a rapid-fire rant while pointing at the door he was currently blocking.

Yazzie stepped away from the window to allow her safe entry when suddenly his arms were grabbed, and he was swept along with the group as if being encouraged to join an Israeli folk dance. His mood was not festive, however, as five members of the mob peeled off into an alleyway with him in tow. The towering brick walls on either side brought gloom to the dirt path they took. A water rat was startled from its hiding place at their passing as a left turn took them farther from the clean, bustling streets of commerce.

Were they a bored street gang looking to rough up a hated American occupier or perhaps something more sinister? His question was answered when the gang of five was greeted by two more members waiting with their feet solidly set a shoulder's length apart and their arms crossed at their ultimate destination. The new additions were the ones in charge, not his dance partners.

Good, Yazzie thought, *I don't have to feel bad about killing them.*

The two thugs in front turned around to face him. Knives were unsheathed. "So," the cocky young leader said in broken English as he approached. "What you going do, old man?"

The two men holding his arms released their grip and stepped back to watch the show. Without a moment's hesitation, Yazzie, in a single fluid movement sent the thug's knife flying with his left hand as he struck an upward blow with his right elbow to the young man's jaw. A sickening crack was heard as his jaw broke and his neck snapped back. The thud of his skull hitting the dirt was all but missed as Yazzie moved seamlessly from attacker one to attacker two. The second man's attempted strike was blocked with Yazzie's left arm as the heel of his right hand struck under his jaw in a violent upward motion. There was a second sickening crack as his head was jolted backward and a dull thud was heard as his body also hit the ground.

Yazzie quickly dropped into a crouch and retrieved the sharp-bladed tantō dropped by one of his victims. He grasped the hilt of the weapon with the blade running up his forearm as he stood to face them. The entire incident was simple, efficient, and took less than five seconds. The remaining three men from the mob were shocked into immobility. They had never witnessed anyone move so blindingly fast and with such devastating results.

Yazzie's fight-first talk-later approach had its desired effect. The three miscreants left standing no longer felt secure in their position, even though they outnumbered the old man three to one. They understood that their situation had just changed dramatically. His speed, his skill, and the way he held the tantō increased the likelihood to about 100% that at least the first of them to strike was going to be maimed or killed. None of them wanted to be that man. Their hesitation caused the two in charge to angrily shout orders in Japanese.

Yazzie turned his head slowly to look at the tallest one on his right, then feigned a slight movement to the left and inwardly smiled when the young man jerked back. They had some skills but were novices compared to his years of training. He glanced at the two at the end of the alley and suddenly understood. They were not here to instruct but to observe. To ascertain Yazzie's skill level before entering into the fray. They were the real threat.

Yazzie was not willing to wait for the three novices to work up their courage or get organized. He would take down the closest one and move into a better position with his back to the wall. The squat one behind him, on the edge of his peripheral vision, would be the first to move, Yazzie surmised. His position at the rear gave him a better opportunity both to take Yazzie down without getting injured himself and to improve his standing with the two yelling orders. His toad-like face and heavy body had probably never impressed anyone, so this was his big moment.

Yazzie spun around and blocked the man's knife arm with his forearm turned in toward his body to ensure that his veins would be protected from what was coming next. As the arms of the two men met, Yazzie's knife hand shot out with the blade, slicing his opponent's neck, neatly cutting open the carotid artery. Then, flipping his hand over, he pulled it back again, cutting the artery a second time. Yazzie then swiftly moved into a position with his back against the wall with the intent of edging out of the secluded area.

Blood spurted from the neck wounds with every heartbeat. Though the man clamped his thick hands over his sinewy neck, his fate was sealed. His compatriots never acknowledged his situation, as the two men at the end of the alley had seen enough. They began to move forward with the intention of ending the confrontation when a noise from the connecting alley caught their attention. To Yazzie's surprise, they immediately disappeared down the narrow walkway, leaving him alone with the last two of his five abductors. These two, knowing they were out matched, were willing to allow his getaway until they saw their champion round the corner of Yazzie's escape route. The white six-foot-eight giant renewed their resolve as they leaped forward to engage. Yazzie dispatched them as efficiently as he had the others As the tall man descended upon his position, Yazzie pulled the gun from the middle of his back and shot him twice in the chest.

The giant managed several more strides until he was within an arm's reach of Yazzie before coming to a teetering stop. A look of disbelief widened his eyes as red stains saturated his chest and he fell to his knees. The sound of footsteps coming up fast caused Yazzie to swing his weapon around as a dark-skinned man skidded to a stop.

Panting, he held his hands up in surrender as he breathlessly asked, "You okay?"

Yazzie's eyebrows knit together at the question as he held the gun steady.

The man smiled and brought his raised hands together in a prayerful pose, then gave a slight bow of his head as he said with admiration, "You are as good as they said. Shalom, my friend."

And with that, he turned and quickly disappeared the same way in which he came.

CHAPTER 38

"Your ass will be on the first transport back to the U.S. if you go anywhere near Hayakawa, the clerk, or the import/export business. Do you understand me, Tamar?" Mac barked.

"They tried to kill him!" she yelled back.

"I will not let you endanger yourself, the mission, or the team members that will undoubtedly have to save your butt because you can't control your temper."

"I can't just sit here and let them get by with it! I won't!" she returned defiantly.

"Helen, contact Quinn," Mac directed without skipping a beat. "Get transport arranged. Farnsworth, contact the MPs, tell them we need an escort for a hostile prisoner to the airfield."

"Yes sir," he said, quietly avoiding Tamar's seething glance.

"You can't! Tell him, Uncle."

"You had better have someone there to meet the plane in D.C. or she'll be on the next flight back," Yazzie replied serenely.

"Oh…" she huffed as she flopped into a chair and began a tirade in Yiddish.

"What's she saying?" Hale asked loudly to be heard over the rant.

"Nothing I can say without making Helen blush," Yazzie shouted back.

"All right, young lady. That is quite enough!" Helen said sternly, with hands on hips. "You are being childish and selfish. I understand the need to blow off steam, but now you are willing to endanger all of us for your foolish revenge? Frankly, I expected more from you."

The room went quiet with nothing except Tamar's heavy breathing breaking the silence. After a few seconds that seemed to be an eternity, Farnsworth asked guiltily, "Am I still calling the MPs?"

"No!" Tamar snapped, as she folded her arms and clamped her mouth shut.

Mac looked at her intently for a moment then turned his gaze to McCann, who had been standing silently in the corner. "I have an assignment for you, Billy. I need you to dip your toe into the Tokyo nightlife. Can you drink, carouse, and pick up women without getting stupid?"

"Aye," he responded with a wide grin. "I've been training my whole life for this assignment, sir. Just who would I be picking up now?"

"811 down the hall. Not that Farnsworth here isn't pretty, but we need to know if her interest goes deeper than a passing flirtation. Also, the clerk from Mr. Hayakawa's place. Did she get a good look at you?"

"A good look, no sir," McCann responded honestly. "But we've been staking them out for close to two weeks now. I can't say she never noticed me."

"That's okay. Just don't seek her out right away. See if she comes to you. Tamar, you and Tommy boy will go along. Can Billy trust that you'll have his back?"

"Yes," she said tightly. "But if a fight breaks out the clerk is mine, do you hear?" she asked, pointing her finger first at Geoffrey, then at McCann.

"Uh, sir…" Farnsworth said hesitantly. "Wouldn't it be better if…"

"No, it wouldn't. 811 fancies you, so you'll just have to take one for the team. Laugh, drink…moderately," Mac said, looking pointedly at McCann. "Flirt, talk them up, but absolutely *do not* leave with them. Do not leave your drinks unattended and do not forget that they could be dangerous and may not be alone. Tamar, if it looks like either of them is in trouble, make a scene and everybody gets out. Got it?"

"Oh, I am excellent at making scenes," she said with a confident smile.

Mac gave her a piercing stare as he reminded her, "Blow this and you're on the first transport out, got it?"

Her smile faded as she nodded solemnly.

"What if the clerk recognizes her?" Yazzie asked with concern.

"I will cover," she answered quickly, not wanting the assignment to be pulled. "I am not as demure as my doting uncle thinks. I sneak out of the hotel room regularly when he is otherwise occupied."

Mac was silent for a moment. He then looked at Yazzie, who gave a slight nod of approval.

"We'll look after one another, sir," McCann assured him. "Don't you worry about that. I can hold my liquor better than anybody in all of Japan and if a disturbance is needed, I can always start a fight."

"Start a fight? Why on earth would you start a fight?" Geoffrey asked, aghast.

"A distraction, mate. That's what it's all about. Besides, what's not to love about a good brawl?" McCann asked with a broad grin and a chuckle. Tamar nodded in agreement.

Hale watched in amusement as Mac rubbed his forehead and muttered, "An Irishman, an Englishman, and a Jew walk into a bar…what could possibly go wrong?" Sometimes it was good not to be in charge.

"All right, just stay alive and don't kill anybody else if possible. Yazzie's already used up our body quota for the decade. Got it?" Affirmative nods all around allowed him to continue. "Bring the car around, will ya."

"Will do, boss," McCann said before he went whistling down the hallway.

"You have made him a very happy man," Hale said as Farnsworth turned back to his machine.

"Tamar and I will escort Yazzie back to the hotel and tend to his few little injuries if you're sure you don't need us," Helen said, gathering her things. She paused as Yazzie and Tamar rose and headed for the door. "Considering that we haven't been in town long enough to really annoy anyone, and what happened to Yazzie, do I have to say be careful?"

"We'll walk out with you," Mac said, planting a soft kiss on Helen's forehead as he slipped his arm around her waist. "Lock the door behind us, Farnsworth."

The ride to the meeting place was brief as the location was within blocks of their office. It was only an abundance of caution that caused Mac to call McCann's chauffeuring services into play. They were expected, so after showing their I.D. an efficient young man escorted them to the conference room where a middle-age bald man with a polished silver cloverleaf insignia on his uniform was pacing and Makoto Fujita sat quietly with his hands folded neatly on the table.

"I'm sorry. Have we met?" Hale asked as he extended his hand to the Lieutenant Colonel.

"So, are you the one that took my man and one of my machines?" He returned without preamble.

"Pardon?"

"Farnsworth, Geoffrey Farnsworth. Are you going to try and deny it?" he asked with his color rising. "What I want to know is who you know that you were able to pull him from my team?"

"President Harry S. Truman," Mac answered quietly.

The irate officer glared at Mac for a moment then replied, dripping with sarcasm, "Right, of course. The President, I should have known." He then turned back to Hale. "When do I get my man and my equipment back?"

"When this assignment is finished," Hale replied firmly.

"And what assignment would that be? Don't worry, I assure you I have the clearance to be read in."

"We'll read you in on ours if you'll read us in on all the intel your team has gathered," Mac interjected casually. Then as the officer turned to stalk out of the room, Mac continued. "I hope you know that we are on the same side, Colonel.

We each have our jobs to do and if you don't interfere with my team, we won't interfere with yours."

"You already have," he spat before exiting the room.

"You are aware that he works in intelligence, yes?" Fujita interjected as he rose from his seat. "Your people will most assuredly be investigated by his team after this altercation."

Hale stepped forward and shook Fujita's hand. "It's nice to meet you, Mr. Fujita. We have heard good things about you. I am Major Donald Hale, and this is General John Magruder."

"Good to meet you," Mac replied blandly, without any acknowledgment of their previous meeting.

"You look familiar," Fujita said as they shook hands. "Have we met before?"

"I don't believe so," Mac responded, then laughed. "But you know how it is, all of us Americans look alike."

"Yes, yes, I've heard that to be the case," Fujita agreed with a smile. It seemed their previous meeting was to be their little secret. Of course, if this Major Hale was unaware of General Magruder's unusual method of entry and exit, it made perfect sense. "Please sit. The chairs are quite comfortable. I imagine there are many so small as to be uncomfortable for a man of your size."

Mac smiled as he remembered the child-sized chair in Fujita's room thinking, *smart ass.*

"Mr. Fujita," Hale began as Mac closed the door. "I will come straight to the point if you don't mind."

"Of course."

"Do you know the owner of an import/export business named Benjiro Hayakawa?"

"Bennie? Yes, of course. He is a retired Admiral from the Imperial Japanese Navy and was my commanding officer during the war."

"An Admiral," Mac repeated. "Wow, it's amazing he had the time to build such a large and successful business while working his way up the ranks."

"It was a family business started by his father and uncle. He inherited his father's half after his death during the war when Bennie was away. He partnered with his uncle upon his return until his death last year. Now it is just him. It was rumored that his uncle's many contacts around the world assisted him in his way 'up the ranks' as you say."

"How so?"

Fujita paused to frame his response. "Bennie's father was a very good man, honorable. After his death, the business built on his reputation began to fail. As the business declined, his uncle became more willing to accept less reputable clients. Not to say he did anything illegal, I wouldn't know that, but it was commonly known that he sometimes did not know the contents of the boxes he was shipping."

"He wasn't afraid of being caught?" Hale inquired.

Fujita smiled. "He was known to do favors for people of wealth and position. They protected their names by protecting him."

"Do you have any idea why good ol' Bennie would try to have a member of my team assassinated before they even met?" Mac asked casually.

Fujita's eyes widened at the accusation. He was silent for a few moments, then sighed. "So, it's true…you see, at one time Admiral Hayakawa was the head of the Japanese version of your military intelligence. It had been rumored that though he retired from the Navy, he retained that function and continues to report directly to the Emperor. I had no way to confirm, of course, but I have seen the two of them together."

"Does Hayakawa have the ability to tap into phone calls in the building currently occupied by General MacArthur?" Hale asked.

"Would your intelligence people be able to manage such an elementary task? We are not as backward as you seem to think, Major. I cannot say conclusively, but I would assume so. A great deal of the city is connected underground by waterways and tunnels. Many utilities use the tunnels for access."

"I've heard that you are a trusted advisor to the Emperor. Has he ever mentioned Mr. Hayakawa to you?"

"No, however, once when I happened to see them together at the Palace I informed the Emperor of the rumors surrounding his business and cautioned him to take care about being seen in his company. He said that he knew nothing of his business. All he cared about was that everything the Admiral did was for the greater good of Japan."

"Well, Mr. Fujita, just one more thing. We came across several maps in what we believe to be an enemy's camp. Would you be able to look at them and tell us if you see anything unusual?" Hale asked as maps were laid out on the table. "We are particularly interested in the Marianas Island that's circled."

Fujita's face hardened as he gave the documents a perfunctory glance. "I know very little. Their approximate location. That's about all."

"So, nothing unusual we should be concerned with?" Mac interjected.

"No," he said flatly.

"Good, good. I ask because my wife has been working with a Christian group that is anxious to begin missionary work there. Actually," Mac said with a laugh, "she had to be interviewed about her connection to the organization because of you."

Both Hale and Fujita gave Mac a puzzled look. "I do not know your wife," Fujita finally said.

"No, of course not. It was your acquaintance with the leader of the group that sparked the questions. I believe you went to school with Abigale Brennan. What a small world, eh? First, you meet her in the United States and now she's coming here."

Fujita's face was furious as he suddenly stood, knocking his chair on its side. "Bastard! You heartless bastard! You know she can't go there!"

Mac's face looked grief-stricken as he quietly said, "I'm sorry, but there is more at stake here than you know, Makoto. So much more."

CHAPTER 39

"Hey, hey diddle dee, dee, hey, hey diddle die, die. Raise a glass to a bonnie lass and…"

Farnsworth heard the Irish tune being sung with gusto as soon as he entered the nightclub. He spotted McCann with a beer in his raised hand, serenading a girl sitting at the end of the bar. His ability to make a ho-hum night into an event had garnered him an entourage already. Geoffrey started when someone grabbed his hand.

"Hi!" 811 said breathlessly. "Billy said you were coming, so I've been watching for you. I'm over here."

She pulled him through the couples cheek-to-cheek on the dance floor to a small table in the back. "I can't believe you're here. I mean you didn't seem too interested the other day, so I was really surprised when Billy said the two of you were looking for a good place to go."

Farnsworth nodded at the barkeep as he held up an empty cup, and then sat down and looked around uncomfortably. "This isn't anything like an English pub," he said finally. "Billy said it would probably be the same."

"I've never been to an English pub, but I would love to go to one someday. I'm Irene, by the way," she said, holding out her hand.

"Oh, yes, I guess we haven't been properly introduced, have we? Geoffrey," he replied, taking her hand in his.

"Oh," she sighed, "I just *love* your accent. I nearly melted into a puddle on the lift when you first spoke. You never hear anything like that in Indiana. That's where I'm from Riley, Indiana. Well, it used to be Lockport but then they changed it to Riley, I don't know why. Anyway, me and my best friend Betty Sue decided we just had to get out of there, it was sooo small like only about a hundred people in the whole town, I mean going to Terre Haute was a huge deal because it was so big. Anyway, we made a pact the summer before we started high school that we were gonna see the world when we graduated. That was June of 1939."

She stopped for a moment to catch her breath and sip her drink as the memories of that carefree summer passed before her.

"Then the war started," Geoffrey prompted as the drink he ordered with nothing more than a nod of his head when he first sat down was delivered.

"Yeah," she said sadly. "I don't think Betty would have come with me though, even if there hadn't been a war. She met Jerry in the 11th grade, and she was a goner. Head over heels in love, you know what I mean? So, I went ahead and joined the Army Air Corps right out of high school. Daddy taught me how to fly the crop duster when I was just thirteen, so they signed me up to fly aircraft from the factories to the forward areas. I volunteered to come here after the war ended. Now I mostly do clerical work like taking dictation at meetings and then typing it up. What do you do Geoffrey?"

Her softer tone and the innocent batting of her eyelashes at the question threw him off for a moment as across the bar he heard, "Hey, hey diddle dee, dee…"

"Oh, I uh…"

A buxom blonde walked up to the table as he began to speak. "Hi Irene," she said, as she stared directly at Geoffrey. "Who's your friend?"

Irene looked annoyed. "This is a private conversation, Doris. Besides, we were just getting ready to dance. Right, Geoffrey?"

She stood, so common courtesy demanded he stand also, but what to do with his drink? Magruder said emphatically not to leave it unattended, and the hungry panther look in Doris' eyes made him inclined to see the wisdom in the order. So, he 'accidentally' knocked it over, spilling it across the table. "Oh dear," he mumbled as he attempted to mop it up with a napkin.

"Oh, don't worry. Doris doesn't mind cleaning it up while we dance, do you, sweetie?" Irene said with a flip of her hair as they vacated the table for the dance floor.

As he turned away from the mess, someone bumped into him, nearly knocking him back into his seat. "Oh, I'm sorry," he began, as he looked up and saw Tamar.

"Oh no, it was all my fault," she said smoothly. "Are you alright?"

"Quite alright, no harm done," he replied as Irene slipped her hand into his and led them to the dance floor.

Tamar left Geoffrey to 811 and easily slipped in and out through the crowd, making note of faces and eavesdropping on conversations. When the clerk from the import/export business was spotted, she found a vantage point from which she could keep an eye on her without being obvious.

Her previous rage had subsided into a controlled determination to see justice done, regardless of how long it took. She would be patient. After all, her anger was never really about the clerk; it was because she hadn't been there. They had snatched her uncle, the one she had sworn to protect, right from under her nose. It wouldn't happen again.

"Hey good looking. You here with anyone?"

Tamar looked up to see a baby-faced young man with a crew cut. He held a beer in one hand and seemed not to know what to do with his other hand, first stuffing it in his pocket then pulling it out again. She had seen him and his friends trying to pick up a couple of girls by the entrance. She had noted that they were incredibly bad at it.

"No, would you like to sit?" she offered, thinking a woman sitting alone might be suspicious.

"Really?" he said in astonishment. "Uh, I mean, thanks."

He took a seat as his friends, watching the miracle in real time, hooted their approval.

"Oh, but perhaps you would rather not be seen with a foreigner. It is against your American regulations to… how do you say, canoodle with non-Americans."

He snorted out a genuine laugh as he relaxed a little. "Fraternize, the word is fraternize. Yeah, we're not supposed to fraternize with the enemy. But you aren't Japanese and we're just sharing a table, right? Hey, can I buy you a drink?"

"No," Tamar responded, as she watched the clerk rebuff a prospective date. "I don't drink much as it makes me act… inappropriately. Is that the right word?"

She actually saw him gulp as he responded. "Yep, that's the right word alright."

Geoffrey and 811 left the dance floor and resettled at a different table. She excused herself and headed toward the bathroom. Tamar considered following but stopped when the woman who had caused him to spill his drink earlier quickly sidled up to the table the moment she left.

"So, you know about Americans, huh?" the young man asked, trying to regain Tamar's waning attention. "Oh, my name is Block, by the way, Jonathan Block. But everybody just calls me Chip. You know the American saying 'a chip off the old block'? Anyway, it's better than being called John which is what a lot of folks call the toilet."

Chip reddened slightly once he realized he was talking about toilets to the most beautiful woman with which he had ever had an actual conversation. "Sorry ma'am," he stammered. "I didn't mean to be vulgar."

"My name is Tamar, Chip, and what is vulgar about calling something what it is?" she asked, turning her lovely eyes his way. "People spend far too much time not speaking plainly in my opinion. I am Jewish and we are taught to speak plainly. It is a virtue, not a vice." At his lack of response, she asked, "It bothers you that I am a Jew?"

Tamar heard 'hey, hey diddle dee, dee, hey, hey diddle die, die' being belted out across the bar in a strong Irish brogue, then saw McCann hoist a petite Japanese woman to sit on his shoulder. She squealed in delight from her perch as the others around joined the merriment, laughing and clapping.

"Oh, no, not at all," Chip answered, a bit embarrassed. "You see, well… um… actually you're the first one I've ever met."

"So," Tamar asked in a sultry voice as she watched the clerk watch McCann. "Now that you've met one, what do you think?"

"I was wondering if all Jewish women are as beautiful as you."

Tamar laughed. "That's a very good answer, Chip. You know, perhaps I will have a drink after all."

The young man's face lit up at the suggestion. He then hurried to the bar to procure what he hoped would make this an extremely interesting night. As he made his way through the crowd Tamar turned her attention to Geoffrey, who had succumbed to the seductive interloper and escorted her to the dance floor. Miss 811 returned from the ladies' room and was without a doubt unhappy at this turn of events. He was definitely in trouble, but not the type with which she was willing to assist.

McCann left his adoring crowd and stumbled his way toward the bathrooms. As he passed Tamar, he fell against a young woman and gave Tamar a sly wink. "Aye, begging me pardon, miss. I'm well on my way to being ossified, and I gotta find the jacks."

Chip returned to the table with two beers and placed one in front of Tamar. "Sorry, I forgot to ask what you wanted. Is beer okay?"

"Yes, I like beer," she returned, then took a sip. "Chip, I heard several people talking about a murder. Did something happen?"

"Oh yeah. There were a bunch of bodies found in an alley," he said. Then he moved his chair around closer to Tamar and lowered his voice. "They think it was gang-related, but MacArthur was not happy about the whole situation."

"You know," Tamar looked around cautiously then lowered her voice to match his, "General MacArthur?"

"I'm in transport," he said in a normal tone but made no move to scoot his chair back to its previous location. "Which basically means I drive the big wigs wherever they need to go. Funny thing, though, they always seem to forget I have ears. Oh, I'm not complaining, mind you, I hear all the good poop just by keeping my mouth shut and my eyes on the road."

McCann exited the facilities with a convincing uncertainty to his gait and yelled, "Another pint, my good man," to the bartender. Hayakawa's clerk finally made her move and intercepted him enroute to the bar by tripping and falling headlong into his muscular body. "Whoa lassie, what's yur hurry?"

"I've been utterly humiliated," she said with a catch in her voice. "I've been stood up. He was supposed to be here an hour ago. You Americans have no decency when it comes to women. Please just let me go."

"Aye, no lass. We must have a drink on it, for it can only be one of two things. Either he's a fool and we must raise a glass to my good fortune, or the poor bastard is lying dead, and we must raise a glass for the same reason. I'm buying!"

The bartender brought two pints of beer and set them down, sloshing a little over the edge as he hurried to the next customer. "Have I seen you someplace before?" she asked, giving him a little sideways glance.

He took a swig from his glass, then answered. "Aw, sure look it. I only been here for nigh onto two weeks now, but I suppose you coulda seen me."

"Yes, I'm certain of it. I've seen you across the street from the business where I work. You aren't watching us, are you?"

McCann gave a lopsided drunken grin then put his finger to his lips. "Shhh. It's a secret. You wouldn't want to get me in trouble, now would ya? Hey, what's your name, anyway?"

"I'm Kaori."

"Kaori, that's a beautiful name. I'm Billy, like the goat." Then McCann threw back his head and guffawed at his silly joke.

Kaori laughed politely as McCann took another quaff of his beer. "I love secrets, Billy," she said as she leaned over and put her hand on his thigh. Her fingers traced up and down the crease of his trousers as she said, "Tell me yours."

"Well, lassie," he said jovially, "it wouldn't be much of a secret if I told you now would it?"

"You're teasing me," she said with a pout as she withdrew her hand and wrapped it around her glass.

McCann took one of her slender hands from the frosty glass and kissed the back of it before placing it back on his thigh. "Go way outta that now," he said with a grin. "We be gettin' along just fine now, aren't we? I be chasing a rat, is all. I'm the cat watching the hole to see when the dirty little Kraut will poke out his head."

"So, what makes you think your rat would be coming to our import/export business?"

"What?" McCann asked dumbly after another swallow. "Burger man will for certain be looking for a place to lie low like the flop house next door to ya. And when he slithers in, I'll be there. Why would he come to you?"

McCann's attention faded before an answer was required as he turned to wave at some of his entourage at the end of the bar. That's when her hand slipped from his thigh and signaled two men that had been loitering near the entrance all evening.

Tamar picked up on the subtle gesture from her vantage point and abruptly rose from her seat. She saw the two men begin moving through the crowd from the entrance and another two converging on McCann's position from the rear. Without a word to Chip, she quickly moved forward and was almost on him when Billy bounced himself up to sit on the bar and began a loud refrain as he lifted his glass.

"Hey, hey diddle, dee, dee grab a sweet lass and follow me." He then hopped down, threw Tamar over his shoulder, and began to belt out his song again with half the bar joining in. "Hey, hey diddle dee, dee. Hey, hey diddle die, die…"

He wove in and out between the tables with Tamar kicking and issuing threats as other gents followed suit, tossing women over their shoulders, and joining the parade, singing and laughing their way into the street.

Geoffrey jumped to his feet when McCann started the conga line heading out the door and was about to make his apologies to Irene and call it a night when he saw her face. The look of hope in her eyes was unmistakable. *Oh bugger,* he thought then, *what the hell,* as he threw the delighted Irene over his shoulder and sang, "Hey, hey diddle dee, dee…"

CHAPTER 40

Benjiro Hayakawa looked up from his desk when Yazzie's entrance jangled the bell over the front door and a broad smile spread across his face. "I was wondering when you'd be back," he said as if they were old friends.

"Your business trip was cut short, I see," Yazzie returned as he approached. "Bad weather?"

He laughed pleasantly at the little jab. "Yes, yes, bad weather for certain. Have a seat. What brings a man of your reputation to my humble business?"

"I am merely here to introduce my new import/export business in the United States and to see if perhaps we can do business. What reputation do you speak of?"

"I am well acquainted with the Irgun," Hayakawa returned easily. "We have done much business together and you are very good customers. I supply quality machinery and parts that allow you to make your weapons and ammunition to fight your war with the British, and I am generously compensated. It works out well for both of us. Had I known you were Irgun earlier, friend, my suspicions would not have been aroused at your sudden appearance."

"And your men would still be alive, I imagine," Yazzie returned coolly.

Hayakawa shrugged noncommittally. "The question is why are you here with the Americans? That is very strange."

"The Americans and I have common goals at the moment. Only a fool would refuse to use tools he had at his disposal, yes?"

Hayakawa gave Yazzie a shrewd look as he leaned back in his chair. "So, what really brings you here?"

"Revenge. What else is there?"

"Hans Bergmann. Yes, I know who you are looking for," he said flatly. "Your Irishman should learn to hold his liquor."

"He is American," Yazzie returned as if that was explanation enough.

"Yes, they pride themselves on a discipline they do not possess. However, at least in this case, it is good that the beans were spilled. You see, I have an interest in Mr. Bergmann as well. Perhaps we can work together."

"What is your interest in the filthy Nazi?" Yazzie asked without emotion.

"He took something that belongs to me. I want it back. After I get my property, you can do whatever you want with him. What do the Americans want with him?"

"Information, then to take him to trial for war crimes. Although, I have a feeling he will meet with an unfortunate accident before he gets to their trial."

"That means nothing to me, as long as I get what's owed me," Hayakawa said with a flip of his hand as if the entire thing bored him. He then abruptly switched topics. "What business do you have with Makoto Fujita?"

Yazzie leaned forward in his chair. "You send your men after me without so much as a conversation, then are surprised when your subordinate is questioned? I don't believe it."

Hayakawa gave a slight smile that faded quickly, then carefully responded. "You should know Makoto is not a well man. The war affected his mind. I have been protecting him since his return so that his family's name is not maligned, but he is not well. What did he tell you?"

"The Americans questioned him, so he told me nothing. If he told them anything of import, they did not share it with me. Just because we currently work together doesn't mean they trust me," Yazzie returned.

"Hmmm, I see," Hayakawa uttered as he sized up Yazzie's response.

"So, tell me," Yazzie said, pulling a handkerchief from his pocket to carefully polish away an accidental fingerprint from the armrest before returning it to his pocket. "How is it that your operative, Kaori, recognized my name on my first visit? Seeing how you didn't know of my glowing reputation at that time, eh?"

Hayakawa smiled from his oversized chair as he neatly folded his hands in his lap. "Lovely little Kaori, an operative? What would make you believe so?"

"Don't insult my intelligence. She is not nearly as effective as you seem to think. How did she know my name?"

He shrugged and gave a little chuckle as he gave up the ruse. "Ahh, children today are not nearly as cunning as treacherous old men like us, are they? Your name came to us from another source. From Amsterdam actually."

"You have an interest in the diamond trade then," Yazzie stated more than asked.

A look of surprise flitted across Hayakawa's face before he could stop it.

"A Jew with an interest in the diamond trade, imagine that. How unusual, eh?" Yazzie responded sarcastically. Then he paused as if considering his next words carefully. "Samuel Gassan is an old friend. I had heard that his dear wife was ailing, so I stopped to enquire as to her health. Of course, the conversation eventually turned to business, as usual with us, and I told him of my new venture in America. I do believe we will be doing business together soon. Now, tell me, why are you spying on my friend?"

Hayakawa looked annoyed. "Mr. Gassan is a competitor. He moves valuable things much as I do. You will find out that our business is very cutthroat," he said, drawing an imaginary knife across his own throat. "You will learn to watch your competitors also if you are to stay in business."

Yazzie's face remained serene as he wondered how much more time Mac needed to explore the tunnels ten feet under the floor where he currently sat.

"So how is she? Mrs. Gassan, I mean," Hayakawa asked with suspicion.

"Not well, I'm afraid," Yazzie replied with regret. "Not well at all."

*****

315

After Helen left to check in with Quinn in D.C. early in the morning, Mac and Yazzie had inter-dimensionally translated into a tunnel under the Emperor's Palace and traced one leg of it back to Hayakawa's import/export business. Stacks of empty and damaged crates and boxes provided cover as they neared the business, but further inspection was required. So, it was decided that Yazzie would pay a visit to Hayakawa and keep him occupied while Mac did a little more exploration.

If Hayakawa was still involved with clandestine operations for the Emperor, as Fujita assumed, he would have a communication center somewhere convenient. Since he had not been seen entering or exiting any other business frequently, they guessed that it was underground, probably right below his own real estate. Since believing it and knowing without a doubt are two different things, Mac was intent on proving their theory one way or another.

After Yazzie's departure, Mac remained in place for a few minutes, watching and listening. The tunnel was dank and musty smelling. Faint sounds of water could be heard nearby, making Mac believe that the tunnel ran close to an underground canal. Wiring was strung along the top of the tunnel, some for the lights swinging overhead and others diverting off into unseen rooms. He took out the Minox Riga camera he had borrowed from Tamar and got ready to capture as much information as possible.

The only person moving about was a petite, dark-haired woman who exited one room and walked away from Mac's position to enter a room further down the tunnel. Hayakawa's unlikely clerk, no doubt. *She must not need much sleep*, Mac thought as he remembered the loud snores rattling the walls of McCann's room this morning.

The first door on his right was locked, so he did a partial translation rather than remaining exposed in the tunnel while picking the lock. The Greys showed them this technique during their training because so much less energy was required than for a whole-body move. Dimensional travel allowed for different levels of movement. Going through a door or wall was the equivalent of going for a stroll as opposed to taking off on a fifty-yard dash. Very handy when you needed to conserve energy for a possible hasty escape.

Once the light switch was found, he understood why the room was secured. Contraband: the room was filled with it. Undoubtedly Hayakawa was involved in the black-market trade. Crates of sugar and rice were stacked along the walls with boxes of vegetables and dairy goods. Additional crates with USA stamped on the side in bold red letters were most certainly filled with wheat grown stateside and shipped over to assist the starving occupants of Japan. How he had managed to commandeer America's gift into his possession, Mac couldn't begin to guess.

Three large storerooms were packed in a similar manner. Hundreds of crates and boxes were stored below ground rather than in the warehouse to avoid inspection. Two smaller storerooms housed items such as ammunition, weapons, mechanical parts, and additional scarce dry goods like tobacco, coffee, and tea. Photographs were taken, but nothing so far suggested anything other than Hayakawa had a heart of stone when it came to his starving countrymen.

Mac checked his watch and knew Yazzie's visit would be drawing to a close soon. He turned off the lights and opened the door a sliver to check for company before exiting and noticed an increase in activity. One of Hayakawa's employees exited the room next door to where Mac was and stood in the tunnel discussing a piece of paper two others were sharing. The three then entered a room just on the other side of a set of stairs. Now was his chance. He darted down the tunnel and into the adjoining room. Jackpot! Hayakawa's communications center! He didn't take time to examine anything but took pictures of all the electronics as quickly as possible.

Mac cursed under his breath. Even though he was done in record time, the room's occupant was already backing out the door down the tunnel right when he was ready to make good his escape. Going for broke, he used a variation of the partial translation they affectionately called 'the Flash'. A substantial amount of adrenalin made this move easier, which at this particular moment he had in spades. The equipment operator glanced back to add a last comment to the ending conversation and Mac sped across the tunnel and through the door across the way, praying no one was currently in residence.

Stopping just inside the door, the utter darkness enfolded him. He held his breath for a moment, trying to hear over his rapidly beating heart. Nothing… no one was coming. He had made it. His breath came out in a sigh of relief as he turned to feel along the wall for a light switch. Then he froze. *It can't be.* In the impenetrable darkness, he breathed in through his nose, and there it was. A particular odor; strong and pungent. He found the switch and flipped it on to see three sets of bunk beds sticking out from the far wall. Two four-drawer dressers, one on either wall to the right and left, and two chairs tucked under a small wooden table in the center of the room were the only other furniture in the room save a chamber pot in the corner to his immediate left.

A glance at the contents of the chamber pot as he walked further into the room turned his stomach as the stink of it reached his nose. Wooden bowls about six inches in diameter sat on each dresser filled with fragrant oil, but one whiff of the blankets on the beds confirmed what he already knew.

"It worked!" Helen said jubilantly as she translated into the room, startling Mac to the point that he hit his head on the bunk above the bed he was inspecting. "Someone came to inspect the tunnels under the White House, and we got 'em!"

"Helen, what in the hell are you doing here?" Mac whispered furiously.

"What…wait…where are we?" she asked, dropping her voice as she looked around.

"We are under Hayakawa's import/export business. You have to go…now."

"You told me you were working in the hotel room today. That's why I centered on you for the trip back," she whispered, to justify her presence. She sighed a bit peeved then said, "I will go on one condition."

"What's that?" he returned, more than a little irritated himself.

"Tell me why Shalanaya are living under Hayakawa's store," she said, wrinkling her nose.

The doorknob suddenly turned, and Mac bolted forward, engulfing Helen in a bear hug as he translated both of them out of the living quarters of the enemy.

CHAPTER 41

"It was completely undignified," Tamar said as the office door swung open. "I was carried out the door like a sack of potatoes."

"I've carried sacks of potatoes, she's much heavier," McCann said jovially to Hale. Tamar stuck her tongue out at the observation. "Besides, you had a look like me mum when she had a switch in her hand, and someone was gonna get a beatin'. I figured it was time for us to get out of there before trouble started."

Geoffrey looked up bleary-eyed at their entrance from his seat in front of the machines he was currently unlocking for another day of work. "*Before* trouble started? The MPs showed up, mate."

"Well now, it isn't really a party unless the MPs show up, is it now?" McCann asked, grinning unapologetically. "You know, Major, maybe I should hit the bar a couple more times in the next few weeks, you know, just to keep up my cover."

"I didn't need to be rescued; you know. I can take care of myself just fine," Tamar said petulantly.

"Aye, I figured that sis, but you may have gotten poor Geoffrey here torn to shreds. Those two she-cats had their claws out over him now, didn't they? If a fight had broken out for real, they would have gone at it for sure."

The three amused comrades looked over at Geoffrey for comment, who was busy trying to open a tin of aspirin. The top popped open, and he fished a couple of tablets out. "Don't start with me. I have a handsome hangover and will now most certainly have to dodge Irene for the rest of my assignment here."

"What did you find out about her?" Hale asked as he pulled up a chair.

"What? Oh," Geoffrey said as the lid was snapped back into place. He dropped the tin into his shirt pocket as he continued. "She's from Indiana and flies planes. Wanted to see the world, that's why she joined up. She's one of seven children, the oldest girl. Two of her brothers joined up before she did. One was injured and sent home…"

"Whoa, whoa, what I meant was did you find out anything useful? Did she ask about your work, who we were, what our assignment was?" Hale pressed.

"Oh, I see what you mean. No, nothing like that. She mostly wanted to hear about England. She saw a book of famous paintings when she was in school and particularly liked English country sides. Fell in love with the place, sight unseen. She hopes to visit after the war."

"And now she's found a tour guide, a native to boot, that can escort her around to all the sights and whisper the history of each one in her ear," Tamar teased.

"Yes," Geoffrey snapped back. "I am very well versed in the history of England and would do an admirable job as a guide, however, my plans for the immediate future do not include Irene or any other woman for that matter. Right now, I simply wish for the pounding in my head to stop and for Sergeant McCann to tell me exactly how he can drink so much and look fresh as a daisy the next day."

McCann looked quite pleased that someone acknowledged a skill at which he excelled. "Well, it helps to be Irish. I was sneaking sips of me da's Guinness from when I was just a wee lad. It built up my tolerance for sure."

"You did very well undercover," Tamar commented. "Did you have training in the Army?"

McCann looked over at Hale, who just shrugged his shoulders. "Well…my training was a bit more, um, informal let's say."

The uncharacteristic hedging got both Tamar's and Geoffrey's attention.

"What does that mean?" Geoffrey asked, as there was a knock on the door.

Hale answered to find Irene carefully patting down her hair. "Oh hi," she said. "Shirley told me that Geoffrey stopped by my office earlier. Is he here?"

Hale looked over at Farnsworth with raised eyebrows.

"You stopped by her office? Why?" Tamar whispered.

"To thank her for a nice evening," he whispered back as he headed to the door. "It's called being polite."

"Poor sap is practically engaged, and he doesn't even know it," McCann said quietly to Hale as Geoffrey stepped into the hallway.

Irene glanced nervously past Geoffrey into the room, and he turned to see Hale, McCann, and Tamar perched on the edge of the desk, directly across from the door like three birds on a wire. He reached in to pull the door closed and whispered, "Don't let McCann start his story until I get back."

Tamar ran to put her ear against the door. "He must be whispering. I can't hear a thing. I need a glass."

Since the show had been canceled, the two men left their perch and took seats. "Where is your uncle this morning, sleeping in?" Hale asked.

"He was gone when I checked in on him, but I know exactly where he went," she said, a bit piqued. "Back to see Hayakawa. He's being reckless."

"He knows what he's doing, Tamar. And after what happened earlier, we certainly know he can handle himself in a sticky situation," Hale countered.

Tamar turned from the door and looked solemnly at Curly. "He's the only family I have left," she said quietly as she went to gaze out the window.

"Well, if it's any comfort to ya, Magruder was missing this morning, too. You can bet the two of them are getting into trouble together." McCann answered. "Did you see the General's face when he heard about the attack on Yazzie? It was like somebody sucker-punched him. If you're going to sucker punch someone like him, you better put him down with that first shot, because if you don't you can bet he's gonna make you pay."

Geoffrey walked in, closing the door behind him. "I don't want to talk about it," he said, holding up a hand to stop any questions. His three coworkers laughed, knowing they would weasel every detail out of him at some point. "So," he continued as he sat down, "tell us about your *informal* training, Billy."

"Well," McCann said, as he leaned back in his chair and looked at the ceiling. His eyes softened, and a smile played about his lips as the memories ran through his mind like the painted ponies of a children's carousel. "Me Da was a peace officer in Ireland before we immigrated to the States. He is a decent man that always worked hard, kept his nose clean, and loved his family. But his brothers…now that was something else altogether. Me Da had to get them out of more than one scrape with the law."

"How did he do that and keep his nose clean?" Farnsworth asked with interest.

"It was a fine line for sure, but it's like the old Irish saying, 'a family of Irish birth will argue and fight, but let a shout come from without and see them all unite'. It wasn't much of anything at first. Buy someone a pint to forget a slight, take a brother by the ear to apologize, and such. Once," McCann laughed, "nothing could be settled except that old man O'Dell get a free shot at me Uncle Liam without him laying a hand on him in return. Now you have to remember that me Uncle Liam was a six-foot-five red-headed wild one and no one ever beat him in a fight. That O'Dell said it was the most glorious day of his life, bragged about popping Uncle Liam for the rest of his days."

"So, what happened to change things?" Tamar inquired.

"I guess you could say that Ireland happened. Got involved with the freedom fighters, they did. That was more than a pint could settle."

"Freedom fighters? You mean the Irish Republican Army. The IRA is nothing more than an underground paramilitary revolutionary group," Tamar interjected.

McCann raised his eyebrows in amusement. "You're gonna lecture me now on relatives involved in underground revolutionary groups? Your Uncle being with the Irgun and all."

Tamar shot Hale a dirty look.

"Oh, now, like he had to tell me. You think a poor dumb Irishman couldn't figure out that a Jew of your uncle's age taking out a half dozen young bucks by his self doesn't speak of higher training?"

"The Irgun are patriots!" Tamar returned defiantly.

"Aye, and that's how my uncles saw themselves as well. I would think you would understand better than anyone what men are willing to do to be free." McCann looked past Tamar to Geoffrey and asked without animus, "Do you want to take a shot at my heritage now, Brit? Defend your right to rule and all."

Geoffrey pursed his lips but said nothing.

"Well, you wanted my story, so here's the rest. Me da's brothers got in deep. So deep that they were told to murder an opposition leader; to sneak into his house and kill him while his wife lay sleeping next to him. You take a life in the face of battle that's something you live with, but murder a man in his own bed? It was more than they could do, even for freedom. That's when the threats started. Me da and me uncles taught me to have eyes in the back of me head," McCann said, smacking the back of his head for effect. "I was nine years old, and I learned how to fight, how to spot a liar, how to play a role. Survival, Geoffrey my man, that was my training. That is how I came to be the affable Irishman that I am."

The room was silent when he finished, then finally Hale cleared his throat. "So, are we still a team?" he asked as he looked at each one in turn. "Do you still have each other's backs? Do you trust the others to watch your back? If the answer to any one of these questions is no let me know now because I won't endanger anybody because we can't work as a team."

The tension in the room was heavy as the door swung open and Mac, Helen, and Yazzie entered. Immediately sensing the stress, they stopped at the door and Mac asked, "Are we interrupting something?"

"No sir," McCann immediately replied, as if he were standing at attention.

No, no, they all replied as they broke apart and moved to various parts of the room. "We were just reviewing the intel gathered last night," Hale responded. "811, whose name is Irene by the way, appears to just be interested in Geoffrey's pretty face and English country sides. We are expecting an announcement of their engagement any day now."

Tamar and McCann snickered as Geoffrey returned blithely, "I can't help it, I just have that effect on women. One look at this mug and they're goners."

"I can believe that dear," Helen said as she patted his shoulder in passing. "You didn't make coffee?"

"I'm sorry Helen. I didn't even think of it," Tamar responded. "Here I'll go get the water."

"No, I'll go. You need to stay and report your intel," Helen returned as she took the pitcher and headed to the door. "Don't worry Geoffrey," she added with a twinkle as she exited, "if I run into Irene I'll talk you up."

Geoffrey's eyes widened at the declaration, and he opened his mouth to protest but she was gone and he was left looking like a fish out of water. Tamar and McCann burst out laughing and Mac thought, *well whatever was going on it's over now.*

"Okay, Geoffrey's impending engagement aside, what did we learn last night?" Mac asked.

"I met one Jonathan Block, nicknamed Chip," Tamar started without preamble. "He's Army and works in transportation which means he overhears a lot of bits and pieces of information. MacArthur is aware of your confrontation in the alley, Uncle, though it has been chalked up to a gang-related incident and not associated with us. A great deal of MacArthur's time is spent breaking up the zaibatsu. The families in control of these financial coalitions wield far too much power and it's believed that their existence will prevent Japan's economy from recovering. Other than that his concerns at the moment seem to be leaning toward the immediate needs of Japan such as getting enough food and rebuilding. Chip knew nothing of diamonds, precious metals, or the like."

Helen re-entered the room with her water and went straight to the percolator. Mac looked at McCann and none of the brash Irishman of the previous night was present in his response. "Well sir, there are a lot of fishing boats being employed to ferry goods from one of the Mariana Islands to Tokyo. Can't say for sure if it's our island or not. I heard that they make better money with the ferry work than from fishing which is real interesting considering food prices are high right now."

"What are they ferrying over?"

"That's just it, they don't know and as long as the money is good they don't much care. The funny thing is sir it's year-round, not seasonal so it's not anything harvested and we're talking about a fair number of craft."

"How long have they been doing this?"

"Since way before the war they said. The most interesting bit sir is that the guy running the docks wherever they unload is said to be a giant white guy well over six-foot tall who it's rumored was recently killed in a knife fight. Don't know for sure, but he could be the big man that had a go at Yazzie."

"What docks?"

"It shifts from load to load. At the time they leave to pick up their load they're told where to unload. Sometimes it goes in trucks, sometimes into another boat. It's never left on shore."

"Hmm, moving that much merchandise would require quite a bit of organization," Mac said thoughtfully. "An import/export business would be very handy if the product was moving out of the country."

"Yes," Helen returned, "but the question remains, who is the customer?"

"There is no darkness, nor shadow of death, where the workers of iniquity may hide themselves," Yazzie quoted from the book of Job. "We will find them."

CHAPTER 42

MacArthur's headquarters in Tokyo was a giant beehive of activity. Men and women all working independently, yet all with the same overall purpose. They were to solve the ten-thousand-piece jigsaw puzzle of putting Japan back together again after its complete decimation from a war their military leaders had provoked with the world. It was not an easy task and every person in every position was needed if that goal was to be accomplished.

Each floor of the multistory building in the heavily guarded compound was buzzing with activity. Every department within every floor was assigned specific tasks to be completed, some with unchangeable drop-dead dates, others with more flexible "see if it's possible" dates. The plaque on the door of the Communications Department commanding officer's office had "Lt Colonel John Smith" printed in no-nonsense block lettering. It was a simple sign that belied the complicated world of encrypted communication codes his department was charged with intercepting and deciphering. His appointment carried the hope that he and his team would decipher the enemy's codes before another world war broke out. It was a daunting task.

The no-nonsense name plaque made the office's occupant smile every time he entered, for John Smith was not his real name. It was a pseudo-name, the alias, if you will, of a very talented cryptanalyst who simply wanted to work in his chosen field. The field in which God had given him exceptional talents and whose uncanny analytical skills could sway the winds of war. His name before jumping at the chance to work on "special projects" for Douglas MacArthur was Captain Joseph Rochefort.

Rochefort had been just a young Captain when he and his team at station HYPO in Hawaii deciphered the Japanese Navy's most secure cipher system, allowing the U.S. Navy to deliver a crippling blow to Japan in June 1942. It was their translation of an intercepted communique and brilliant counter-move to confirm their suspicions of its meaning that had correctly determined and confirmed that the Japanese navy was headed to Midway Island. That had allowed the Americans to position themselves correctly to intercept the unsuspecting enemy navy.

It was a magnificent feat that undoubtedly saved thousands of American lives, but it was not a triumph celebrated by everyone. In fact, jealous counterparts stationed at OP-20-G in Washington D.C. moved to take credit for the code break with the politicos in the nation's capital even though they had dismissed the Rochefort team's early calls for action on the discovery. They simply refused to believe a young Captain stationed at Pearl Harbor could achieve more than their brain trust of code breakers in the Capital. It was fortunate for the nation and the men under his command that Admiral Chester William Nimitz sided with Rochefort and the Station HYPO team and moved on the intel.

Being thus proved wrong, the OP-20-G quickly moved to banish Rochefort from cryptanalyst work permanently by promptly reassigning him to a position where he would not be part of the encryption conversation. He was "dry-docked" and left to obscurity in hopes no one would ever know who actually saved the day for America at Midway Island. The alias provided him by several resourceful people familiar with his abilities allowed him to quietly continue his work without the knowledge of the OP-20-G glory hounds in D.C.

He had found a home working for MacArthur after the war, utilizing his skills to intercept messages between Russia, Germany, China, and Japan. MacArthur had no doubt the Russians would try to weasel their way into the rebuilding of Japan. That way they could take credit for the turnaround and convince the Japanese people that a great debt was owed to Russia for their economic rebirth and not the United States. They were devious that way, and it had proven successful in the past. Credit yourself with assistance someone else provided and take any associated rewards in the future.

Smith's (aka Rochefort) world was neat and orderly, as well as deliberately low-key. He worked methodically in his new position to drill into the communication logs, searching for pearls of Russian secret messages. His tidy world was given a start as he opened his office door and found a smartly dressed middle-aged woman standing next to his coffee pot gently blowing on a fresh hot cup of joe.

"Who are you, and how did you get in here?" he demanded as he stood rooted in the doorway.

"Good morning, Colonel," she replied pleasantly. "The coffee is hot. I just finished making it," she continued as she held up the pot in an offer to pour him a fresh cup. "Isn't the electric percolator the most marvelous invention?"

He looked at her quizzically before answering. "No, no coffee, thanks. Now just who are you and why did my staff let you in my office?"

"Oh, well they may be under the impression that I'm an old family friend here to pay my obligatory respects seeing how I'm distantly related to your mother through marriage," she returned as she took a seat and straightened her skirt.

"You know my mother…" he said uncertainly as he moved to stand behind his desk.

"Oh, my goodness, no, not at all. But you have to admit it worked rather well to get me an audience with you, Joseph."

His face turned ashen. "It's John, Lieutenant Colonel John Smith."

"Of course, it is," she returned with a wink. "My mistake. You have to allow a dotty old lady her little mistakes."

He sat down hard in his chair and scooted under his desk. "What do you want?" he asked with the implied threat understood.

"I am Helen Magruder. I believe you've met my husband, General John Magruder," she said sweetly as she sipped her coffee.

"Magruder! That son of a bitch took Farnsworth, my best cryptologist then tried to convince me that the orders came directly from Truman! What is he planning to shanghai from me this time?"

Helen sighed and shook her head with a knowing look. "I know, I know, my husband does tend to have an ill effect on some people. He just doesn't have a pleasing way about him sometimes."

"A pleasing way?!" Smith pushed the chair back and stood. "You know in my career, I've met some real…" Helen innocently raised her eyebrows in anticipation as she casually sipped her beverage, causing him to rethink his response. "…some real nasty, backbiting, underhanded, two-faced, no good, lying…you know what, just leave. Get out. I'm not interested in whatever you're peddling."

Helen sat unmoved by his outburst. She sipped, then carefully sat the beverage on his desk. "I don't really care for these mugs. I much prefer a regular coffee cup. The mugs are much sturdier, it's true, but the sides are too thick; it's difficult to drink from without dribbling."

The Colonel folded his arms across his chest and held his ground. "Go ahead and expose me, I'm not going to help you."

"Expose you! Oh my, you misunderstand me completely. Like you, we aren't even here. Once we realized who you were, I told Mac that if anyone could help us it was you. He, of course, was a bit pessimistic, but I said let me talk to the young man." Helen leaned toward him and said in a conspiratorial whisper, "I'm actually much better with people than he is, but don't tell him I said so."

The Colonel could feel a headache coming on as Helen quietly attempted another sip from her mug. "Are you certain I can't fix you a cup of coffee? You're looking a little peaked. I think I have a tin of aspirin in my purse. Do you need some?"

"I'm not going to get rid of you, am I?"

"Well, how would it look if I left so soon? After all, we haven't seen one another in years, and we have a lot of catching up to do."

The Colonel sighed in surrender.

"I knew your mama raised you right. You would never kick your mother's kin, distant or not, out of your office without hearing them out."

"But we're not related! You don't even *know* my mother."

"Not technically, I suppose," Helen said with a smile while waving his logic away with a sweep of her hand. "But that doesn't mean that we can't be like family, Joseph – I mean John."

"Lord help me," he muttered under his breath as he sat down. "What do you want, Mrs. Magruder?"

"Oh, I just need you to look at some photographs," she said as a large tan envelope was pulled from her belongings and handed across the desk.

He grudgingly pulled the photos out and quickly sifted through them, one by one. He glanced up at Helen and pursed his lips, then went through them again, slowly taking in every detail. "It's a nice setup, professional. Where are these from?"

"Here in Tokyo under an import/export business owned by…"

"Benjiro Hayakawa, it has to be Hayakawa," he said as she nodded confirmation. "I knew it. I knew he wasn't out of the game. I investigated him when I first got here, but he's an oily one. I couldn't find anything that could definitively tie him to current events. You're sure this is his set up?"

"Oh yes, there's no doubt," Helen replied.

"How did you get these photos? Are they recent?"

Helen smiled. "Come now, Colonel, you can't expect me to tell you all my secrets. A girl has to keep a few things under her hat, but I can say that they are very recent."

He sat back in his chair and contemplated Helen for a moment as she quietly sipped her coffee. "I have questions."

"Undoubtedly."

"Why is your husband here in Tokyo? Why bring his team here?"

He was surprised when Helen didn't deny anything. "We, you don't mind if I include myself, do you?" At the negative shake of his head, she continued. "There has been intelligence indicating that the United States may have a previously unknown enemy. Mac's team was assigned with finding out if there is a new threat or not, and our investigation has led us here."

"What does General MacArthur say about this visit?"

"He doesn't even know we're here and we would like to keep it that way," Helen said, then continued sweetly. "He has enough on his mind at present, don't you think? Why burden him with something that may turn out to be nothing but a red herring?"

"Okay, I'll bite," he said with his guard still clearly up. "Just what is it you think I can help you with, Mrs. Magruder? Captain Farnsworth could easily have identified the equipment in these photos so don't try to convince me that's all you want."

"I wouldn't think of it, Colonel, and please call me Helen. No, we need to know if you've run into any languages you've been unable to translate."

He smiled at her lack of understanding as to what they did in his unit. "Decryption is what we do here, Helen, and I have analysts fluent in more than fifteen different languages and dialects. We work with unknowns every day."

"I see," she said with a sigh.

"May I ask what Makoto Fujita has to do with this? He was waiting for your husband and one Major Hale when I saw them the other day."

"He's just another piece of the puzzle. How do you know him?"

"Everyone knows Fujita. Some say he's crazy, but I've never seen any sign of it. He's smart, articulate, and highly respected."

"That's what we found also," she said as a bulky tan envelope was pulled from her oversized purse. She slid the package across the desk. "There are voice recordings in here with a mixture of English and an unknown language. Would you be so kind as to listen and tell us if you recognize it?"

"You have access to a magnetic tape recorder?" he asked with astonishment as he looked in the envelope. "Just who are you working with that you have that kind of equipment?"

"Some wonderful people at Groom Lake in Nevada," Helen said with a smile as she rose to leave. John Smith gave a little snort of disbelief at her assertion. "It has been so lovely talking with you, Colonel. I do hope to see you again soon. By the way, has anyone recently approached you with a strong scent?" Helen asked from the doorway.

"What?" This woman was all over the map. He couldn't figure out if she was a bit touched in the head, or if she was just excellent at keeping her targets off balance.

"You know too much perfume or aftershave. Maybe just a strong distinctive odor."

"Uh, no. Nothing like that."

"Oh good, good. It's so unpleasant to have your senses overpowered by an odor, whether it be pleasant or unpleasant. Don't you think?"

He furrowed his brow at the lady and at the question itself. It was a puzzle. She was a puzzle.

Helen paused a moment before taking her leave to read the sign that had hung in every office Joseph Rochefort had ever occupied: ***We can accomplish anything provided no one cares who gets the credit.***

"So true," she said quietly, "so very true."

CHAPTER 43

"So, did the kids get off on their trip?" Helen asked as she sat down on the sofa in their living quarters. It was a small space to meet, but they could talk freely here as opposed to the office, where they constantly had to be careful not to be overheard.

"Kids?" Yazzie said with amusement.

"I'm sure Curly, Tamar, and Billy don't think of themselves as kids, Helen," Mac responded. "And, yes, they took off this morning. They should get to Osaka this afternoon barring any issues."

"Do you think we can trust the information Hayakawa provided?" Helen queried. "After all, we know for a fact that he's working directly with the enemy."

"The information, yes. Hayakawa, no," Mac replied.

"He still believes the diamonds to be in play," Yazzie explained. "As long as he believes there is a chance of getting them back, he'll provide good intel. He thinks he's using us to do his dirty work."

"But we know it can't possibly be Bergmann that was spotted as he is after all very, very dead. Why send the *young people* to do Hayakawa's bidding?" she came back, emphasizing her change in reference to the other team members.

"A man speaking German in Japan tends to stand out, dear, and America is still interested in justice regarding the war. Rest assured that they will find him and determine how to proceed. This is what Hale and McCann were doing in Germany before they were assigned to us," Mac responded.

"And Tamar as well. Although I believe her tactics were somewhat more lethal than the gentlemen," Yazzie added before changing the topic of conversation. "So, I was quite pleased to hear that our redeployed sensors were successful. Are you ready to brief us on what's happening?"

"Oh, it's very good news!" Helen said, scooting forward in her seat, anxious to share the latest events. "The person that tripped the sensors is a human female and her name is June Watts. She's not a government employee, thank heavens. We've certainly found enough traitors in the government's employ already. However, she was tracked from the time she left the tunnels and one of her first stops was to have lunch with her boyfriend…CIG employee Lt. Jack Hornsby."

"Quinn's assistant?" Mac voiced in surprise.

"The very same," Helen confirmed, with a nod of her head.

"Well, we may have found our leak," Yazzie stated. "Have they determined whether he was colluding with the enemy?"

"It seems he was completely ignorant of her duplicity," Helen clarified. "He was absolutely devastated at finding out the truth and has volunteered to resign his commission. Quinn, however, is inclined to keep him on and use him as an asset."

"How is Quinn taking the revelation that his office was the leak?" Mac asked with concern.

"Oh, I've never seen him so upset," Helen said with all seriousness. "I was there when he briefed Truman on what his men had discovered. He took full responsibility and immediately resigned from his position. Thankfully, the President promptly rejected that idea."

"A visit may be in order," Yazzie said to Mac. "No one can understand what he's going through better than you and we need him functioning at 100%."

"I was thinking the same thing," Mac replied.

"Oh, but then," Helen responded quickly, "he, President Truman that is, reminded Quinn how that originally he had been slow to accept the immediate threat of the alien presence but then the assassination attempt made him a believer. Then he says (he's quite brilliant you know) so now that you know there is an actual threat are you going to let them take you out of the game? They used you, Colonel, are you going to just let that pass?"

Yazzie and Mac smiled at the Commander-in-Chief's understanding of how a soldier's mind works. Turn remorse into a white-hot firebrand of anger, morph an unfruitful emotion into a weapon. Motivate the good ones to use the tactics of the enemy meant to destroy them into an unbreakable determination to track them down like the dogs they are.

"Then the President asked him if his men, the ones that briefed him on Miss Watts, no longer respected his command. If they had voiced a vote of no confidence. Quinn said it was just the opposite. They reminded him that the big bad had murdered one of their own and said he must fight to keep his position so that justice could be done for their teammate."

"And Truman was agreeable to that?" Mac asked.

"Oh yes, he seemed quite pleased. He told the Colonel that no one else had experienced the unforgettable presence of these particular enemies of the United States as he had. No one else could possibly understand the entirety of what they were up against."

"Well, that's certainly true. There's no reason to believe that the Greys would be amenable to another alien showcase in the Oval Office any time soon," Yazzie speculated. "And what about Colonel Quinn, was he on board?"

"Yes," Helen replied. "But the look on his face – well he wasn't the same. It was as if any doubts as to the intentions of the Shalanaya and Anakim were gone, and every ounce of possible mercy had evaporated. Heaven help anyone who stands in the way of his exacting revenge on the ones responsible for abusing his staff."

Mac gave a halfway grin as he commented. "You have anyone in particular in mind for the wrath of Quinn?"

"Actually, yes," Helen said as she took a deep breath before continuing. "That's the other thing I had to tell you. The other person Miss Watts visited was none other than Randall Smithers the second."

"The third. You mean our boy Randall Smithers the third."

"No," she said expressly. "I mean his *father*."

"The whole family is in on it?" Mac said with wonder. "Are they certain?"

"Not yet. They are investigating him, and he's being watched for now. But you can be sure if he is involved that he's more than just a courier," Helen responded.

"Junior didn't give up dear old dad during his interrogation," Yazzie observed. "Not even a hint of anyone else's involvement. Is he that good under pressure or is it possible that he doesn't know of his father's involvement?"

The trio chewed on this thought and the implications of it all for a moment in silence. "Was there anything else, dear?" Mac finally said.

"Just that they're making great progress at Groom Lake. There are new discoveries every day, however with so much more to do, it seems slow to them. They discovered that the Shalanaya have a type of gland that is the source of their odor. They are postulating that it is an oil gland that lubricates their skin." Helen smiled as she added, "That particular discovery stunk up the lab for days."

The men grunted out laughs that said 'better them than us' then Mac turned his attention to Yazzie. "What's the news from Amsterdam?"

"We were not the first to notice that there was a new supplier of diamonds. The community of jewelers in Amsterdam is small and very competitive and normally they would never share information about customers. However, the perfection of the gems caused them to come under scrutiny immediately. The apprehension of the businessmen got the attention of the Irgun and caused them to take an interest in their origin." Yazzie smiled as he paused for effect. "They also have traced them to Tokyo. I have been told that the man who assisted me when I was under attack was Irgun and had been made aware of my presence here. When he saw me abducted, he intervened but had not been authorized to reveal himself, so he quickly left once he was certain of my safety."

"Have they had any success in finding…" A knock on the door interrupted Mac's question.

"Geoffrey must have gotten lonely in the office," Helen said with a smile as she rose to answer the door and left the two men to finish their conversation. The cheerful salutation on her lips was cut short when instead of amiable Geoffrey, she found an intense Japanese man waiting on the other side of the door.

"I have come to speak to General Magruder," he said at her hesitation. "May I come in?"

"Yes, yes, of course. Where are my manners?" Helen continued, standing aside to allow him entry.

The two men rose at his entrance as Mac and the stranger locked eyes. "Yazzie, Helen," Mac said at last, "I would like you to meet Makoto Fujita."

"Mr. Fujita," Helen exclaimed, "it's so nice to meet you at last. I must apologize for my reaction at the door. I was quite expecting someone else and though I've heard a lot about you we've never met. Please sit, sit," she said as a chair was offered.

Fujita slowly sat down while examining the two new faces and the others followed suit, with Mac moving to the sofa with his wife. "They know?" he asked Mac. At the nod of his head Fujita continued, "and they have the same abilities of entry and exit as you?" After a moment's hesitation, Mac again nodded in answer. "How many more?"

"Just the three of us that we know of," Mac responded.

"Are you human?"

"Oh, my goodness," Helen exclaimed. "Just tell him. He already knows about the aliens and has undoubtedly suffered more for that knowledge than any of us. I am so sorry for what you've been through, dear," she said, directing her attention to Fujita. "I would never dismiss your suffering by trying to say that I know how you feel."

"It's a yes from me," Yazzie chimed in. "We agreed that decisions like these had to be unanimous. What's your vote, Mac?"

The General considered the implications carefully for a moment, then quietly inclined his head in agreement.

"Yitzhak Shimon at your service," Yazzie said, extending his hand. Fujita hesitated a moment, then cautiously took his hand. "Yes, we are all three quite human and have been conscripted into this battle against the alien presence here on earth. Our knowledge of the creatures is limited, and we would very much like to hear all that you have learned from your experiences so that we can send as many of them as possible directly to Sheol."

Fujita smiled at the possibility of the ones who had murdered the men under his command being sentenced to a place of darkness and torment for eternity. "You said conscripted, that you were conscripted into the battle. By whom?"

"Well, that's a little harder to explain," Mac answered, trying to formulate a sufficient answer that wouldn't scare him off.

"By aliens then," Fujita stately flatly. At their obvious surprise, he continued, "I have had much time to think of nothing else but the island and what happened there. If there are two alien races, I thought perhaps there are more. You know there are two different types of aliens on earth, yes?"

"Yes," Mac answered. "The huge monstrosities are called Anakim. The pale, almost human-looking ones are called the Shalanaya. The ones that contacted us we call the Greys."

"Why did they contact you?"

"The three of us in particular? We don't know. Humans in general – because if the Anakim are not stopped here on earth then the Greys' planet is next," Mac replied.

"Strong motivation indeed," Fujita agreed quietly. "And they gave you abilities beyond human capabilities to assist in the fight."

"Exactly."

"Hmm, I see," Fujita murmured as he thought. After several moments, he continued, "I have come here to offer my services. I will tell you everything I know and lay down my life if necessary, *but* you must promise me that no one will be allowed to go to the island for missionary work or any other reason except to kill the evil ones."

"Of course," Mac returned.

"Promise me on your wife's life," he persisted.

"I promise you, Makoto," Helen said solemnly, "that I will do everything within my power to prevent any more death or destruction by these beasts." Mac and Yazzie agreed with Helen's statement and promised in turn to do the same.

Fujita relaxed a little at their unity then smiled as he continued, "So, I must ask, of course. Will the Greys do for me what they have done for you?"

The trio laughed, then Yazzie responded. "They made it clear they intend to be involved as little as possible in taking down the Anakim. They occupy themselves by observing other cultures strictly without interference and with their quest to reach the heavenly tenth dimension. I believe they would not have made contact in this instance either had they been at all certain humans could overcome their enemy without assistance. So, to answer your question, not at this time but who knows how they will feel in the future."

"I see…if I may ask," Fujita started uncertainly, "how did you come to know of me and my experiences? I was told that all records of my report would be destroyed."

Mac looked at the floor for a moment before answering. "The Greys gave us your name as a witness that the alien presence was already on earth. You were to verify their assertions."

"They knew of me?" he asked, puzzled. At the apologetic look in Mac's eyes, he understood. "They watched as my men were murdered and did nothing. They saw the torture and did not move to stop it. I thought they were to be our allies!"

"They are currently not our enemies," Yazzie returned, "however that doesn't mean they are our allies."

"They are not like us, dear," Helen said. "They are aloof from any sentimental attachment. Any qualities of mercy or grace are saved for their own race. You see…"

A knock on the door interrupted the conversation.

"I'll get it, Helen," Yazzie said as he stood up. "Please continue."

He took a moment to stretch on the way to the door, then opened it only to see the face of a man for whom he had forged papers several years before. It was not the man himself that had requested his services, as arrangements had been made through a third party. However, he remembered the job because of the unoriginality of the name – John Smith.

"Where…" Mr. Smith started without a preamble. Seeing Helen on the sofa, he pushed past Yazzie and continued. "How did you know? Tell me that. How did you know someone with a peculiar odor would contact me?"

CHAPTER 44

"Geez Louise," Mac intoned with a roll of his eyes. "What is this Grand Central Station?"

"Colonel Smith, is something wrong?" Helen asked from her seat on the sofa.

"Why did you ask me about meeting someone with a peculiar odor?" he responded. "Are my people in danger?"

"Did someone threaten you?" Yazzie asked with concern, as he followed him back into the room.

"No, no one threatened me."

"Good to see you again, Colonel," Fujita said as he vacated his seat and offered it to the newcomer.

"Don't bother, Makoto," Mac said. "He's not going to be here long."

"I'll be here as long as it takes to get a straight answer out of you," he returned hotly.

"Colonel," Yazzie said evenly. "Just tell us what happened."

"I left for a staff meeting and an hour later returned to my office to find it had been ransacked by someone who left a pungent odor. That's what happened."

"Did they get the recordings or photos?" Helen asked.

"No…" Colonel Smith paused to take a breath. "No, I had stacked them on top of a box I was taking with me."

"Did they take anything else?" Yazzie asked.

"No, I assumed they were looking for the items you gave me."

"I'm so sorry, everyone. I watched and would have sworn I wasn't followed," Helen apologized.

"You may not have been followed, Helen," Yazzie assured her. "There are several ways they could have known you two met."

"And just who is *they?*" alias John Smith asked pointedly.

"Here's what you're going to do, Colonel," Mac said, ignoring his question. "You came to pick up your distant relative, Helen, for lunch. The two of you are going to eat and chat about old times. You absolutely will NOT discuss anything we just mentioned here. Not even a whisper."

"I don't take orders from you, *General.*"

"Do you want your men to be safe or not?" At his silence, Mac continued. "You've got to sell it. You two are related but haven't seen one another in years. That is your only connection. Common courtesy demands you share at least one meal. Get your coat, Helen. We will be in touch to share what we can, but right now you must not spend any more time here just in case they are watching. Understand?"

The Colonel was not happy. However, he allowed Helen to tuck her hand into the crook of his arm and usher him out the door. The three men remaining in the room heard her say as the door closed, "I'm so sorry I held us up, dear. I thought you said you'd be here at half past."

"Are you certain they will be okay?" Fujita asked with concern.

Mac smiled. "We each have our strengths; Helen's is dealing with people. The Colonel is going to come away from this lunch believing that they really are related."

"Or at least wishing they were," Yazzie agreed, nodding his head. "Besides, she does possess, how did you say it, unique methods of entry and exit if there's trouble."

"How many people know of your abilities?"

"Besides the three of us? You are the third, right behind the President of the United States and the Director of the Central Intelligence Group."

Fujita's eyebrows went up in surprise. "Your team does not know?"

"It is something the three of us have discussed many times," Yazzie responded gravely. "Whether to tell them. Would knowing put them in more or less danger? And when we do tell them, will they still feel safe working with us?"

"At this time, we feel it's to our advantage if no one knows, especially the Anakim and Shalanaya. It's better for our enemies to underestimate our abilities as long as possible," Mac clarified. "We definitely don't want them to realize we're getting assistance from the Greys either. It may change their plans from covert to overt and that would not be good for the human race."

"No, it would not," Fujita said thoughtfully. He then sighed heavily, knowing that his story must be told once again. When he first started to speak, the words stuck in his throat and choked the very breath from his lungs. After several deep breaths, he began again. "We were on a mission when we first saw their aircraft. It sped through the sky at an amazing speed. At that time, we had no idea what it was or who was in it but the speed at which it traveled was like nothing we had ever seen before."

"If I may ask," Yazzie interjected apologetically, "what was your mission?"

"Movement had been detected around the Mariana Islands," Fujita answered. "Admiral Hayakawa was unaware of any Japanese operations in the area, so he sent us to covertly observe and report back our observations. We were ordered not to engage, however when we lost contact with our aircraft we had no choice but to disembark to find our missing man."

Mac and Yazzie could see the pain and regret on his face and did not interrupt the telling of his story again. They also had events in their lives that were better left buried and forgotten and wished with everything in them that Fujita's experiences could be left to fade into nothing. But they knew it could not be so.

"We lost contact with him, so we went to the last place of transmission - the island. We tried to get him on the radio and watched for any signs of enemy presence. We saw and heard nothing. The time finally came when we had no choice. We had to look for our pilot. So, a search party of ten, including myself, was formed and we went ashore. It was quiet...beautiful...peaceful. The sun was warm, and I remember thinking how good it was to leave the sub for a time. As we were discussing how to divide up into search parties their ship reappeared, and we watched as a beam of light shot forth from under the craft. We didn't understand what was happening at first. Not until we saw our boat lift out of the water in two pieces like an inverted vee that we realized it had been cut in half."

"Cut in half!" Mac exclaimed. Fujita's silent nod left them speechless.

"Each end immediately sank with the middle where it was cut breaking the surface until it followed the rest of the boat down into the deep. My entire crew, save the nine who had come ashore with me, were gone in a moment," he said sadly. "Over the next few months of terror, we each wished that we had gone down with them."

"How is that possible? How can a beam of light cut through steel?" Mac asked no one in particular. "That sounds like something out of a Flash Gordon movie."

"If the light uses intense heat, it would explain something I saw while working for the Irgun," Yazzie said thoughtfully. "An arm was found (we never did locate the rest of the body). It was neatly severed, but it had been cauterized at the point of separation so quickly and completely that we were able to extract blood from his vein. This was, um, nine months ago I believe."

"So," Mac said gravely, "a new weapon that's beyond anything we currently have on earth. We always knew it was a possibility."

"It's not your fault, you know," Yazzie said while staring intently at Fujita. "You had a man down; you surveyed the area and precautions were taken. Anyone in your position would have done exactly the same thing."

"Thank you," Fujita acknowledged quietly while fighting the emotions that always accompanied the memory. He finally cleared his throat to regain control of himself and continued. "After the island, when I was questioned, I sounded mad. Speaking of creatures and atrocities, they couldn't possibly imagine. I can't tell you how many times, how many people I told my story. Each, of course, wanted me to start from the beginning. Reliving it over and over again just about did drive me mad. Finally, Admiral Hayakawa came to me and said never to speak of it again to anyone. He said he would destroy all records of my confessions and that he would get me transferred to Hiroshima for a fresh start."

"After we were given your name, I looked for you and was able to trace you to Hiroshima. However, I could find nothing after that, so we assumed the worst," Yazzie said.

"I'm not surprised," Fujita responded. "I wasn't there long. You see, Hiroshima was at that time a communications center and a key port for shipping; many troops were assembled there. There was also much manufacturing of parts for planes and boats as well as bombs, rifles, and handguns."

"My understanding has always been that it was a significant supply and logistics base," Mac said.

"Yes, there was much happening there," Fujita agreed. "That's why I thought it would be a good place to blend in and be so ordinary that no one would pay any attention to me or my story. The Admiral had me assigned to the communications center where I would finish my years of service quietly in a menial job."

"The communications center, you say?" Yazzie asked.

"I never served one day there," Fujita confessed. "Transportation had been arranged to take us to our new assignments, but I never got on the truck. I left and made my way to a ship heading back to Tokyo."

"Why? Did you see something that changed your mind?"

"No, it was not what I saw, but what I *smelled*. Something I hadn't smelled since the island; something that made my blood run cold. I went to the Admiral upon my return to warn him of the threat, but he thought I imagined it," Fujita said with disgust. Then in a softer tone, he admitted with a sigh, "Who knows, maybe I did. Maybe I was obsessed, to the point that my mind created something that wasn't there. As it turned out it didn't matter as two days later the Americans dropped the atomic bomb on Hiroshima, and it was all gone. God forgive me, but though I was saddened for the loss of my countrymen, I was happy to think that *they* were dead."

Mac and Yazzie looked at one another before Mac spoke. "They were there. The Shalanaya had their own communications operation running right alongside Japan's in Hiroshima during the war according to the Greys."

"Yes," Yazzie confirmed, "it was only the destruction of their command center that set back the alien takeover. And it was then that the Greys realized the threat to their own planet and began discussing whether to interfere in human history."

"They were there?" Fujita asked in disbelief. At their solemn nods, he repeated in stunned acknowledgment, "It wasn't just me, they really were there."

"We found a map in D.C. that indicated Hiroshima was at one time their base of operations," Yazzie continued. "According to that same map, their new base is on the island hence why we're here. However aerial reconnaissance photos show no facilities."

"They wouldn't," Fujita responded. "It's all underground – at least it was when I was there."

"Underground? How?" Mac asked.

Fujita leaned forward in his seat. "Their aircraft can also act as a submarine. As I said they fly at amazing speeds but can also hover like a helicopter. Have you actually seen one? A helicopter I mean."

"Amazing, absolutely amazing crafts," both men agreed.

"Yes, I'm hoping to ride in one someday," Fujita admitted with childlike wonder, then continued in a more serious vein. "Make no mistake, their technology is far more advanced than anything I've seen in Japan or the United States. The aircraft can fly directly from the air into the water and remain there for days. I imagined they had some type of docking station underwater, but I never got a good look at it."

"What made you think so?"

"There was a heavily camouflaged door on the side of the island where the craft always entered and exited. They each had a ring that was used for access."

Mac's face lit up. "Oh, tell me the hand you cut off had a ring…"

"Oh yes," Fujita beamed. "Yes, it did."

"We need to get to the island," Mac affirmed. "We need to find that ring and see if it opens what we all think it will open."

CHAPTER 45

"I'm so sorry to bring you out on such a frightful day, Major," Helen said apologetically as the wind whipped her skirt around her legs.

"No problem," Curly responded as he turned his collar up to shield his neck from the bluster. "It's refreshing actually after being confined to a jeep for the last few days."

"I was so happy to hear that everything turned out well. Mac told me the German scientist was delighted to see you. He said that the poor man had been kidnapped?"

"Yes," Hale said, unable to suppress a grin. "When he heard Tamar speaking German, he ran across the room and caught her up in a bear hug much to her displeasure. We had to practically pry him off her. He instantly became the stray pup she had rescued, and he followed her everywhere. That's why she went with McCann this morning instead of me to drop him off to the MPs."

"Oh my," Helen said as they turned a corner, and the wind nearly knocked her off her feet. "So, he's headed to the States?"

"Eventually," Hale said as he wrapped his arm around Helen to steady her. They leaned into the wind and pushed ahead. "He's going by way of Pullach. He'll be interrogated there, and we've promised to try to locate his teenage son who was left behind. After that, if everything checks out he, or the two of them if his son is found, will be headed stateside."

"Oh, that poor boy! He must have been terrified when he couldn't find his father."

"He told Tamar that he and his son had discussed what to do should anything bad happen. If the kid stuck to the plan, we may have a decent chance of finding him."

The wind died suddenly as they turned off the street acting as a wind tunnel and the rush of blood their bodies had produced to warm them in the bluster brought a sudden flush to their cheeks. Helen patted her head to make sure her scarf was still secure over her hair as they arrived at their destination.

Lieutenant Colonel John Smith stepped from a doorway as they walked up. "I wasn't sure you would be able to come in this whirlwind," he said as he bent to kiss Helen on the cheek.

"I had to enlist Major Hale here to assist me. It's a good thing I did. I would have most certainly been blown out to sea without him. You two have met, haven't you?" she asked.

"Briefly," the Lieutenant Colonel responded as he extended his hand. "Good to see you again, Major."

"Sir," Hale responded succinctly as they shook hands.

The Lieutenant Colonel then reached into his pocket and produced a small item, causing Helen to put her hands to her chest and sigh in delight. "Oh, I'm so happy you found my glasses, dear. I looked everywhere and was certain I'd lost them for good." The spectacles were withdrawn from the case and perched on her nose as she continued, "Now I can read without looking like I play the trombone."

The two men laughed as the lost item was returned to its case and placed in her purse.

"It was so sweet of you to come out of your way to deliver these. Please let me buy you a cup of coffee or tea."

"Well, that's what you do for family," Colonel Smith returned, much to Major Hale's surprise. "But I'm afraid I'm on my way to a meeting with General MacArthur and can't today. Another time?"

"Of course, I understand," Helen said as she affectionately patted his cheek. "We'll make it another time, dear." And with that Lieutenant Colonel Smith took up the briefcase leaning in the doorway he had stepped from and hurried down the street to attend to business.

"I had no idea you two were related," Hale said as they turned to head back to the office.

"Only distantly," Helen said. "But family is family, isn't it?"

Something in the way she responded gave Hale pause, but he squelched the interrogator's side of himself and didn't question her any further on the matter. "What do you say we take a different route back? I think if we take alleyways, we'll get less wind. Unless you have another errand to run?"

"That's a brilliant idea, Major, as it is exactly what I was going to suggest!" Helen said with a sparkle. "There's nothing important enough to keep me out in this weather any longer than necessary, so please lead the way."

They bypassed the main road and turned down an alley running parallel to it. After pressing up against the wall for a moment to allow an old truck to lumber by with its load, they saw no other movement as the weather had driven everyone inside to bunker up until the storm had passed.

"So, did anything interesting happen while we were gone?" Hale asked as much to distract them from the darkening skies as for the information the question may provide.

"Well, I finally got to meet Mr. Fujita," Helen said as she picked her way past something unpleasant on the ground. "He seems to be a lovely man."

"Fujita!" Hale exclaimed, thinking of their previous meeting when he had cursed Mac and stormed out of the room.

"Yes. It seems he and Mac had a disagreement before. My husband does tend to rub people the wrong way sometimes," she said with a sigh. "I personally think it's from being a general for so long. Anyway, I believe everything has been straightened out now."

Hale was silent for a moment as he wondered what could have created such an about-face from their last meeting when he suddenly stopped dead in his tracks.

"What is that smell?" he asked.

Helen knew exactly what odor he was referring to, as it was the very same aroma that had caused her to wrap her hand around the derringer in her purse moments before.

"What is that damn smell? Do you smell it?" he asked as he spun in place, taking a step this way then that trying to locate its origin.

Helen saw him first. She threw herself against Hale's shoulder as hard as she could to move him from the bullet's trajectory. Falling to one side, Hale's gun was unholstered on his way down at the sound of the first shot. He rolled over and fired three shots center mass into the assailant when a single pop from Helen's gun jerked his head back and dropped him to the ground. Hale ran over and removed the weapon from the hit man's reach, then checked for a pulse. Finding none, Hale turned back to Helen.

"What in the hell…" he started, then saw her ashen face and blood seeping through the shoulder on her coat. "Oh, dear God," he breathed as he scooped her up in his arms and began running down the alley. "Don't worry, I'll get you to Mac!"

"No," she whispered. "Yazzie. I need Yazzie."

Then abruptly his surroundings changed, and Hale nearly dropped her when his forward momentum from the alley crashed him into Yazzie – in their office!

"How…what…" Hale stammered as his mind reeled and his arms went weak.

Yazzie caught her just as the office door opened and Tamar and McCann walked in laughing. "Clear the desk, clear the desk," Yazzie yelled as Geoffrey jumped from his seat to comply. Yazzie laid her carefully on the desk as Geoffrey swiftly removed his shirt to place under her head.

"What happened? Answer me, dammit!" Mac demanded as he shook Curly by the shoulders.

"Ambush. We were ambushed," he finally managed to get out with his eyes still riveted on Helen.

Tamar pulled the knife from her boot and handed it to McCann, who had moved to the opposite side of the desk to assist Yazzie. Helen's coat and clothes were quickly cut away and her shoulder exposed.

"Where? Where were you? Who did this?" Mac grilled the practically incoherent, utterly stunned Hale. The guilt swept over him as his mind tried to comprehend the events of the last few minutes.

Tamar carefully took the small weapon still clasp in Helen's hand and set it aside as Yazzie uttered a curse in Yiddish. "Poison," he stated, as Geoffrey was instructed to lift and suspend Helen's shoulder from the surface of the desk as Yazzie placed his hands several inches from each wound. "Go! Go, I've got this!" Yazzie ordered Mac, never lifting his eyes from Helen.

Mac's eyes welled up with tears and he shook with emotion as he looked at the face of the person that meant everything to him. Then he turned to Hale and said, "Just visualize where it happened. I'll get us there from that." He took one last glance at his wife, then took Hale's shoulder and they disappeared from the room.

Tamar's mouth fell open as Geoffrey's wide-eyed stare told her this was new to him, too. McCann didn't even lift his eyes as he carefully wiped away the burnt orange liquid bubbling out of Helen's wounds with the shirt he had removed and torn in half.

"Here," McCann said, throwing Tamar the half not in use. "Wipe it off the desk and don't touch it. You don't know how it enters the bloodstream." Then turning his attention to Yazzie, he asked, "Do you need the med kit, sir?"

At his affirmative nod, Tamar volunteered to retrieve it. She carefully cleared the mess from the desk, noticing that the liquid had left an etching on the smooth metal surface. She then placed a piece of cloth under the wound to catch the dripping poison and dashed from the room.

After several moments of silence, Geoffrey leaned toward McCann and quietly inquired, "Is this normal?"

"There's not a single damn thing normal about any of this, mate."

"That's what I thought," he replied, and then fell silent.

The bubbling from Helen's wound had just begun to slow when Tamar burst through the door with Curly close behind. He was out of breath and had clearly run back to the office as fast as his legs would carry him. The color of the seepage from Helen's wound had been slowly changing from orange to blood red as beads of sweat broke out on Yazzie's forehead. McCann grabbed the kit and prepared alcohol swabs to cleanse the wounds.

"Where's Mac?" Geoffrey asked with his distinctive British reserve kicking in, completely ignoring the million other questions that needed to be asked. "She'll want to see him when she wakes up."

Curly glanced at his cryptanalyst without any of his customary everything-will-be-okay confidence, then looked down at Helen. "We located the assailant, determined him to be deceased, then the General left to deliver the body and weapon used in the attack to Colonel Quinn in Washington, D.C. I ran back here as quickly as I could."

"Oh," was all that was said as a pregnant silence filled the room.

A soft groan from Helen broke them all from their individual revelry. Smiles broke out all around as McCann chortled, "Well bless my soul. The lovely lassie decided to join the party!"

Helen's eyes fluttered open and after assessing the situation by the looks on her friends' faces said, "Well, I guess the cat is out of the bag. Isn't it?"

CHAPTER 46

The four weary veterans pushed through the door and silently filed in after their debrief on all things alien. The bar was missing all its usual revelry as preparations to open took place.

"We not open yet," a small Japanese man said from behind the bar as they each took a seat around a table situated in a back corner of the room. "You hear? We not open yet. No beer, come back later."

The four remained in their seats and briefly glanced at one another, then avoided eye contact as they each processed all they had just heard from the General, Yazzie, and Helen. It was the damndest briefing any of them had ever been to.

The Asian man ran up to the table after shouting orders in Japanese to a young man sweeping the floor. "We not open yet," he repeated with his hands on his hips. Then suddenly he broke out into a crooked smile. "Okay, okay, for you, okay. We love Americans. They drink much beer. I bring something."

Geoffrey was the first to break the silence after the man hurried back behind the bar. "Well, it's been quite a day, hasn't it?" The lack of response caused him to continue nervously. "Well, it's probably nothing to all of you. I know you've seen a lot more action than I have. This is probably nothing to you…"

Two more workers came through the front door and the little boss man paused in the preparation of their beverages to shout unintelligible instructions to the late comers. The woman said something back that sounded more like sass than an apology, but the man stayed mum and quickly walked past them into the back room. The young man that had been present when they entered had paused his sweeping to take in the scene but resumed with renewed enthusiasm when his boss shot a look his way as the four drinks were delivered.

"Okay, I bring beer, but not free, okay? You pay."

Major Hale pulled out his wallet and said, "I got this." Then threw a couple of bills on the tray. The boss was all smiles as he retreated, and they each lifted their glasses to sip quietly.

"It's a hell of a thing, isn't it?" McCann said, as he leaned back in his seat and sighed. "And you two knew nothing about it, you say?" At Hale and Tamar's negative responses he continued, "I always had an itch on the back of my neck about this one but figured you two knew a hell of a lot more about what was going on than I did. It's damn disconcerting to think you were in the dark too."

"I can tell you I suspected nothing was amiss," Geoffrey chimed in relieved that someone else had finally spoken.

"Oh, go way outta that now. I never thought for a minute you were in the know Geoffrey my man," McCann said, with a little of his usual Irish swagger shining through. "Dumb as a post you are."

"Thank you," Geoffrey replied sarcastically. "Thank you very much. I propose we raise our glasses in recognition of ignorant dogfaces everywhere who are the first to fight and the last to know what the hell's going on."

As their glasses clinked, a worker came from the back and passed the table carrying two crates to the bar.

"I can't believe they suspected Irene," Geoffrey said with wonder.

"It was the perfume," Tamar observed. "Heavy scents…" Tamar paused as the bar worker passed by to procure another load. "Heavy scents are a red flag."

"Irene spilled a bottle of cologne on her clothes, is all. It took a few washings to get it all out. But, of course, they had no way to know that, did they?"

"Look at that," McCann said, nudging Hale. "He's defending his future missus already, takin' her part and all."

Geoffrey rolled his eyes as the others laughed, then they fell silent again, just drinking their beer and keeping their thoughts to themselves as they watched the workers ready the establishment for business.

"So," Geoffrey finally said as he leaned into the group and lowered his voice. "Have any of you had…encounters? You know with the…you know…flying monkeys?"

Three pairs of eyes slowly widened at the question as Hale asked, "What in the living hell are you talking about?"

"You haven't even finished one pint, mate. You can't be back on your heels yet," McCann added, shaking his head.

"I was trying to use code, Irish. We can't very well just say *it* out loud now can we?" As his three compatriots laughed, Geoffrey continued. "Think about the Wizard of Oz film. The flying monkeys did the dirty work of the wicked witch, right?"

"I hated those damn monkeys. Gave me nightmares right up until I went squirrel hunting and pictured their ugly faces on every one of the little bastards I hit. Made squirrel stew," Hale said with a smile while licking his fingers. "Mighty tasty."

"So, what we talk about?" the bar boss asked as he stepped to the table, wiping his hands on a bar towel.

"Flying monkeys," Tamar said with a sly look at the others at the table.

"Oh, monkeys mean!" the little man said with disgust. "My sister live in Philippines, she tell me. They throw things and scream loud. They throw rocks and they sheet. Nasty mean creature smell very bad. I stay away from moneys whether they fly or not. You want another round?"

At their nods, he hurried off to get their order and Hale turned to Geoffrey with a smile. "My apologies, old man. You nailed it. The topics of our discussion are mean and smell bad. They do the bidding of their evil masters and I'm quite certain that they would throw their *sheet* given the opportunity."

"They scream also," Tamar added knowingly, as she recalled the animal like scream that came from Truman's would-be assassin. She paused as a worker hurried past the bar's earliest customers. "I knew something was off when we fought. She was too strong for her size, but I let the notion slip away because of who the target was. It is sobering to think how close they got. You heard it too, didn't you, Curly?"

"I was focused on my target, but I remember thinking 'what the hell was that?' as I ran. Then someone kicked me in the head and the world went dark," Hale returned drily, giving Tamar a look.

She shrugged noncommittally and continued, "Their eyes go black, like they have nothing but empty sockets." She shivered involuntarily at the memory.

The look on her face made Geoffrey unwilling to pursue any more questions about the incident. "Well, we know that the Major had a monkey encounter earlier today," he stated, trying to keep the conversation going.

"Yes," he said somberly, "and thanks to Helen I'm here to talk about it."

"Sir," McCann returned as he recognized the tone of imagined failure in Hale's voice. "There's no way you could have known he was wearing a body armor that would stop a bullet. She had information you didn't have, and she acted on it appropriately. I personally think she must have a wee bit of Irish in 'er. She's quite a gal."

"Here's to Helen!" Geoffrey said as he raised his glass. "Here, here," they all responded, as they followed his lead. "So, what about you?" he asked McCann, as he wiped his mouth. "Do you have any monkey tales?"

"Me? None that I know of, but I've smelled 'em and seen the mess they leave behind. Course that coulda been the work of the wicked witch herself and not the flying primates what serve her."

"So, what do we do now?" Hale solemnly asked the table. "They said we could opt out, get reassigned if we wanted. It won't reflect on our records."

Tamar smiled. "I will forever be by my uncle's side no matter who the enemy. He is my only family."

Hale looked at McCann. "Hell, a bad guy is a bad guy, right? Some flying monkeys wear a swastika, some wear a white hood, these just stink. They're no different. Evil is evil. Gotta take it down no matter what it looks like. I'm staying."

At Hale's look Geoffrey quickly replied, "I'm in." The surprise must have clearly shown on each of their faces, as he explained. "Look, I know my military experience has been vastly different from any of yours, but once you know something you can't un-know it. This is a real threat - as much as any enemy in any war. I can't walk away; I won't walk away. Besides, the way I see it, the odds are much better with the General, Tamar's uncle, and Helen than without them."

"And how about you, sir?" McCann asked, knowing the answer before any response was given. The Major had never run from a fight in his life.

Hale took a sip from his glass and quietly responded. "From what we were just told, we're probably outmatched. Their technology is far more advanced than ours and they have weapons we've never even heard of. We're just learning about them, and they've been studying us for years." He paused to look around the table. "Helen nearly died from a simple through-and-through on her shoulder. You get that, right? I don't know that we can win this one. The General and Yazzie, along with Helen, were conscripted into this fight, we've got a choice. Think about it, they were given outrageous skills so they could survive, and they still almost got her. We, on the other hand, have no such protection. We've only got our wits and determination to defeat a superior enemy force. We're in a damn poor position militarily."

"So, what are you saying, Major?" Geoffrey pressed.

"I'm saying this isn't a time for bravado. If you have any doubt, any hesitation, opt out now. I know this isn't a fight our training has prepared any of us for…but if you're in, you've got to be 100% all in the fight. I know these two knuckleheads love a good brawl," Hale said giving a nod to Tamar and McCann, "and it seems that I've already got a target painted on my back, but you've got more brains and common sense than the three of us combined. Are you sure this is what you want to do, Geoffrey?"

Geoffrey leaned back in his chair, not sure whether to be pleased at the compliment or offended at the lack of esteem of his colleagues. "Well sir…" he replied thoughtfully before slamming his fist on the table, startling some of the patrons starting to make their way into the room. "I'm saying, hell yes, I'm in this fight! Let's go kick some flying monkey ass!"

McCann and Tamar smiled and raised their glasses, chiming in "to the extinction of flying monkeys!" as Hale motioned the pretty lady bartender over. "My friend here has just made a momentous decision. How do you think he should celebrate the occasion?"

"Oh, in Tokyo we have many ways to celebrate," the five-foot beauty said seductively as she moved over to rub Geoffrey's back.

At first Geoffrey thought this was simply to be an initiation into the big boys club, but there was something in the Major's steady unblinking gaze that gave him pause. Then his eyes widened in recognition, and his face paled as the petite brunette stepped behind him and bent to whisper a decidedly inappropriate suggestion into his ear. It was there – the smell of heavy perfume, beer, and an unidentifiable musky sweat stink not entirely masked by the other two.

"Welcome to the circus, brother," Hale said as he lifted his glass to the newest member of his unit.

Geoffrey shrank from her touch at which she laughed and said, "Oh, you shy. I like the shy ones. They so willing to learn."

"You really shouldn't do that in front of my girlfriend," Geoffrey choked out with a summoned strength he certainly didn't currently feel. "She's the jealous type."

At that, Tamar pushed her chair back and stood to her full five-foot-eight height to look down menacingly on the threat. Fastening her emerald eyes on the enemy she said, "Get your hands off my man," with violence in her tone.

"I not know, I not know," the Shalanaya seductress replied as she ran to the safety of the bar.

Tamar walked around the table and pulled Geoffrey to his feet by his collar. "Let's go, baby," she said as she brushed his lips with a kiss. "I'm tired of this place." Then she took his hand and led the way to the door with her hips gently swaying.

Hale and McCann were clapping and cheering as they rose to follow. Whistles and hoots of approval from the incoming customers followed the four friends out the door as the small Japanese barkeep said, "Damn, monkeys! Monkeys mean!"

CHAPTER 47

"I'll do it," Mac insisted.

"You most certainly will not," Helen returned. "It's my job and I'll do it."

"Sweetheart, you were shot yesterday. You need to rest. It's too much."

"I know very well what happened yesterday, Mr. Magruder. That doesn't change the fact that the assassin's body is currently decaying in Colonel Quinn's safe house and needs to be moved."

"I…"

"I am perfectly fine," Helen cut in before Mac could make his case. "Yazzie did an excellent job of removing the poison and fixing me up, thanks to the Greys little gift of healing imparted to the Rabbi. And besides, the doctors would be suspicious if you showed up to Groom Lake instead of me. I'm their contact and I fully intend to continue in that capacity."

"No. Do you hear me? No, it's my duty to assess the mental and physical well-being of those under my command and make assignments accordingly. You've never suffered an injury like this before and can't know how it will affect you."

"Don't try to use that I'm-the-General tone with me because it won't work."

"You said you would respect my lead. When we got into this mess, you said you could separate our personal relationship from the job. The fact is that I *am* the General, and you agreed to follow my command."

Helen stood silently for a moment. "Okay, I'll do what you say if you can answer me one thing. If this decision is based solely on the mission and not on me being your wife, would you forbid Tamar or Curly or Yazzie or anyone else on the team from performing their assigned duties if it were one of them that got shot then healed?"

Mac sighed in agitated frustration and ran his hand through his hair. "Damn it all, Helen. Why are you making such a big deal about this?"

"Why are you?" she shot back defiantly. As they glared at one another from across the room, she finally sighed in resignation. Then quietly lessened the distance between them and slid her arms around Mac's neck. "Thank you for wanting to protect me. I really do love you for it, darling, but you have other things that need to be done that I simply can't do. You know you do. How about this? I promise that if I feel any ill effects at all, I'll come back straight away. I'll leave that body to rot and come home, I promise."

"I almost lost you," Mac choked out as he pulled her body against his. "I've lost men in battle before and it was hell, but I wouldn't be able to recover from losing you that way. I love you, Helen."

"I know, I love you too," she sighed into his ear as she placed a soft kiss on his neck. "There is one small silver lining to me getting shot though."

Mac pulled back and looked at her like she was crazy. "I don't think so."

"But now I have the cutest little scar on my shoulder," she returned. As her husband rolled his eyes in response, she continued. "I think your scars are very alluring. Don't men think scars are sexy?"

"I was there when it happened, dear. I had to leave you lying there. I don't think I'll ever find that stinking scar sexy."

Helen pulled his face to hers and kissed him until she felt his body respond. She pulled away a little breathless and said, "It has come to my attention that in all the hustle and bustle of our new life that I've been missing you."

"Mmm," he responded, nuzzling her neck. "Have you now?"

"Yes," she replied, as he pulled her into another kiss. When he released her and returned to softly planting kisses down her neck and shoulder, she continued.

"I know we don't have time to, you know, really do justice to how much I've missed you right now, but I was thinking that when we both get back from our assignments, we could steal away to the cabin for a date."

Mac smiled into her neck, then pulled away from her with a mock scowl. "Shirk our duties? Madam, you sound absolutely scandalous."

"I thought maybe I could change your mind about my scar. It really is the cutest little thing."

"I don't know, that could take a while," Mac responded, allowing his smile to return at the pleasant thought of all that her convincing would entail.

"So, is it a date?"

Mac thought about the dozens of times Helen had made similar dates. Every time he left on assignment, in fact. Every time there was a possibility that he wouldn't return, she would make a date. Then she would tell him how much trouble he'd be in if he stood her up. There were never any tears, no sniveling, no emotional outbursts when he left - just a date planned for a time after his return.

"It's a date," he promised, crossing his heart with his index finger. She then smiled and disappeared from the room. "And you had better not stand me up, woman," he added softly as he joined Yazzie and Fujita who were waiting in the Rabbi's room.

The arsenal laid out on Yazzie's bed spoke of a successful raid on Hayakawa's secret storeroom. A series of handguns, rifles, grenades, ammunition, and other useful paraphernalia filled the sleeping area.

"This should do nicely, don't you think?" Yazzie said with a grin.

"Looks like you got everything except a cannon," Mac returned.

"He didn't have a cannon," Yazzie responded with regret. Then he brightened and said, "There was a bazooka we left behind. Shall I go get it?"

"I don't think we'll need a bazooka just for a recon mission. If we do, then we were completely unsuccessful in getting in and out unnoticed," Mac replied.

Noticing Fujita's disconnection from the conversation and reserved demeanor, Mac could only imagine what thoughts were racing through his mind. To return to the scene of your nightmare couldn't be easy.

"Are you sure you're up for this?" Mac asked quietly. "We've got your directions from the plane to the hollowed-out tree. We can probably find it from that."

Fujita's attention snapped back to the present as he replied, "Without a doubt you will need me to find it. I am ready to go. Do we have the scent?"

"That will *not* be applied in this room!" Yazzie stated emphatically as a tactical vest loaded with gear was zipped up. "I have to sleep here tonight."

Mac suppressed a smile as he said, "I don't know maybe we should at least open it up and give it a sniff."

"Not happening," Yazzie reiterated without hesitating in his preparations.

"It will most definitely provide essential cover from the Anakim. Their eyesight is poor; however their sense of smell is highly advanced. I stayed alive by rubbing rotting fruit and feces on my body while there. Perhaps it would be safer to apply it in advance," Fujita added solemnly.

Yazzie looked up and saw the serious faces of his two compatriots. "Oh hell," he muttered before both Mac and Fujita could no longer cover their mirth and snorted with laughter. "Bastards," was heard as Yazzie snatched the vial of Shalanaya scent procured from the Groom Lake scientists and placed it in his pocket, zipping it shut with finality.

"Are we ready?" Mac asked.

The three clasped one another hand to wrist, forming a human circle then moved inter-dimensionally from their present location as Yazzie quoted from the 143rd Psalm. "Deliver us, oh Lord, from our enemies; in You we take shelter."

Fujita had to trust Mac and Yazzie that this inter-dimensional travel was not only real, but safe. They had been modified to physically accommodate it. He had not. Would he die in the process? He was filled with apprehension but determined to see if it was actually possible to travel from one place to another on earth without using conventional travel methods. If it worked, a whole new world of possibilities could open up to mankind and he hadn't yet determined if it would be for the better or worse. For now, he could only follow the lead of his new allies and see what happened.

The controlled air of the living quarters shifted to the humid, heavy air of the island as they manifested in the jungle. The thick canopy overhead filtered out what little moonlight was available and caused any sound daring to break the imposed silence to drop to the earth in submission. Yazzie quickly produced the vial, and each man applied the Shalanaya stink to their persons without protest. Their guiding landmark, the Seiran aircraft launched from Fujita's submarine so many years ago, had become overgrown with foliage and swallowed up by its environment, leaving only one pontoon visible to speak of its presence.

Fujita immediately dropped into a squat to quiet his reeling thoughts. *My God! It's real! This cannot be an illusion; it's too real. We're actually on the island. This is the remains of the aircraft. Covered in island fauna, but still here.*

Every hint of the man they met in Tokyo was suddenly gone as he became once again the only survivor on an island of hostiles. An intensity enveloped him and, just as the jungle had consumed the plane, Fujita's return had left a mere skeleton of the person he was hidden underneath his overpowering survival instinct. He sniffed the air and listened, turning his head this way and that like an owl on a branch. Convinced they were alone he reached back and patted the damaged airplane pontoon, the only witness to his previous time there, and whispered, "This way."

The nimble Japanese sailor led them quickly and quietly through the brush, weaving through branches and vines, and hopping over protruding roots along the way. Mac and Yazzie kept pace as best they could with their taller frames hindering them from displaying an agility equal to their guide. All three remained as silent as gravestones and on high alert, listening for any movement in the dense brush. When Fujita stopped up ahead, the two following tensed and readied for action.

When they approached, Fujita held up his hand like a stop sign, then dropped to the ground and disappeared on all fours into the matted foliage. The air was dead and still and full of the musty smell of decaying leaves. They waited back-to-back, each watching and listening, but the soft rustling of underbrush was the only sound as beads of sweat from the intense humidity trickled unnoticed down their faces.

Mac and Yazzie looked intently for the hollowed-out tree Fujita spoke of but saw nothing except an expanse of jungle that looked exactly the same as what they had just made their way through. Privately they wondered if perhaps his time away from the island had dulled his sense of direction and they were in the wrong spot. But he soon emerged and the triumphant smile he wore told them their fears were unjustified. Several long bony fingers were summarily removed and discarded into the brush as the object of their quest was held up for inspection.

The Anakim 'ring' was almost the size of a human man's wristwatch and was mounted on what looked like a piece of ancient Crusader's chainmail. Beyond that the intense darkness made any further inspection unfruitful, so the prize was stowed in Fujita's pocket, which was slowly zippered closed to mask the sound as they proceeded to their secondary objective.

As vegetation thinned and the sound of the gentle lapping of waves was heard, they knew the shoreline was approaching. Skirting along the edge of the jungle, they made their way toward the encampment. The powerful odor of the Anakim floated inland on the ocean breezes, warning the trio of their presence long before the grunting and growling of their guttural voices was heard.

All three men were now alert to the immense danger that surrounded them.

A small cargo ship was docked at the pier and wooden crates were being loaded by the albino looking Shalanaya laborers. Apparently their off-world assignments did not warrant the same physical modifications as those who would mingle with the inhabitants of earth as with minimal observation several differences could readily be spotted from the Shalanaya currently taking up drawer space in Groom Lake.

They observed the enemy in his natural state for a few moments; taking note of every detail that in time might be used against them in battle. One shirtless worker displayed a rib cage that extended from the throat down to his pelvis. Their anatomy allowing the ribs to float in a movement resembling the spine rather than remaining stationary, like human ribs attached to a sternum.

As they observed, a disagreement between the two Anakim on-site broke out in a shouting match that sounded like an intense dog fight, with fierce barking and growling. The fracas ended when a shove caused one to lose his balance and fall into the water. The depth of the water could have been easily overcome by his ten-foot height had he been standing; however, the shallow depth where he fell would not allow him room enough to get his legs underneath him so he could force himself to an upright position. His heavy head and chest sunk like an anchor below the surface, and it became clear the creature would drown if something were not done to help him.

The offending Anakim then pushed a couple of Shalanaya dock workers into the water to rescue his kinsman. They struggled in vain to lift the immense frantic creature out of his predicament, however his thrashing panic and intense weight was simply too much for them to overcome.

After several tense minutes, the Anakim remaining on the pier barked an order to the Shalanaya in the water to abandon their efforts and return to work. Neither the Anakim nor the Shalanaya gave a backward glance to the place of their comrade's demise but continued with their tasks as before.

While all attention was focused on the other side of the pier, Mac and Yazzie had slipped to the shoreline leaving Fujita hidden in the brush with a rifle pointed toward the enemy in case they should be discovered. The two men focused all their energy on the task at hand as they carefully inserted their hands inter-dimensionally through the wood crates one by one and grabbed a handful of whatever was inside. Once retracted, the obtained samples were carefully placed into envelopes brought for this purpose. The Greys' training had taught Mac and Yazzie how to translate only parts of their bodies to move transparently through solid objects in this way. It saved energy and was certainly more convenient than trying to pry open every box for a sample.

Fujita's trigger finger tensed as one of the pale dock workers paused to peer over the edge of the pier where Mac and Yazzie had been standing. The movement was chalked up to imagination by the Shalanaya as the two men appeared next to Fujita.

"For the love of Mike, don't fire that thing while we're traveling inter-dimensionally," Mac whispered as he and Yazzie each took an arm. "We have no idea where the bullet would land."

Then the jungle was left to itself once again.

CHAPTER 48

"I'm sorry your assignment here was cut short, mate," McCann said as he tightened the strap securing the Enigma machine to a dolly. "It's been a pleasure working with you for sure."

"I didn't know the General was considering sending you back so soon. I'm sorry too," Tamar added regretfully.

"He didn't send me back. I requested the transfer," Geoffrey replied. At their surprised expressions, he continued. "Look, Lieutenant Colonel Smith doesn't have anyone to watch his back, and he really doesn't know what he's up against. The whole unit needs protection, and I can work from there as well as I can from here, right?"

They all nodded their heads in respect at his decision to forego his own personal preference to stay and to return to protect his teammates.

"You know you can't tell them the truth, right?" Hale asked quietly.

"I wouldn't know where to begin," Geoffrey said with a mirthless smile. "How do you convince people that flying monkeys really exist?"

The four laughed at the reference, then Tamar gave Geoffrey a quick hug and asked, "Lunch sometime?"

"Of course," he replied as the door was opened and the armed escort entered to take control of the equipment.

"What about Irene?" McCann inquired.

"We spoke," Geoffrey replied as he trailed the equipment from the room. "I think she'll be better off if she's not connected to me right now."

The others knew what he meant. There was always that fear, that thought, that possibility of the enemy going after an innocent just because of their connection to you. The threat of peripheral casualties was a very effective means of control.

They watched as Geoffrey walked down the hall and packed into the lift with the soldiers and their precious cargo. Only when the lift doors had silently slid closed did they step back into the office.

"We've got a short window on this," Hale said as McCann prepared to heft the remaining dolly into rolling position. "Colonel Smith and Geoffrey are going to be in the lobby making a scene and keeping everyone distracted so we can get the SIGABA out the back and on its way without any delay. You ready?"

Tamar stuck her head out the door and looked down the hall. "Irene is standing in her doorway," she said, stepping back inside. "Want me to take care of it?"

"Can you handle this alone?" Hale asked McCann, patting the dolly. At his affirmative nod, Hale continued. "We'll meet you out back."

"I'll whistle if I need you, Major," McCann said with a grin.

Hale pushed Tamar into the hallway, then stuck his head back in. "Make it a wolf whistle," he returned mischievously. "Tamar will love that!"

As they started walking toward Irene's position, a casual conversation was started.

"I wasn't expecting his assignment to be cut so short, were you?" Hale began.

"No, not at all. The office won't be the same without him," Tamar replied.

"Hi," Irene said as they passed. "Are you talking about Geoffrey?"

They turned to address her question, positioning her back to their office door.

"Yes," Tamar replied, sweeping a hand through her hair as the dolly nosed its way into the hall. "We knew he was only on loan, but we had hoped he would be able to stay longer."

"I hoped he would be here longer too," Irene returned softly as McCann puffed his way out of the office. "He's such a sweet guy."

"Very easy to work with," Hale said lamely as he tried to think of something pertinent to add.

"Say," Irene said, inadvertently reviving the dying conversation. "I saw you two running full speed down the hallway yesterday. Was everything okay?"

They saw the muscles standing out on McCann's arms as he turned the corner to the service lift, and their minds immediately shifted to their efforts to save Helen's life.

"We were racing," Tamar replied smugly. "And I won."

"You cheated," Hale replied, following her lead.

"I did not. You're just a sore loser," Tamar said, giving Irene a little wave as they turned to continue on their way. "See you later."

"You tripped me," Hale returned, giving Irene a departing nod.

"There were no rules," Tamar said, giving Hale a little shove.

"Everyone knows you can't trip someone in a race. It's an unwritten rule," he replied, pushing her back.

Irene watched the argument progress down the hallway when suddenly both began to gain speed, jostling and shoving one another in an effort to reach the stairs first. Irene shook her head, completely baffled by the competition, then returned to her office as they disappeared into the stairwell. Reaching the ground floor, still jockeying for position and out of breath, Curly stopped dead in his tracks and blocked Tamar from the exit as he heard a long, loud wolf whistle echoing off the steep walls of the alley.

"Trouble," Hale told Tamar as he unholstered his weapon and eased the exit door open. They could hear the conversation taking place by the service entrance down the alley.

"Now Kaori darlin' you're looking mighty fine tonight, *mighty fine*," McCann said as he casually leaned up against the truck he had surreptitiously borrowed earlier in the evening. His demeanor was relaxed; however, he was acutely aware that Hale and Tamar were on their way and was hoping they would show while he drew out a conversation with Hayakawa's lovely personal assistant. "But I'm sure we could have a lot more fun if you'd ditch these two blokes, and it was just you and me."

He looked with interest at Kaori's two bodyguards and wondered just how good they might be if it came down to a fight. They were well-armed and clearly not Japanese. From the smell of them, he was fairly certain he was having his first face-to-face monkey encounter.

"My boss wants to know where his property is. We know you found the German," she responded as her pistol remained leveled at his chest and she ignored his primitive advances.

"Oh, now, lassie, I told you the truth. We found a German for sure, just not your German. We still be looking for Bergmann now. You tell Hayakawa we'll sure enough return his property as soon as we find that dirty little Kraut."

Kaori's eyes narrowed in disbelief. "We gave you good intel and you give us nothing. Why should I trust you?"

"U.S. Army green runs through these veins. Nobody truer on earth."

"Hah," she returned, spitting on the ground in front of McCann. "You bomb my people, then expect us to be grateful that you have invaded our country. You Americans are disgusting."

"Oh, I see. So, now you want to discuss the little matter of who bombed Pearl Harbor without provocation to start the whole war?"

"Shut up! I'm tired of hearing your lies. Mr. Hayakawa expects payment, and he always gets paid. What's in the box?" she asked, motioning to the dolly.

"How the hell should I know?" McCann returned with a shrug. "My boss says move it; I move it. That's all I need to know."

"You," she said to the Shalanaya hit men accompanying her. "Get it in the truck."

The two men obediently lowered their weapons and went to do as they were told. The mystery box was wheeled to the rear of the vehicle and hefted, dolly and all, into the back of the truck. McCann watched the process without a hint of concern.

"I appreciate the assist darlin', but I got this," he said as he pulled keys from his pocket and turned to go. "Good seeing you again lassie, but I gotta be on my way or my boss will give me hell for being late."

Kaori motioned to one of her compatriots to retrieve the keys as she ordered McCann to stop. "You won't be going anywhere tonight, Irishman. This is ours now. My employer says thank you for the down payment."

She smiled in triumph as one of the Shalanaya snatched the keys from McCann's hand and hopped in the front seat, while the other secured the tailgate in the rear. Her smug smile faded into fury as the truck engine failed to turn over.

"What's wrong with it?" she raged, catching a glimpse of McCann's knowing smile. She drew her weapon up tensely while the driver hopped down and went to open the hood. "What did you do?"

A knife was at Kaori's throat before she was even aware of Tamar's presence.

"Lower your weapon," Tamar whispered in her ear while the rear guard froze, not knowing how to respond. "Now!" she demanded at Kaori's hesitation.

Kaori's hand slowly dropped to her side, unwillingly pointing the pistol toward the ground as McCann broke into a grin. "It be good to see you, sis. Lookin' at meetin' my Maker there for a minute I was," he said jovially. "Where's the Major?" At the sound of a body thudding to the ground at the front of the truck he said, "Oh, there he is."

The distraction of Hale's appearance was all the encouragement the remaining Shalanaya needed to quickly raise his weapon and let loose a barrage of bullets. All three hit the ground with Tamar, trying to pull her captive down with her, but Kaori wrenched herself away and was left standing over them, the victor.

"No, no, no…" Kaori admonished as she wagged a finger at McCann and Hale when they reached for their side arms. "Do you want your girlfriend to live?"

They carefully eased their hands away from their weapons.

"Two fingers, remove them with two fingers and toss them over here to me."

"You're bleeding," Hale said conversationally while both men stood and gently tossed their weapons five feet short of her position.

"That's because the bitch cut me!" she spat, as she swiped at a trickle of blood flowing down her throat.

"No," Hale said, pointing to her arm. "Your friend over there shot you."

She looked at Hale with suspicion but chanced a glance at her arm, only to see blood flowing from where she'd been grazed. "Damn," she said, moving her weapon from one hand to the other. "It's a good thing I am equally deadly with either hand, yes? Now fix the truck or she dies."

McCann held his hands up in surrender. "No tricks, lassie. Just take it easy," he said as he slowly bent to reach under the driver's seat.

"You removed the distributor cap?" Hale said with amusement as the missing part was extracted.

"Of course," McCann returned with a snort. "I didn't want someone to steal my stolen vehicle while I was upstairs."

"Shut up and fix it!" Kaori demanded, as her head suddenly twitched to the side and her weapon involuntarily jerked away from her captive.

"The same ammo that shot Helen?" Tamar asked Hale as she realized that their strategic position may have just shifted dramatically.

"When you dance with the devil, you may be the one to get burned," Hale returned, knowing that it was already too late to save Kaori from the poison now coursing through her veins.

Suddenly her eyes rolled back in her head, and she fell stiffly to the ground. Her body convulsed as her weapon lay useless beside her. Hale and McCann dove for their weapons when two shots reverberated off the walls. They snatched their guns from the dust and rolled to one side just in time to see the glassy-eyed stare of the Shalanaya gunman before his body joined Kaori face down in the filth of the alley.

Tamar grabbed Kaori's weapon and scooted up against the wall while Hale and McCann slid to the protection of the armored truck as they waited for the newest player in the game to reveal themself.

"One flying monkey down," was heard yelled from the shadows.

Hale cocked his head in bemusement and said, "Geoffrey?"

"One and the same," he responded, stepping into the light. "So don't shoot me."

They rose from the dirt, all smiles.

"Good timing, mate," McCann said as he checked the down combatant for a pulse and removed his weapon.

"I did shoot him in the back, so it wasn't very sporting of me I'm afraid," he replied.

"Well, in your defense, his back was to you," McCann replied.

"It was him or us," Hale said grimly. "I'm glad you chose us."

"Not that I'm not grateful, but what on earth are you doing here?" Tamar asked.

"Funny that," Geoffrey explained. He held up a sexy silk stocking and said, "Miss Irene somehow managed to put one of her stockings in my jacket pocket. I just discovered it and thought I had better bring it back to her. She can't be going around with just one stocking, now can she?"

"So, *Irene* put the stocking in your pocket," Hale said with a small smile.

"Well, of course, old man, you don't think I would snatch it along with her white cotton knickers, do you? What kind of British officer do you take me for?"

CHAPTER 49

"So, you briefed Begin?" Quinn asked tersely.

"Of course," Yazzie replied. "I may be working with you Americans for now, however, I must eventually go home to Menachem. I would be foolish to provoke his distrust by my failure to communicate."

Quinn sighed in resignation, knowing that what was done was done. However, he had to ponder the wisdom of releasing information this sensitive, even to an ally. How would this affect their course of action? Of course, he had to admit that if he were in Yazzie's position, he would probably do the same thing.

"I assure you, Colonel, I told them nothing they didn't already discover on their own. If you remember, the Irgun were the ones to tell *us* of the sudden uptick in the availability of rare earth metals such as titanium and uranium."

"And you gave them some of the samples you and Mac retrieved from the island," Quinn stated with displeasure. "You do realize that the United States has no formal relations with Palestine or Mr. Begin. I'm not sure President Truman would be at all pleased to know that we are sharing information with an organization outlawed by our closest ally."

"I am aware. No offense, but you did have three operatives working undetected in your War Department," Yazzie reminded Quinn without accusation. "Who's to say if they also have access to your laboratories? Two independent tests are better than one, yes?"

Quinn sighed. "Perhaps, but if the testing were to pique your countrymen's curiosity, it could get them killed. After all, they don't really know who they're up against."

"A fact I am keenly aware of," Yazzie admitted. "This is why I reported that the United States is currently running an operation in Tokyo that should be avoided at all costs lest it be discovered by the enemy. I assured Menachem I would relate his offered assistance."

"And he was good with that?"

Yazzie shrugged. "It is of little importance whether he is satisfied or not, eh? What can he do? But I would warn you that his patience will not last forever."

"I can certainly believe that," Quinn muttered under his breath. "On the other hand, he has more than enough on his plate in Palestine. An operation on the other side of the world should be of minor interest to him."

"You do not understand Menachem Begin. He sees the whole world as a possible threat to his people. An operation anywhere in the world may have an impact on the Jews in Palestine as far as he is concerned. He will take nothing for granted."

"I may have underestimated him," Quinn admitted. "He may have a more complex worldview than I had been led to believe."

"He has been underestimated by the British for quite some time now. It has always worked in his favor," Yazzie noted with a coy smile.

"Indeed," Quinn agreed. After shuffling a few papers on his desk while attempting to organize his thoughts concerning the remainder of his morning, he continued. "I was surprised to see you, Yazzie. Usually, Helen is assigned this task."

Yazzie restrained a smile as he remembered Mac showing up at his door this morning clean-shaven and smelling of aftershave. He was all geniality during their briefing and was impatient to be off with his lady on their 'date'. No doubt Helen had reminded him that there were times when war needed to be put on hold while romancing one's adoring wife.

"They had other business to attend to today. I'm certain Helen will be back with you soon, Colonel. I will do my best to fill her shoes," Yazzie replied.

Quinn waited to see if any further information was to be offered concerning their whereabouts. When the immutable Jew remained mum, Quinn grunted an unintelligible comment, then continued. "So, how is she doing? The whole episode had to be quite a trauma for a lady."

"She's doing surprisingly well, actually," Yazzie responded. "She seems oddly pleased to be a part of the team rather than sitting at home waiting for news even if it means getting shot."

"And the team, I understand they were informed of the genuine situation. How are they?"

"Shaken, certainly," Yazzie replied thoughtfully. "Especially Major Hale. Moving inter-dimensionally unexpectedly is unnerving enough, but when you were unaware that such things are even possible it can cause you to question reality as you know it."

"Is he fit for duty?" Quinn asked with concern. "Things seem to be escalating and I won't leave him in a compromised position if he needs time to deal with recent events."

Yazzie shifted in his chair as he considered the question. "Actually, the truth seems to have answered a lot of questions for him. His understanding of the required change in our strategy and our position militarily seems to exceed that of the others. While the method of learning our secret was unfortunate, he has dealt with the truth of it extraordinarily well. They all have."

Quinn paused to consider Yazzie's assessment for a moment before continuing. "So, the Enigma and SIGABA machines were delivered to Colonel Smith without issue?"

"They were delivered but not without issue. An attempted theft of one device was dealt with appropriately by Major Hale and the others. Colonel Smith is delighted to have Farnsworth back under his command and is equally happy with the additional equipment."

"Was Smith briefed on the situation?"

"As much as was possible. However, I would be remiss not to mention that he certainly knows the information provided was incomplete. He is a man given to solving puzzles after all."

"Farnsworth understands that this is very restricted knowledge, correct? He knows not to confide any privileged information to his commanding officer or anyone else?" Quinn asked.

"Of course," Yazzie answered. At Quinn's look of uncertainty, he continued. "You forget that Captain Farnsworth is a man privy to the secrets of many nations. His unassuming personality causes people to underestimate his fortitude and resolve. It can be of great benefit to have your enemy underestimate you but most unfortunate for your superiors to do the same."

"Yes, I suppose that's true. Well, if that's all, there is other business I must attend to," Quinn stated, as he rose from his chair.

"You are going to interrogate the captured alien then, yes?" At Quinn's look of surprise, Yazzie confessed that Helen had apprized Mac and himself of the good news that very morning. At last, they had one still breathing that could be questioned.

Yazzie motioned Quinn back into his chair. "Then there is something that may be beneficial for you to know before you begin. Helen and Colonel Smith quite cleverly constructed a signal if he had something of import to relay; he was to return her lost spectacles. He triggered the signal on the day she was shot. In all the fuss their meeting was delayed."

"I imagine so," Quinn said, impatient to be in the interrogation room with the new prisoner.

"Lieutenant Commander Fujita went to speak with Smith in her stead. It seems the Colonel found something suspect in the tapes from the tunnels."

This news got Quinn's immediate attention. "They were able to decipher the alien language already?"

"No. I'm afraid that would be expecting too much. No, it was not what was said in their language, but in *ours*. In English."

"My people listened to those tapes several times and didn't pick up on anything. What exactly does he think he heard?" Quinn asked with a furrowed brow.

"A single word, actually…fault," Yazzie answered. "You see, his team had intercepted several messages from the Soviets that were simply a string of numbers. When he heard a voice on the tapes laughing about how it was 'nobody's fault' something clicked. He verified his hunch and found that the numbers correspond to the latitude and longitude coordinates of three known fault lines in the United States; the San Andreas which runs up the west coast, the New Madrid which runs from Texas up the middle of the country, and the Ramapo Seismic Zone on the east coast."

Quinn leaned back in his chair. "What exactly does he think it means?"

"He wasn't certain but let me ask you a question. Can you imagine a better way to disable and immobilize the United States than to initiate three catastrophic eruptions simultaneously?" Yazzie queried with a cock of his head. "There wouldn't be a single area in the nation that wasn't affected. All resources, including finances and manpower, would be pulled home to deal with the aftermath. In addition, you would be hard-pressed to protect yourself against your enemies let alone assist other nations in their recovery efforts."

The magnitude of this scenario was reflected in the grim look on Quinn's face. "Do they have the capability to do this?"

"Fujita reported that a beam of light from one of their flying crafts cut his submarine in half during the war as he watched. This was how he and his men came to be stranded on the island. Only immense heat could do that. Imagine that kind of heat being shot directly into a fault line for a time, building up pressure. If this is their plan, we have surmised only one reason for their delay. The Pacific continental plate lying under the San Andreas extends, in God's divine wisdom, all the way to the Marianas Trench."

Quinn thought about this momentarily. The idea of protecting one's vulnerability immediately sprang to mind. In war, you should always be aware of your greatest assets and strive to shelter and protect them as much as possible. If these aliens had the same mentality, they would strive to protect their greatest resource as well. "Their mining operation could be affected," he stated flatly.

Yazzie nodded in agreement before continuing to his next point. "Truman's new doctrine establishing the U.S. as willing to provide political, military, and economic assistance to all democratic nations under threat from external or internal authoritarian forces has set the communists back on their heels a bit. According to my Irgun contacts, Stalin believes the rumors that Truman issued ultimatums to both France and Italy that if they did not move against the rise of communism in their nations, all financial assistance would be terminated, and he is furious."

"Yes, we've heard the same about Stalin from our sources also," Quinn stated, without confirming or denying the truth of those rumors. "So, you're suggesting that the intercepted coordinates may indicate a plan to attack and weaken America so severely that we are removed from the recovery of European nations. We are decimated and the rest of the world falls into chaos, leaving Stalin free to move in and take over while the aliens continue their mining operations without interruption."

"That would be our consensus, yes."

Quinn took in Yazzie's comments and pondered the ramifications if his information was correct. The very thought made his gut wrench. America would be in shambles and the rest of the world would inevitably fall to the communists. It all seemed like a precursor to Armageddon. In fact, in Quinn's mind, it sounded worse than Armageddon.

"How reliable do you consider Fujita's account of events? He suffered great trauma during the war and some records allude to him having a nervous breakdown. Could his memory be faulty?"

"It is possible, of course," Yazzie admitted. "However, we have found him to be of sound mind. Everything he told us has been true thus far."

"Damn," Quinn muttered in resignation. "I was hoping you would say he was completely unstable."

"Perhaps the captured alien will be able to confirm or deny our suppositions," Yazzie offered. "Where was he captured? It is a Shalanaya, yes?"

"Yes. He was taken into custody as he exited the tunnel system under the White House. He didn't resist, which is suspicious in and of itself," Quinn said with a frown. "He swears he is working on behalf of his ruler. He was sent to undermine the work of the Anakim here on earth. It's all very bizarre and frankly, I am having a difficult time rationalizing all this, even with what Mac displayed to us in the Oval Office. We've had him under continuous observation and have moved him several times, but who knows if they have a way to track his whereabouts that's beyond our ken."

"Has he said anything else?"

"Oh, apparently he's quite the talker, according to my men. He says he is a member of the royal high court of Shalna and has been asking to speak to the royalty of this nation. He insists that he must report back to his Queen, whoever that is. He says he and the queen are doing their best to avoid any conflict with the earth. They want to put a stop to what the Anakim have been doing here for a couple of hundred years."

"Interesting," Yazzie replied. "Could it be true, do you think?"

"I don't know. I've been trying to figure out how to interrogate a creature not of this world all morning," Quinn admitted. "Would you possibly have time to sit in with me? Perhaps your time with the Greys would be of benefit in this instance."

"Well," Yazzie responded, as he stood up. "It took you long enough to ask. What are we waiting for?"

CHAPTER 50

The interrogation room was chilly and brightly lit with overhead fluorescent lighting. The walls were devoid of any décor, with only the requisite large, one-way mirrored window and the door breaking the continuity of the four walls.

Quinn was sitting with his folded hands resting comfortably on the steel table where he was seated. Yazzie stood serenely in the corner, waiting for the entrance of their captive.

"My apologies for not bowing at my entrance, good sirs. My current restraints prohibit me from moving freely. Your most capable sentries have informed me that it will not be taken as an offense on your planet," the Shalanaya prisoner said with a slight dip of his head.

"No offense taken," Yazzie replied with a slight inclination of his head as he silently sized up the creature they had come to know as an enemy.

His face was smooth and flat without a single wrinkle or distinguishing mark, giving him the appearance of a department store mannequin. His hair was fair and wispy, like a young child's and the eyes were a translucent gray. The only spark of color about him was a gold tattoo of what appeared to be an official seal on the top of his right hand.

The guard pulled out the chair directly across from Quinn, causing the sound of the scraping against the concrete floors to echo off the walls of the deliberately bare room. He then unceremoniously pushed the prisoner into the seat.

"I am Mordecai, emissary of her royal highness, the beloved Queen Jehosheba the First, ruler of the planet Shalna. It is imperative that I speak with your high leader as soon as possible," the captive began without prompting.

"Well, there's no way in hell that's happening," Quinn replied with a slight smile as he settled back in his chair.

Mordecai looked taken aback momentarily, then humbly bowed his head. "You have my profuse apologies, sir. I was severely inappropriate to make such demands. I will take whatever punishment you deem necessary without complaint, as I have shamed my Queen and my people. I beg you not to hold my impertinence against my most beloved Queen."

Mordecai's head remained bowed as Quinn's eyebrows drew together in consternation and he muttered, "What the hell?"

"I do believe he's waiting for your pronouncement of judgment," Yazzie said from the corner with a smile. This was going to be one of the more interesting interrogations he had ever witnessed.

The emissary remained in that submissive position as Yazzie continued. "You may raise your head on one condition – you must tell us why you are here. If you lie, we will most certainly hold your Queen responsible."

Quinn shot a look back at Yazzie when Mordecai remained motionless. "Perhaps because you were the one offended, you must be the one to release him," Yazzie surmised with a shrug.

"Raise your head and answer the question," Quinn responded roughly.

"It is with great eagerness I comply," Mordecai answered as he raised his head to look at Quinn again. "For I have been sent with a message to your high leader. The illustrious Queen Jehosheba wishes you to know that we are not allies of the Anakim. We are an enslaved nation, as you will also be if they are not stopped. My Queen pledges to assist you in your resistance in any way within her power."

"Why would she do that?" Quinn asked. "Why not use her power to free her own people?"

"Alas, our resistance came too late. It was believed that diplomacy could resolve our differences, that a covenant could be established so we could live side-by-side in peace," Mordecai said with genuine regret. "But they are dishonorable covenant breakers with evil intent and not to be trusted. My Queen hopes that our sacrificial assistance in your battle may cause the Most High God to show great mercy on Shalna and help us in our struggle for freedom."

"How long has your planet been under Anakim control?" Yazzie asked quietly from the corner, feeling a certain connection to a people struggling to regain their status as a sovereign nation.

"Four hundred cycles now," he returned sadly. "There have been many battles in that time, but all to no avail. We continue as an enslaved nation, causing some of our subjects to lose hope. It is much to our shame that some have willingly rejected their Queen and now assist the Anakim of their own volition."

"And you expect us to just believe you?" Quinn asked unsympathetically. "Let me tell you something Mordecai, I don't give squat about any planet other than the one I'm on. This nation, this planet, is what I'm dedicated to protecting. How do we know you are even telling the truth?"

Mordecai nodded his head in approval. "You are an honorable man. You care about your people and would lay down your life to protect them. You need not confirm my assertion for I know it to be true, for I am as you are. I am here to protect and serve my Queen and my people. I understand that you have it within your power to end my life and I also understand that if you don't end me, the Anakim most certainly will."

"Why do it then?"

"For honor, of course. I have dedicated my life to my Queen and will most joyfully release my life in exchange for hers," Mordecai said with a lift of his chin as if it were an understood truth. He then sighed, and his body sagged as his pronouncement of unwavering devotion ended. "The Anakim have until now allowed my Queen to live unharmed. She remains on the throne to mollify the masses and give them false hope of freedom one day. However, I greatly fear that her days of security grow short. If the Anakim no longer need our females to breed, it is quite possible that they will abandon Shalna after its destruction as they have done to so many other planets before us. So, you see, it is absolutely imperative that I do everything in my power to protect my Queen and my people – even if it means my life. I will trust the Great God of heaven to receive my spirit into his eternal presence."

Quinn sat frozen in place momentarily as Mordecai's words ushered a horrible new possibility to light. "What do you mean *if they no longer need your females to breed?*"

The emissary looked at Quinn, then at Yazzie with some puzzlement. "Surely you understand that the Anakim are a dying race. They are sterile so require other races to propagate their species. Shalanaya females have been found in the last 200 cycles to produce an inferior generation. Anakim produced by human women have been found to be far superior. Their breeding has brought relief to the Anakim. They believe their progeny dilemma is solved. That should be good news for Shalna, but the reality is if they can depend upon human females for procreation, they have no further need of Shalna or its people. We are dispensable. They will proceed with the conquest of earth."

Quinn's stunned silence caused Yazzie to approach the table. "We were under the impression that they were strictly interested in this planet's natural resources."

"Yes," Mordecai responded, "of which human females are a part."

"And when did the Anakim conclude that they can just conquer earth without a 'by your leave' to the inhabitants of this planet?" Quinn asked angrily. "What makes them think they can just waltz in here and take over?"

"Perhaps," Mordecai responded, not understanding the nature of a rhetorical question, "it is because they have succeeded so many times before."

Quinn motioned Yazzie to sit beside him as his mind reeled at this new revelation. He needed time to process the possible repercussions if this were true, so he abruptly changed the course of the interview. "Why did the Anakim send you here?"

"They have not been able to communicate with this location for some time. As it is a vital link in their communications stream, its lack of function has affected their ability to connect. A human asset was sent but deemed unreliable, so they sent me believing me expendable should I be apprehended," Mordecai responded.

"Why would they trust you? If they know your loyalties lie elsewhere, why would your word mean any more than the human asset?" Quinn asked.

"Because they know I would never endanger my Queen. If I try to deceive them in any way, the great Queen Jehosheba will pay the price for my deception. What they would do to her before allowing her to die is beyond horrifying. And I have no doubt they would do it publicly to demoralize the people of the realm."

"So, they just sent you here alone - with no oversight?" Quinn responded, his voice dripping with doubt.

"No, I was to report to the commander of this area, a human whose name is The Second. It was he who gave me a key to the tunnel system and sent me to inspect it. I was to report back to him my findings in seven days' time, tonight if my calculations are correct."

Both Yazzie and Quinn had to wonder if this was simply a ploy on Mordecai's part to gain release. However, he had given them an answer to something they had been investigating themselves. Miss June Watts, the human female Quinn's men had been tailing ever since she tripped the sensors in the tunnel, had indeed reported back to her superior in the Anakim terrorist cell. None other than Randall Smithers *the second*.

"May I be so bold as to ask, if it would cause no offense, the fire in their headquarters…was it an accident?" Mordecai asked timidly.

Quinn considered his response, then casually leaned back in his chair and replied, "Oh, hell no. We torched the place after killing those in residence."

"You were able to overcome the Anakim?" Mordecai asked with awe.

"Oh yeah. Killed a couple of Shalanaya as well," Quinn deliberately added to test his response.

Mordecai straightened in his seat and then returned solemnly. "If they were stationed here they were greatly trusted by the enemy. Traitors to their people and the great and honorable Queen Jehosheba. I consider them justly executed for their crimes. Thank you for your service to Shalna and her beloved Queen."

"We would return their bodies to you; however, they have been found to decay very rapidly here," Yazzie inserted diplomatically.

"Oh, I am not surprised," Mordecai responded. "Though you have much water on your planet, your air is very, very dry. The Shalanaya require much moisture to remain healthy. During periods of drought our bodies produce a lubricant to survive – perhaps you've noticed the aromatic scent?" At their affirmative nods, he continued. "If the duration of arid conditions continue long enough, a Shalanaya will most certainly suffer adverse effects."

Though the use of the term 'aromatic' to describe the musky stink of the Shalanaya seemed questionable, Quinn decided to let it go. "What do you know of the Anakim's plans for the earth?"

"They, of course, do not share their strategies with me. However, I can tell you their intentions at this point are not that of wanton destruction. That will come when they are finished with you. This does not mean they are above targeted destruction. Two most honorable Shalanaya tribes ceased to exist when the Anakim destroyed an entire Shalna island territory. They left not a single one alive to continue their lineage, then brutally displayed horrific trophies to the Queen to assure her future cooperation."

"Who are the Anakim, and how did they come to be on your planet?" Yazzie asked.

"For you to understand I must share a little of our history if I may." At Quinn's assent, Mordecai continued. "Our planet had been without war for many generations, causing us to become arrogant in our belief that we had become far too civilized to engage in any such monstrosities again. We grew so complacent and full of pride that when several Anakim came posing as ambassadors claiming to be descendants of a Shalna tribe sent to a distant planet during the war years we accepted them."

Mordecai bowed his head for a moment at the memory of that first meeting. Their claims that they had been horribly disfigured by the atmosphere of the hostile planet to which they had been sent. How they asserted the planet was dying and that their tribe would most certainly perish altogether were they not allowed to return home. All their pledges of peace and friendship in exchange for a return to the place of their origin.

"You see, they had a ready answer for each of our questions and appeared pitiable and worthy of our compassion. After all, they had suffered so after courageously leaving all that was familiar to assure the continuance of our kind should the war claim our entire race. By the time we realized the peaceful coexistence the Anakim had purported was a sham, and their intent had always been to take control, it was too late to stop them. They had infiltrated every level of government and industry. It was not long before their act of civility was abandoned altogether and replaced with fear, intimidation, and brute force."

An involuntary groan made its way up from his diaphragm, and Mordecai let out what sounded like a primal growl. "Each resistance brought new punishments," he said in anguish. "A virus that killed thousands of Shalanaya in a brutally slow manner was released, Shalna's stability was shaken, her majesty the honorable Queen Jehosheba's family was brutalized…"

"Whoa, wait, what do you mean Shalna's stability was shaken?" Quinn asked intensely.

Mordecai's tone was grim at the remembrance. "The very terrain beneath our feet moved violently creating great crevices. Entire cities were swallowed up; death and destruction were everywhere. A great canyon remains to this day extending from the palace gardens visible from my Queen's living quarters to the mountains of Edad as a solemn reminder to never defy them again."

Quinn and Yazzie exchanged glances as Mordecai described with precision the effects of an earthquake. Knowing that they had not mentioned the suspicions stirred by the interception of the fault line coordinates from the Soviets gave his testimony greater weight. And it caused them to lose any hope of their hypothesis being incorrect.

"But we have no choice, don't you see?" he asked passionately. "We must resist regardless the consequences. Our very hearts are breaking to be free once more… at any cost."

CHAPTER 51

"So, Miss Watts is being tailed by Hoover's men now, Master Sergeant?" Colonel Quinn asked.

Mumford smiled as he looked straight ahead. "Worked like a charm, sir. I drank a little, then I drank a lot and started shooting my mouth off about the cute little Commie I was assigned to tail. Case said I could have been an actor, sir, if it weren't for the fact that I love breaking heads so much."

"I'm sure. But did they buy it?"

"Oh, yes, sir. Hoover's dog boy was so smug when he told me I'd been relieved of my assignment because I couldn't hold my liquor he actually giggled. A disgusting display I'll treasure all my life, Colonel."

The men in the room laughed.

"She doesn't seem to be a major player anyway, sir," Mumford continued. "Mostly delivers messages from Smithers the second to his son. There's no indication that sonny boy knows his father is running the show. She's made multiple contacts with a couple of other people on the government payroll, but it's unclear if they are traitors or not. Their names are in my report."

"Okay, let them go for now. Hoover will check them out for us, I'm sure. What about Mordecai? Did he stay on plan?" Quinn asked.

"Yes sir. The little man is as strange as a three-legged duck, but he's got guts. Met with the elder Smithers, then followed the route we gave him to the letter after he was cut loose. He deliberately knocked Case down on the street and whispered 'new assignment' as he apologized about fifteen times while helping him to his feet. We'll keep our distance for two days as planned unless our orders are changed."

Quinn looked at President Truman for confirmation.

"Stay on plan but keep watch to ensure his safety. Intervene if he's in danger," Truman responded as he rubbed his chin thoughtfully. At Mumford's nod of acknowledgement, he continued. "I'll let you get back to it if that's all, Master Sergeant."

"Yes sir. Thank you sir," he returned smartly as he saluted the Commander-in-Chief then quietly left the room.

Those in attendance remained silent as the door clicked closed behind Mumford. Each of them had been in battle. Each of them had been in command and responsible for the lives of others serving under them. And each of them had at one time or another led those souls into battle, knowing they might not return. But this was different – sending was always different than leading. And each of them felt unreasonable pangs of cowardice and guilt for expecting this very capable soldier to go and face the enemy without them.

President Truman stood to pace the Oval Office in agitation at Mumford's exit. "So let me run through this again, gentlemen. This Mordecai is an alien, from an undiscovered planet named Shalna located outside our galaxy. He is here claiming to be an ally of earth and desiring to assist us in the destruction of the Anakim, who are a present danger to this planet, and who also currently enslave his planet. Is that about it?"

"Yes, Mr. President. He says the Queen of his people wishes an alliance with earth although he has been honest enough to admit some of his people have been collaborating with the Anakim both on their home planet and here as well."

"Similar to collaborators in Europe during the Second War," Truman reasoned. "And he says the Anakim have been working behind the scenes here on earth for what, a couple hundred years or more?"

"That's what he told me," Colonel Quinn provided. "He confirmed our suspicions that their intentions have currently shifted from simply stripping us of our natural resources to world domination. That's why they have been working with the likes of the Nazis and Japanese, encouraging them to start wars. But we inadvertently disrupted their plans by defeating the Germans."

"That, and destroying their headquarters at Hiroshima," Mac added for emphasis.

"How inhospitable of me," Truman said absently. "And now, we're being told that they have concocted yet another plan to get them back on track. Is that correct?"

"Yes, Mr. President," Quinn replied.

Truman stopped pacing long enough to look carefully at Mac and Quinn. He sighed heavily as he wondered just how trustworthy this Mordecai was, and then strode back to his desk. He sat heavily in his comfortable chair and leaned back to further study the two men facing him.

"You do know this sounds like the bottom half of a double feature at the Bijou, don't you? There is no way the American public will believe there are aliens walking undetected among us here on earth. That's just outside the realm of intelligent thought, gentlemen. Hell, I've seen them personally right here in this office and still have a hard time believing they exist."

Mac and Quinn studied the shine on their shoes intently, knowing that the President's observations were dead on. They had both dealt with the unmitigated disbelief of seasoned soldiers when they were told the truth. How could the public be expected to digest all of this?

"How can I possibly get the American people on board with this? To believe in something they have never seen for themselves. How do I convince them that we must enter another war, with aliens no less, and risk losing yet more American lives?"

"Don't tell them anything," Quinn interjected. "Mac and I both agree 100% with your observations, sir. The public simply could not comprehend anything like this. That's why this war should be fought covertly. If we win, the public never has to know."

"Lie to the American people? That goes against every instinct and principle I hold dear! I don't want to become known as another one of those lying, hypocritical politicians! Wasn't I the one who said, if you can't stand the heat, get out of the kitchen?"

"While you were still a Senator, yes sir," Quinn acknowledged.

"No doubt about it. Completely covert would be the best way to go, Mr. President," Mac emphasized. "But as you know, the likelihood of information being leaked is always there. Should that happen confusion and distrust fueled by the ever headline-hungry media could affect the integrity of this office. So perhaps there is an acceptable alternative."

Truman watched Mac and Quinn without comment and waited for an explanation.

"Blame the Russians, sir," Quinn said bluntly. "Everyone in this country has already seen what Stalin has planned for eastern Europe. His subjugation of the people in Berlin, Hungary, Czechoslovakia, Romania, all point to communist domination."

"We just say that our efforts are aimed at preventing further Russian dominance," Mac added. "No one will dare disagree with whatever needs to be done to stop Stalin and his henchmen. The public saw what happened when we ignored Hitler. We would be letting everyone know that the United States will not be manipulated or coerced by any communist regime."

"So, we would sweep our efforts against the Anakim into the fight against communist aggression," the President mulled over to himself. "That might work. God knows we have enough problems with those Russkies, anyway. It won't be hard to convince people that we must act strategically to stop their insidious advance around the globe."

"And the Russians are genuinely involved in this anyway," Quinn proffered. "Mordecai only confirmed what our Communications Division in Tokyo had already told us. Russia is without a doubt a part of this. Intercepted intelligence highly suggests that the Anakim are already working with them. Apparently, they were making inroads to Stalin's inner circle even before Hitler's failure. We are confident that a new Anakim communications station has already been established in Moscow to replace the ones lost in Berlin and Hiroshima in the war."

"Are you telling me that Stalin is actively seeking alien help to take over the world?" Truman asked.

"I wouldn't put it past him, sir. He just doesn't understand that the Anakim have no intention of keeping their pact with him any more than Hitler did," Mac added.

"Operation Barbarossa," Truman reminisced. "Hitler launched a surprise attack on Russia despite the agreement he had signed with them regarding the dispersion of European nations after they had been conquered. After the Russians were no longer of use in the war effort, he decided all of Europe should be his. So, he reneged on his agreement with Stalin and tried to take him out as well."

"Well, they were two peas in the same pod, sir," Mac offered. "Stalin was probably thinking after Hitler suffered all the losses of war in conquering Europe he would step in and take over Germany with all of their new territory. Hitler just happened to pull the trigger first."

"My thoughts as well," Truman agreed. "Now that wily old Stalin thinks he can make a deal with an alien race to conquer the world in the name of communism?"

"To be honest with you, Mr. President, he may be unaware of who he's dealing with."

"How so?"

"The intercepted communiques indicate Stalin has had multiple conversations with those he believes to be wealthy industrialists from America with communist leanings. It's been inferred that they are men of power and position that have access to advanced technologies and scientists. Have you ever heard the saying when it seems too good to be true it usually is? Frankly, the whole thing has a striking resemblance to shell companies the SSU would have used to set someone up," Mac added. "Maybe it's on the up and up but I think it's more likely that Stalin's been duped."

"His ego is such that he probably thinks it doesn't matter who is on the other end of the conversation anyway. As long as the goal is achieved he figures the collaborators can be outmaneuvered and dealt with later just as he dealt with Hitler," Quinn surmised. "Everyone seems to think they are the chess master."

"What does that make us, Colonel?" the President asked earnestly.

Quinn paused momentarily. "The lowly pawn trying to outfox the queen, I guess."

CHAPTER 52

Truman stood and walked to the window overlooking the White House grounds below. A cigarette was retrieved and lit, then placed between his lips. He inhaled deeply and exhaled a billow of smoke before turning back to face Mac and Quinn.

"How much time do we have before the Anakim make a move on America?"

"We believe they have already set their plan in motion, Mr. President," Mac answered quickly. "That's why we're here."

Quinn reached into his briefcase and pulled out a folder filled with paperwork. He slid the hefty file across the desk as Truman returned to his seat.

"That file contains what we know so far, sir," Quinn stated. "It is a combination of our own findings and what we've been told by the two interviewees with firsthand experience of the Anakim — Fujita and the alien. I have interrogated the Shalanya Mordecai extensively and if what he says is true, the aliens already have a plan of attack that will make Pearl Harbor look like a walk in the park."

"Could it be hyperbole, Colonel?" Truman asked grimly, glancing up from the unopened folder lying before him.

"I wish I could say yes, sir. But we have facts gathered by several independent intelligence agencies that support our analysis that his assertions are credible. He was consistent in his rendition of his planet's history with the Anakim, regardless of how many times or in what manner he was asked. He had none of the standard tells that he was lying, however that obviously could be because he isn't human. He seemed eager to provide information regarding the enemy's strengths and weaknesses when questioned and also offered unsolicited information. Yazzie and I were with him for several hours and we both found him to be genuine."

Truman picked up the file and first tested how much it weighed before glancing at the manifest within. He silently thumbed through the documents, his eyes alternately widening and narrowing at the information he read.

"It is probable," Mac began once the folder was set aside, "that they have an extensive underwater complex in the Marianna Trench. We estimate that it has been in operation for several hundred years now."

"That's where the diamonds have been coming from?" Truman asked.

"Yes, diamonds and other rare earth metals the Anakim have mined to utilize for their own purposes. Some have been used to finance their operations here, but primarily they are shipped back to Shalna to support Shalanaya technology and weaponry according to Mordecai."

"It's in this trench that they have hidden at least one aircraft that can fly as well as maneuver underwater," Quinn interjected. "There may be more. Either way, it's something we cannot replicate with our current technology, and according to the alien, it is being armed to perform the first strike. A strike we cannot defend against."

Truman's face went pale as he contemplated the implications of this information. The United States had been bloodied by the Japanese on December 7, 1941 but was able to mount countermeasures leading to eventual victory. But that was under Franklin D. Roosevelt who convinced the American public to believe in the United States and its ability to overcome any enemy. A lot had happened since then.

"From all appearances, sir, this alien race has technology superior to anything we currently have available," Quinn stated. "According to Mordecai, they have developed a weapon that can shoot sound waves like a ray gun. I know it sounds a lot like Flash Gordon, but the weapon was actually used on Shalna and when directed deep into the planet, those sound waves created quakes — massive quakes."

"A series of numbers were intercepted from Russia, sir, that correspond to the coordinates of three major fault lines within this nation," Mac added as he leaned forward in his chair. "If those sound waves can create massive earthquakes without a fault line present, just think what would happen if the weapon was targeted directly into the most unstable part of a fault. Once started, the quake could cascade for miles."

"The loss of lives could be in the millions, Mr. President," Quinn confirmed. "We have calculated that the casualties sustained would be far higher than the projections of allied losses if Japan had not surrendered and we had been forced to invade. That is not hyperbole. That's a fact. The destruction would make what we did at Hiroshima and Nagasaki look like child's play."

"My God. Those projections predicted over one million American lives and over ten million Japanese civilians would be lost. It would have been a mass annihilation of human life," Truman said.

"The loss of life would be devastating, but the damage to infrastructure would be equally so," Mac added. "Communications would be down, food and supply chains disrupted, and medical facilities unable to meet demand. There's more, much more, but you get the idea. With such widespread and catastrophic destruction, would we even be able to defend ourselves? Roads would be impassable, and airstrips destroyed. Utilities would undoubtedly be affected. Without electric, gas, or clean water, our defenses would be so severely limited it is probable that we would be overrun."

The President turned and looked solemnly at the other men in the room. His face bore the agony of a man faced with an impossible decision. But he was the only one who could make the choice and only he would bear the responsibility of the consequences.

"And even if we managed to fend off the aggressors, full recovery would likely take decades," Truman said solemnly.

"Yes, sir," Quinn confirmed. "We have been able to confirm that several recent unusual earthquakes around the world were presumed to be caused by an outside force like a sound wave. It is now believed that these incidents were trial runs prior to their actual attack here. The sound wave weapon is aboard their ship, and I simply cannot guarantee that we have the capability of stopping it once it's airborne. We do not have anything that can match the speed and weaponry on that ship."

"Now, Mordecai believes that only one of these weapons exist here on earth," Mac interjected. "So, if the ship is destroyed or incapacitated, then the weapon is not a threat. However, to have a chance of success it is imperative that we incapacitate their ship prior to it becoming airborne."

"I didn't mean to imply that all is lost, sir," Quinn said apologetically. "They do have weaknesses. According to Mordecai, the Anakim being sent to earth are not the cream of the crop. They are here because they are thought to be expendable and have basically been abandoned on earth. Because this isn't a plum assignment and due to the logistics of maintaining control on Shalna while attempting their take over here, they are running on a skeleton crew. They absolutely must have the assistance of humans to succeed."

"This is why the Shalanaya have been vital to their success here. Traitors are far more likely to work with someone who looks like a Shalanaya than someone who looks like the Anakim," Mac said. "If their collaborators knew who they were really working with, I think they would reconsider their alliances immediately. Of course, both the Shalanaya and the Anakim have physical limitations here as well. The scent emitted by the Shalanaya is actually a chemical breakdown of their bodies due to a lack of moisture. Subject them to hot dry conditions for an extended period of time and they will be incapacitated and eventually die. And ironically, even though their base of operations is underwater, the Anakim can't swim. Yazzie, Fujita, and I saw this firsthand on our visit to the island."

"So, how do you suggest we proceed?" the President asked somberly.

"We strike first and hard. There are three main areas of concern: the Marianas Trench, the island and their base there, and their communications center in Moscow," Quinn responded.

"Known key players must also be taken out of play. Perhaps Papa Smithers could develop tax problems that land him in federal custody for a while," Mac suggested with a smile. "My team can deal with Hayakawa. As for the communications center, sabotage would be ideal, but simply keeping the Russians occupied at the time of our attack so they can't rush to assist the Anakim would work. Perhaps our Irgun friends could provide an anonymous distraction for Stalin and his troops?"

"So, our only option seems to be to find a way to destroy this race of beings before they destroy us," the President concluded. "There's a lot riding on this, gentlemen, so here's my question. How do we know the information provided by this Shalanaya Mordecai can be trusted? How do we know this is not a scheme to get us to do the Shalanaya's dirty work? How do we know if he is really a captive of the Anakim? He could be duping us into another war; a war we are not sure we can win."

"I don't believe so, sir," Quinn responded. "My men and I have interrogated the Shalanya extensively. We believe he is telling us the truth. He is too afraid not to."

"Afraid of us?" Truman asked.

"No sir. Once he found out the Greys had enhanced Mac, Helen, and Yazzie's capabilities enabling them to move between dimensions, whatever that means, and gave them who knows what other powers, he was actually greatly encouraged that we stand a chance of winning. He is afraid of the Anakim, for sure, but he is terrified of the Greys, and it shows. He is telling us everything he knows, Mr. President."

"Makes you wonder if we shouldn't be wary of those Greys as well, doesn't it?" he asked rhetorically.

The other two men in the room remained silent as they processed what the President had just said. It wasn't like the thought hadn't already crossed their minds. The Commander-in-Chief had simply said aloud what they all had been thinking. It was yet another issue with aliens that hadn't been discussed to date.

Then Truman went on, "And we're banking on the word of one alien that the world is in jeopardy? That the United States must step in once again to save the day?"

Mac pointed to the folder Quinn had delivered to the President and said, "Not only Mordecai's word, sir. We have information from our intelligence sources and the eyewitness account of the former Japanese naval officer Fujita about the aircraft's capability. How it had no problem taking out his surveillance aircraft as well as his submarine. And that's only one alien craft, sir."

"My God," Truman sighed.

"And with what we have learned from communications intercepted by Major Farnsworth in Tokyo, it confirms the Anakim are preparing a first and massive strike."

"He is the one working with MacArthur's staff?"

"Yes, sir. A fine officer. A brilliant communications analyst."

"We now know where they are. We also have a good idea of what they have to work with. We know what they have done to other alien races and what they plan to do here. There is no question that this is a clear and present danger to the American people — and to the world," Quinn answered forcefully.

"Mr. President, if I may?" Mac asked quietly. At the nod of Truman's head, he continued. "Sir, we must remember that they are not trying to destroy the earth — their intention is to subjugate us, which may be far worse than death. The choice seems clear to me, and I believe to both of you as well. We cannot sit by and allow these creatures to decimate the earth. If we do not act immediately, it may be too late to save ourselves or anyone else."

CHAPTER 53

The building sat near the Chiyoda railway station, located in the once thriving Marunouchi manufacturing district. Even after two years, the area remained a charred reminder of the horrible devastation and loss of life during Operation Meetinghouse carried out in March 1945 by the United States Army Air Forces. The operation that cut Tokyo's production capabilities in half and effectively brought the war to an end two months later.

Proximity to the Emperor's Palace was the only reason this building was still largely intact and able to be commandeered for their purposes. After a hasty refurbishing, it was in use once again. Not by the Japanese government, but by former submarine commander Makoto Fujita and his associates.

The relentless rain beat against the tin roof of the warehouse, forcing the occupants to raise their voices in conversation. "How's it going?" Mac asked, while looking at the stacks of merchandise surrounding him. "Looks like you've been busy."

Yazzie grinned as he wiped the sweat from his face. "Hayakawa isn't going to know what hit him. Kaori's disappearance, along with merchandise stored directly under his warehouse. It's bound to unsettle him a might. So, what's the news from D.C.?"

"It's a go," Mac said, stepping closer and lowering his voice so the news wouldn't echo through the building. "The package is enroute. We have seven days. Where are the girls?"

"We've been working in shifts. They went back to the hotel to catch a few hours of sleep."

"I see a few unfamiliar faces. Irgun?" Mac asked. At Yazzie's affirmative nod, he continued, "Did Menachem have a problem loaning us a few more people?"

"Not once we promised him arms in return," Yazzie said as a worker with crates stacked on a dolly was waved past them. "We are a very practical people. Besides, maybe he expects with more eyes and ears on site he will gain information as well as weapons."

"No doubt. Did you have time to sweep up?" Mac asked cryptically, thinking of the new highly trained operatives now in the building. He hoped that no additional "ears" were found in their office or hotel rooms.

"Hale recruited Farnsworth to assist. They're at it right now. McCann is assisting Fujita. It seems Billy was built for black market trade."

"So, you're sure Hayakawa will know it's his merchandise hitting the circuit?"

"Oh yeah, he'll know. Colonel Smith and Farnsworth have started dropping breadcrumbs in various fictitious phone calls and communiques, suggesting Kaori is going into business for herself," Yazzie responded.

"And can we be certain that Kaori's body will not be discovered?" Mac asked.

Yazzie hesitated a moment before answering. "Oh, they will never find her body. I have a friend who is very knowledgeable about poisons. She was very interested in studying this new one."

At Mac's startled look, he continued. "Don't worry, she is very discreet, and she knows nothing of its origin. Finding an antidote will be her top priority. Besides, I thought Groom Lake could use a little help. Helen said they were concerned about the number of bodies showing up."

"The number of alien bodies or just bodies in general?" Mac asked. "Were they asking questions?"

"No questions, but she could tell they were uneasy. I can't blame them. We've taken, what, a half dozen or more dead aliens to them. They've got to be wondering what's happening topside."

"Groom Lake is one of the most secure facilities in the world. The people working there are aware of the unusual and secretive nature of their work. They won't say anything," Mac assured the practical Jew.

"True but dropping off a human body might just have put them over the edge of reason," Yazzie said as he stepped away to direct the placement of new merchandise.

Mac had to agree that there was a certain logic to what Yazzie said. His mind whirred with the details of the operation ahead. Hayakawa was no push over. He had been involved in the spy game for a couple of decades and they had to assume he would check every detail coming his way before condemning his most trusted employee. Too little proof and he wouldn't buy the ruse, too much and he would smell a rat. They needed him paranoid and unstable, unable to trust anyone. He had to be so involved in pursuing the traitor in his midst that he was unable, or unwilling, to assist his alien allies once their operation started.

"I talked to McCann about spending some time hitting a couple of bars tonight," Yazzie stated when he returned. "He could throw around a little money. You know, buy a few rounds, slap a few backs, get the word out about the new player in the black market. It's risky as Hayakawa would connect him back to us if he found out the source, but he's willing."

"I agree. Too risky at this point. I don't want to put him in that position if we don't have to. Besides, it's our MPs we need to act on this information. They are already watching black market activity. We just need a couple of those crates with a great big USA painted on the side to hit the streets and the Army will get involved. I'm assuming Hayakawa or the Shalanaya have infiltrated or at least have contacts in the military police. The blotter will be one way he'll verify if this is a set up or not. Nothing confiscated goes in or out without being entered on the blotter, and you can bet he knows that. When American wheat shows up, he'll know it only could have come from his storeroom."

"If we do this right, he may even hatch a plan to get his merchandise back," Yazzie agreed. "I wouldn't be surprised if he thinks he can outsmart your military police."

A door clanged shut at the far end of the warehouse, drawing their attention. The two men turned in time to see Hale shaking himself off like a wet dog.

"How's our Captain Farnsworth, Curly?" Mac asked at his approach.

"Mad as hell, but not nearly as mad as Colonel Smith," Hale replied. "We found an interesting item in your room, Yazzie, and a couple more in the Communications Center. Smith is kicking himself for not running a check right after his office was ransacked. You can bet it'll be done regularly from now on."

"Were they removed?" Yazzie asked.

"The one in your room, yes. They are going to feed some false information into the ones in the Comm Center and see where it leads." Hale lowered his voice as he asked, "What's the word from the Oval Office?"

"Green light — seven days." At Hale's expression, Mac continued, "Is there a problem?"

"Don't know for sure, sir, it could be nothing. Farnsworth has been following a conversation out of Russia since he went back to the bunker. Oh, that's what the comm guys affectionately call their offices. Anyway, the two parties have been talking about what's needed to *close the deal*. He said the entire line of inquiry has seemed off, if you know what I mean. That's why he's been tracking it."

"Okay, tell him to stay on it."

"I already did, but here's the thing. The last communique said that the final paperwork will be hand delivered by a courier from Demitre Centre later this week. Farnsworth said the syntax was all wrong and the mention of a company name was odd for a normal conversation. It wouldn't be out of the ordinary, however, if the message was that a courier was coming from D.C."

"Damn," Mac breathed out as he ran his hand over his forehead.

"If it's referring to what we think, our timelines are almost parallel. We'll be cutting it close," Yazzie said.

"Yeah, too close for comfort. Okay, it may be related it might not, but let's keep a close eye on it. Tell Farnsworth to let me know the minute he hears anything else."

"Will do," Hale said as they saw Fujita and McCann's jeep pull into the delivery bay. "Listen, we've been up a solid twenty-four. Okay if McCann and I go hit the rack for a couple of hours?"

"Yeah, no problem. See if Fujita needs a ride too," Magruder instructed. He sighed as Hale walked away and turned to Yazzie. "It's gotta be related…it's just too damn much of a coincidence, isn't it?"

"I would say so, yes," Yazzie responded. "If the Russians are housing an enemy communication center, as we suspect, then it can be assumed that the information coming out of D.C. would be forwarded on to facilitate their attack. The delivery of that information must be stopped."

"If it's coming through Smithers, we may have a chance. But just because he's the only contact we're aware of doesn't necessarily mean he's the only one in play," Mac returned. "Also, any suspected interference on our part may move up their timetable."

Yazzie nodded in agreement as Fujita waved at the departing jeep and started walking their way. His gait displayed his weariness, making the two men wonder what could be so important as to keep him from returning to quarters and a comfortable bed.

"Makoto," Mac said at his approach, "go, get some sleep. We've got this."

"How long have you known Hayakawa has been working side by side with the enemy? How long?" Fujita demanded with a contained fury. "Did you think I would not smell them? That I would not know? Is that how little you respect me?"

Magruder and Yazzie did not quiet or subdue the man until the emotions had ebbed and Fujita fell silent. His eyes were hard, and his breathing labored as he stood defiantly, demanding an answer.

"We did not know until we got to Japan," Mac said. "If the Greys knew, they said nothing to us. It wasn't until our first venture into the tunnels underneath Hayakawa's business that we realized the Shalanaya were working in his warehouse."

"Did he know what was happening on the island? To my men?"

"I don't know. The Greys only told us your name, and that you could confirm the alien presence here on earth. Nothing more."

"We are not even certain Hayakawa has ever seen the Anakim," Yazzie added. "His knowledge of them may rely solely on the personal account of your experiences."

"And yet he continued in partnership with the Shalanaya knowing who they're working with and what they did," Fujita said without a hint of forgiveness in his tone. "That makes him worse than the Anakim and he must pay for his sins."

"His atonement will have to wait," Mac said sternly. "Do you understand me, Fujita? In seven days we're going to bomb the hell out of the Anakim, and we will not hesitate to park your butt in the brig for the next week if you don't guarantee me right here and now that you will not approach or contact Hayakawa during that time."

The stony look and defiant attitude did not seem to wane at Mac's threat.

"Makoto," Yazzie began gently, "there is no doubt in our minds that Hayakawa is guilty of collaborating with the enemies of not only you, your men, and Japan but of the world. So here is the deal — once our operation has taken place, he's all yours. You can do whatever you want, and we will not interfere. Agreed?"

Fujita stood unmoved for several moments, then said, "Fukushū wa watashi no monodesu. Vengeance is mine, for I will surely be God's hand to repay Hayakawa for his betrayal. In eight days, he will see God."

CHAPTER 54

The bell above the door announced the arrival of someone at the front entrance but Benjiro Hayakawa didn't so much as look up from his desk. He was far too important to be expected to stoop to such menial work as greeting a customer and to actually do so never entered his mind. The fact that his assistant was not available to see to the task didn't occur to him. He was a person of reputation and standing that had far more important things to do. Whoever it was would simply have to wait until he was willing to see them, he thought. Then Yazzie strode into his private office and sat without invitation.

"What do you want?" Hayakawa asked gruffly as he returned to shuffling papers on his desk. The deliberate intrusion was an intentional insult he was sure. "I'm busy."

"Is that any way to greet such a valued customer?" Yazzie replied unmoved by his tone or expected convention.

"Very well," he returned with a sigh while pasting on an obviously fake smile. "How can I be of service to you most valued customer?"

Yazzie cocked his head to the side and relaxed back into the chair. "Having a bad day, Admiral? It seems in poor taste to take it out on me after all we've been through together."

Hayakawa snorted out a divisive laugh. "We have been through nothing together, friend. You seem to have imagined a connection where none exists."

"Of course, of course," Yazzie returned with a knowing smile and a wink. "My apologies for making an assumption."

"Where are your American friends? Why are you not with them?"

A look of surprise flitted across Yazzie's face. "I'm not currently spending much time with them seeing that our objective has been met. Our union was only temporary, you see. I will be leaving your nation as soon as our business is concluded."

"Our business?" Hayakawa asked with a touch of humor. "We have done no business together."

"Yes, yes of course. I understand completely," Yazzie returned blandly. "We have no connection at all. However, a recent shipment to my import/export company in America has come up two cases short. An oversight I'm sure, but one that must be corrected."

"You have lost your mind. Go," Hayakawa said irately while pointing to the door. "Leave now. I have no time for your foolish games."

"Don't worry," Yazzie replied unmoved. "Nothing will trace back to you as agreed, but my employers are expecting ten cases not eight. This will need to be made right if you expect to continue doing business with us."

"Ten cases of what?" Hayakawa asked with suspicion.

Yazzie was clearly not amused. "Now who's playing games? I am aware you expressly wished to keep our connection unknown. A desire I would have gladly honored had I received what I paid for. Blame yourself for my intrusion. If you had held up your end of the bargain you never would have seen my face again. Deliver the two missing cases or things will be considerably less friendly next time we meet."

Yazzie stood abruptly and headed for the door. He turned back to see the look of doubt on Hayakawa's face. "If you cannot be trusted to deliver what you promised how can I possibly recommend you to my contacts in Amsterdam?"

"Wait…what?" Hayakawa said as Yazzie reached the door.

"Before you say anything, of course I looked to see what was in the package from Bergmann. I'm not a fool," Yazzie returned without remorse. "And my offer to make introductions was genuine. However, I won't risk my reputation recommending someone unreliable no matter how perfect the stones. Take my advice friend, provide what you promised lest one of my less civilized associates be sent to encourage your compliance."

Yazzie exited the building and dodged his way across traffic. The plan was to duck into an alley before Hayakawa could summon his men to follow him. Once a few winding turns were made he stopped and quieted his breathing. There was no sound save the water rats rummaging for food. It was only then that he relaxed and allowed some of the suppressed tension to release.

"How did it go?" Mac inquired once Yazzie translated into the warehouse.

"Very well, I think," Yazzie replied. "He was confused naturally since not a single event discussed actually happened. He's probably down in his storeroom at this very moment checking inventory."

"Did you mention Kaori?" Hale asked hoping to pick up pointers on deception from an expert.

"No, it would have been disrespectful and unusual to include an underling in our discussion. He would have picked up on the inconsistency immediately. I spoke as if my business had always been directly with him," Yazzie responded.

"Did he believe you?" Hale persisted.

"The idea was never to get him to trust or believe me, only for him to wonder if there was an element of truth in what I said. He knows I could be lying but I told him enough that he'll be forced to verify or disprove my assertions. His perception of Kaori will have changed from one of a missing person to a possible enemy. His inquiries into her disappearance will shift accordingly," Yazzie answered before turning to Mac. "Did Helen get off okay?"

"Yes, she'll be spending the next few days with Munro. The family has been questioning our absence, so she's arranged to spend some time smoothing things over. It's her intention to slip away on occasion to meet with Quinn and monitor her Groom Lake contacts, but primarily she will simply be a mother spending time with her son," Mac said.

"And Fujita, did he accompany McCann and Tamar to Osaka?" Yazzie asked.

"Yes, he was surprisingly cooperative. Even so, it's better to have some distance between him and Hayakawa. We can't let him do something rash that will cause the Anakim to move up their timetable," Mac responded. "Besides, they may need his language skills to get the crates shipped without raising any eyebrows."

"Indeed," Yazzie agreed soberly then smiled. "Menachem will be very pleased with the generous gift from President Truman, I'm sure."

"Well what else were we going to do with those weapons? It's imperative that they not be located by Hayakawa if we want him to believe that Kaori stole them. And it wouldn't be wise to let them fall into the hands of the Japanese while we are occupying their nation. We could turn them over to the military, but they would undoubtedly have questions that we can't answer at the moment," Mac returned. "But Menachem is not our enemy, and he won't ask questions, so let's just allow him to be happy thinking it is a gift from Truman, okay?"

Yazzie dipped his head in agreement and then asked, "Are we on schedule? Is the package enroute?"

Hale furrowed his eyebrows in confusion. "Enroute? I thought we already had what we need here."

"For the island, yes," Mac confirmed. "In fact, we have surplus armory. It would be inconvenient to haul everything back to the States, so a practice drill has been scheduled. We wouldn't want our fly boys to forget how to hit a target. That's why they're going to bomb the hell out of the cove where the alien ship is."

Yazzie smiled at the thought. "Five-hundred-pound bombs?"

Mac nodded in the affirmative. How the operation would go down played through his head. Plane after plane would swoop in and drop their load one after another. They, of course, would have no idea that a facility housing alien creatures lay right beneath the water's surface. They would never know that their training exercise could quite possibly save the world.

"So, what's enroute?" Hale asked suspecting he already knew the answer.

Mac glanced at the floor then locked eyes with Hale. "Atomic bomb. It's the only thing that has a chance of destroying the ship in the Marianas Trench."

"We have one?" Hale asked. "I mean ready to go. Didn't we use the only two in existence on Hiroshima and Nagasaki?"

"That was the rumor," the General replied noncommittally.

"Are they going to do the retrofitting on the base while it's in Nevada or after it gets to San Diego?" Yazzie asked. "Having it encased in a cast iron diving bell is the only way we can get it deep enough to detonate where we need it."

"Quinn is handling the details. Don't worry, it'll be ready," Mac assured him. "He's also sidelining Smithers the second. He's going to be entangled with the IRS for a while. We're hoping he's their only contact and putting him on ice for a time will prevent the package they're expecting from ever leaving the States."

"Okay, Smithers will be out of commission soon and Hayakawa is hopefully so distracted with his own problems that he will be of no help to the Anakim. So, what about Moscow?" Hale asked.

"Working on it," Mac answered with a sigh as he sincerely hoped his plan didn't leave Helen a widow.

CHAPTER 55

"You'll be going into an enemy nation without any point of reference to guide you to your destination. You could wind up being a sitting duck," Yazzie said. "Not only that, but we've never translated carrying that type of devise."

"We were armed when we went to the island with Fujita. We had no issue," Mac stated, fully aware that his argument didn't hold water.

"Those combustibles were encased in metal and were completely within our control. This would be plastique in a briefcase," Yazzie returned. "Even if you manage to step directly into the target area without issue, what would happen if the device exploded while you were translating out? Would a piece of the explosion travel with you?"

"I don't know."

"Exactly," Yazzie continued. "The Greys were very reluctant to answer many of my questions about the logistics of translation. Most of what we know has been learned by trial and error. I'd rather not find the answer to this question through experience."

Mac was silent for a moment. "I know the risk and am willing to take it…it must be done, Yazzie, we both know that. The alien com center can't be left operational and right now we have a small window of opportunity to do the job. But that window may slam shut right after our operation is complete. We just have to figure a way to take it out without starting World War III with Russia."

"Being willing to take the risk doesn't make it a good plan. Have you discussed this with Helen?" Yazzie asked.

"No, and you won't discuss it with her either. It's my decision…"

The remainder of Mac's defense was lost in squealing tires and screeching brakes as McCann swerved into the loading bay. Hale hopped out while the jeep was still in motion and sprinted over to Mac and Yazzie.

"We've got trouble, General. One of Hayakawa's goons was waiting for Fujita when he exited quarters this morning," Hale panted.

"Oh crap. Did he go with him?"

"Yes, sir. I don't think he had a choice," McCann reported. "When we got there to pick Tamar and Makoto up, he was nowhere to be found and she was running like a bat out of hell towards us through traffic trying to keep him in sight. She passed us up in the jeep. I had to tear through an alley and double back to catch her."

"Where is she now?" Yazzie asked soberly.

"She refused to come. So, we left her to watch the building where they took him. Even though we haven't been completely briefed on the op yet we know this could blow up in our faces. What are your orders sir?" Hale asked with adrenaline making his skin tingle and his heart race.

It was like this every time for Hale because it seemed when things were at their worst was when he was at his best. When the enemy was so close you felt like you could hear his heartbeat and your hand was on your weapon before even realizing you had moved. And every thought outside of recovering your teammate was dispelled like a child's soap bubble popping into oblivion at the touch of your finger. He was 100 percent focused U.S. grade A Army badass at this moment and he was ready, scratch that, he wanted to be sent into battle.

Before Mac could open his mouth with a response Yazzie disappeared from the room.

"Damn," McCann breathed out. "I want to do that."

"Where did they take him?" Mac asked.

"An empty building only half of which is still standing about a mile outside of downtown," Hale responded. "This is a new location, sir. If Hayakawa has connections to it we didn't pick up on it before today."

"Okay…" was all Mac got out before Helen translated into the group.

"Mac," she started without preamble, "Quinn needs to meet with you right away. There's big news stateside and he needs to brief you toot sweet."

"We're in the middle of something right now sweetheart," Mac said as he planted a soft kiss on her forehead. "I'll be sure to contact him once things settle down."

"No, he said it was time sensitive and he needed to see you now," she insisted. Seeing his temper beginning to rise at her impertinence she put her hands on her hips and continued. "Listen Mr. Magruder, I am currently supposed to be in the lady's room in the National Museum of Art. Our son is perusing the Pre-Columbian collection but that won't hold his attention long. I have to get back pronto before he storms the doors thinking I'm being held against my will."

"Take Hale," Mac replied looking at his watch. "I'll follow as soon as I can."

And without pause Helen grabbed Hale's arm and they disappeared from the room.

"Janey mac!" McCann exclaimed with wonder. "That's bleedin' massive, it is sir."

"It is indeed," Mac agreed with a smile.

A smile that did a fair job of covering the scenarios, calculations, and probabilities running through his head at the moment. What would change if Fujita killed Hayakawa today? Or if Hayakawa killed Fujita? Or if the team intervened and their connection with Fujita was discovered? None of it was good and none of it was within his immediate control. However, he could do a small preemptive strike to hopefully minimize the fall out and keep the Anakim out of the loop for the next six days.

"Listen I've got to follow Hale to D.C. to meet with Quinn. Get back to the building where the meeting is taking place. If things have gone south you'll be their only backup so are you up to the task Irish?"

"Yes, sir!" McCann said as he snapped to and sprinted for the jeep.

"McCann…" Mac called after him.

"Sir?"

"We're enhanced but we still have our limits. Yazzie can't do it alone."

McCann noted the concern on the General's face as he nodded. "Understood sir. I won't let you down."

As the jeep roared to life and sped from the warehouse Mac patted the sheath securely fastened to his person and stepped from the brightly lit open space into the dim tunnel system beneath Hayakawa's business. He knelt down to give his eyes a chance to adjust as he watched for movement up ahead. He might have assumed it to be an abandoned building if he didn't know better. There wasn't a single sound except a steady drip, drip, drip somewhere behind him.

He stayed motionless a few seconds longer reaching into his years of experience to get any sense of an ambush. Of course, Hayakawa would have to possess mystic powers to have known he was coming as he had not shared this particular plan with anyone, not even Yazzie. It had simply been an idea simmering on the back burner of his mind for a while. One of those "if the opportunity arises" kind of plans. So, when news of Hayakawa's abduction of Fujita came complete with the assurance that Hayakawa and most probably his men were off premises Magruder jumped at the chance.

As he began his stealthy approach to the comm room bile burned the back of his throat. He was hoping to find the equipment room as unoccupied as the hallway, but he knew the odds of that were slim to none. Even if all other work came to a halt, someone would be in that room monitoring communications. He quietly removed the tanto from its sheath knowing there was a high probability he would kill that unlucky soul today.

It was every soldier's conundrum – doing seemingly bad things for good purposes. It was always hard to reconcile. One's head and one's heart didn't always stand in unity on the issue. And some bad things were worse than others. Sending a person, or even a Shalanaya, into eternity without their even knowing that you are in the room was certainly expedient but much harder to reconcile than hand-to-hand combat when only one of you will survive.

And then there was Helen. She knew, of course, he had killed people. She was not ignorant of a soldier's lot; however, he would make sure that the details would be forever absent. Mac was careful to minimize his experiences around her and to leave the worst of it unsaid. Helen still believed him to be a good man even when he doubted it himself. She still saw that unscathed young man that had been nervous to ask her out on a date. The wear and tear of life, of a soldier's life in particular, had not dimmed her opinion nor made her think less of him. She was his anchor, and he was not about to sever that lifeline by unnecessarily including her in this moment.

Mac swallowed the bitterness in his mouth and stepped into the comm room. A Shalanaya sat with his back to the door listening intently to what was coming across the wireless. Mac quietly crossed the room and slit his throat so quickly that the alien's body remained upright in the chair as if still intent on the conversation in his ears, his blood coloring the equipment red.

The tangle of power supply lines was quickly located and a glass of water sitting an arm's reach from the operator's chair was poured directly into the outlets causing sparks to fly and the equipment to hiss and smoke. The reaction shorted out every piece of equipment and left a putrid burning smell hanging in the air. As the blood and water mingled on the console and the popping and snapping continued Mac returned the water glass to its original position, then brushed dirt from the knees of his trousers and disappeared from the room.

"I'm glad you could join us, General," Quinn said calmly as Mac manifested in his D.C. office. "Is everything under control in Japan?"

"Of course," Mac replied.

Quinn tipped his head down and looked over the rim of his glasses without making a response.

"My team will handle it. Now, what's so important that you tracked my wife down while spending time with our son and sent her to get me?"

"It's very good news, sir," Hale said entering the conversation. "Very good."

"First off, your team's intel was spot on. The enemy is expecting information from D.C. Secondly, we lucked out," Quinn said. "The package being expected by the Russians was compiled by Papa Smithers. Who after being jailed for tax evasion called on junior to retrieve a briefcase for him and deliver it to a messenger that has been tasked with accompanying it personally to Moscow."

Mac's face lit up at the news. "So, we have an opportunity to replace the information before handing it off! That is good news!"

"Oh yes, however we can do better than that," Quinn responded all smiles. "The courier Smithers was told to deliver the package to is none other than our very own Shalanaya defector - Mordecai."

CHAPTER 56

"So will Helen be joining us or is she still visiting with family?" Hale asked.

"Currently she is enroute to Moscow," Mac replied.

Moscow? What the hell is she going to do in Moscow? Is it safe? The questions came like a barrage from every person in the room.

"Calm down, calm down," Mac said with his hands up to quell the anxiety on display. "She is on a flight with the Shalanaya defector. However, Mordecai doesn't know who she is, and she has orders not to interact or interfere with him in any way. She is simply watching to see if he's intercepted before the handoff in Moscow. Besides, Munro insisted on seeing his mother to the airport so…"

He could see that they weren't convinced of the sanity of the decision. "Well, she had to fly somewhere," Mac replied with a shrug.

"Listen," Hale said carefully as he again felt the weight of her body limp in his arms. "I know she has abilities, but it doesn't take long for things to go wrong."

"I am aware," Mac said understanding exactly what Hale was saying. He had dealt with the same misgivings before deciding to send her. "That's why Tamar is going to Moscow. Are you up for it?"

"Of course," Tamar said without pause. "What's my cover?"

"You are Helen's niece, born of the Russian immigrant who married her brother. Your mother's greatest wish was to return to her homeland one more time, however she died before that could happen, so now you have returned to scatter her ashes."

"Okay, what is the mission?"

"Find the alien comm center," Mac replied. "Do not breach; just find it. Some of your Irgun brothers will also be in the area searching, however you and Helen have knowledge about the enemy that unfortunately we can't share with them."

"Don't worry, sir, we will sniff them out," she said with a sly smile as she tapped her nose.

"McCann."

"Sir."

"Get the rest of the merchandise out of this warehouse. Move it, sell it, hell, give it away, but get it out of here. Fujita has to give Hayakawa something and we agreed that this location has served its purpose. Leave a little bit of trash like it was cleared out in a hurry just make sure nothing traces back to us." Mac instructed.

"Can you believe the arrogance of that man? The bald-faced, unmitigated gall," Tamar said with disgust. "After Hayakawa abandoned Fujita and his men on that island to the aliens then to turn to him begging for help saying how he had no one else he could trust. Crying about how *he* was betrayed. It is beyond reprehensible."

"I don't know how he kept from taking him out there and then," McCann agreed.

"This place could put Fujita in the crosshairs if Hayakawa finds out he leased it," Hale said with concern.

Mac smiled. "Kaori's name is on the paperwork. Fujita is sharp and strategic; he was thinking ahead," he said with appreciation. He then grew serious as he asked, "How is he holding up through all of this?"

"Counting the days until he can kill the son of a bitch that left his men to be tortured by the enemy, sir," Hale answered.

"I guess it helps to have something to look forward to," Mac muttered with a sigh. "Yazzie, were Farnsworth and Colonel Smith able to tap into the data flow intended for Hayakawa?"

"Yes. They are monitoring all incoming messages. They intend to maintain radio silence as long as possible without drawing suspicion," Yazzie replied. "They don't want anything to tip off the other side that they may not be talking to their allies."

"Good. So that leaves you Hale. How would you like to meet General MacArthur up close and personal?"

"Sir?" Hale returned in surprise.

"Our presence has become known to him. No doubt Hayakawa whispered something in the Emperor's ear who in turn told MacArthur. You know, just to let him know that his contacts have not diminished, and the empire is still his. Anyway, Yazzie and I have been summoned to D.C., so I need you to go in my place."

"Yes sir," Hale responded dreading the meeting already. He was not afraid of the man, but he wasn't stupid either. One wrong word could affect the mission to say nothing of his career. Plus, MacArthur was well known for having a monstrous ego. Finding out that they had been working in Tokyo right under his nose without reporting directly to him probably had not gone over well.

"Stick to the truth as much as possible. We are here hunting Nazi war criminals. One has already been apprehended and returned to Pullach for interrogation, etcetera," Mac instructed. "Apologize for my absence. Tell him I am currently out of the country. I guess I don't need to tell you not to mention aliens or atomic bombs, correct?"

A general snickering went through the room.

"I'll see if I can steer the conversation away from those two particular topics, sir," Hale responded with a smile.

"Okay, everyone has their assignments. Any questions?" Mac asked looking at each person present. After receiving negative responses all around he continued. "All right, get to it. Yazzie are you ready?"

The two old warriors stepped into the Oval Office ready to immediately translate out should anyone not in their closely held circle be present. Finding no one except the President and Colonel Quinn in residence they relaxed and stepped forward to extend greetings.

"Mr. President. Quinn," Mac said with a nod in their direction. "So, how goes the rat race?"

"Some days it feels like the rats may be winning, General," Truman replied. "Please, sit down. May I pour you a drink, gentlemen?"

"Considering I haven't had breakfast yet, sir, I'll pass," Mac said as Yazzie also politely declined.

"Oh yes," the President returned as he poured a liberal glass of bourbon for Quinn and then one equally as liberal for himself. "You are just now starting the day coming to a close here or are you beginning our tomorrow?"

"Right now, I just go by how many days we have left before we bomb the Anakim into oblivion," Mac returned keenly eyeing the two men sipping whiskey. "Please don't tell me there's been a delay."

"No, no delay. Everything is on schedule," Truman returned, much to Mac and Yazzie's relief.

"The package should be delivered to its final destination within 48 hours," Quinn confirmed. "The commander in charge has been given a heads up and we have a secondary briefing scheduled for the day after tomorrow."

"I'd like you to be on-site for that. Is that possible?" Truman asked.

"Of course. It shouldn't be a problem," Mac replied. After a brief pause in the conversation, he asked, "Was that all Mr. President?"

"No. Actually, there is something else we need to discuss. It's about the bombing of the island."

"Oh yes, that's all arranged. A training exercise has been scheduled with our fly boys to coincide with the drop over the trench. If all goes as planned both sites will be totally destroyed in tandem."

"That's the thing, General," Truman said quietly. "There may be extremely valuable weapons and technology on-site in their base of operations on the island. We may not be able to recover anything from the Marianas Trench due to its location, however, we need to salvage as much as possible from the secondary sight."

"This means boots on the ground during the air raid on the island," Quinn said as if everything had already been discussed and decided. "You have the key for the Anakim base Mr. Fujita captured, correct?"

Mac felt Yazzie turn to ice beside him. "Wait, wait, wait. Let's back up a minute," Mac said as he moved to the edge of his seat. "You want me to put men on that island who have no idea that the enemy they'll be fighting is ten-foot-tall aliens that can absorb multiple shots and remain standing? Respectfully, are you out of your damn minds?"

"General, surely you can appreciate what an opportunity this is," Truman responded. "From what we've been told ridding our planet of the creatures currently here does not end the species. There are more, and after annihilating them here the others will undoubtedly be out for revenge."

"We will need those weapons for humanity to survive," Quinn added with resolve.

"Then the weapons and technology recovered will be equally shared with the Irgun, yes?" Yazzie asked calmly. "So that we too may protect humanity?"

President Truman and Yazzie stared at one another in silence each one carefully weighing their next words.

"Yazzie," Quinn jumped in, "these weapons are certain to be unlike anything we've ever seen on earth. They will need to be examined to determine what they are and how to use them. Everything must be kept secret until we've had time to test them."

"My people have brilliant scientists that would be eager to assist in this process," Yazzie returned knowing full well that the sharing of any recovered technology would never happen. "After all, if your government or the facility at Groom Lake are infiltrated again as they have been in the past wouldn't it be wise to have this humanity-saving technology elsewhere as well?"

Quinn's face went red as the worldly-wise Jew sat unmoved by his attempts to brush him and his people away like a piece of unwanted lint.

"Mr. President," Mac responded. "I have no doubt your intentions are good. But, as the Greys were only too happy to point out, we are also barbaric warmongering people like the Anakim. You'll be out of office in a few years, then what? Who will safeguard weapons we shouldn't have against use on other human beings? This is not a good idea."

"And what makes you think the Greys will not make a move against us if we attempt this?" Yazzie added. "Their intention was to give humanity a fighting chance against a more technologically advanced species, not provide an advanced technology to mankind so we could destroy ourselves at an accelerated pace."

"They weren't even willing to fight an enemy to save their own race. I seriously doubt they will make a move against us," Quinn shot back.

"Perhaps they will decide to correct their mistake in trusting us to rise to the occasion," Yazzie returned sharply.

"Don't be naive!" Quinn said as he shook his head in exasperation thinking about how close the aliens had been. About how they had been living in the tunnels under the White House. It was too damn close. "This shouldn't even be a question. Of course, we should recover their technology. We would be fools not to. The United States will safeguard the alien technology and ensure that it's never used against our own kind."

"Oh, c'mon Quinn," Mac said jumping into the fray. "Now who's being naive? That's a promise you know can't be kept. The four of us aren't going to live forever. Do you really think those that come after us will use the same restraint?"

Quinn looked at his predecessor. "I just hope humans survive long enough for that to be a problem."

"Enough," the President interrupted, bringing the room to silence. "Don't think I haven't lost sleep over this decision, gentlemen, because I have. And the consequences are simply too grave to ignore. We must attempt to preserve any and all weaponry and technology located on the Anakim's island base in the interest of self-preservation. General revise your plan to ensure the recovery of anything not destroyed, and I will take steps to secure whatever is discovered for the future protection of earth from invading alien forces. If you respect me and the office I hold then respect my decision."

CHAPTER 57

Several nocturnal after-hours shopping trips supplied authentic Russian shoes and clothing for the group converging on Moscow. Mac and Yazzie left ample rubles in the cash drawers in exchange for the goods, hoping the owners wouldn't find it necessary to involve the politsiya regarding the missing merchandise. Chances were good that the theft would not have been reported even if no funds were left as no one wanted to draw the attention and possible involvement of the Narodnyy komissariat vnutrennikh del — NKVD. Their involvement was never a good thing, it was better to suffer the loss in silence.

Tamar and several Irgun that had been working with them in Tokyo were the first to reach their destination. They arrived separately by varied routes and different means of transportation so that even if one person was detained the operation would continue unhampered. After their arrival contact was to be visual only. The pervasive anti-Semitic narrative holding sway in the Soviet Union at this time was well known. If anyone was being watched, contact could cause the arrest of not only themselves but a brother-in-arms as well.

The papers Yazzie forged for each of them looked authentic and lent each holder a certain sense of comfort. However, there had been thousands of loyal Russian citizens murdered for nothing more than to justify Stalin's expansive paranoia. Papers, no matter how expertly forged, were no guarantee of safety especially if you were found to be a Jew. Despite the danger, they moved forward and were able to locate the alien communications center within twenty-four hours of their arrival.

The neighborhood where it was located was old and solid. The buildings had been constructed to withstand war with heavy stone and block walls covering extensive basements that undoubtedly had been used as bomb shelters in the past. Starovagankovskiy Lane was less than a kilometer from the Kremlin and on it resided the Pravilo Taprum serving up varieties of ale and beer to whoever was thirsty.

Much business was conducted in the Taprum making it a good cover for the enemy's com center. Many people were coming and going every day so their business could be conducted openly without much possibility of drawing unwanted attention. What had drawn the searchers to this particular area was not the busy bar, however, but Mordecai's advice to look for water close by. Moisture was essential to their survival on this dry planet so they would want an ample supply within easy access. The Moskva River that passes through central Moscow with the Kremlin situated right along its banks was their starting point.

The Taprum's proximity to water along with the radio waves emanating from the Russian seat of government just down the road made the location ideal. The alien presence could access Russian transmissions and patch hidden encrypted messages into existing messages. The team continued canvassing the city after finding the local bar lest they were mistaken however Tamar had no doubt of their success once she walked by the entrance of the bar and smelled the unmistakable Shalanaya stench mixed with odors of the libations served.

Once Mac joined the group in Moscow a room was rented on the third floor of the hotel across the street from the bar. This was for visual confirmation of the second item Mordecai said would be present, a large flat antenna on the roof. The antenna, according to Mordecai, was non-human technology that could connect with a floating piece of technology in space that in turn connected with the planet Shalna. It also provided the power needed to communicate with the alien mining facility six miles deep in the Marianas Trench. A contraption was indeed present on the roof. It wasn't visible at street level which made them wonder whether Russian intelligence was even aware of this alien stronghold in their midst.

Yazzie visited the Taprum on Mordecai's arrival day and purchased a tall cold lager beer. Then he positioned himself at a corner table to watch who was coming and going. He perused the Russian paper he brought with him while he sipped and noted the number of Russian intel microphones sprinkled throughout the establishment. There was a single hallway that led to two doors. One was a public bathroom with a constant flow of patrons in and out. The other had a keyed lock and next to no traffic coming or going. It had to be the entrance to the basement and their operations. It was noted that all the Taprum staff were Shalanaya agents.

As Yazzie sat in the enemy's camp enjoying his beverage Helen and Mordecai were disembarking their plane. Helen hung back fussing over her belongings to keep an eye on Mordecai. He had been pulled aside in Poland and the contents of the briefcase were questioned. Security there tried to take the case for inspection, but he argued with them, refusing to relinquish his property until a supervisor with unusually white skin intervened. The planted Shalanaya agent in charge vouched for Mordecai and sent him on his way much to Helen's relief. She wanted to ensure there was not a repeat performance.

Tamar was there to meet her new aunt with hugs and kisses, and they chatted happily as they made their way to the car park. Mordecai was walking just ahead of them. They paused for a moment as Helen searched her handbag for her glasses as he stopped at the cab stand. The driver was handed a piece of paper, presumably with an address, then Mordecai took a seat in the back and placed the briefcase on the floor behind the driver.

The ladies rushed to their vehicle as the taxi departed and retrieved what Helen light-heartedly called the *bomb-case*. Mac had not been amused but it was the only way she could bring herself to touch the thing. Mac had moved inter-dimensionally with the case several times to test its stability before trusting it to Tamar's care. Helen retrieved the small black transmitter from the burial urn she had carried with her the whole trip and dropped it in her pocket. She then briskly picked up the armed briefcase with the accompanying box of shrapnel. The box was heavy even though Tamar said it was only about the size of two hand grenades. Helen tried very hard not to contemplate exactly what she now held in her hands.

"Wish me luck," she said to Tamar with a smile and a wink trying to disguise her rapidly beating heart and palpable fear before she disappeared.

When Helen materialized in the backseat of Mordecai's cab behind the driver, she immediately held her index finger to her lips to hopefully quash any exclamation of surprise from the startled Shalanaya. She slid the palm-size transmitter and the small box across the seat leaving it within his arm's reach, then carefully placed the bomb-case on the floor next to the other. Once the briefcase containing documents was in her grasp, she translated to Mac's location in the hotel room by the Taprum. The whole transaction took only seconds and the driver never noticed Helen's coming or going as he expertly navigated the congested traffic.

In the end, Helen was extremely grateful for Yazzie's suggestion that she center on Mac, her strongest connection, for her exit. She was not certain where she would have ended up without his guiding presence to draw her when she was in such a state. The immediate, emotional bear hug at her appearance in the rented hotel room was most welcome and they stood there embracing for several minutes before regretfully pulling apart.

"I did good, didn't I?" Helen asked shakily.

"You did great," Mac said tenderly brushing a strand of hair from her face. "Maybe I should…"

"No, I'll be fine," she said knowing where the conversation was headed. "The worst part is over."

Mac nodded knowing he had to stick with the plan, but it didn't mean he had to like it. "Maybe when this is all over we should go somewhere, just the two of us."

"It's a date," she said with a smile as he vanished.

"That cabbie drives like a maniac," Tamar said as Mac appeared in the seat next to her. "I'm having a hard time keeping up with him and that's saying something." She expertly dodged in and out of traffic as she spoke while Mac braced himself to prevent being thrown around like a rag doll. "How's Helen?"

"Shaken, but okay. I think she's doing better than I am," Mac returned with a rueful smile. He took a deep breath and shook off the emotion. Assuming the analytical mindset he knew was needed for him and his team to survive what was coming next, he continued. "Yazzie's in place. It all comes down to this."

Tamar nodded as she swung to the curb several spaces from where the cab had stopped to let out his fare. A mental sigh of relief was exhaled when the Pravilo Taprum was indeed the location to which their courier had been directed. Mac and Tamar took their time exiting the vehicle while mentally counting off the seconds. It should take no longer than five minutes. Mordecai was told to get in and out as quickly as possible.

Yazzie picked up on Mordecai's entrance immediately and turned his face away from the affable Shalanaya, praying he would not acknowledge him in any way. It seemed the bar's proprietor had been anxiously waiting for this important guest as he left his station behind the bar as soon as Mordecai crossed the threshold. He met him at the door and then guided him down the dingy hallway. A quick knock on the locked door was answered, a few words exchanged, and Mordecai ushered down the basement stairs.

This was it. This was the moment that would tell the team whether Mordecai was a friend or foe. It was without a doubt the biggest unknown in the plan. Could he be trusted? Yazzie folded his paper and set it aside then calmly took another sip of the lager.

Helen chanced a glance out the window of their rented room and saw Mac take Tamar's elbow to guide her across the street. She then turned back to focus all her attention on the little red light located on the receiver lying on the bed. She was ready for her final assignment of this operation.

Mordecai carefully made his way down the dimly lit staircase knowing that dropping or even jostling the briefcase he held could result in his untimely death. Once his feet touched the cold concrete floor, he breathed out a sigh of relief. Then his heart was nearly torn in two when he stepped into the open space and saw the room filled with his Shalanaya brethren. He had been instructed to place the briefcase on the floor with the scratched flat side directed toward the communication equipment, but he hesitated. Could he do this? Could he execute his own people?

As his eyes swept the room he realized with a start that the technology here was not earthly. No human, nor Anakim for that matter, would know how to construct the network functioning here. Only Shalanaya could have created this highly advanced communication center. *Traitors!* This was not a prison. There were no Anakim on-site forcing their cooperation. They were here of their own free will aiding the enemies that held their home planet and its inhabitants captive.

Mordecai was outraged and wanted to lash out at their disloyalty. How could they not see that it would be better to die for their nation than live in harmony with their enemies? He wanted to rail at them, accuse them to their faces of their crimes but he knew it would not make a difference. They had made their choice so without reservation, he placed the briefcase as instructed. He then retrieved the small heavy box from his pocket and placed it next to the case.

"What is that?" one of the traitors asked.

"I don't know. I was instructed to bring it with the case," Mordecai answered truthfully. They did not need to know who had given him the instructions.

He then nearly panicked when another traitor moved to retrieve the briefcase. Its position was vital he had been told. It could not be moved. "I know you," he blurted out. "Your family was deemed unworthy to serve in the Queen's house."

The traitor stopped and straightened to look with disdain at Mordecai. "I know you as well. You always thought yourself to be better than everyone else, didn't you? But look at you now, doing the Anakim's bidding just like me."

"What I do is for queen and country," Mordecai said proudly as he pressed the button on the transmitter in his pocket. "Long live Queen Jehosheba!"

The little red light lit up and Helen went into action. She translated into the Taprum basement threw her arms around Mordecai then deposited the two of them back in the hotel room. Mordecai's smiling, triumphant face was the last thing any of the traitors saw.

Yazzie felt Helen's presence flit in, then out again signaling it was a go. He flipped the switch on the device he carried with him and then stepped on it as the floor shook from the blast below. Customers screamed in horror and Yazzie put on a terrified face to join them in a mad dash for the door. He was knocked back and thrown to the floor by a burly man with a young woman tucked in the crook of his arm trying to vacate the premises. From his prone position he saw the proprietor sprinting down the hallway to the basement door.

Mac and Tamar stood across the street in the chaos watching for Yazzie's exit while fire trucks were screaming their way to the site of the blast. The proximity of the taprum to the Kremlin undoubtedly aided in the incredibly fast response time. The fire truck pulled up right after a black government car skidded to a stop in the middle of the street.

Four members of the NKVD piled out of their arriving vehicle and caught Yazzie as he staggered out the door. He was helping a woman who had also been tossed aside in the name of self-preservation. She limped away without a backward glance as Yazzie's arms were suddenly grabbed by one of the government men. A gash on his forehead ran a convincing trail of blood down the side of his face.

"What happened?" the NKVD agent screamed in Russian. "Tell me what happened."

Yazzie stumbled and was pulled back upright by the claw-like hold on his arms as the government man waited for a response.

"Podval," he responded weakly in their language. "The basement..."

He was finally determined to be unimportant and thrown aside as an argument broke out inside the building. Politsiya cars joined the fray emptying uniforms onto the street to shake down the crowds for information as Yazzie heard the proprietor telling the Fire Chief that a boiler had exploded in the basement. There were no casualties, he insisted, other than a few cases of imported ale. Voices were raised as the Fire Chief demanded access so they could check it out for themselves when the NKVD agent that seemed to be in charge intervened.

"It seems no harm was done, yes? We will just consider ourselves to be most fortunate to have sustained no casualties," he said with a humorless smile that brooked no resistance. The NKVD man then wrapped his arm tightly around the Chief's shoulders causing the firefighter's body to stiffen and his face to drain of color. As the agent forcibly drew the Chief back to the bar he continued. "I think some vodka would be in order to salute the regretful demise of a fine ale. Yes?"

The proprietor had not been happy at first when he was told several Russian agents had been informed of their operations. His unease had lessened somewhat as time passed when they were found to be very discreet. Today, however, he saw the wisdom of their inclusion and was delighted with the protection they afforded. Free libations were a small price to pay if it meant the absolute carnage in the basement would remain undiscovered.

The explosive device had been devastatingly effective. It exploded outward across the room like a shotgun blast leaving the equipment in unrecognizable pieces while the shrapnel insured the death of everyone in the room. The walls were covered with Shalanaya blood and scattered bits of flesh and bones.

The Irgun watching the rear and sides of the building for escapees appeared around each corner of the building. They signaled Mac and Tamar that all had gone according to plan, none had escaped. One of the men rushed forward to grab Yazzie under the guise of assisting an injured old man, then all of them disappeared separately into the confused and frightened throng. Once certain of the team's secure departure Mac and Tamar turned to leave the chaos as well. Suddenly a member of the politsiya grabbed the front of Mac's coat and began shaking him while screaming in his face.

"What do you know about this? Did you plant a bomb? Tell me!"

Tamar ran to his defense pushing the aggressive young man back. "What are you doing?" she asked in Russian. "He is the Minister of Agriculture of the USSR! We were on our way to the Ministry when the ground shook and the street was suddenly filled with running people!"

Tamar presented him with their Ministry credentials and as he examined them a look of fear filled his face. Apologies were graciously extended as he bowed his head several times to Mac's scathing look. Then he quickly took his leave to harass less prominent and powerful citizens.

CHAPTER 58

"We really haven't had time to talk since everyone got back from Moscow. So how did it go with General MacArthur?" Mac asked as Hale entered the room.

"Great. He said I was going places," Hale replied.

"You must have impressed him."

"Oh yeah, I did. I was professional and straight to the point. Then I looked him straight in the eye while I laid out our mission here. That was when he said I was going straight to the brig if I ever came in your place again."

Mac smiled. "Noted, I'll take care of it when this is over. Did the others get off?"

"Yes sir. Fujita commandeered a fishing boat for the transport of himself, Mordecai, and Quinn's men. They left about an hour ago. The rest of Yazzie's armory went with them."

"Good. Was he able to get everything we need?"

"I think so. There are six panzerfausts most of them coming from Hayakawa's stash. Yazzie also got a box of hand grenades and two American Springfield 1903A4s with M73 scopes. The .30-06 cartridges should cut through any foliage no problem." Hale replied.

"Okay, we'll put Case and Sheperd up high. See if they can't pick off a few of the Anakim as they exit the underground facility. Let's give them the panzerfausts too. They'll have more use for them than those of us on the ground," Mac said. "Was Yazzie's extra day in Russia worthwhile?"

"Oh yeah," Hale replied with his face just beaming. "He relieved the NKVD of enough AK47 prototypes for everyone. It's an amazing weapon, sir. It's a single shot and machine gun in one. 7.62mm rounds with huge hitting power and can fire 550 rounds per minute. We also have M1911 .45 caliber pistols for everyone. Mordecai had to be instructed in how to use his."

"So, what did he think?" Mac inquired.

"Well," Hale said smiling. "He wasn't as impressed with the gun as he was that we managed to overcome the Anakim with such primitive weapons."

Mac laughed. "He took the M1911 anyway though, right?"

"Oh yeah," Hale replied. "But what really charged his battery was the saber. You'd have thought it was his birthday."

"A saber? Where did we even get a saber?" Mac asked with an unbelieving shake of his head.

"It was in Hayakawa's stuff. We had no intention of using it, but once Mordecai saw it that was all he wanted," Hale said with a shrug of his shoulders. "I don't know, maybe it's an alien thing."

"Well, okay but the last thing we should be doing is hand-to-hand with the Anakim," Mac said with a sigh. "I should have been here to help with everything, but the briefing with the captain took longer than expected. You all did an excellent job as usual. Yazzie's idea of using the pontoons on the plane as storage for our stash was inspired." The data, details, and execution of the impending operation raced through Mac's mind. "I hated to leave all the weapon and ammo transport on Yazzie, but I don't want Helen to ever set foot on that Island."

"I was wondering, sir," Hale said. "Why are the Irgun willing to provide all that weaponry. After all, they have their own battles to fight. Are you sure they aren't aware of just exactly who our enemy is in this battle?"

Mac snorted out a little laugh. "You never know with that bunch. They may know everything, but they're a tight-lipped bunch. If they've been told to keep mum, you would never get them to admit to anything."

Hale paused a moment. "Sir, do Quinn's guys know what they're up against?"

"Yes. We ran into both Shalanaya and Anakim in the tunnels under the White House. After the encounter they were briefed on all things alien. I assume that's why Truman sent them. They are not, however, privy to Yazzie, Helen, and my special enhancements from the Greys," Mac responded.

"Understood. So that's why their transport to the island is by boat rather than the Mac or Yazzie express," Hale stated.

"Exactly. No sense in traumatizing them right before the operation. Are you and McCann ready to go?"

"Yes sir," Hale responded with a smile tugging at his lips. "Just so you know, you've made our Irishman very happy sir."

"How so?"

"He gets to use the whiz-bang transport," Hale replied unable to contain his smile any longer. "His words, sir. He's really charged up about it."

Mac shook his head with a little laugh. "Let's just hope he can translate all that enthusiasm to the battlefield Major."

"Oh, we're ready sir. Gonna go take down the big bad."

"I see you've been talking to Mumford, Shepherd, and Case. I haven't had an opportunity to speak with them since their arrival from D.C. except for the briefing. What do you think, are they ready for this?"

"Yes sir. Now that I know they are fully aware of the enemy I have no reservations about going into battle with them."

"Good," Mac said looking at his watch. "The bombing raid will start in about an hour. Go round up McCann and send Tamar in."

When Tamar entered the room Mac could plainly see on her face what he already suspected. She was not happy about being left behind.

"I wanted to talk to you before we left," Mac said as he leaned back in his chair. "I want you to know that you're not being left behind because you're female."

"Why am I being left behind then?" she asked, unable to completely mask her anger. "Did my uncle demand it?"

Mac and Tamar maintained eye contact for a span of time until Mac finally looked down at his hands. "I need you here because I trust you."

A look of surprise flitted across Tamar's face.

"There may be enemy combatants left in Tokyo that we failed to identify. If so, I need someone here that can, and will, take them down. Geoffrey and Colonel Smith will be monitoring communications. That will be their focus. You need to watch their backs and if things go sideways on the island I need you to get Helen out. She will resist, I can promise you that, but you need to get her back to the States…back to our son. Will you do that for me?"

The weight of her new assignment changed her demeanor immediately. It was not a vote of no confidence. No, in fact it was just the opposite, he trusted her. It was both militarily and personally important to him, and he had assigned it to her – just her.

"You can count on me, General. I will take care of them. No worries, you just take care of business on the island. I've got this."

Mac nodded his head and gave her a little half-smile. "I know you do, Tamar. The Lieutenant Colonel gave the rest of his team the day off so it will just be Geoffrey and Smith hunkered down in the bunker. Helen's gone to brief Truman and Quinn; she knows to meet you there. I've got to get going. There's an Irishman giddy as a schoolgirl about our means of transport to the island."

Tamar laughed. "He's not driving for once."

"I just hope he doesn't wet his pants," Mac said with a grin then disappeared from the room.

Tamar took a deep breath of the salty ocean air as she hopped in their jeep to drive to the comm center. She did a slow perimeter check peering into the early morning darkness prior to entering the building. Once assured that all was well, she took the stairs down to the basement to join Geoffrey and the Lieutenant Colonel.

"How's it going? Picking up any chatter yet?" she asked as she entered the room.

"Nothing yet," Geoffrey responded.

"Good," she replied. "Listen, I'm going to do a walk-through and make sure no one else is in the building. I'll be back in a few."

The two men gave absent nods as they concentrated on what was coming through their earpieces. Tamar climbed the stairs to the top floor and made her way down checking offices and closets floor by floor for intruders. Bathrooms, clear. Stairwells the same. She started checking that windows were secure on the second floor. All was quiet.

She noticed the sun was just starting to dispel the inky darkness as she made her way back downstairs to the basement. The Airmen were probably readying their aircraft for the bombing drill about now she thought. Suddenly she stopped short and listened. Conversation. Not Geoffrey or the Lieutenant Colonel's voice. Then she smelled it. *Oh hell!*

Tamar drew her weapon and silently descended the few remaining steps. She slipped into an equipment room tucked under the stairs and took a crouched position behind the door. From her vantage point, she could see Hayakawa and five, no six, armed Shalanaya. Were there more out of her line of sight?

"My Enigma machine was sabotaged, you see," Hayakawa stated serenely. "So, I thought I'd borrow one of yours. Two of your men were in the bar last night, Lieutenant Colonel. They were discussing plans for their day off so I thought it would be an ideal time to confiscate what I need. However, I was not expecting the building to be occupied. It is most unfortunate you are here gentlemen. Yes indeed, most unfortunate…for you."

Tamar estimated that she would be able to get off two clean shots before taking fire. She knew those two shots had to hit their marks if they were to stand even a small chance of coming out of this alive. She didn't have a shot at Hayakawa, so the Shalanaya that seemed to be his number two was the first to go down. Her second shot immediately followed taking down the one controlling a dolly loaded down with the desired Enigma machine. The dolly slammed forward with a bang as the alien's grip released and he fell backward flat onto the concrete floor.

She didn't slow her response. In rapid-fire her third shot grazed Hayakawa's arm as he ducked for cover, then all attention turned to the equipment room. Shots echoed off the walls as Lieutenant Colonel Smith dropped to the floor and Farnsworth dove across the gunmetal gray desk for the weapon he was forced to abandon there earlier. He snatched up his handgun and took out number three from his prone position as he slid across the smooth surface. It was the perfect height to aim directly at the alien's heart – exactly where a human appendix would be.

As Geoffrey slid off the desk and scrambled for cover, Lieutenant Colonel Smith came up with the service pistol that had been taped under his desk. He locked on Hayakawa as the coward dashed for the exit. The shot meant for the Japanese spy, currently in bed with the enemy, instead took down the fourth alien when Hayakawa dodged behind him for cover.

"I brought donuts!" Helen chirped as she suddenly appeared in the middle of the war zone.

Hayakawa didn't take time to consider where she came from. He simply grabbed her around the waist and positioned her between himself and the gunfire.

"Stop! Stop right now or she will die. You know I won't hesitate to sacrifice her for myself."

The shooting immediately stopped, and the room went silent.

"You," he said pointing to Tamar's sanctuary, "out here now."

Tamar slowly emerged with her hands in the air.

"Slide your guns to me. All of you, now!"

The weapons were placed on the concrete floor and slid across the expanse to Hayakawa's feet.

"Dear Lieutenant Colonel," Helen said as she extended *three fingers* along the arm around her waist. "I am so sorry to bring you into all of this." *Two fingers.* "It was never my intention to disrupt your life." *One finger.* "I hope you can forgive me."

As the last finger retracted Helen took hold of Hayakawa's wrist and disappeared from the room with her captor. Ready for her move Geoffrey and Tamar simultaneously grabbed the concealed weapons nestled in holsters in the small of their backs and fired on the last two Shalanaya gunmen as they gaped at the previously occupied empty space.

Helen and Hayakawa landed on a pier at the island. The gun slipped from the panicked Hayakawa's hand and tumbled off the wood slats into the water. When Helen felt his strength fade, she wrenched away from his encircling arm and left him there bleeding and alone wondering if his sanity had been stripped away.

She reappeared in the communications bunker with her derringer in hand.

"Oh," Helen said with a twinge of disappointment. "It seems you have things well in hand. There's no one left to shoot."

"What just happened?" the stunned Lieutenant Colonel Smith asked.

"We really need to talk dear. I will explain everything," Helen promised. "But there's no time now. You must man the comms just now."

Smith glanced at Geoffrey and Tamar. "You two don't seem to be as stunned as I am. You knew what was going to happen, didn't you?"

"Another time, Lieutenant Colonel," Helen insisted. "You really must stay on task. Lives may depend on it."

"I'll collect on that promise," Lieutenant Colonel Smith told Helen as he retrieved his headphones from the floor. "Guaranteed."

"I'll take care of the bodies," Tamar said as she grabbed the hands of one of the deceased. "I'll put them in the equipment room for now."

"Excellent idea," Helen said as Geoffrey put his weapon back into the leather holster that no longer felt uncomfortable resting against his back.

"When did you start carrying a side arm and another in your back?" Tamar asked as she passed by enroute to her destination.

"Ever since I met your uncle," he replied as his chair was scooted back into place and he sat down. "He can be quite unsettling."

Tamar smiled broadly at Geoffrey's inadvertent compliment to her uncle as she slid the lifeless body into place. "Where did you take him? D.C.?" Tamar asked Helen as she grabbed another alien's arms and tugged him in the direction of the new morgue.

Helen looked quite pleased with herself as she replied, "No, somewhere a little more tropical."

Geoffrey and Tamar started laughing. "You didn't! The island?"

"It seemed fitting that he should be witness to his ally's complete destruction," Helen replied sweetly. "Donut anyone?"

CHAPTER 59

McCann wobbled uncertainly after his whiz-bang transport with Yazzie to the island. His legs were unsteady, but he was smiling from ear to ear with his white teeth gleaming from his already blackened face.

"Janey mac, that's bleedin' massive that is," he breathed out quietly.

Mac smiled as he pulled his AK47 into place and used it to point the direction to Fujita's downed aircraft. With weapons in hand Mac took the lead with Hale and McCann following closely behind. Yazzie brought up the rear. All four men went silent as they carefully made their way through the darkness and dense brush. All their senses were heightened as their training and experience took over and every thought was now on the mission before them.

They emerged from the thick brush to find four rifles pointed in their direction and a saber ready for action. Recognition caused each of the men to break into a smile and lower their weapons. Everyone had already geared up and smeared black shoe polish like paste on their exposed skin for camouflage. A mixture of animal and Shalanaya scent had been applied to each person except Mordecai lest they be sniffed out by the Anakim.

"Failure is not an option, gentlemen. Ready?" Mac whispered as all nine heads leaned together.

Thumbs up all the way around released them to go their separate ways. Mac, Case, and Sheperd headed toward the entrance of the underwater alien ship where Fujita believed their communication equipment was housed. The air raid would be concentrated on this cove, and they were hoping to hell the ship wouldn't be able to get airborne.

Hale, McCann, and Fujita took a route through the dense vegetation that would take them to the backside of the Shalanaya camp. Meanwhile, Yazzie, Mumford, and Mordecai skirted the shoreline to the docks and the front of the same encampment. Anakim barracks had been built around the meager Shalanaya huts to provide their slaves with incentive to obey without question.

It was unknown exactly how many Anakim were housed on the island. However, each group knew their assignment and each man knew they could be vastly outnumbered. What strengthened their resolve was knowing the atrocities and abominations that would be committed against earth and its inhabitants by the Anakim if they failed.

Mac's team reached their first destination and Mac pulled down the red fabric marking the tree he and Yazzie had scouted out earlier. Case shinnied up the tree without comment to get settled before the air raid started. Mac and Sheperd continued to the second nesting place where Sheperd, like Case, made his way up to a lofty perch out of sight.

Mac made his way through the dense underbrush to the entrance then squatted in a tangle of vegetation letting the early morning darkness envelope him. He listened for a moment as birds began their waking calls and mosquitos took flight. Once convinced the coast was clear he quietly emerged and pointed his flashlight straight into the air and lit the small beacon three times. The two nesting soldiers now had a point from which to determine line of sight and distance. Then Mac melted back into the jungle and made haste to his next stop.

Yazzie, Mumford, and Mordecai heard the lapping of the waves against the shore as they made their way just inside the tree line. The darkness was changing to grey with the rising of the sun as they hurried to get into position. They spotted the pier with a small craft tethered in place through the fading moonlight and knew they were right on schedule.

Suddenly Yazzie stopped and held up his hand. They squatted in place and tried to determine from which direction a muffled rustling of brush was coming. Then the sound was on them before retreat was possible causing the trio to sink back into the brush hoping to disappear into the foliage. A Shalanaya with an arm full of sticks missed stepping on Yazzie's foot by inches, but no one moved or made a sound. When the early riser continued on his way relief washed over them thinking a chance encounter had been averted, but a quick change in direction to retrieve another branch for his stack caused him to fall headlong over Mumford scattering his gathered collection.

Mordecai jumped from his hiding spot to confront his countryman. His feet were solidly planted with his knees bent. The hilt of his now drawn saber was in his left hand in front of his face with his right hand covering the left. Then a menacing hiss came up from deep in his diaphragm that startled even Mumford and Yazzie.

The Shalanaya's eyes went wide when he heard the hiss and wider still when he saw the golden seal on Mordecai's right hand. He scrambled off Mumford, his task forgotten, to lay prone before Mordecai. "You have come," he said with humble adoration. "Queen Jehosheba has sent you to rescue us at last."

Mumford and Yazzie glanced at one another without saying a word then took a knee to scan the area while Mordecai engaged the Shalanaya.

"Where does your allegiance lie?" Mordecai demanded fiercely.

"My allegiance will always be with Shalna and the glorious Queen Jehosheba," he replied into the dirt.

"What is your name?"

"Gideon, noble sir," he replied still not daring to raise his head.

The saber was lowered to his waist as Mordecai asked, "What are you doing out here, Gideon?"

"I have come to gather wood for the fire to cook food for the Anakim as I do every morning."

Mordecai looked at him intently for a moment before asking, "Are you willing to fight for your freedom and the freedom of Shalna?"

Gideon dared raise his head to look at Mordecai as a deep guttural hiss was his only reply.

"Gather your sticks and return to camp. Tell the others to ready themselves. Today we will overcome the Anakim for our glorious Queen and country," Mordecai proclaimed.

Gideon did not hesitate to do as he was told. He quickly gathered his bundle of sticks and ran back to camp to tell the others the joyous news.

"They will fight," Mordecai said as the saber was put back in place. "They will fight to the death for their Queen."

Yazzie gave a quick nod of acknowledgment as he and Mumford stood to continue to their appointed position.

Hale, McCann, and Fujita were emerging from the jungle behind the encampment as the others moved to get into place by the shore. They slowed when an unexpected commotion was heard up ahead.

"Wait! Wait! Don't you know who I am? You can't kill me."

The three men stayed hidden as an Anakim came into view with none other than the honorable Admiral Benjiro Hayakawa clutched in his hand.

"How the hell did he get here?" Hale asked himself.

"I work with you, I'm on your side!" Hayakawa pleaded.

"Is that so," Fujita said calmly as he stepped out of hiding with his weapon at the ready.

Hale and McCann quietly cursed as they drew their weapons into position and watched helplessly as their teammate exposed their presence.

"Fujita!" Hayakawa exclaimed in relief. "Fujita, undoubtedly God himself has sent you here this day to deliver me."

The startled Anakim snorted out a menacing growl to warn Fujita from coming any closer as he yanked Hayakawa off his feet and used the Admiral's body as a shield between himself and Fujita.

Hayakawa saw the icy cold look in Fujita's eyes and decided to use it to his advantage. "They killed your men, Lieutenant Commander. They tortured your crew and sunk your ship. Now is your time to exact revenge on your enemy. Kill him, kill him!"

What Hayakawa didn't realize was that Fujita and his teammates had been instructed to only take head shots if possible. A headshot would take an Anakim down even if they were wearing bullet-resistant clothing. What he also didn't realize was how the line of sight had changed when the Anakim lifted him off the ground. Fujita's short stature and the Anakim's great height meant that for him to obey orders the trajectory of the bullet had to angle upward through Hayakawa's forehead into the Anakim's ugly face.

"Not a problem," Fujita said without emotion as he brought the AK-47 to his shoulder and pulled the trigger.

Their faces erupted as the single bullet passed through Fujita's two most hated enemies. Blood spurted out of the Admiral and mingled with his captor's blood as the two allies collapsed together in a heap.

Fujita turned back to Hale and McCann and took his place beside them. "It had to be done," he said without apology while avoiding eye contact with either man. And without a word the three of them moved into position praying that the crack of Fujita's weapon wouldn't bring swarms of Anakim down on their heads.

Mac had reached the far side of the island where according to Fujita the native islanders were being held. His assignment was to take out the Anakim sentry guarding them before joining the others. They didn't want the natives to be wiped out in the name of efficiency nor them being used as leverage against them once the fighting began.

He smelled him before he saw him. The Shalanaya had a distinct odor for sure, but the Anakim just stank. Mac crept closer and heard a child crying then a roaring growl. He fought his way through a wall of vines and penetrated them just in time to see the Anakim guard bring his weapon into position to take out a man and the boy he was sheltering in his arms.

Mac quickly stood and took a shot that the Anakim never saw coming. A bullet to the back of his head caused him to lurch forward then stiffen and fall to the ground like a felled tree. The man gripped his child tight as he dove out of the way of the giant's path.

For a moment Mac stood with his eyes locked on the Anakim body laying quiet and still on the ground ready to take a second shot if necessary. Once convinced of the certainty of his death Mac relaxed, lowering his weapon slightly until he saw the horror on the faces of the two natives. The man pointed behind Mac and yelled an unintelligible warning. He didn't need to understand the shouted words to know what was happening – there was a second sentry.

He attempted to bring his AK-47 back into position as he dove to his right twisting his body around midair in an effort to see his enemy. Even so, the Anakim's backhanded blow was not completely averted. The beast still managed to make glancing contact with Mac's torso throwing him fifteen feet into the jungle.

Mac struggled to breathe after the blow knocked the wind out of him. His eyes blinked furiously as he tried to regain his vision and force his senses to function. Heavy footsteps coming his way kicked his survival instincts into action and he used his feet to push his damaged body deeper into the thicket. Desperate attempts to pull the AK in to his chest were unsuccessful and as the footsteps grew closer a different set of instincts set in.

If I'm going down, Mac thought, *he's coming with me.*

Without hesitation he pulled a hand grenade from his jacket and stuck a finger through the loop in the pin. He paused with sweat trickling from his face and the seconds seeming like minutes until the beast stood directly over his hiding place. His hand tensed ready to jerk the pin from its position when the Anakim bent to finish the job.

Crack, crack.

The Anakim's face exploded as the bullets exited spraying Mac with the enemy's blood. The beast fell forward and as Mac rolled to avoid his collapse the pin was inadvertently pulled from the hand grenade which was then instinctively dropped by Mac as he rolled. A muffled *boom* was heard as the device exploded beneath the Anakim's heavy body then everything went quiet as Mac panted into the brush.

"That was a little overkill, wasn't it?" Yazzie asked drily as he came to stand over his longtime friend.

"Well, I already had it out. It seemed a shame to waste it," Mac returned sarcastically as Yazzie extended a hand to pull him to his feet. "What are you doing here?"

"I felt your distress," Yazzie returned. "So, I came."

"You felt my distress? What the hell does that mean?"

"I don't know how else to explain it. I was compelled to come. Can you fight?" Yazzie inquired as Mac groaned when he bent over to retrieve his weapon.

Mac gave Yazzie a what-do-you-think look as he looped the AK-47's strap over his neck and said, "Let's go."

Yazzie evaluated his compatriot's condition for a moment then commented. "You just better hope that Helen didn't get the same message I did."

CHAPTER 60

The steady hum of the B-25 bombers headed toward their target was getting louder as Mac and Yazzie joined the others at the encampment. The sky was becoming more gray than black as the rising sun lit the heavens to start a new day.

Mumford took a second glance when he saw Magruder. "You look like hell, sir. I trust the other guy looks worse," he said as he turned back to look down the barrel of the rifle currently aimed at the Anakim barracks.

"Let's just say that two of the ugly mugs aren't a problem anymore," Mac returned grimacing at the pain he was trying to ignore. He was unable to give credit where credit was due without divulging how they managed to traverse the island so quickly, however Mac was positive that without Yazzie he would have been the one who was no longer among the living. It had been too close for comfort.

"Excellent," Mumford mumbled as he smiled at the news.

Mac shook his head and rubbed his ears as a humming sound grew stronger. It made him wonder if being belted into kingdom come had affected his hearing. It wasn't the B-25s, no, it was much closer. "Am I hearing things?" he asked quietly. "What the hell is that sound?"

Yazzie and Mumford glanced at one another as Yazzie replied, "There's been a few new developments with the Shalanaya since we last saw you. They apparently vibrate when they're gearing up for war."

"They what…?"

Mac looked at Mumford for further explanation when a roar went up across the camp. It had been surmised that the first air strike would be what brought the Anakim out in mass. However, the discovery of Hayakawa and his captor crumpled together in death had sounded the alarm early.

Two shots sounded from the other side of the compound. Then doors slammed open as several half-dressed Anakim emerged to find out what the disturbance was about. Mumford fired several rounds in rapid fire taking down two in succession and injuring a third before he was able to dive back into the barracks.

"That's for Collins, you bastards," Mumford said never lowering his weapon or losing his concentration as his friend and teammate's death motivated him all over again.

Witnessing the death of two of their Anakim tormentors caused the Shalanaya captives to buzz like a hive of angry bees. They were not unaware that they would be blamed, and punished, for the attack regardless of the role they played. So, when one of their brethren boldly set fire to a building housing the Anakim others were delighted to follow suit.

The wooden buildings ignited like torches as the human envoy began firing. From a crouched position they set their AK-47's for machinegun fire then aimed high hoping to take out a few of their towering enemies before they were able to leave quarters while avoiding accidentally shooting any of their teammates stationed on the other side of the compound.

A B-25 bomber flew over their heads as the Anakim tumbled out of the flames engulfing their shelters. The people on the ground engaging with the beasts breathed out a little prayer for Case and Sheperd. They prayed for their aim to be good, their nests to remain hidden, and for the bombers to be on target. But most of all they prayed that the alien aircraft would not be able to take flight.

As gunfire erupted in the camp the first plane's payload was released. Case and Shepherd tensed in their lofty positions hoping to hell that the pilots were on target and wouldn't shake them from their perches. The bombs whistled toward their coordinates, and they heard the splash, splash, splash as each bomb hit the water then watched as water shot into the air at each blast. Seconds later the door they had been patiently watching opened and their targets began to file out trying to figure out what was happening.

Their sights were set. The two sharpshooters had agreed to work in tandem. Case fired first and a body hit the ground. As he grabbed the bolt to expend the now empty cartridge and ready the next round Shepard took his shot and another alien body dropped. As Shepherd operated his bolt action, Case's second shot found his next victim who was staring in confusion at the bodies on the ground. Shepard caught his second target while he was still in the entrance trying to find his way over the mounting bodies.

A second B-25 flew overhead, and another payload whistled its way into the cove. Explosions sounded one after another as the water reached for the sky again and again. An Anakim pushed his way past the bodies by the entrance and aimed a weapon at the departing aircraft. A shot from the treetops put a bullet through his temple causing the deadly beam of light destined to drop the plane into the sea to go wide.

Suddenly the two snipers saw their worst fears manifesting. There was movement beneath the surface as the alien craft began to rise out of its watery hiding place. Another series of bombs were released as the practice drill continued and the no longer secured alien craft was caught by the violent waves emanating from the blasts before it could completely emerge. Rocking and tipping back and forth, completely at the mercy of the sea, the hull broke the surface of the water then dipped back down again.

Both men pulled one of their panzerfausts around with the same idea in mind. These weapons could stop a tank, why not an alien aircraft? They had one anti-tank warhead in each weapon which meant they each had three chances to save the world. They waited until the hull rocked back to the surface then fired at the visible portion of the ship with their first weapon. The launch tube was quickly tossed aside once the warhead had deployed and the second weapon pulled into place.

The proximity of the ascending craft to the water's surface now gave their shots contact with something solid. Case and Sheperd continued hammering the hull with blast after blast until they saw a hole appear in the sea as the craft dipped back down and water poured into the damaged vessel infiltrating the interior.

As the alien ship took on water frantic Anakim poured onto shore. The duo in the treetops realized that the others had not been exaggerating when describing the beast's fear of water. This observation helped them keep their focus as a stream of the enemy left behind by their own kind poured out of the tunnel now disconnected from the drowning vessel. Aim, fire, bolt action, aim, fire, bolt action, again and again reloading when necessary, as smoke billowed from the encampment behind them.

Every building in the encampment was now ablaze. Anakim began fighting their way out of the flames and smoke, now enraged that their slaves would think they could overcome them. Unaware of the human presence, they fought the Shalanaya for dominance and control as they had on Shalna. Mordecai and his countrymen used the adrenalin generated by their vibrating anger to fight for their freedom.

Gideon and his army would draw the Anakim in and Mordecai would be waiting with his saber. The weapon was nothing but a blur as he expertly danced a dance of death with his enemy. He whirled and squatted, then jumped in the air spinning like a top as blood gushed from his enemies at every slice of the blade. Once an Anakim was wounded the Shalanaya warriors would swarm in and finish him off.

The humans were stunned to see the physical prowess of the odd little man they had come to know as an ally and friend. He was a surprisingly fierce combatant, and mesmerizing to watch. Pulling their attention back to the action, the men circling the perimeter of the camp started picking off the Anakim with weapons in hand. They protected Gideon's army, the ones forcibly taken from their homes and enslaved, as they ignored the flames and poured out unleashed fury on their captors.

The roar of a B-25 overhead blended into the chaos of the battle as Mac signaled Yazzie his intent to depart. He materialized in a sheltered spot under Case and Sheperd just in time for a couple of hand grenades to explode in the middle of a wave of Anakim desperate to reach dry land. Mac's ears were ringing as he saw an ugly alien head tip back to search the treetops. He didn't allow the thing to even get his weapon into position before taking him out.

Mac abandoned his spot as the enemy pressed inland toward his position. He quickly moved back about thirty feet toward the encampment then stopped to look and listen. When pounding footsteps were heard coming up fast behind him Mac ducked into a thicket hoping the enemy had not seen his detour. The Anakim raced by without a second glance. That was when he realized they were not after him – they were headed to the encampment.

Mac suddenly materialized beside Hale yelling, "They're coming!"

The words were barely out of his mouth when the first Anakim broke through the trees at a full run. Mac turned and opened fire with the alien nearly on top of them. Insanity ensued. The survivors from the alien aircraft were ready to fight, but so were their opponents. It was man against beast, each willing to fight to the death for their way of life.

McCann lobbed a hand grenade into the onslaught signaling the shift of the battlefield. Yazzie and Mumford picked up on the cue and left the last few wounded Anakim from the encampment to Mordecai and Gideon's lot. They ran across the smoldering ashes of the buildings toward the action as a second grenade exploded. Mumford took a knee and fired on an Anakim that had lifted Fujita off the ground by the throat. The beast released his prey only when his head snapped sideways, and he fell to his death. Fujita stood and gave Mumford a thumbs up while rubbing his neck.

Yazzie didn't stop but ran straight into the middle of the Anakim overtaking his teammate's position. They were losing ground but not for long. He hooked his arm around McCann as he passed and translated them both to a position behind the enemy. Mac, seeing Yazzie's approach and understanding his intent, lowered his weapon and dove toward Hale's position grabbing his ankle just as an Anakim absorbed several shots to tower over his smaller enemy. His ham sized fist caught nothing but air as the two men he meant to destroy with his own two hands disappeared before his eyes.

The tide had turned and the Anakim went down one by one. As each body dropped the scene became quieter. The beast's roaring ceased, the gunfire lessened, and the men began to cautiously step from their positions. The grayness had dispelled, and the sun was up over the horizon as they began to take stock.

"Damn, we did it," Hale breathed out in amazement. "We actually did it."

Giddy joyful laughing commenced as the humans came together one by one. The question of whether to take prisoners or not was quickly resolved when Gideon and his Shalanaya countrymen fell on the bodies of their tormentors and slit each one's throat in celebration. Case and Shepherd came out of the brush to join the team with weapons at the ready but broke into ear-to-ear grins when they saw that the enemy was no longer a threat.

The gaiety was cut short when Mac asked, "Where's Fujita?"

The group immediately grew somber and dispersed to find the ninth member of their unit.

"Over here," McCann yelled as he stooped to find a pulse.

Fujita's eyes fluttered open at McCann's touch. "Did we get them?" he asked quietly as the others gathered around one by one. "Did we get them all?"

"Every last one of the ugly bastards and I intend to dance me an Irish jig momentarily," McCann replied with a false enthusiasm. "You'll for sure not want to miss it, so you hang on and we'll get you fixed up for the party."

Yazzie took a knee on the other side of Fujita and prepared to violate his vow of nondisclosure by applying his healing skills to his fellow warrior. The dying man took Yazzie's hand.

"No," Fujita said with a weak smile. "No. I have fulfilled my vow and had my revenge. Everything is as it should be. I will die here on the island as was destined. God is so good. He extended my life so I could avenge my men. Please bury me here, please promise me. It is where I belong."

Every head was bowed, and tears flowed through the grime and blood on the faces of the seasoned warriors as Mac silently nodded his agreement.

CHAPTER 61

The two pilots fell into lockstep with the third when he exited the administration building into the predawn darkness.

"What the hell was that all about?" the third man asked without looking at his compatriots.

"A nondisclosure agreement? Like we don't know to keep our mouths shut?" one of the others replied likewise keeping his face front and center.

"We already have top secret clearance then they send the U.S. Attorney General in person to get our John Hancock's? Something big is up."

"Did you get the 'you'll never see life outside of Fort Leavenworth again if you talk' threat?"

"It didn't sound like a threat to me. Sounded more like a promise."

"You think we're getting ready to start World War three?" one asked chancing a glance at the other two pilots as they turned down the road lined with planes in shiny silver rows.

"We're getting ready to bomb a Russian underwater storage facility they probably think is indestructible. What do you think?"

"Destination already has a reputation seeing how Fat Man and Little Boy took to the air from this base. Seems like they don't want any press on this one like they got last time."

"Yeah, I'm sure that's it. They don't want to scare away all the white-legged tourists coming to get a tan on Tinian Island."

The three laughed at the thought then fell silent as they approached the crewmen getting their aircraft ready. They watched the preparations silently for a moment then faced one another. The senior most man (at all of 28 years old) put forth a fist then the other two added their fists to the tower.

"Let's go scare the crap out of some fish and above all…"

"Don't get dead," they all said in unison.

There was little banter back and forth between the crew as they worked like a well-oiled machine to prepare the three aircraft for the mission. Maybe this was because of the familiarity of the tasks or maybe it was because they all recognized what no one was willing to say out loud - this mission wasn't normal. Even though the higher-ups tried to give it the appearance of ordinary not a single person was buying it.

The United States wasn't at war with anyone, and they all knew there wasn't an enemy target within the fuel parameters. In fact, there was nothing but open water. Then there were the bombs. Both of similar weight and bulk but one of them was encased in an iron bell like contraption. And then there was the tiny little detail that it was an actual honest-to-God atomic bomb! Just what did the Russians have below the water's surface that required such firepower?

The sky was beginning to lighten as they each boarded their assigned Boeing B-29 Superfortress bombers. Helmets were strapped on and tightened, and instrumentation was checked as they pushed any questions aside and cleared their minds to zero in on the task at hand. Engines were fired up as they went through their mental checklist by rote just like any other mission ticking off each task in their heads as it was completed.

Ghost Rider was to take the lead. Ranger was to follow with Phantom bringing up the rear. The USS Chewink was in the water to track the effectiveness of the deployed bombs and radio in a battle damage assessment. The Emergency Rescue Boat Squadrons, or ERBS as most sailors called them, had been activated and were already in the neighborhood just in case.

Geoffrey and Colonel Smith had been given permission to tap into the ship's comms and were just now readjusting their headphones after the shootout with

Hayakawa. They were sitting in the Bunker like a couple of flies on the wall listening to mission preparations as Tamar stacked Shalanaya bodies and Helen distributed donuts.

"Comms, checking comms. This is Ghost Rider. Over."

"We've got you loud and clear Ghost Rider. You are cleared for takeoff on runway one. Over."

As the plane with a 141-foot wingspan left its spot and made its way to the runway, Ranger reported in.

"Comms, checking comms. This is Ranger. Over."

"We've got you Ranger. Ghost Rider is moving into position on runway one. Proceed to runway two and hold. Over."

"Comms, checking comms. This is Phantom. Over."

"You're loud and clear Phantom. Proceed to runway three and hold. Over."

"Will do but try to get me in the air in time to catch that beautiful sunrise, will ya? I hate to waste all that film just recording a bomber's butt. Over."

The controller smiled. "Request noted, Phantom. We'll see what we can do. Over."

When Ghost Rider received word to take off, the propeller-driven heavy bomber revved up its four engines to pick up the speed necessary to get the bird and its cargo airborne. He eased up off the runway and began the onerous task of getting the aircraft up to thirty-one thousand feet without burning out any of his engines.

As Ghost Rider lifted off and headed to the prescribed coordinates, Ranger rolled his head from side to side then shook out his arms to release the building tension. Never in a million years did he think he would be the one tagged to drop an atomic bomb, but here he was getting ready to send a bunch of fish to hell and back.

"Ranger, you have a go."

"Roger," he replied as he earnestly hoped his grandmother was praying for him right now. Ranger's wheels were barely off the ground when Phantom received the go ahead.

"Okay, here we go," Phantom said. "Be sure to smile for the camera, boys."

Ghost Rider reached his destination and released his payload then smoothly tipped the huge aircraft into a turn and headed back toward base. The bomb sank into the deep before exploding and he saw the water shoot into the air over his right wing as he headed home.

The Chewink's sonar picked up the detonation and sent word to the flyboys comm center to adjust Ranger's release one mile southeast of Ghost Riders drop. Ranger adjusted his trajectory as instructed.

"You got your cameras rolling, Phantom?"

"You betcha. It'll be the best footage that no one will ever see."

Ranger smiled at Phantom's little joke – mostly because he knew it was true. He took a deep breath then let the air out in a sigh as his coordinates told him it was time to release his payload. "Bye-bye Tiny Tim," he said under his breath. That's what his crew had named the bomb. If you had A-bombs named Fat Man and Little Boy naturally Tiny Tim would come next, they had surmised in a moment of levity.

Ranger tilted his heavy aircraft to swing home but saw no spray of water. The iron casing surrounding the bomb, he had been told, was added to get the bomb to sink to a greater depth before detonation so he wasn't surprised there was no show. He leveled out his aircraft and relaxed back into his seat for the trip home now that the atomic bomb was no longer in residence.

Then Phantom suddenly exclaimed, "What in the holy hell is that?! Look out!!" as a silver disk the size of a football stadium suddenly shot out of the water.

Ranger stiffened at the warning as an airborne craft like nothing he'd ever seen before streaked passed him in a blur. His gunners opened fire with everything they had. The machine guns shot rapid fire rounds as the M2 20 mm cannon released the 20-caliber mm projectile from the tail position. The cannon missile made impact just as a beam of light shot out of the alien craft and ripped the

B-29 in two depressurizing the cabin and sending the fuselage hurling toward the deep blue ocean.

The ERBS raced in the direction of the wreckage hoping to hell that the crew wouldn't be trapped in the fuselage and sucked under the surface beyond their reach. The Chewink's crew, already at battle stations per the captain's orders, activated the two 3"/23 caliber anti-aircraft cannons mounted on deck and began firing projectiles at the enemy. They fired one after another while the alien craft engaged with Ranger's B-29. The first shots were direct hits to the underside of the craft causing it to wobble like a top. The sailors continued to fire as the strange craft turned to engage.

The crew assigned to the sonar and other seismic devices tried to ignore the roar of the anti-aircraft cannons as they manned their posts. Data was retrieved and immediately forwarded to those waiting for the information. They followed the bomb as it dropped through the murky depths and recorded the detonation when it occurred just before touching the ocean's floor. A huge structure was seen miles below the surface that was damaged but reported as not completely destroyed. They assumed the structure to be the target of this exercise, however they had no time to think about its purpose or who put it there.

Topside the alien craft had drawn near taking several hits before targeting the ship with the light beam. As the ship broke apart Phantom recorded the enemy craft as it attempted and failed to regain its equilibrium. It dipped and spun like a carnival ride before jetting out of sight.

CHAPTER 62

"Where shall we begin, gentlemen?" President Truman began as the four of them settled on the sofa and chairs in the Oval Office. "Will Helen be joining us? She hasn't been injured in some way, has she?"

"Oh, no sir she's fine," Mac replied. "She's visiting the good doctors at Groom Lake. I understand they are being moved to different quarters."

"Yes," Truman replied. "We've realized that their research has outgrown their assigned space. They will be relocated to a larger and far more secure area."

"Will they also be tasked with examination of the weaponry recovered?" Mac inquired.

Truman glanced down at his hands resting comfortably in his lap as he considered his response. "The medical and technical areas of research will be housed in the same facility, however, the number of personnel assigned to the task will be increased significantly and compartmentalized. Their location and nature of the work will be classified Top Secret and only those approved for special access will have any knowledge of their existence."

Mac smiled. "And let me guess, I don't need special access."

"That is correct," Truman responded quietly. "I am actually acting on your advice General. You had concerns about alien technology falling into the wrong hands, about it being used against humans. And I assured you that steps would be taken to secure any and all knowledge regarding alien life and/or technology."

"So, you only have yourself to blame for your exclusion," Yazzie interjected with a hint of irony.

"I don't know why you're gloating. You've been cut off as well," Mac returned.

Yazzie tried to hide a mischievous grin and turned his attention back to Truman. Quinn and Mac followed Yazzie's gaze with puzzled looks.

"I met with Menachem this morning," Truman confessed.

"You *met* with him, sir?" Quinn asked.

"Yazzie arranged the meeting and *transportation*," the President stated firmly. Quinn paled and opened his mouth as Truman held up his hand to squelch the tirade that was sure to come. "I am well aware of the, let's just say, unusual nature of the appointment with Mr. Begin. And for the record, Yazzie, it was a onetime event."

"Oh my God," Quinn said rubbing his forehead as a multitude of scenarios ran through his head of what could have gone wrong.

"We have come to an agreement and made a pact, or a covenant, as Menachem calls it. Since we are, as far as we know, the only two peoples on earth that are aware of the infiltration of two alien races we have become allies. We will work together to ensure the security of the human race." Truman paused for a moment then continued. "This includes sharing the research and ensuring the protection of any information regarding alien species and technology."

Quinn and Mac sat silent for a moment as they digested this new revelation.

"As it turns out the Irgun knew much more than we thought."

As all eyes turned on Yazzie he held up his hands and stated, "It wasn't me, I shared nothing. I didn't need to. They saw many of the same things we did and came to the same conclusions, that's all. The only thing they had not seen was an actual Anakim."

"And now that the Irgun are assisting on the island, they are privy to that information as well," Truman said dryly.

A smile tugged at the mouth of the wily old Jew, and he replied with a shrug, "I thought you could use the help."

Mac coughed into his hand to hide his smile at the craftiness of his longtime friend. They had both known that Menachem and the Irgun would most certainly be stonewalled regarding any information about the world's newest enemies once the alien technology was procured by the United States. Yazzie just made sure that his people stayed in the loop.

"How did it go on the island?" Truman asked, steering the conversation back to the matter at hand.

"There were two human casualties, Makoto Fujita and Admiral Benjiro Hayakawa," Mac responded.

"Hayakawa? He was on your team?" Quinn asked.

Mac glanced at Yazzie before responding. "He was not. My wife brought him and left him on the island."

"Helen?" Truman asked with raised eyebrows. "Helen killed him?"

"No, of course not," Mac replied with disdain. "Hayakawa threatened members of my team in Tokyo and tried to kidnap Helen during an attempted robbery of U.S. military communication equipment. She simply relocated him to the island. Fujita later executed him for collaborating with the enemy."

"She was brilliant, actually," Yazzie said with pride. "Cool under pressure. She's my protégé you know."

"Executed him without a fair trial, General?" Quinn asked ignoring Yazzie's delight.

"He had been captured by the Anakim," Mac said as pictures of the bodies of the men that had been skinned and tossed into the churchyard graves in Germany flashed through his mind. "Trust me, I've seen how they torture and kill their prisoners he was better off being shot."

Truman refrained from commenting on the moral and legal complexities presented here. "Will either of them be missed?"

"Fujita was disowned by his family after his return from the island talking about alien monsters. When it was determined he was crazy they cut him off. They won't come looking for him," Mac replied. "As for Hayakawa, MacArthur received an anonymous tip about arms and contraband being stored in his basement. We put the word on the street that he fled to parts unknown after he heard of the impending raid, sir."

"Very well. How goes the clean up on the island? All Anakim present were terminated, yes? And what about the Shalanaya?"

"Yes sir, all Anakim were dispatched," Mac confirmed. "And as it turns out not all Shalanaya are fans of the Anakim. Mordecai recruited his brethren, and they were instrumental in completing the operation. They are now assisting with the recovery of technology from the downed alien craft as it turns out they can hold their breath for an exceedingly long time. It is only the salt in the water that limits their efforts."

"Any plans on how we're going to get them home?"

"They're not going home."

The President raised his head to look at the men sitting across from him. "Say again."

"They can't be sent home, sir. Their return to Shalna would alert the Anakim still in residence that the balance of power has shifted on earth," Mac said. "It would most certainly bring more of their kind here before we are ready for them."

"That is to say nothing, Mr. President," Yazzie added, "of what unspeakable things they would do to those Shalanaya who returned home."

"Yes…I see," Truman said while mulling the situation over. "So, just what do you propose we do with them?"

"They will remain on the island, sir. After some coaxing, the native islanders have agreed to share the space with them."

"This absolutely must be contained, gentlemen," Truman said emphatically. "The public can never know, must never know about the events that took place on that island. How can we be sure that the islanders and Shalanaya will stay mum?"

"The islanders have lived there for generations, sir. They're born there and they die there. No one leaves. Their priority is rebuilding and repopulating right now, that's all. In the unlikely event that word should get out we can spin it as old island lore. As for the Shalanaya, Mordecai is stuck here too, sir. He's taken responsibility for his people. We'll make sure he understands what's at stake during our debrief with the team. Any other Shalanaya located on this planet will be relocated to the island until their situation at home is resolved."

President Truman sat back in his chair and sighed. "It looks like that bit of legislation is coming just in time, eh Quinn?"

"Yes sir."

"It is quite possible that all this alien madness can be lost in the transition. It could be most fortuitous actually."

"Legislation, sir?" Mac asked.

"The National Security Act is currently being debated in the Senate. Once approved it will move to the House of Representatives. Hopefully, it will be voted on and approved later this month. I believe I mentioned my intention to break up the building of J. Edgar's intelligence kingdom in one of our earlier meetings?" Nods around the room encouraged the President to continue. "It's been a couple of years in the making but I'm thinking it will not only be good for the nation but for our purposes as well."

"In what way sir?" Quinn asked.

"This change will be huge. The Department of War will be renamed the Department of Defense. Much better don't you think?"

"Indeed," Yazzie confirmed.

"It will restructure our Army and Navy and create a new Air Force that will fold into one National Military Establishment. Now don't you worry General we'll work it out for the Army to keep its air forces and the Marines will stay as an independent force under the Navy. A National Security Council, or NSC, will be established to assist with the coordination and communication of information within our intelligence communities. The new Central Intelligence Agency will in effect replace the current Central Intelligence Group and will report directly to the NSC who will in turn report to me. They will act in an advisory capacity to the Commander in Chief on matters of national security in the realm of domestic, foreign, and military policies."

"This sounds like a massive undertaking, sir," Mac said as the implications of it all swirled through his head.

"It is," Truman confirmed. "But what better time to quietly create and bury a clandestine unit tasked with the location of aliens living among us?"

CHAPTER 63

President Truman stood and walked silently to his desk. He extracted a bottle of Wild Turkey from the bottom drawer and four glasses. When his questioning look brought nods from the other three men, he then poured two fingers into each glass. Quinn retrieved three of the four glasses, then he and the President returned to their seats. Mac and Yazzie accepted the proffered beverage and each of the four men took a sip before the conversation resumed.

"So," Truman began. "I understand that the bombing of the underwater Anakim facility was not as clean as the operation on the island."

"No sir," Quinn responded. "Unfortunately, you are correct. We lost one B-29 and the USS Chewink. Three were lost from the plane with only the pilot surviving, seventy-five souls lost from the ship with twenty-seven survivors."

"Too damn many," Truman sighed. "Was the target destroyed?"

"Damage assessments received from the Chewink before she went down indicate that there was severe damage, but the alien facility was not completely destroyed. However, I can say with about 85% certainty that there were no survivors," Quinn answered.

"And how do we know that?"

"We know for sure that the outer shell was compromised, and the facility took on water. At that depth, no human could have survived once the pressurization was interrupted let alone make it to the surface. If Anakim physiology is similar to ours it is highly unlikely that there were any survivors *unless* the facility has compartmentalized pressurization units protecting other areas independently,"

Quinn assured the President. "Regretfully, a physical inspection is not an option as it's approximately 30,000 feet or five and a half to six miles down."

Truman silently sipped his whiskey for a moment.

"I understand there was an airborne plane recording the events," Yazzie said breaking the silence. "Have its films been reviewed yet?"

Quinn looked at Yazzie with surprise that top-secret military information was known by an outsider. He then turned to Truman for the go-ahead. A silent nod from the Commander in Chief allowed him to continue. "The film is on its way to Groom Lake for safekeeping. A hand-selected team will be reviewing the footage."

"Don't worry, we'll be coordinating with your people on the findings," Truman said cutting off Yazzie's question before it was asked.

"I heard the alien craft was damaged," Mac said, thinking about the men lost. "Hopefully it was damaged badly enough to prevent the attack planned by the Anakim from being initiated."

Truman and Quinn glanced at one another.

"What?" Mac asked after observing their loaded look.

"The damn thing crashed in New Mexico," Truman responded.

"What?!" Mac gasped.

"So, they tried. Even after sustaining heavy damage, they still tried to carry out their plan," Yazzie commented before breathing out a Psalm. "You have also given me the necks of my enemies, so that I destroyed those who hated me..."

"We don't know if that was their intent or not. If it was, they failed," Quinn stated.

"Where is the ship? Did anyone see it?" Mac asked with concern.

"Oh, hell yeah. Some damn fool public information officer sent out a press release stating that the 509th Operations Group had recovered a flying disc," Quinn stated shaking his head in disbelief.

"Flying disc?" Yazzie asked.

"Oh, that's right you haven't been here to witness the brand spanking new unidentified flying objects craze," Truman said. "UFO, that's what they're calling them."

Mac leaned forward to rest his elbows on his knees while cradling his head in his hands. He sighed deeply as he massaged his temples with his fingertips. "So, how did it get out? It wasn't my group."

"Nor the Irgun," Yazzie quickly added.

"No, it was one Kenneth Arnold, a private pilot, who reported seeing a series of nine unidentified flying objects whizzing past Mount Rainier at about a thousand miles an hour last month," Quinn said.

"Nine?!" Mac and Yazzie exclaimed in tandem.

Truman held his hands up to quell the panic in the voices of two men that had solid reasons to react as they did. "Slow down. We don't know what was actually seen by the pilot, if anything. I was concerned myself at that first report but I'm certain that if there were seven more ships docked somewhere here on earth they would have activated them by now."

"*First* report?" Yazzie asked.

"Yes, everybody and their brother up in that area have reported sightings in the last few weeks. Nobody wants to be left out of the excitement I guess," Truman replied.

"It was Arnold's description that led the press to tag them flying saucers or flying discs. News outlets are certainly making the most of it," Quinn said. "I've even heard that a motion picture studio has plans to make a movie about aliens invading earth."

Yazzie smiled. "Art imitating life, eh?"

Truman agreed grimly.

"But when you can't head it off, use it. Right General?" Quinn stated. "The PR story was retracted, and the public told that it was simply a conventional weather balloon that went down. Rumors are swirling about a government coverup which isn't necessarily a bad thing."

"No," Mac said thoughtfully. "No, it's not. It's so very every man's nightmare and Hollywood's involvement simply adds to the delightful conspiracy. It will hopefully turn into nothing more than idle barber shop talk…provided, of course, that no physical evidence is recovered."

"The U.S. Army Air Forces recovered the alien craft and bodies. Everything is currently being housed at the Roswell Army Airfield, hence the need for a larger facility for our alien research," Truman responded. "I've already spoken with Menachem about engaging some of your scientists for the new venue, Yazzie."

"You might be interested to know that the German scientist your team recovered in Osaka has been reunited with his son, who is even more brilliant than his father if the reports we've received thus far are accurate. That's why the boy's father took such great precautions. He didn't want him to be conscripted into Hitler's stable of scientists," Quinn said. "They are both very excited to be coming to America to work on this new project."

"Do they know what the *project* is?" Mac asked.

Quinn smiled. "Of course not. However, it will be interesting to find out if any of Hitler's technology has alien roots as we have suspected."

"Yes indeed, very interesting," Yazzie commented.

"Not to hijack the conversation, Mr. President, but it was never said how the loss of lives on the B-29 and USS Chewink are to be explained," Mac said. "Any mention of a ship going down by the Marianas Islands is sure to draw unwanted attention."

Truman looked at Quinn who responded. "The Chewink was decommissioned in February, at least that's what the paperwork will show, and will be used for submarine target practice off New London, Connecticut at the end of this month. The seventy-eight crew members that disembarked from the Chewink are to be sent home by Navy transport. Unfortunately, that aircraft will crash into the ocean before reaching its final destination. There will be no survivors."

"So," Mac responded soberly, "their families will never know that they died saving the world."

CHAPTER 64

"The honorable Queen Jehosheba is most pleased with the outcome of your battle with the earth-bound Anakim and sends her congratulations," Mordecai said with a bow of his head. "She is most hopeful that this good fortune will extend to our battle for freedom on Shalna. She wished me to convey to you that there is currently no indication that the Anakim on Shalna are aware of occurrences here."

The dozen or so people in the room just stared.

"How the hell would you know what someone said on another planet?" Mac asked after a moment.

"While you were reporting to your esteemed leader, I was doing the same," Mordecai said with a smile.

"And just exactly how did you do that?"

Now Mordecai looked confused. "I am her emissary."

Yazzie rubbed his whiskers to cover his grin while Mac counted to ten. "Okay," Mac said plastering a smile on his face. "That still doesn't answer the question."

The blank look on Mordecai's face and the frustration on Mac's caused Helen to intervene. "Mordecai, dear, can you communicate with your Queen while you are here on earth?"

"Of course. I am her emissary."

"Yeah, yeah of course," Mac said to Yazzie sarcastically. "Of course, because he's her damn emissary. Don't you think that would have been a nice piece of information for us to have known before now?"

Mordecai stared in amazement. "You mean your emissaries can not contact your President when they are off-world? That must be most…disconcerting."

Mac stared at the little man for a moment biting back the response that was on the tip of his tongue. Then he abruptly turned away muttering as he rubbed the back of his neck.

"Yes indeed," Yazzie replied in amusement. "Very disconcerting. You will be making regular reports to Queen Jehosheba?"

"Most certainly."

"And she'll let us know if the Anakim activate to move against us?"

"Of course, we are allies. We have the same enemies and have fought side by side in battle," he said relieved that whatever he had said to displease the General had now been straightened out. "However, it is her sincerest wish to speak to you directly when opportunity allows."

"Do you have everything you need on the island, dear?" Helen interjected, trying to head Mordecai off from blurting out just exactly how a meeting would be possible. "It is unfortunate that you can't go home quite yet."

"We are very happy to stay here if it means our families will remain safe. And yes, we are quite well cared for. It is good for my people to be busy, working with earthers to build shelters, gather food, and assist with the recovery of technology from the Anakim aircraft. We are most pleased to be at your disposal."

"Good," Mac sighed. "Because we may need your help finding the rest of your people scattered across the planet. We intend to bring any Shalanaya found to the island to live with you there until you can be transported home. Any disciplinary action to be taken will be up to you, Mordecai."

Mordecai smiled broadly as he bowed before Mac. "That will be most pleasing to the illustrious Queen Jehosheba."

"Farnsworth," Mac said as Geoffrey came to attention. "Your country wants you back. So, it seems you will be able to take Irene on a tour of the English countryside after all."

A little titter of laughter went through the small group as McCann elbowed the blushing Geoffrey.

"However, rest assured that we know how to find you if we need you. Colonel Smith, you'll return to your post in San Francisco, California, and continue your command of the floating dry dock ABSD-2."

"Of course," Smith replied resolutely as he thought about the boredom his transition from John Smith back to Joseph Rochefort would entail.

"I do, however, expect your linguistic translation assignment to be completed," Mac commanded as a broad smile appeared on Rochefort's face. "You can be certain I'll be in touch."

"I look forward to it sir," he replied with pleasure.

"The President has spoken with Mr. Begin and they have agreed that our next moves should be decided together as we are the only ones aware of the threat at hand. Yazzie will be heading up a group of yet to be chosen, what do you call them? Oh yes, mighty men under Menachim's guidance. I assume they will be what we would call hell raisers," Mac said as he addressed the rest of the room. "Tamar, there is a good chance you will make the cut given the stated criteria."

Tamar smiled coyly running her hand through her hair. "Oh yes, I'm quite certain I am capable of raising a little hell as well as any man."

"Mumford, Sheperd, and Case," Mac continued. "You will return to D.C. tomorrow on military transport and will remain under Colonel Quinn's command. Changes are coming to our nation concerning national defense and the gathering of intelligence, gentlemen, so I cannot speak as to your next assignments. Do understand that I have pull with your boss – and won't hesitate to use it if I need you."

"Wouldn't have it any other way, sir," Mumford replied to the accompanying nods of Sheperd and Case.

"Damn, I hate being picked last," McCann said to Hale with a sigh.

Chuckles all around the room changed to groans of protest as Hale replied with a grin, "I prefer to think the General saved the best for last."

"You both are returning to Pullach for now. I will make contact in Germany after resettling Helen at home and clearing up a few loose ends in D.C."

"Will I continue to be a liaison with Groom Lake?" Helen asked.

"Undetermined at this time but unlikely," Mac said. "The investigation into all things alien just got exponentially larger with our recent successes, dear. The need for our services in that capacity have for all intents and purposes ended."

"Well, I'll just have to speak to the President about that," Helen returned while fluffing her skirt to remove a noticed wrinkle. She looked up to a host of smiling faces. "Well, I can't just sit home baking cookies when I know what's at stake now, can I?"

Mac turned to Yazzie with a sigh. "The Greys had no idea what they started when they selected her."

"I don't know," Yazzie replied with a smile. "Maybe they did."

Mac just grunted an unintelligible response to his wise old friend. Then he took a moment to look around the room at each face and realized that even though they had been strangers to one another just a few months ago, they were now family. Helen was gently brushing the hair back off Tamar's shoulder as they spoke. The daughter she'd never had. Yazzie and Smith were making plans to meet up in San Francisco for a meal. McCann had pulled out his Irish brogue to amuse Mumford and Hale as Geoffrey compared biceps with Sheperd and Case. Brothers all.

It was something many outside the military didn't understand, couldn't understand. How your experiences change you, knit you together. Loved ones sit at home with their sameness of days and expect their soldier boys to come home as they left. But it can never be so. The sights, the sounds, the pain and fear, the close calls and sudden death. Knowing that sheer damn luck could mean the difference between losing your life or taking one. It all changes a man. It is a change that cannot be explained, it must be lived to be understood. The people in this room understood and that understanding would bind them together across the miles. No matter where life would take each of them. No matter how much time passed. The next time they met that inexplicable bond would be there as strong as ever.

It was a crazy life. A compulsion to fight and protect those that would never understand or appreciate the sacrifices made. A desire to stand in the place of the naive so that they can remain in that state of blissful innocence. Taking on all the violence and suffering, shouldering all the torment to ensure a quiet peaceful life for the ignorant masses. Crazy.

And now the Anakim. At least their coming would have all mankind fighting a common enemy instead of one another, wouldn't it? *Ah, we'll probably find a way to muck that up too,* Mac thought with a sigh. The people in this room plus a handful of others. That was it. That was the sum total of humanity standing between alien destruction and human history. Of course, they would fight. They had to fight because they were the only ones that knew about the real war.